PRAISE FOR MICHAEL MCBRIDE

"Thrilling entertainment."

— *PUBLISHERS WEEKLY* ON MUTATION

"McBride writes with the perfect mixture of suspense and horror that keeps the reader on edge."

— EXAMINER

"McBride's style brings to mind both James Rollins and Michael Crichton."

— SCI-FI & SCARY

"Highly recommended for fans of creature horror and the thrillers of Michael Crichton."

— *THE HORROR REVIEW*

"Michael McBride literally stunned me with his enigmatic talent and kept me hanging on right up until the end."

— *MIDWEST BOOK REVIEW*

ALSO BY MICHAEL MCBRIDE

FEARFUL SYMMETRY

MICHAEL MCBRIDE

PRETERNATURAL PRESS
DENVER, COLORADO

First paperback edition published by Preternatural Press

www.michaelmcbride.net

Cover Design by Michael McBride

ISBN-13: 978-0-692-26087-6

ISBN-10: 0-6922-6087-0

Second Edition: February 2022

10 9 8 7 6 5 4 3 2 1

For Tobin von der Nuell

PROLOGUE

Yarlung Tsangpo River Basin
Motuo County
Tibet Autonomous Region
People's Republic of China
October 17th

Today

The branches of the camphorwoods and elms whipped his cheeks and clawed at his eyes despite his best efforts to shield them with his forearms. The wet leaves threw water into his face. He could barely see the narrow, muddy path through the darkness and the fog and the suffocating forest. Every muscle in his body burned from the exertion and his pulse pounded loudly in his ears. He could barely hear the roar of the river over the storm lashing the upper canopy, which sealed off what little starlight managed to permeate the dense clouds. If he strayed from the trail, he was a dead man. Probably already was. He could feel his lead shrinking by the second and there was nothing he could do about it.

The Yarlung Tsangpo urged him on with a rumble so loud he could feel it in his chest. The path sloped steeply downward. He slipped in the runoff sluicing across the path and slid into a rhododendron that mercifully allowed him to gain his balance once more.

A crashing sound behind him.

He didn't dare look back. He knew exactly what it meant.

Whatever separation he had created between them had evaporated.

He wasn't going to make it.

More crashing sounds uphill and to his left. The cracking and snapping of breaking wood. Boughs swayed violently in his peripheral vision.

He wasn't going to make it.

A strobe of lightning froze the world around him like a snapshot. It reflected from the droplets of water hovering around his head, the rivulets draining through the canopy, and the broad, leathery leaves that crowded him from all sides at once. He saw the bend ahead, marked by a pile of stones where a cairn had once stood. The trees beyond it positively shook.

And then there was nothing but darkness again.

He wasn't going to make it.

Thunder grumbled overhead as he burst from the forest and was assaulted by the driving rain. The wind screamed through the valley, clearing the omnipresent fog and causing the suspension bridge over the river to sway. The rickety wooden construct spanned the six-hundred-foot chasm carved by the Yarlung Tsangpo, three hundred feet straight down. It flowed high and fast and churned with uprooted trees and debris.

The camphorwoods had grown over and around the bridge. Vines reached from their branches and entwined with the aged ropes. The trees on the steep escarpment below grew up through the gaps between the wooden slats. He had to duck underneath the faded and tattered prayer flags that whipped at his head as he sprinted out onto the bridge. The ruckus of his boots striking the ancient, moss-covered planks was barely audible over the river. He was grateful he couldn't hear the cracking noises of the warped boards threatening to give way underfoot.

He drew the ice axes from either hip on his climbing belt without slowing and prayed the picks would be sharp enough to do what needed to be done.

Five hundred feet.

He was out of breath and on the verge of collapse. Through the gaps he could see the brown river raging. It was so far down there. So far . . .

Four hundred fifty feet.

A ferocious gust swung the bridge nearly thirty degrees, forcing him to lunge for the rope rail. He slipped on the wet boards. Fell to his knees. Glanced back in time to see a shadow emerge from the shivering branches that concealed the mouth of the path.

He wasn't going to make it.

He pulled himself to his feet and sprinted for everything he was worth.

Four hundred feet.

Three hundred fifty.

He wasn't going to make it.

Taking his chances with the river wasn't an option from this height. The impact would be like landing on concrete. Even if he managed not to break his legs, he'd be swept under before he could catch his breath.

Another glance back.

The shadow stood silhouetted against the forest, framed by the ropes. Another shadow materialized from the trees and fell in behind the first. Neither of them moved. They just stood there, watching him.

Waiting.

Three hundred feet.

Halfway.

Why weren't they coming after him?

The answer struck him hard enough to halt his momentum.

He looked up toward the other end of the bridge in time to see more shadows materialize from the underbrush and eclipse the trail.

It was all over now.

He turned and watched his pursuit slowly advance onto the weathered bridge.

Spun to see the others on the opposite end do the same.

He'd never stood a chance.

He leaned over the rope and looked down at the water speeding past far below him. The trunks of massive trees fired downstream. The troughs hid jagged boulders beneath the rising river.

The wind momentarily abated and the heavy raindrops struck his shoulders like pebbles. He closed his eyes and turned his face skyward.

When he lowered it again, the cold water drained from his nose and chin. He opened his eyes and appraised the Black Diamond Cobra ice ax in his left hand. It had a reverse-arched carbon fiber shaft with a four-inch serrated pick on one side of the head and a hammer on the other. He adjusted his grip on the rubberized handle, at the end of which a bungee cord connected it to a carabiner hooked to his belt. Hefted its weight. Less than two pounds. Looked at its twin in his right fist.

If this was the end, then he would at least go down swinging.

He raised the ice axes high and stared first one way, then the other. A flash of lightning illuminated the hunters at either end of the bridge.

"What are you waiting for?" he shouted.

The echo of his voice was swallowed by a clap of thunder.

And the drumroll of running feet striking the decrepit bridge from both directions at once.

PART I

Hidden Lotus

1

Johann Brandt Institute for Evolutionary Anthropology
Chicago, Illinois
October 3rd

Two Weeks Ago

"You wanted to see me, Dr. Brandt?"

"Ah, yes. Jordan, my boy. Do come in, won't you?"

Dr. Jordan Brooks stepped inside and quietly closed the door behind him. Entering the enormous office of the founder and chief financier of the entire institute never failed to amaze him. It was like a museum unto itself. Enlarged and framed photographs of Dr. Johann Brandt in the field covered the walls. Nearly three-quarters of a century's worth, Brooks figured. They traversed the spectrum from black and white to color, and all of the myriad shades in between. Brandt was readily identifiable in each of them with his regal profile and almost pompous bearing. He had the presence of a stage actor and stood apart from the other subjects, yet somehow seemed to bring them into the perpetual glow that radiated from him. That and, of course, his trademark black spectacles. The pictures had been taken at major anthropological digs all around the world, from Lake Turkana in Kenya to the Serengeti in Tanzania; the peat bogs of Scotland to the Denisova Cave in Siberia; and from the Nazca Desert in Peru to the petroglyphs of Alberta. Brandt beaming as he held human remains and stone tools and all kinds of relics for the camera to see.

Climate-controlled display cases on pedestals showcased the partial and complete skulls of the human lineage from the apelike *Ardipithecus ramidus* and *Homo habilis* through *Homo erectus, Homo neanderthalensis* and *Homo sapiens idaltu*, culminating in *Homo sapiens sapiens*, the skull of which wore a pair of Brandt's old glasses to comedic effect. There were fossilized hand and footprints, idols, tools, grave goods, and everything in between. A near-complete history of mankind in one room.

Yet for as intimidating as the office was, it was nothing compared to the man who had personally collected every artifact, the giant in the field who sat across the room, silhouetted against the bank of floor-to-ceiling windows over-looking the massive courtyard with the hedge maze filled with bronze statues of all of the incarnations of humanity.

Dr. Brandt pressed a button on the arm of his wheelchair and the windows changed from crystal-clear to a solarized gold reminiscent of the foil NASA used. He spun the chair to face Brooks, who failed to hide his expression of shock.

Brandt smiled and waved away his reaction.

"I know how I look. Believe me, my young friend. I see that same look on my face every time I catch a glimpse of my reflection." He laughed and the momentary tension vanished. Brandt's laugh had that effect. It was infectious, and somehow seemed to encapsulate everything he was in a single sound: warm, brilliant, open and honest. No one could meet the man and not be affected by him. He was simply one of those special people who rose above the crowd and disproved the old adage that only the good died young. "Come, come. There's something I must show you."

He thumbed the control knob on his chair and blew past Brooks, who followed him through the maze of pedestals to a short hallway at the back of the office. Brooks had never been back here before and was surprised to watch Brandt speed right past the bathroom and the closet and stop in front of what appeared to be an ordinary wall at the terminus.

Brandt removed the oxygen tubing from around his ears and the cannula from his nose in order to slide his necklace out from beneath his collar and over his head.

Brooks had seen its ornamentation before. The charm was a three-inch-long section of four tapering, spade-shaped human vertebrae. They were the texture of stone and the color of clay and despite the inherent ugliness, represented an archaeological finding unique in all of the world. Brandt had found it himself in the Great Rift Valley, near the Congo, and prized it above any other object in his personal collection, for it was the validation of his life's work, proof positive of the theory of evolution.

It was a vestigial human tail.

Brandt caught him looking, grinned like a child, and pulled the bones apart to expose the key hidden inside. He cast a wink back over his shoulder and slid aside an electrical outlet cover. Behind the false façade was a metal panel with a single lock in the center. He inserted the key, gave it a twist, and then removed it before the entire wall slid back into a recess and revealed an elevator cab with mirrored paneling.

Brooks saw the reflection of Brandt's smirk before settling on his own dumbfounded expression. He followed Brandt inside and turned to face the doors as they whispered closed.

"How long have you been the director here, Jordan?"

"Apparently not long enough to get the full tour."

"Then it's high time we rectified that, my boy." He smiled. "Push that bottom button, would you?"

Brooks did as instructed and, with a hum, the cab descended. He watched Brandt in the mirror. The old man wore an amused expression that belied his age, unlike his old-fashioned, double-breasted Canali suit, which made him look like he'd stepped right out of the twenties. Brooks, in contrast, never failed to look rumpled, no matter how hard he tried to keep himself from tugging at his collar and pushing up his sleeves and adjusting his slacks. He was better suited for field-work, as his physique and mannerisms attested. There were times when he felt as though the deal to become director had been struck with the devil — and, in a sense, it had — as it was the price he had to pay to fund his own research. Yet in his eight years at the Johann Brandt Institute, he'd never even suspected there was an elevator in Brandt's office, let alone a sublevel separate from the others. It was one thing not to be told when he was a graduate student, and maybe even during his years as a department head and assistant director, but he'd been the director of operations for nearly four full years now. Nothing should be allowed to go on within these walls without his implicit approval. Or at least his knowledge.

As soon as the doors parted, he understood why the secret had been so closely guarded.

The elevator opened upon a chamber approximately twenty feet wide and the length of the entire building. He realized the main sublevel where they received, stored, and curated artifacts was just on the other side of the wall. Either he'd never noticed the basement was smaller than the floor above it or this section had been poured at the same time as the initial foundation, sealed off, and buried. Considering construction on the original building, which had grown and metamorphosed into the architectural marvel that it was now, had commenced in 1978, the secret Brandt housed down here was one he'd been prepared to keep since before Brooks was even born.

"You'll be able to see better if you actually step out of the elevator," Brandt said as he rolled down the main aisle of his own personal exhibition. An exhibition of a much different nature than the one in the office above their heads.

Brooks followed slowly. His footsteps echoed from the walls. The air was dramatically cooler and the humidity was controlled to help preserve the delicate relics. He was just about to ask Brandt where he had secured so many rare and remarkable objects when he recognized the gleam of pride in the benefactor's eyes. Like everything in his office, Brandt had personally collected these, too. Suddenly, he realized there was far more he didn't know about his boss and mentor than he ever imagined.

There were rows and rows of long glass cases, inside of which were plaster casts of faces mounted in such a way as to appear to be looking right at Brandt as he rolled past. They were discolored by age and crumbling in spots, but the care that had been invested into their creation was readily apparent. This was the foundation of evolutionary anthropology back in the late thirties and early forties, although from a different school of practice than the one in which Brooks had been groomed. Scientists had traveled the world with their calipers and eye charts, measuring and comparing every possible physical dimension from weight and height to the length and width of noses, eyes, and foreheads. They'd established conventional ranges of eye color, dimension, and acuity for the different races and creeds. And then they'd immortalized the faces of their subjects in plaster.

It was a horrible process during which the subjects were forced to close their eyes and mouths and breathe through reeds inserted into their nostrils while layer after layer of plaster were applied to their entire faces. Over their noses and eyes. In their ears and hair. The experience took hours and was often described as similar to being buried alive, which was why indigenous peoples tended to vanish when white men arrived and many early scholars shied away from its practice. In fact, there was really only one faction notorious for its use.

The government-sponsored scientists of the *Nationalsozialistische Deutsche Arbeiterpartei.*

The Nazis.

The pictures on the walls confirmed Brandt's involvement. Were it not for the eyes and the smile, Brooks might not have recognized the man in the pictures — who barely looked out of his teens — as the elderly gentleman he'd known for nearly a decade. In most, he was bearded and wearing heavy wool sweaters and coats and hats in the field, where he mugged for posterity with his expedition mates in front of tents in remote locations or greeted foreign rulers and dignitaries at whose identities Brooks couldn't even begin to speculate. There were black and white photographs of bundled men leading trains of overburdened mules up steep switchbacks and across glacial fields of ice, animals previously unknown to science and since driven to extinction by the men who "collected" them, and Brandt with natives of all nationalities as he poked and prodded with calipers and rulers and needles with a smile on his face.

And then there were others.

Men in pith helmets with the twin sig runes of the *Schutzstaffel* insignia. Men in gray uniforms readily identifiable by the SS eagles and death's heads on their peaked caps, by the *Sigrunen* and rank on their black collars, by their knee-high black boots and, most notably, by the swastikas banded around their arms. These were the same men doing the exact same things, only to a different type of subject. To naked men, women, and children, emaciated and branded, young and old, on the verge of death. Filthy and terrified. Surrounded by guards with rifles and in overcrowded barracks and behind barbed wire fences with smokestacks in the background, churning the ashes of their kin into slate-gray skies that wept cold rain.

Brandt was in nearly all of them. The same man whose eyes and smile had undoubtedly had a much different effect on his subjects behind the fortified walls of Dachau.

"I am an old man," Brandt said. "Much has changed during my ninety-five years on this planet. Everything, in fact. We live our lives in the times, as you'll one day learn. Judgment is reserved for subsequent generations; history is written by the victors of wars."

He turned around in his chair to face Brooks, who couldn't bring himself to meet the old man's stare.

"I was just a child when the French and Belgians invaded the Ruhr and seized my father's land as compensation for the unreasonable and punitive reparations demanded by the Treaty of Versailles, which my country had been unable to pay. Our families met soldiers with a display of passive resistance. They responded by executing more than a hundred civilians, among them *mein vater.*" He cleared his throat. "My father. I was three years old when he was bayonetted before my very eyes. I knew nothing of reparations or finances, nor did I care about the resulting hyperinflation that doomed our economy. All I knew was fear. And as I grew older, hatred. Like the rest of my generation. And that combination is a recipe for disaster, as history has shown us since. Maybe we knew as much at the time. But even history can't show us how it all could have played out any differently."

"There's no justification for the atrocities you committed."

"I committed no atrocities. Mine were crimes of inaction. Or perhaps failure to recognize the need to act would be more accurate. Maybe even deliberately so. You have to understand that this was a time of great scientific and technological advancement. A wonderful time to be a scientist. We were all swept up in it. Fields like theoretical and atomic physics, aerospace and genetic engineering were in their infancy and we made enormous strides thanks to the active support and funding of a government with its own agenda, which we believed at the time aligned with ours. Our prized evolutionary anthropology was elevated from a speculative pseudoscience to legitimacy by the office of the Ahnenerbe, Heinrich Himmler's society for the study of Germanic ancestral heritage. He used his power and position as Reichsführer of the SS — the state police — to advance his personal theories about the enlightened origins of the German people, whom he believed descended from a mystical Nordic race that escaped the sinking of Atlantis, fled across the Gobi Desert, and settled high in the Himalayas, in a holy place known as Shambhala. These were the ancestors who would prove that the Germanic peoples were not meant to be ground beneath the heels of their European oppressors, that they were inherently superior. It wasn't about the Jews. Not then, and not to us, anyway. It was about finding proof of the transcendence of our bloodline, about showing not only our own people that they were better than those who held them down, but the entire world. And thus, it was to academia and the field of anthropology that the Ahnenerbe turned when it commenced its quest to find the origins of the Aryan race."

"The Atlanteans who fled their sinking city and settled in the highest mountains on the planet."

Brandt smiled.

"I know how it sounds now. So many of us believed it because we wanted to. Because we needed to. Despite how fantastic the legends sounded, even at the time. It wasn't about the blond-haired, blue-eyed ideal. That was propaganda of Western creation. Did anyone really think that men with dark hair and eyes could sell such a notion to an entire nation? It was about the bloodline, the lineage. We were all caught up in the populist *völkisch* movement and the concept of returning to the greatness of our roots. Most of us, anyway. I didn't buy into any of that, but I kept my feelings about the matter to myself. I was an anthropologist with a blank check drawn on a seemingly inexhaustible account with the freedom to truly advance my field. I might not have believed in the existence of Himmler's Aryan race, but I did subscribe to the theory of human evolution and set out on my own personal quest to discover the origin of the species."

Brandt turned his chair and drove beside the long rows of preserved faces. He gestured with his left hand as he spoke.

"At the time, I believed ours to be a collection of races descended from common ancestors. Still do, really. I traveled the world taking measurements with calipers and rulers and scales and all of the tools they now chuckle about in schools. I found the consistent differences between the peoples of this planet, the subtle physical variations that developed through the eons thanks to geography and the climate, behavior and society. I catalogued the spatulate-shaped incisors, advanced musculature, and *steatopygia* of the African peoples and the epicanthal folds and brachycephalic skulls of the Asian races." He waved at the cases, where men, women, and children, most of whom were undoubtedly long gone, stared back at him with perpetually blank expressions. "I studied the brow ridges and nasal bone configurations of the indigenous tribes of South America and the traits both common and unique to Pacific islanders isolated by water and time. The subtle similarities between the Jews in Dachau and the peoples of Arabic descent, and their more prominent similarities to their fellow Germans, despite the lengths to which my colleagues went to demonstrate otherwise. And in all of them I found the commonalities of an analogous evolution — the trunk of the family tree of man, if you will — and yet I also found countless points of divergence I felt — and still feel — were distinct enough to warrant subspecies classification. But only once in all of my travels and explorations did I truly encounter something — shall we say — unclassifiable."

"Why are you telling me all of this? Why now?"

"My boy, if there is one thing I understand, it is the nature of mortality. I may not be afflicted with some fatal disease, but I assure you, I am dying. It is simply the fulfillment of my biological destiny, and my time will come sooner than later."

"I can't offer you absolution."

"I seek none. The choices I've made along the journey have been my own. They were educated, and yet informed by the times. Were I to have the chance to live my life again, I would certainly make the same choices in the same historical context. Science has never been a field beholden to morality. Roentgen sacrificed his own wife to radiation when he discovered x-rays. Marie Curie nearly blinded herself and suffered from anemia caused by carrying radioactive isotopes in her pockets. I merely utilized my station to gather the data that proved to be the foundation of a field devoted to the study and advancement of mankind. The world is and will be a better place for the existence of this institute and the dozens of others like it."

"So why bring me down here? Displaying any of this will destroy the reputation of the institute and cast a pall over the entire field."

"You remind me a lot of myself. A lifetime ago, anyway. Ambitious and adventurous, with a lust for knowledge and discovery for its own sake. Not for the money or the acclaim or the prestige, but simply because there are mysteries out there to be solved using clues hidden all around the globe, from the deepest oceanic trenches to the highest snowcapped peaks. Your work with the evolutionary impact of viruses is beyond anything I could have imagined in my wildest dreams when I exhumed my first partial hominin skull. You are the worthy inheritor not just of the leadership of the institute, but of my greatest discovery, one I've spent the majority of my life trying to understand."

Brooks stopped and looked around him before affixing his stare on the frail old man's back.

"We're *nothing* alike. I would never sacrifice my soul for my research."

"Soul? Let me know when you dig one of those up."

"My morality then."

"Morality is dictated by the prevailing winds of the time. Were our roles reversed, I have no doubt you would have made the same choices I did."

"I think maybe we should head back upstairs. I have actual job duties—"

"I haven't shown you what I brought you down here to see."

"I've seen enough."

"You haven't seen anything yet."

The whirring sound of Brandt's chair echoed in the vast room as he led Brooks toward a central display case taller and wider than all of the others, with its own set of environmental controls. It was dark inside to protect its contents from the damage of even the weak ultraviolet radiation emitted by the fluorescent lights. Brandt pressed a series of buttons on the control panel built into the pedestal and, with a shushing sound, the glass became transparent and the internal lead shielding retracted.

Brooks found himself staring at the plaster mold of a face simultaneously both like, and completely unlike, all of the others. He stepped forward and appraised it. Turned and stared at Brandt, who smiled indulgently and tented his bony fingers in his lap. Looked back at the object in the case. It was positively surreal.

Millions of thoughts collided in Brooks's head as he scrutinized the object in the case. He managed to pluck four words from the tumult without once so much as blinking.

"When do I leave?"

2

Pai Village
Motuo County
Tibet Autonomous Region
People's Republic of China
October 12th

Five Days Ago

Brooks shuffled out of the lodge that had been billed as the "Grand Scenic Resort." In reality, it was little more than a rectangular wood-frame structure built on two-foot block stilts to keep it above ground that was hard and frozen and snow-packed nine months out of the year and flowing with mud and seasonal runoff during the remaining three. The walls were composed of irregular planks and the construction was shoddy even by backyard fencing standards back home. The exposed roof joists were covered by a patchwork of sheets and blankets, which also served as the doors over the open thresholds and the curtains covering the cutouts that passed for windows, a superfluous luxury considering he could see straight through the gaps between the slats. The resort claimed it was the foremost attraction in Motuo County and received four stars for its accommodations on a scale that must have been established by the frogs that had descended from the forest beneath the mist to take shelter under the floorboards, through which he could not only hear the cacophonous croaking, but see them squirming and flopping on top of one another through the cracks below him as he lay on the warped elm slab that passed for a bed.

All five of them had been crammed into that one room, four along the back wall and one lengthwise beside the feet of the others, with barely enough space to walk between them. The outhouse was spacious by comparison and the smell was almost preferable to the continuous exposure to the wind and rain that passed straight through the walls and extinguished the diminutive flame in the stove they had lit for heat.

All in all, though, he'd stayed in worse.

He found a seat on a planed stump and wrapped his arms around his chest. He watched an elderly woman crumble brick tea and salt into a cauldron over the fire while he waited for the others to drag themselves out of bed, which, on a frigid morning like this one, was easier said than done. Especially considering they all knew they had a long, arduous day ahead of them. Several, in fact. Each of which promised to make this look like a night at the Ritz.

Pai Village was internationally renowned as the springboard of the brutal trail to Motuo and their ultimate destination in the low-lying valley of the Yarlung Tsangpo River, enclosed on four sides by the towering Himalayas. It was a biome unto itself, completely isolated from the rest of the world, and the only one of China's 2,100 counties to remain inaccessible by road, despite numerous attempts to construct highways that were thwarted by mudslides and avalanches. An air drop would be risky, thanks to the unpredictable weather, tempestuous winds, and mist-shrouded peaks, even if one could find a pilot willing to risk creating an international incident and being fired upon by the Chinese entrenched in the mountains, defending their borders from the "autonomous" Tibetans to the southwest and the Indians to the south, who themselves grew increasingly wary of the red tide rising to the north with each passing day. Thus the necessity for the four-day trek, which had required a staggering amount of money to bribe a Sichuanese trail boss named Zhang to escort them since westerners were forbidden from entering Motuo — "hidden lotus" in Tibetan — which Buddhist scripture designated the purest and holiest region due to its unique contiguous environment where frozen peaks descended into sub-tropical jungles.

Brooks gratefully accepted a steaming wooden bowl of tea and a dollop of yak butter, which melted into the brew as she stirred it with her gnarled finger. His nod of thanks elicited a beaming grin and she shuffled back to the fire and commenced with arranging the ingredients for the morning meal. The sun was still an hour from rising, but already the curious Lhoba people eyed him from their windows, doorways, and alleys with open suspicion while he drank his tea and his colleagues emerged from their shared room and crossed the bare earth to warm themselves by the fire.

Dr. Warren Murray was the Assistant Director of Hominin Studies at the Brandt Institute and President of the Department of Evolutionary Biology at the University of Chicago. At forty, he was the elder statesman of the expedition, but carried himself as though he were even older than that. He was a native Australian who immigrated to Texas during his formative years, earned his undergraduate degree at NYU and his doctorate at Harvard, and had the unique accent to show for it. He was the most widely published of them by far, yet had remarkably accomplished that feat with a minimum amount of actual fieldwork. As an academic, however, his fingers had ready access to the purse strings of benefactors Brooks had never even met and his refined good looks — with his almost feminine lips and soul-deep blue eyes — generally got him whatever he wanted, which, in this case, had been to insinuate himself onto a high-profile expedition that would allow him to put to rest once and for all the rumors that he was soft. Knowing Warren, he'd probably also arranged endorsement deals and media exclusives, which was more likely the case.

He was the first to join Brooks beside the fire and greeted him with a grunt. He beckoned the woman with a snap of his fingers. For as surprised as he was when she dropped the yak butter into his tea, he was even more repulsed by the unwashed finger she used to stir it. He mumbled something incomprehensible under his breath while he stared at the yellow swirl diffusing into his tea.

"Sleep well, Warren?"

"If you call tossing and turning on a lumpy wooden slab all night sleeping, then yes, I slept magnificently."

"You're lucky you slept at all with that chainsaw roaring," Adrianne Grayson said as she emerged from the blanket that served as the front door. She had her sleeping bag wrapped around her and a woolen Tibetan hat with earflaps over her blond hair, and still managed to pull off the look. With her blue eyes and the freckles on just the very tip of her nose, she was positively adorable. She was twenty-six, but looked eighteen, and one of the most ambitious graduate students Brooks had ever interviewed. She was a doctoral candidate from Penn whose thesis about the effects of vector-borne diseases on population models dovetailed nicely with his own regarding the physiological effects of viruses on human evolution. Thus the reason she had all but beaten down his door to join his department.

"I have sinus issues, you know." Julian Armstead swatted the blanket out of his way as he followed her. He had curly dark hair, a long face, and a straggly goatee. He was the kind of guy who wore socks with sandals and undoubtedly wouldn't pass a surprise UA, but he'd spent more time in the field than any graduate student who applied. Most of it was in more tropical locations than the one towering over the small village, where he'd probably done little more than comb the underbrush for mushrooms and marijuana, but he was an experienced climber, which was what had initially attracted him to Northern Arizona's prestigious anthropology department in general and the sheer red plateaus and gorges of Sonora specifically. His doctoral thesis, while ill defined, revolved around the idea of creating a pharmacopeia of ancient holistic remedies that he not-so-secretly intended to use to impress his old man, the managing director of U.S. operations for pharmaceutical giant Bristol-Myers Squibb. And then sell it to him at a cost that would avenge every childhood slight. "And a deviated septum. It's a legitimate medical condition. There's nothing I can do about it."

"I can think of plenty of ways to take care of that for you. I've heard the quickest way to learn to breathe through your nose is by having someone hold a hand over your mouth."

"You wouldn't dare."

"I wouldn't?"

Adrianne sat on a rock beside Brooks and rubbed her hands together over the fire. The silver polish on her nails reflected the flames. She must have just had them done before receiving his last-minute invitation. Julian crouched beside her, but moved when the smoke blew into his face. The old woman laughed and clapped him on the back when he started to cough.

"Everyone make sure to eat and drink your fill," Brooks said. "We have a rough journey ahead of us."

"How far is it to the next camp again?" Warren asked.

"Only five thousand feet—"

"That's not even a mile," Julian interrupted.

"—straight up."

With the clopping of hooves, their trail boss, Zhang, appeared from the road on the other side of the wooden hovel, leading a hairy mule. Its breath plumed around the bit in its mouth. All of their packs were strapped to its back in a gravity-defying mound. Their hydro bladders were holstered on its flank for easy retrieval. The last thing they could afford to do was become dehydrated, especially as they ascended into the mist surrounding the peaks.

Zhang beamed, showcasing a smile lacking the two front teeth in the upper row. His skin was wrinkled and leathered by the elements, his dark eyes hooded, and his slender frame concealed beneath multiple layers of clothing. His black braids hung from beneath his fur-rimmed hood. He gestured to the mule like a showcase model presenting a new car.

"You like?" he said.

"That's a world-class mule, for sure," Brooks said. "You didn't steal it, did you?"

"No, no. I buy. I pay with money I find in bag here."

His smile grew impossibly wider.

Brooks regretted asking. He didn't trust Zhang as far as he could throw him. Anyone whose primary skill set involved moving unnoticed across hotly contested borders without incurring the wrath of the Chinese or the Indians or any of the bands of thieves stalking these trails suggested he was accustomed to smuggling a lot more than tourists through the mountains. That Brooks had already heard him converse in Tibetan, two different dialects of Chinese, a kind of pidgin Indian, and passable English suggested he was also a lot smarter than he wanted anyone to believe. His rural bumpkin façade might have been just for show, but his allegiance to the money they were paying him seemed genuine enough.

A reddish-orange aura spread across the jagged horizon to the east as the sun prepared to rise.

Brooks stood and turned to face the Himalayas. Somewhere up there was what he had traveled all this way to find. He could feel it. There was just one thing that continued to gnaw at him, despite his best efforts to rationalize it away. If Brandt had known it was up there all this time, why had he not returned to gather more evidence to share with the world? After all, it was a discovery of the highest order, a revolutionary finding that would change the field of evolutionary anthropology forever. And why would he wait until death was imminent to share what he had found with Brooks, when any of his predecessors would have jumped at the chance to be a part of history?

Or maybe Brandt had done the exact same thing with them and had simply withheld that information from Brooks. Perhaps Brandt himself had returned on numerous occasions and been unable to find what he had simply come upon by accident the first time. For all Brooks knew, he was just another in a long line of anthropologists Brandt had wound up like tin soldiers and turned loose in the Tibetan wilds. After all, as he had learned only recently, it wasn't out of character for Brandt to hide the truth. Who knew if there was really anything up there at all? He couldn't rule out the possibility that the plaster cast was an elaborate fake. Or perhaps he just didn't want to.

None of it mattered in the grand design. If there was a chance that Brandt's story was true and the discovery of a lifetime was up there, then it was a chance he had to take. In this case, even returning home empty-handed wouldn't be considered an outright failure. This was the adventure he needed to break out of the monotonous routine into which he'd settled. This was what he had envisioned for his life when he first realized that anthropology was his calling. One of the four most remote areas on the planet awaited him, where few humans had ever set foot, and even fewer Westerners. If there was one place where life could have evolved and thrived in complete isolation, this was it.

Brooks felt a surge of adrenaline and turned to face the others.

"All right people. Are you ready to make history?"

3

Duoxiongla Pass
Motuo County
Tibet Autonomous Region
People's Republic of China
October 12th

Five Days Ago

A damp fog clung to the steep foothills through which they trekked for the majority of the morning. At best, the visibility was maybe a quarter of a mile; at worst, Brooks could barely see the others, mere feet away. The path was formed from smooth stones the size of baseballs, polished by hundreds of years of brutal wind and seasonal runoff, and glazed with a layer of ice that made it nearly impossible to remain upright. The ferns and rhododendrons enclosing the path sparkled with a layer of frost that seemingly turned from water to ice at will. The meandering route followed the topography, skirting granite escarpments hundreds of feet tall and bridging whitewater streams that plummeted from the mist and raced unimpeded down the mountainside. Only occasionally did the snowcapped peaks appear high above, taunting them.

Somewhere beyond them was what they had traveled all this way to find.

Brooks had never experienced weather even remotely like this. It didn't rain or snow as much as the air itself seemed to turn to ice against what little bare skin remained exposed. It felt as though microscopic organisms were taking bites from his cheekbones and forehead. He tried not to dwell on the cold because he knew it was only going to get worse.

He wore a hybrid hoody that zipped up to his nose, almost high enough to conceal his neoprene balaclava. The jacket had a Pertex shell and synthetic microfiber thermal insulation that was supposed to be nearly impervious to everything the environment could throw at it, but he doubted the manufacturer had ever tested it in wind like this. It buffeted him with such force that he'd taken to walking nearly doubled over and bracing himself with a walking stick. The skin around his sunglasses was abraded to such an extent that it was dotted with blood. There were even times when he had no choice but to drag his pack behind him for fear of the wind using it to lift him like a kite. He knew better than to complain, though, not that anyone would have been able to hear him over Warren's incessant griping.

It was almost a relief when they finally ascended from the fog and into the snow, where at least they occasionally felt the presence of the sun on their bodies, despite the howling wind that battered them with snowflakes.

The path vanished beneath the seamless accumulation, the top layer of which was crisp and sounded like Styrofoam when they broke through it. The first time Adrianne fell, she slid nearly fifty feet straight down the mountain before she managed to catch an ice-rimed granite pinnacle. They all strapped on their crampons after that. The spikes made the mere act of walking difficult, but they granted solid traction. Most of the time, anyway.

Zhang claimed to know exactly where the trail ran beneath all of the snow. He wore a parka with fur reminiscent of a lion's mane around the hood and a gap-toothed grin that never left his face. He shouldered the mule's haunches when it balked at some of the steeper switchbacks and brushed the frozen spume from its muzzle. When it tired he fed it one of the dried roots he stored in his jacket pocket and kept clenched between his molars like a toothpick.

"You eat, you no get tired so fast," he'd said and laughed when Julian spit the offered piece onto the ground and shoveled snow into his mouth.

"Christ, man! It tastes like ass!"

"You no like ass? Good news for Dorje."

He clapped the mule on its flank and urged it faster.

Despite his initial reaction, Julian persevered and made seemingly endless notes about the root. He believed to it be of the *Rhodiola* genus, but couldn't be certain of the species. Whether or not the effects were psychosomatic, he claimed to feel less fatigued and mentally sharper and searched for the source plant in the windswept lee behind every rock outcropping.

Faded prayer flags beaten to ribbons by the wind snapped with such force that they nearly bent the sticks to which they were moored to the ground. Mountains of talus reared up from the accumulation at random intervals, rubble left behind from crumbled cairns and structures that Adrianne said were originally built some forty thousand years ago by a nomadic tribe known as the Qiang, who herded long-horned Tibetan sheep through these mountains and erected these stacked-stone domiciles as shelters from the elements. What little remained of the largest of these dwellings hardly deterred the insistent wind long enough for them to eat protein bars and drink what little water remained thawed in the hydro bladders against the mule's flank.

The trail grew even steeper from there, forcing them to crawl in spots.

By the time they reached the summit of the trail, it already felt like they'd been climbing for days in the thin air. The sun vanished behind the clouds and the storm commenced in earnest, sheeting sideways with such ferocity that the snow looked like the fin of a shark where it blew from the peak of Mt. Duoxiongla. It froze to their clothing on contact and somehow found its way under their sunglasses and inside of their clothes. Or at least that was how it felt. It became impossible to separate the wind from the frozen needles it hurled through them in the same fashion as a tornado impelled blades of grass through telephone poles. They had to shout to be heard and none of them risked looking up from the treacherous footing.

The mule Zhang had apparently named Dorje brayed when he drove it over a slick precipice, beyond which there appeared to be nothing but open air. It locked its legs and skidded down the narrow switchback, its burden threatening to send it careening over the edge. The wind blew so hard across the northeastern face that the snow had no chance to stick. The loose talus was covered with ice and slid out from beneath their feet, tumbled down the path, and bounded out over the sheer pitfalls.

At the top of an especially steep section, the mule planted its haunches on the ground and refused to take another step. Zhang gave a sharp tug on the reins, but it didn't budge. He braced his feet and tried again. The mule lost traction and slid down at him so fast he had to lunge uphill to keep from being plowed over the edge. The mule righted itself on trembling legs within inches of plummeting to its death.

"We have to unburden her!" Brooks shouted over the screaming wind and reached for one of the straps.

Zhang slapped his gloved hand.

"You must not make lose balance! She will get cargo down!"

"The trail's too steep!" Adrianne shouted. "She'll fall to her death!"

"You no understand. This what mule do."

"I've had just about enough of this nonsense!" Warren shouted. He pushed past Julian on the narrow trail. "I need to get off of this infernal mountain before—"

He lost his footing and slid on the ice, a scarlet-jacketed blur streaking past their feet. With a scream and a spray of snow, Warren fired down the path and launched out over the rocks and into the storm.

Brooks dove for his colleague's hand. He caught a fleeting glimpse of the terror on Warren's face.

And then he was gone.

4

Excerpt from the journal of
Hermann G. Wolff

Courtesy of Johann Brandt, Private Collection
Chicago, Illinois
(Translated from original handwritten German text)

November 1938

I t is hard to believe that a mere six months ago I had never set foot outside
of the Fatherland, nor had I any reason to believe I ever would. Now,
here I am, half a world away from the only home I have ever known and
standing on the brink of this new and wondrous frontier. The vessel that
ferried us from Genoa to Ceylon — across the Mediterranean and Red Seas
and the Indian Ocean — is but a distant memory and already I feel like I
have known my new friends all of my life, even though we were only recently
introduced. We were all recruited for the expedition by the Ahnenerbe — upon
Augustus König's recommendation and Heinrich Himmler's personal insis-

tence — *from the ranks of the Schutzstaffel and academia. None of us had the slightest idea what we had been volunteered for, only that declining such an honor would not be a prudent choice. Not that we objected. Let it not be said that when the Reichsführer promised the world, he did not deliver. Not only would we have the unprecedented freedom to pursue our professional agendas, upon our return we would be granted the highest academic standing offered by the NSDAP.*

By the time we reached Calcutta, the staging grounds for the journey to come, our group was as tight-knit as any family, with the exception of König, who maintained separate quarters to demonstrate his authority even when we transferred ships in both Colombo and Madras, on the Bay of Bengal.

While the rest of us explored the sweltering, seething streets of Calcutta, experiencing the outrageous contrast between squalor and excess, and haggling with merchants who would sell their very souls for the right price, König sought refuge from streets that reeked of the impoverished in the wilds, with only his rifle to keep him company.

None of us cared, for we were boys turned loose in a fairytale land, albeit one inflicted upon the land like a festering wound, between the ricelands and the bustling bay. We drank whisky [sic], took tea, and gorged ourselves upon festive-colored meals that curled the hair in our nostrils, singed our tongues, and passed through us like fire while we awaited news from the Viceroy in Simla, who ultimately granted our request — thanks in no small part to pressure exerted by Berlin — to travel on to Sikkim, where we would again find ourselves ensnared in a morass of bureaucracy and diplomacy.

Unlike its repugnant Bengali cousin, Sikkim is a majestic land. It is a steep slice of land rising from within sight of the ocean up into the clouds, like a great tent spike driven into the black heart of an otherwise vile and uncivilized land. The narrow-gauge train that carried us as far as Siliguri reminded me of a toy I played with as a child, especially as it passed through forests of bamboo that towered thirty meters over our heads and across trembling wooden bridges that spanned waterfalls of such violence that their roar drowned out even the omnipresent ruckus of the engine and the clamor of the wheels. I filmed it all with an awed sense of fascination for which words alone are insufficient. It was as though I were on a faraway planet, surrounded by species of flora and fauna so unlike anything with which I was familiar it is as though they shared no commonalities whatsoever. I found myself thinking that if there were indeed one place in this world where the roots of our mystical Aryan origin could be hidden, it was this.

The monsoon rains fell warm and with such ferocity it was as if the globe had been suddenly turned upside down and the seas had become the skies. The very hillsides crumbled before our eyes, opening chasms through which the floodwaters swept with murderous intent. One mudslide nearly buried half of the train and it took us three days to dig it back out. While König hunted this strange land on his own, of course.

Every stop along the way found Johann Brandt with his calipers and eye charts, measuring and cataloguing the native populations with a boyish grin on his face. Despite his inability to communicate with the natives, nearly every man or woman he approached allowed him to poke and prod to his heart's content, thanks to his natural charm and charisma. We are not even close to our destination and already he has accumulated more plaster casts of faces than we can comfortably accommodate and has crates filled with racial and hygienic documentation for the Kaiser Wilhelm Society and its eugenicists, with whom he is in frequent contact.

Kurt Eberhardt and Otto Metzger are content to take in the sights and sounds and the unusual culinary delicacies made from Lord only knows which kind of meat and seasoned with spices forged from the flames of hell themselves. Like me, their mission lies ahead of them and there's little we are able to contribute, outside of documenting everything we see for posterity.

Looking back now, I hardly remember Ghoom or Darjeeling, for the moment the snowcapped Himalayas reared from the horizon and impaled the clouds, I could think of nothing else. It was unconscionable to even imagine that we would soon be up there, standing on top of the world itself, where few men have ever dared venture. It was a feeling unlike any I had experienced before. Metzger described it as a physical sensation of euphoria, like the moment before climax, but that was too commonplace an occurrence to do it justice.

We are on the verge of making history — whether or not we find mythical Shambhala and the tracks of our Aryan ancestors — and the film of our expedition will be not only the first of its kind, it will play in theaters and universities alike. It will be a documentary of historical significance that will allow us to bring the same sense of awe we feel right now to an entire generation of Germans who have known little more in life than the taste of shoe leather from the heels of their oppressors.

From Kalimping we traveled by auto, while our supplies completed the final leg of the journey to Gangtok heaped on the backs of yaks. The dwellings reflected an interbreeding of the neighboring styles, from the Indians to the Chinese, and especially the Mongols. The monasteries and temples stood apart from and towered over the adjacent structures and could be seen from every vantage point. Their walls were slanted and their windows made of paper. Their ornate eaves made them look like they were wearing enormous golden hats. The streets were bare and windswept and as hard as marble. They led upward into hills bristling with trees that reminded me of those back home.

Everything appeared dirty, from the tattered prayer flags snapping on the constant gales to the whitewashed buildings to the people themselves. Even the sheep and goats herded down the main thoroughfare were a shade of brown I found more than a little repulsive.

We passed men and women dressed in a style beyond my limited comprehension. Monks in red robes chanted mantras and counted prayer beads with such speed it was impossible to believe they could keep accurate count. There were chortens with spinning prayer wheels, like slabs of meat on vertical spits, and offerings of objects of all types, from the exquisite to the mundane and everything in between. Incense filled the air in fingers of smoke that dissipated on the breeze. Eyes followed our procession, from faces chafed by the elements and eroded by age. We were accompanied the entire way by the clatter of prayer wheels that looked like rattles and made a distinctive clicking sound when their handles were spun between two rubbed palms.

We passed from nomadic communities where entire families lived in tents alongside their herds to homes built from stacked stones and hovels of the most primitive materials to palatial manors as the town ascended the forested mountain in defiance of gravity, it seemed.

And over it all lorded the distant Himalayas and our gateway to Shambhala. Unfortunately, before we could even get a peek at Tibet, we had to seek permission inside a ramshackle building that looked just like all of the others, with the notable exceptions of the Union Jack flying from its ramparts and the uniformed officers of the British Indian Army watching our approach from the balcony.

5

Five Days Ago

Brooks scurried to the rocky ledge in time to hear Warren scream, before the furious wind swept the sound away. Through the blowing snow Brooks saw him, seemingly floating in midair.

"Help me!" Warren shouted.

He dangled from the mule's reins, his legs flailing over the mist, hundreds of feet straight down. He'd managed to grab hold with his right hand, but couldn't seem to reach it with his left.

The mule brayed and skidded closer to the edge on the loose talus. Palm-size stones tumbled over the edge and fell past Warren, who stared up at them with an expression of sheer desperation. He'd lost his sunglasses and his eyes were wide with terror. His tears froze in his lashes.

Brooks reached out over the nothingness. The wind threatened to pry him from the ledge.

"Grab my hand!"

Warren swung his left arm, but didn't come anywhere close. The movement caused the mule to slide even closer to the edge. Her legs trembled. Zhang wrapped his arms around her flank and braced his feet. Adrianne and Julian grabbed the straps they'd used to lash down their packs and pulled with everything they had.

Warren closed his eyes when a wave of rocks cascaded down onto his face.

Brooks could see the man's grip on the rein slipping. The mule lowered her head clear down past the ground. The muscles and tendons in her neck stood out as she fought the treacherous footing in a vain effort to inch away from the precipice. Even her most concerted efforts cost her ground she couldn't afford to lose. If they didn't get Warren's weight off her reins, both of them were going over.

Adrianne lost her footing and fell. The mule slid right up to the very edge. She stamped her feet and raged against her fate.

"Listen to me, Warren. You have to do this now. Grab my hand!"

He made another feeble effort and was rewarded with a rain of stones.

"I can't reach!"

Each time the mule slid, Warren dropped farther away. As it was, Brooks barely had a grip on the rock around which he'd wrapped his left arm and he could feel the wind against his chest. He extended his arm as far as he could reach. Any farther and he'd lose his own tenuous balance. He looked Warren directly in the eyes.

"Either you take my hand now or you're going to fall."

Zhang hollered and slapped the mule's flank. She strained and took a half-step back, bringing Warren momentarily closer. He reached again for Brooks as the talus gave way and the mule slid right back to the edge. Warren nearly lost his grip with the sudden drop.

"You can do this, Warren."

"Don't let me fall, Jordan!"

"I won't. You have my word. But if you don't go now—"

Warren lunged and caught his hand before Brooks was ready. He felt his grip on the rock slip and the toes of his crampons clatter across the ice. Warren released the rein and grabbed on with his other hand.

The mule bucked backward and knocked Zhang to the side. Loose rocks poured over the edge.

Brooks bellowed as he slid over the ledge, his eyes locked on Warren's. The fog rolled past far below his feet.

Weight on his legs, arresting his slide. The ledge bit into his abdomen. He stared straight down at Warren. He could feel the other man's grip slipping, his gloves peeling from his hands.

Warren looked up at him with an almost resigned expression.

"Please, God. Don't let go."

Brooks felt arms wrap around his left leg. Fists curled into the back of his jacket. He shouted with the pain as he was pulled back over the ledge. The stone bit into his chest, clipped his chin. It felt like both arms were going to rip out of their sockets. And then he was tasting snow.

The pressure abated and he raised his face just far enough to see the others hauling Warren up onto the trail. He rolled onto his back and bellowed up into the storm in triumph.

Warren was on all fours, trembling, when Brooks stood. He looked from Adrianne to Julian and finally to Zhang and thanked each of them with a nod. Had they not come to his aid when they did, he would have either been forced to release Warren or fall to his death alongside him. He rubbed the mule's smooth cheek, then extended his hand once more to Warren.

"What do you say we get the hell off this infernal mountain?"

Warren clasped his hand and struggled to stand. He looked as though he were about to say something, but instead blew out a long, pent-up breath and started tentatively down the decline.

Brooks did his best to put the near-tragedy out of his mind as they negotiated the slick path, which leveled off, if only slightly with each foot of descent. It led them into the lee of a rugged ridge, where they were spared the brunt of the wind. With the surge of adrenaline waning, Brooks felt an overwhelming sense of exhaustion that threatened to deposit him right there in the snow, but he drew upon reserves he didn't even suspect he had. Eventually, the frosted leaves of the groundcover peeked out from beneath the accumulation. The brittle crust gave way to slush even slicker than the ice in the higher regions. Fortunately, the path had widened enough that it no longer felt as though they were walking an icy tightrope over the abyss. The mist rode over their ankles and waists as they descended into the thick fog, which clung to them in the absence of the wind.

Another quarter-mile and the snow retreated into memory. Rhododendrons encroached from all sides, wet with the drizzle that hung in the air as though in defiance of gravity. For as quickly as the temperatures had plummeted, they rose even faster. The cool air combined with the layer of sweat beneath their suddenly sweltering clothes caused the goosebumps to rise almost electrically.

It struck Brooks how few people had ever made it this far, to a place that seventy years ago had been unknown to the Western world. For as magical as it felt to him, he could only imagine how it must have felt to be Brandt and his party, the first to penetrate the shroud of mystery that hung over this entire region, where only a select few indigenous people had ever passed, most of them nomadic herdsmen whose bones had turned to dust long before the first permanent settlements were erected.

They wended through narrow valleys cut by whitewater streams, which flowed nearly straight down and with almost unnatural speed. Birds came to life in the thickets and frogs chirruped from the branches and the moldering detritus. A premature dusk crept down from the high country, staining the cloudy sky momentarily crimson before the shadow of Mt. Duoxiongla fell heavily upon them.

The wooden roofs of several small dwellings materialized from the trees and the mist. They'd finally reached Lage, the first layover point on the arduous journey. Smoke from a cooking fire filtered through the valley and Brooks smelled a heavenly aroma that reminded him of how hungry he was. He felt victorious for making it this far and surviving the harrowing trials of the mountain pass, but he had to caution himself that the journey had only just begun.

This was still only the first day.

PART II

_____

THE FOREST OF THE NIGHT

6

Four Days Ago

The accommodations in Lage made the hovel in Pai look like the Ritz. It was a ramshackle wooden structure propped above a black pool of stagnant water on rough-hewn wooden blocks, the same kind they used to fashion the lumpy beds and the prison bar-like dividers between the room they shared and the main portion of the dwelling, which itself was little more than a dingy space arranged around a cooking hearth. There was an outhouse crawling with insects of all kinds and the only potable water came from a stream a short walk away, but after the day they'd endured, they were grateful for such comforts. Even Warren was uncharacteristically quiet the following morning. There was nothing like sleeping on a log with knots bruising your back and flies buzzing around your head to instill a little humility.

Their hosts had no contact whatsoever with the outside world, but were kind and generous. An older woman named Norba served them *kalep borkun* — a kind of flatbread made from tsampa — from a smoking skillet and goat milk so fresh it was still warm. Adrianne commented that its collection must have been the cause of the bleating that had awakened them before dawn, but none of them dwelled on it. They had another long day ahead of them and were thankful for the hot meal and the curiously sweet drink.

They left Lage behind at the foot of mist-ensconced Mt. Duoxiongla and entered the steep maze of valleys leading from the sub-alpine temperate zone into what qualified as a jungle by anyone's definition of the word. Impenetrable snarls of lychee, longan, and durian trees grew from nearly vertical steppes, alongside which a stone path barely wide enough to place both feet beside each other wended. There was no way Dorje would have made the journey, even had Zhang not unilaterally made the decision to leave her behind. The added weight from their packs made negotiating the terrain a feat in itself. Brooks wondered how even such a large animal could have borne their combined weight. Worse was the understanding that had the mule not hauled their gear over the pass, they likely never would have made it. It was a grim reminder of the fact that they were academics, not adventurers, and whatever feelings of invulnerability they carried with them were illusory. Warren had nearly died and, if they weren't careful, someone else just might. He shook his head to dispel the memory of staring down at Warren as he slid over the edge and seeing nothing but the fear in the man's eyes and the clouds far below him.

Chinese ficus trees sent out climbers and runners in an attempt to strangle the life from the other trees, ensnaring them in an inescapable wooden net. Hornbills trumpeted from the upper canopy and occasionally flashed through the sporadic columns of light that penetrated the vegetation. Geckos scurried up the trunks of trees and calote lizards — colloquially called bloodsuckers — scampered across the dead leaves. Boas hung over the thick boughs like glistening brown gobs of taffy. Zhang reminded them that the predators here knew no natural enemies. The last thing they wanted to do was startle a tiger or a king cobra basking on the trail.

It was impossible to believe that less than twenty-four hours ago they'd been trudging through snow and ice at the top of the world. Now it was all they could do to keep their skin covered so as not to feed the whining clouds

of mosquitoes. Their clothes clung to their sweat and hampered their movements. It was a relief when the rain started to patter on the treetops and drip
to the ground around them. The humidity made it feel like they were trying to
breathe underwater, but not nearly to the extent of the storm when it finally
cut loose.

Brooks had never seen rain quite like it. The drops beat the broad leaves
from the branches and released a steady barrage of hard-husked fruit. Water
poured in streams from the upper reaches, raced across the already slick path,
and fired from the rocky steppes in impromptu waterfalls. Their clothes were
drenched before they had a chance to do anything about it, but at least they no
longer had to worry about the mosquitoes and the snakes. The streams rose
and washed out their banks, sending tangles of uprooted foliage downhill,
where the lowlands were already flooded. Mud sluiced through the maze of
trunks and roots and spilled across the trail, nearly hiding it from sight.

Zhang led them toward a yellow granite escarpment that appeared to have
been thrust upward from the mantle by some great tectonic upheaval.
Epiphytes bloomed from where they'd taken root directly in the cracks
between the slithering vines. They were nearly upon it when Brooks saw the
mouth of a cave and dashed out of the rain. Their footsteps echoed in the
darkness. Brooks looked back past the others and through the entrance, which
looked like it had been sealed by a waterfall. He flung the water from his hands
and wrung out the front of his shirt.

"Where the hell did that come from?" Julian asked.

"You no worry," Zhang said. "Rain like this not last long."

Brooks surveyed his surroundings as his eyes adjusted to the darkness.
Prayer flags had been strung overhead, across what appeared to be a natural
karst formation. Some grew colonies of mold, but most were fairly new and in
good repair. Offerings of fine linens had been draped over the speleothems on
the limestone walls. Waist-high cairns of stacked stones stood near the walls, at
the base of which several pots filled with white sand rested. Sticks of incense
stood from them like stubbed cigarettes. The algae on the walls had been worn
away where hands had used the contours of the cave to guide themselves
deeper into the darkness. The sound of condensation dripping from somewhere ahead of him was loud enough that he could distinguish it from the
roar of the storm.

"What is this place?" Adrianne asked.

"This *Dayandong*. It mean 'Big Cave.' Very holy place."

Brooks slipped out of his backpack and walked away from the others. He followed the dripping sound toward the rear of the cave, where a small pool with phosphorescent blue water shimmered. The surrounding walls had been carved into various incarnations of the Buddha, each with different hand gestures, or *mudras*, which symbolized unique and important teachings, from wisdom to spiritualism and balance with nature. Offerings of all types rested at the feet of each one. There were scarves so old they'd deteriorated to strands of silk and coins and trinkets rusted to the point that it was impossible to tell what they once were.

One Buddha stood apart from the others, its visage dramatically more detailed and humanlike. It loomed over the pool as though guarding it, its eyes seeming to follow Brooks as he approached. He stood directly before the pool and looked down into the water. It didn't shimmer because of phosphorescent organisms as he had initially suspected, but rather from the sheer quantity of gemstones covering the bottom. There had to be a fortune in precious stones down there. The thought of men and women making the perilous pilgrimage to this grotto just to throw away their jewels was incomprehensible.

"Are they real?" Julian asked.

He knelt beside Brooks, reached into the water, and pulled out a fistful of uncut emeralds and rubies and jade that sparkled in even the wan light. Zhang grabbed his wrist and squeezed, for the first time his grin gone.

"These offerings not for you."

"Okay, okay. I was just looking, for God's sake."

He dropped the gems back into the water and cautiously pulled his arm from Zhang's grip. Their trail boss knelt and smoothed the stones along the bottom of the pool. He whispered something in Chinese. Brooks caught just enough to recognize the word *liánmǐn* — to have mercy. Zhang glanced into the Buddha's lap, then quickly away.

Brooks followed his stare to the statue. The Buddha sat cross-legged with its right hand raised, the palm facing outward and the fingers extended, and its left hand supinated in its lap. Cradled in its palm was what at first looked like a handful of white pebbles, or perhaps bits of ivory. Brooks leaned closer and realized they were anything but stone.

They were teeth. Most of them undeniably human. He didn't know enough about animalian dentition to guess as to which species supplied the remainder, but they were obviously canines taken from a large predatory species, likely a tiger.

The hairs rose on the backs of his arms and neck and he stifled a shiver. He turned away and saw sunlight through the mouth of the cave.

When he looked back, the grin had returned to Zhang's face.

"See? I tell you rain stop soon. Now we leave."

And with that he struck off into little more than a drizzle.

Brooks shouldered his pack, glanced one final time at the grotto, and walked out into the oppressive humidity with the others.

The rain fell just hard enough to spare them from the mosquitoes, which allowed them to concentrate on their footing. The mud made the trail even more treacherous, in many ways even more so than the ice. Far below, the stream flowed high and dark, just waiting for its opportunity to claim them with a single misstep. It wasn't long before the path leveled and wended off into the trees, where the footing was only marginally better, but at least if they slipped they wouldn't careen to their deaths from the top of the cliff.

The others marveled at the brazen snub-nosed monkeys that hopped within inches of them before darting back into the trees and screeching playfully. Even Warren amused himself by setting pieces of dried fruit on his shoulder and waiting for the creatures to hop down onto his backpack and snatch them. Brooks smiled outwardly, but couldn't seem to shake what he had seen in the grotto.

Six years ago he'd been summoned to Sri Lanka as a representative of the Brandt Institute to assist in the classification of hominin remains unearthed by a monsoon, near ruins dating to the fifth century and the reign of Dhatusena. He quickly determined the bones belonged to *Homo erectus*, the third such discovery on the island, and spent the remaining few days of his assignment exploring the ancient ruins with a British archaeologist named Dr. Emma Crandall, who had taught him to appreciate the history of the early Ceylonese dynasties, especially following the arrival of Buddhism during the second century BCE, when the nation as a whole essentially devoted itself to spiritual and humanitarian pursuits. Their early architecture was revolutionary and they were credited with establishing the first hospital, before the Indians and Europeans with whom they traded returned with invading armies. Most impressive were the statues of the Buddha, which had been meticulously tended through the millennia to such extremes they might as well have been recently carved.

Emma taught him about the *mudras*, or hand gestures, and their respective meanings, as well as a good number of other, more intimate things he remembered quite fondly.

The central Buddha in the grotto had its right hand raised in what was called the *Abhaya mudra*, or the Gesture of Fearlessness. The left hand, which cradled the teeth, formed the *Kataka mudra*, or Flower-holding Gesture, frequently used to hold venerated objects of some kind, although how the teeth qualified was a matter of speculation. It was the *mudras* of the two adjacent Buddhas that left little room for interpretation. Both had their hands raised in front of their chest, crossed at the wrists, palms out, middle fingers bent. It was a *mudra* known as *Bhutadamara*, or the Warding Off Evil Gesture. Combined, the three gave the impression of blessing the traveler for the journey ahead, one which — if the value of the offerings was any indication — promised to be even more perilous than they anticipated.

Brooks was still pondering the significance of the human and animal teeth and how they might relate to what he had seen in Brandt's private exhibit beneath the institution when the jungle retreated just enough to allow the sun to reach the ground, where waist-high grasses proliferated. The monkeys that had been following them no longer shrieked from the trees. In fact, there was no movement in the upper canopy whatsoever. No birds flitted from one shadowed enclave to the next; no lizards basked on the trunks. Only the mosquitoes continued to swarm, although in nowhere near the same numbers they once had. The ground was spongy and eagerly accepted their footprints. And worse.

Julian cursed when he stepped right out of his shoe and planted his socked foot in the mud. He gripped his shoe by the laces and pulled. It didn't budge. He wrapped the laces around his fists and put his body into it. The mud gave with a slurping sound and deposited him on his rear end.

Adrianne and Warren, who stood back and watched, burst out laughing.

Julian flung his sopping sock at them before inserting his bare foot into his shoe.

Brooks used the opportunity to tighten his own hiking boots. From one knee he could barely see the others over the tops of the tall, black-spotted weeds, which swayed at the behest of a gentle breeze. He looked back down and saw a print in the mud. It was old and nearly washed away by the recent storm, but enough of it remained that he could see the deep, smeared impression of the forefoot. The toes were large and teardrop-shaped, suggestive of long nails or claws. The way the rain had eroded it, it was impossible to tell which species had left it, only that whatever did was very large. It could possibly have been made by a Tibetan macaque — one of the largest species of old world monkeys in Asia — only if there had been heel contact, the impression had been washed away. From the right angle it almost looked like the paw print of a large cat. The slippery mud distorted both the size and shape—

"You're bleeding," Adrianne said.

"Not funny," Julian said. "I think we've all had more than our share of fun at my expense."

"No. Seriously. Right there. On the side of your neck."

Julian dabbed beneath his left earlobe and drew his fingertips away bloody.

"Jesus Christ. I didn't feel any—"

"You're bleeding, too," Warren said.

Brooks stood and saw the crimson smear on Adrianne's arm where Warren was pointing. There was blood on his extended arm, too.

Warren shrieked when he saw it spiraling around his forearm and dripping from his wrist. He wiped it on his side and looked back at Brooks with a panicked expression. A droplet of blood rolled down his forehead from beneath his hairline.

Sweat trickled down Brooks's neck and over his clavicle as he fought through the weeds to join the others. As he neared, he saw Adrianne's bare legs. They looked like they'd been cut to hell by sawgrass. Julian's were the same. Warren's socks were already drenched with the blood trickling down his legs. Zhang's arms were positively slick with blood.

Brooks wiped what he thought was sweat from his eyes and caught a glimpse of the back of his bloody hand.

"What the devil is going on here?" Warren asked.

Brooks looked up at his colleague in time to see something dark fall from the canopy and alight on Warren's right ear. He flicked at it and a dribble of blood followed the arch of the conch.

"Oh, God," Adrianne said. She started dancing in place and swatting at her legs.

Brooks looked down and found his legs dripping with blood. He looked at the long blades of grass, at the black spots all over them. They weren't tiny buds like he'd unconsciously assumed.

They were leeches.

Something struck his shoulder and he nearly cried out. He brushed it off and looked up to find the undersides of the broad leaves covered with leeches, which dropped down upon them like rain.

Before he knew it he was running after the others, leaving the grasses smeared with blood in his wake.

7

Johann Brandt Institute for Evolutionary Anthropology
Chicago, Illinois
October 5th

Twelve Days Ago

"I want the opportunity to examine it for myself," Brooks said.

"You question its authenticity?" Brandt looked up from his computer and raised an eyebrow. The expression on his face was one of amusement. "I assure you it is real. I made the cast myself, with my own hands. I smoothed the contours and traced the bony structures. I had no reason to seek either verification or validation from other sources."

"If you want me to lead this expedition, then you're going to have to let me examine it."

"Curiosity's got the better of you, does it my boy?"

"I can't help but wonder why — if it's legitimate, as you claim — you didn't bring back the remains from which it was cast. Or why you wouldn't have showcased your findings for the entire world to see? We're talking about a discovery of the highest order sitting in the private collection of the founder of one of the foremost institutions devoted to the advancement of evolutionary studies. Tell me you can't see the inherent contradiction from my perspective."

"Let me ask you a question, Jordan. And do take your time to think about it before you answer. I want you to carefully consider the ramifications before speaking. Do you think you can do that?"

Brooks nodded.

Brandt smiled, removed his spectacles, and rolled out from behind his desk. He beckoned to Brooks with a wave of his gnarled hand and guided him once more toward the elevator. He waited until they were both inside the cab to speak. Brooks watched the old man's face in the reflection on the inside of the doors. Over the past few days, all of the little doubts his initial excitement had allowed him to set aside had begun to nag at him. He had more than a few questions, and he needed to answer them before he set off blindly for a region of Tibet where westerners, especially Americans, were unwelcome.

"Consider everything you know about the lineage of the human species. Go all the way back to the first mammalian forest ape, the progenitor of the three major genera: *Pan*, *Gorilla*, and *Homo*. It is this single ancestor, common to all three, that serves as the trunk of our family tree. This is the lone commonality from which two branches diverged more than eight million years ago, one of which evolved separately into the great apes; the other into mankind and chimpanzees. The first divergence one can arguably state to be the antecedent of man would be *Australopithecus afarensis*, nearly four million years ago."

The elevator door opened upon the display room, the thought of which had become increasingly uncomfortable for Brooks.

"I know all of this, Dr. Brandt. What I don't know is where this discovery of yours fits in."

"The foundation of evolution is patience, my boy. You must open your mind to the possibilities and the implications of each. As I said, don't rush to judgment."

Brooks had already exhausted his patience. The old man had the answers to the questions that plagued him and he was in no mood for the song and dance. He needed facts, not justifications. It took superhuman restraint, but he managed to stay his tongue. He gestured for Brandt to proceed.

"Thank you." Brandt rolled out of the cab and down the main aisle. "Where was I? Ah, yes. From *Australopithecus* comes the terminal branch of genus *Paranthropus*, which coexisted for a time with several species from our direct *Homo* lineage. *Paranthropus* was considerably larger than *Australopithecus* and evolved with a larger brain and heavily muscled jaws designed to feed primarily on plant matter. Tubers, and what not. Unfortunately, that path also led to it becoming a common prey species that was eventually hunted to extinction by the mammalian megafauna of the time.

"The evolution from *afarensis* to *africanus* that spawned the entire *Homo* branch, on the other hand, was much more significant. The dramatic increase in cranial capacity, with doubling in size from *habilis* to *erectus* and again to *heidelbergensis*. Major growth in both height and weight and a staggering increase in mass and musculature. But the most important facet of their evolution wasn't the development of the use of stone tools, as most would have you believe. Nor was it the mass migration out of Africa, which itself led to a dozen analogous subspecies. It was the gradual progression to an omnivorous diet. This is most clearly evidenced by the evolution of the teeth themselves.

"*Australopith* canines were markedly underdeveloped and microwear on the molars suggests a grinding chewing motion and a largely frugivorous diet. The *Paranthropes* could be considered to have devolved, as they developed larger molars and premolars that functioned to help break down tougher plant materials. Conversely, chemistry confirms that early *Homo* species not only ate significantly more meat, but also preferred it to the diet favored by the now extinct *Paranthropus*. This started a trend toward smaller, sharper teeth that coincided with the almost exponential increase in brain size. Essentially, the success of mankind's evolution was dependent upon its transition from prey to predator. It was only as the rate at which the brain developed outpaced its physical transformation that mankind's evolutionary ascension plateaued at the level of apex predator, its modern incarnation. For all intents and purposes, humanity realized that its evolutionary advantage was its intelligence, not its predatory nature."

Brooks watched the memorialized faces of emaciated Jews pass in the cases and realized just how wrong Brandt was. Or at least that some men embraced the bestial aspect of their heritage.

"Gorillas, on the other hand, evolved long, sharp canine teeth, but retained the smaller cranial vault and, curiously, a predominantly vegetarian diet. The canines are largely vestigial, I would imagine, yet their importance as a threat display cannot be understated. As is the case with chimpanzees and bonobos, which are mainly frugivorous, but will resort to eating anything they can get their hands on as a 'fallback food,' even smaller monkeys, in times of scarcity. Both genera exhibit the same rounded jaws and prominent dentition as *Homo sapiens*, while retaining more ferocious canines and smaller brains. What does that tell us? That modern man needs no threat display, that evolutionarily speaking, he's confident he sits on top of the food chain, that he has evolved *into* the physical embodiment of a threat. Are you following me?"

"Yes," Brooks said, although he had absolutely no idea where Brandt was going with this line of thought.

Brandt stopped before the main display, killed the tinting, and lowered the lead liners to reveal the plaster cast, which turned slowly on its pedestal to be viewed from all angles, like a mask on the wig manikin.

"Now look at the size of the cranial vault compared to the three extant hominin lines. Look at the shape of the face. The relative prominence of the cheekbones, orbits, brow, and nasal arch. The humanoid prominence of the teeth and jaws. Now imagine how these teeth compare to all three lines and tell me where this individual fits into the entire evolutionary tree, from the very first forest ape through modern chimps, gorillas, and men."

The realization hit Brooks so hard he had the urge to sit down. He looked at Brandt, who leaned back in his chair, laced his bony fingers, and smiled at the revelation that must have been written all over Brooks's face.

"So now, my boy, I'll ask you the same question you asked me. Do you understand why I kept this discovery to myself, especially considering the political climate during which I made the discovery?"

Brooks could only nod.

"And do you understand why I devoted every waking moment of my life to fostering an environment conducive to learning everything we can about human evolution? Why in the years during the reign of Hitler's Reich I used the opportunity to gain as much knowledge as I possibly could about my own species, despite the moral implications and, as you say, the ultimate forfeiture of my soul? Why I was a willing participant in the perpetuation of evil when a man of my intellect and societal standing by all means should have, at worst, walked away?"

Brooks looked at the face turning slowly in a circle, its sightless eyes scanning the room, lord of all it surveyed.

"Do you understand why, with all of the advancements in DNA

sequencing and cloning, the physical remains must never be brought back here? And more to the point, do you understand why I'm now passing the torch of its stewardship on to you?"

The enormity of the responsibility Brandt bestowed upon him was overwhelming.

"Do you understand how our entire species would react if this ever saw the light of day? This is no mere mutation or anomaly, Brooks. This is, potentially, the next phase in the evolution of mankind."

8

Hanmi
Motuo County
Tibet Autonomous Region
People's Republic of China
October 14th

Three Days Ago

They arrived at the layover point in Hanmi after dark and spent a good portion of the night burning off the leeches by the light of a campfire that produced more smoke than flame, thanks to the what little damp wood they were able to gather. The majority of the parasites had either sated themselves and fallen off or had been painfully excised en route. Those that remained had swollen to nearly three times their original size and produced a smell like a cross between singed hair and burnt rubber with the application of the tips of the smoldering sticks.

They used nearly every last inch of gauze and tape from their emergency medical kit to cover the wounds that showed no indication that the bleeding would stop anytime soon, at least not until the anticoagulatory effects of the enzymes in the leeches' saliva waned.

The blood loss served to amplify their exhaustion and they slept the sleep of the dead on the bare floor of a structure made of decayed pickets and situated on blocks that wouldn't support the warped building much longer. The sheets draped over the bare rafters were weathered and admitted the early morning fog, which crept in well before sunrise.

Brooks awakened to the sound of sheep baaing in the rocky fields and a headache caused by the loss of so much fluid. They ate in a faint drizzle that evaporated in the heat of the fire and listened to Zhang converse with the old man who served them porridge he called *tholma* and an earthy brick tea. The caffeine helped ease his headache and he slowly rejoined the land of the living.

"He say we go through 'leech zone,'" Zhang said. "You supposed to swing stick ahead of you to knock them off weeds. They angry when it rain."

"I thought you'd made this journey before." Warren looked up over the lip of his bowl as he tipped back the last bit of *tholma*. "Shouldn't you have known about this 'leech zone'?"

"Who say I not know?"

Zhang said something to the old man in Tibetan and they both laughed.

"Ask him if there have been any tiger sightings around here lately," Brooks said.

He felt the weight of his colleagues' eyes upon him and turned to watch the old man's *Riwoche* horse, a miniature species barely larger than an average pony. The horse sensed his attention, nickered, and swatted at the flies on its haunches with its long tail.

Zhang spoke to the old man, whose reply was brief and elicited a gap-toothed smile.

"He say there always tigers around. You just no see them."

"That's comforting," Adrianne said.

"Why do you ask, Dr. Brooks?"

Something about the way Julian asked suggested that Brooks wasn't the only one to have noticed something.

Brooks stared to the east, toward yet another range of fog-shrouded mountains. There was no point in alarming them unnecessarily. A solitary footprint more than a day old was undoubtedly nothing to worry about, even if it did belong to a tiger and not a macaque, which was starting to feel more and more likely in retrospect. And besides, tiger attacks were incredibly rare, especially on people traveling in groups.

"No reason."

They set out under a gray dawn and made good time across the rocky plateau, where they passed cairns of indeterminate age and the rubble of structures that gave no indication as to what they might once have been. The trail grew steeper and even rockier from there as it ascended into the clouds. The streams flowed narrow and vertical and crashed down onto rocks reminiscent of the teeth of a dragon. They were forced to crawl over the steeper sections to compensate for the weight of their backpacks and shivered with the damp mist and the caress of the cool wind. Aged prayer flags snapped from branches wedged into the gaps between the loose boulders, from which not a single tree grew. They fell repeatedly and tore their pants and skinned their knees, but anything was preferable to the siege at the hands of the bloodsucking leeches.

At the summit they rested in the lee of an outcropping on top of which the furious wind snapped the stringy remains of multicolored prayer flags faded to a nearly uniform dirt-brown color. They made a concerted effort to stay on top of their hydration regimen, which was exceedingly important at higher altitudes. They ate jerky and herbs that tasted like grass. Julian had packed them in plastic baggies and assured them that the combination would increase their stamina and slow the rate at which they fatigued. Considering how their legs felt after so many days of sustained exertion over the rugged terrain, no one griped about the taste or the fact that the effects of Julian's holistic remedies were undoubtedly psychosomatic.

The descent was much more gradual and the rhododendrons that grew beside the trail shielded them from the brunt of the wind. There were even points when the sun penetrated the mist, dried their clothes, and warmed their bodies. The path widened as it led them out of the foothills and into a lush temperate forest. They all beat the bushes and weeds with their walking sticks, despite the fact that none of them had seen so much as a single leech since leaving Hanmi. Their bandages had been victimized by their sweat and the humidity and had fallen off long ago, leaving the wounds exposed. Most of them had scabbed over, but enough remained raw to darken their socks and pants, which they were forced to look at with increasing frequency due to the heaps of yak dung spotting the path.

As the forest closed around them, the sound of the river grew from a whisper to a roar. Only it wasn't a single river, but a series of waterfalls cascading a hundred feet down a sheer escarpment and bludgeoning the breakers, filling the air with spume. The path terminated at the mouth of a suspension bridge that had to be a quarter-mile long and made from mismatched planks warped and saturated by the constant exposure to the water.

For as decrepit as the bridge felt, the view from it was even more magnificent. The mist sparkled all around them like millions of tiny prisms. Far below, the violent collisions of the warring streams merged into a single turquoise body that would eventually join with the mighty Yarlung Tsangpo near where they would cross into Motuo and reach their ultimate destination.

On the far side of the bridge was a tiny lodge run by Menba villagers who peeked out at them as they passed from behind the tapestries hanging over the windows. They followed the procession with their eyes, but never made any attempt to hail them, even as they had to push through the herd of black sheep with curlicue horns blocking the narrow trail.

"Menba and Luobo no like outsiders," Zhang said. "They welcome you into home, as is tradition. Then they poison food. This is holy place. They no want anyone else in it."

"We should register a complaint with the chamber of commerce," Adrianne said.

Zhang laughed as though he understood the joke and prodded the sheep out of his way with what Julian called his "leech stick."

Brooks glanced back and caught a glimpse of a sun-leathered face before the man reached out from behind the tapestry and swing the wooden shutters closed with a loud clapping sound. There were deep gouges in the exterior of the shutters where it looked as though something had attempted to claw through them. The front door was similarly scarred.

The structure was barely out of sight behind them when again the forest closed around the path, beside which a pyramidal cairn had been erected. It was draped with so many prayer flags that it looked like an enormous heap of dirty laundry left to rot in the elements. A single pole stood from the top of it and served as the attachment for the string of flags that stretched off into the forest. On top of it, speared through the hole in the base of the cranium, was the skull of a yak with wild, curled horns.

A cloud of flies swirled around it, incensed by their intrusion. They were fat and bloated and buzzed lazily as they again alighted and crawled across the decomposing fabric and the mess of bones scattered around the base, to which a length of rusted chain was bolted.

Zhang waved them away and crouched over the freshly butchered bones. There were still knots of meat and tendons at the joints and there were sections where it looked like the bones had been gnawed. They were brown with dried blood and the long bones broken, presumably in order to get to the marrow. He stood and the flies again descended upon their meal.

"Why did you ask about tigers this morning?" Warren asked.

Brooks blew out his breath.

"I thought I saw a track at the point where we entered the field of leeches."

"And you didn't think that was maybe worth mentioning?"

"I saw no reason to frighten anyone. We knew there were tigers up here when we set out. And I don't think we have anything to worry about." He nodded to the remains of the yak. "It looks like they're being well fed."

Brooks turned his back on them and started down the trail once more.

"What else aren't you telling us?" Warren asked.

"Some things are worth the wait."

And with that Brooks struck off into the trees, which gradually transitioned from rhododendrons and azaleas to tropical figs and lychees. The air grew warmer even as the sun continued its unwitnessed descent above the canopy. The forest life again filled the trees with hoots and squeals and sounds Brooks could hardly describe, let alone attribute to any specific species. Their return was every bit as sudden as their cessation had been. He wondered if the others had noticed the same thing.

He felt guilty keeping anything from them, especially something as earth-shattering as what Brandt had shown him to convince him to launch this expedition. There was no way he could explain it to them though, not in any believable way. He would have thought Brandt senile had he attempted to merely tell him about the plaster cast. It was one of those things you had to see to believe, the kind of flight of fancy easily enough dismissed without a second thought. Even seeing it in person hadn't been enough. Brooks had needed additional time to digest what he'd seen, to contemplate it from every possible angle, and then he'd made Brandt show him again to dispel his lingering doubts.

Soon enough they'd see for themselves, assuming they were able to find it again after so many years. Then they'd have no choice but to believe and they'd understand why he'd been unable to tell them. If they even still cared by then.

The ground trembled, subtly at first, but with increasing intensity as they continued to the east. The Yarlung Tsangpo beckoned louder and louder until it was all they could hear.

Brooks's heart raced. He turned to see the expressions of anticipation on the faces of the others. They, too, understood the implications. They were about to enter a place where only the occasional monk was permitted to tread, where even the indigenous people refused to go for any length of time for fear of spoiling its sanctity, and where few westerners had ever gone before. They were about to penetrate the hidden lotus.

On the other side of the river lay Motuo and what Brooks was certain would be the greatest discovery of the twenty-first century.

9

Excerpt from the journal of
Hermann G. Wolff

Courtesy of Johann Brandt, Private Collection
Chicago, Illinois
(Translated from original handwritten German text)

January 1939

I t became soon apparent that Sir Basil Heatherton, the political officer at the British Mission in Gangtok, whom we initially suspected of trying to delay our departure for mystical Lhasa while awaiting formal approval from the embassy in London, had no intention whatsoever of granting our request. Tensions between our two nations back home deteriorated by the hour and there was much legal posturing over the means by which the process of reunifying the Germanic peoples had commenced. Heatherton's relationship with both the Sikkimese and Tibetans was already strained, and rightfully so, thanks to the history of British Imperialism in India, while across the border the Tibetans *prepared to go to war, if that was what it took, to extricate the fourteenth Dalai Lama, little more than a child, from the clutches of the Chinese, who themselves were in the midst of fighting a bloody war against the Japanese. With the training and economic support of the NSDAP, of course.*

Ultimately, it was Brandt who formulated the plan to use our frustration and impatience to our advantage. We made a grand scene of demanding to cross the border and then an even grander show of leaving Gangtok when the sanctimonious political officer rebuked us. Once we were confident Heatherton had sent word of his triumph back to England, we doubled back through Bootan [sic] and traveled several weeks out of our way into Assam to the east.

We followed the Brahmaputra River through the Sadiya Frontier Tract and crossed into Tibet without major complication. We encountered Ngolok bandits who were easily routed by several warning shots fired at the hooves of their horses. König collected species previously only thought to be legendary, most notably the [shaggy] shapi and the ferocious dhole. Brandt examined every subject we passed with his calipers and rulers, despite slowing our progress to a maddening extent. Eberhardt and Metzger gathered rocks and every artifact they could get their hands on, and charted the geography and took magnetic readings from the soil. All the while I gathered plants and flowers and filmed everything I saw. Little did any of us suspect the trials that lay ahead of us.

Our initial assumptions proved erroneous. We believed the passage from the Sadiya Frontier would allow us to circle around the Himalayas to the north and reach Lhasa in a roundabout approach. If there were a way of doing so, we certainly did not see it. By the time we recognized that our route was leading us straight into the mountains, it was too late to turn around, or at least not without wasting even more valuable time and running the risk of being forced to return to Gangtok with our hats in hand. König firmly believed we would eventually reach our destination by staying the course and that surely the banks of the Yarlung Tsang-po [sic] would prove no more treacherous than its Indian incarnation as the Brahmaputra to the south, which was indeed the case for the first few days, after which we learned exactly why the British had chosen to squat on the passage from Sikkim and why we had encountered an utter lack of resistance through Assam.

The banks of the river grew first rocky, then impassible, detouring us ever eastward onto narrow paths cut by nomadic herdsmen and wild game. We were reluctant to abandon our entire mule train, but guiding so many overburdened beasts along the rugged switchbacks nearly halted progress and we knew all too well the gamble we were already taking. We had no choice but to send the majority back to Darjeeling where they would be unburdened of our collections, which would be crated and shipped back to the Fatherland. Of the five mules we kept, four survived the journey to the village of Laga [sic]. The animal carrying Eberhardt's supplies and equipment lost its footing on the icy pass, slipped, and plummeted hundreds of feet down through the mist to its death, taking with it the Sherpa who'd been shouldering its haunches.

We were relieved to encounter the village beneath the driving storm shortly after nightfall and were received with steaming bowls of thenthuk *and blood sausages. The natives blessed us with a shelter made from raw timber and wood for a fire, for which we were more than grateful. The wind doubled its efforts and the snow turned to blowing ice that felt like needles when it struck our skin. That night we slept better than we had since arriving in Gangtok and sang the praises of our hosts for their hospitality, clear up until the moment we reached the stables where we had hitched our mules and found them gone. Our Sherpa guides had abandoned us, as well, much to König's chagrin. He had developed a fondness for the young man with the omnipresent smile he had taken to calling* Sonnig [Sunny].

Fortunately, we had the presence of mind to bring our valuables into the shelter with us. Brandt, especially, bemoaned the loss of so large a portion of our supplies, but busied himself measuring and casting the faces of the villagers while he waited for the rest of us to ready ourselves for the journey into the Himalayan Mountains, which loomed over us like an impenetrable fortress. Penetrate them we did, though. We attacked with axes and picks and ropes and fought for every meter we ascended. The bitter wind abraded our cheeks and lanced through our parkas. Our breath turned to ice in our beards and eyebrows. Our heads ached from the altitude and the dehydration. Still, we persevered and made camp in the lee of a peak we named Mt. Sieg [Victory]. Too exhausted to even notice the falling temperatures, we bedded down and slept [like] the dead until we awakened, shivering and coughing, with the first light of dawn to filter through the storm clouds.

The following day was one of descent. For as hazardous as the climb had been, picking our way down perilous sheets of ice and slickrock was even more so. Traction on the talus was poor at best and crossing the arrested rockslides threatened to turn ankles. When we finally reached timberline, we were spared the brunt of the wind and snow for the balance of the day until we reached the plateau where we decided to camp amid the rhododendrons and azaleas and beneath a ceiling of clouds so low we could nearly reach up and touch it. We boiled droma roots Metzger exhumed and ate the snow cocks König, who grew ever more distant, shot during one of his increasingly frequent disappearances.

It was the next morning when he came to the realization that we were much farther from Lhasa than we had thought and that if we did not increase our pace, we risked not only being at the mercy of winter high in the Himalayas, but the British discovering our ruse — thanks to the mutinous Sherpas — and attempting to outflank us and block our road to the holy city. He drove us hard through the morning and by the time we reached the Metog Lho pass, which marked the final leg of the descent to Motuo, he had essentially abandoned us altogether. We occasionally saw him far ahead on the path or materializing uphill from the dense fog, crouching to inspect something in the snow. He had always seemed to be separate from the rest of us, and at no time was it more apparent than during the final approach to Motuo. He came from wealth rather than academia and was renowned for his skills as an explorer and hunter, rather than his potential for scientific discovery. The most noteworthy difference between us, however, was his almost religious devotion to the more esoteric beliefs of the Nazi party. The majority of us have known hardship and the daily frustration of watching the rest of the world vilify our heritage and celebrate the impoverishment it forced upon us. We were all swept up in the völkisch movement and the idea that we were better than the circumstances into which we'd been born, that ours was a bloodline that once flowed through the veins of gods. None of us more so than König.

It is difficult to describe the distinction. Ours was an abstract belief in the nobility of our remote ancestry, while he believed that we were the direct descendants of the surviving rulers of Atlantis, the progenitors of our Nordic roots, the Aryans themselves. It is no small coincidence that he is also the lone man among us who is not a scientist. He is several years older than the rest of us and the only one to have been orphaned by the war. He has no memories of his father and knows him only through the legends we had all heard. Walther König not only amassed a fortune from his travels around the globe, but also returned with rare and unusual treasures of all kinds and tales of people we scarcely believed truly existed. Ferocious beasts he collected on his myriad expeditions featured prominently in every museum across Europe. It was in his enormous shadow that

Augustus König essentially raised himself, utilizing his vast inheritance and rage for the loss of a father he deified to drive himself to conquer the world. Perhaps it was this quest to prove his personal worthiness of the König blood — the Blood of Kings, as he called it — that initially attracted him to the search for the Aryan Race, which he was obsessed with proving still survived to this day.

For as little as the rest of us subscribed to the theory of a master race of Atlantean origin, he more than compensated for our combined lack of enthusiasm. So strong was his belief that it was he who insinuated himself into the good graces of the Ahnenerbe, organized the expedition, and provided the funds that even Himmler himself had been unable to secure for us to wait out the British in Gangtok. The four of us — Brandt, Eberhardt, Metzger, and myself — were selected for our scientific specialties and objectivity. More precisely, we were skeptics, although none of us would have dared so say aloud, especially around König, who perhaps believed even more fervently than either Himmler or our beloved Chancellor. In his mind, König was convinced that we would find more than mere proof of the existence of the Aryan Race when we ultimately reached Lhasa, we would find the first clue as to where they had gone from there.

The majority of the day passed without interaction with König, who flitted in and out of the fog as we descended from the blowing snow into evergreen forests where the precipitation fell as rain, and finally into temperate zones where my comrades practically undressed as we walked. Despite my initial discomfort, I alone elected to remain fully clothed, for I was raised near the swamps of the Bodensee and recognized the kind of habitat that attracted mosquitoes and other bloodsucking insects of their ilk. They mocked me when I cautioned them. I might have been a naturalist in the strictest terms, but I had been selected for my skills as a filmmaker, not my scientific specialty, a fact none of them let me forget with nicknames like blumemann *[flower man] and* käfersammler *[bug catcher].*

It served them all right when the rain brought out the leeches, which dropped from the trees and attacked from the tall weeds. I taught them how to clear their path by swinging a stick, although not until they had been drained of a good amount of blood. And my laughter ceased. I did try to warn them, after all.

It wasn't until late afternoon, when the mist crept down from the mountaintops and settled into the valleys and the rumble of the Yarlung Tsang-po [sic] turned into a roar that we finally caught up with König.

A steady drizzle fell on the treetops and dripped to the muddy path all around us in drops the size of marbles. As we had throughout the day, we came upon König squatting on the ground, his face mere inches from the earth, gently running his fingers over the mud. Metzger called out to him, but he appeared oblivious to our presence. He merely stood, walked a few more feet, and then crouched again. When he finally rose once more, he walked away from us toward the near-deafening sound of the river and stood framed in the mouth of a rope bridge over a deep gorge with the howling wind tossing the trees around him.

I recognized it as a moment of significance and commenced filming the silhouette of this man we all knew and yet didn't know, this explorer who had led us to the top of the world and then down into the most holy of sites, the hidden lotus that was Motuo, a jungle captured by the Himalayas and jealously guarded where few men could ever reach it.

König stood there for several minutes while I filmed him. The others used the respite to shed a layer of clothing and change their sodden bandages. When he turned to face me, it was as though he had just awakened from a deep sleep and was surprised to find the rest of us behind him. He slung his Browning over his shoulder, smiled that boyish smile of his, and with a tip of his pith helmet, struck off across the bridge.

I filmed the others as they filed onto the decrepit bridge behind him and braced themselves against the wind. Once they reached the other side, I hurried back to gather my gear, which I had set down near where we had first come upon König squatting in the mud. His footprints were deep and clearly defined, but the one he had been studying and tracing with his fingertips, the footprint I was certain couldn't have been more than a few hours old, was like nothing I had ever seen before.

10

Two Days Ago

B rooks closed his eyes and savored the warmth of the sun on his face. The skin on his cheekbones and around his eyes still burned from the harsh elements in the higher elevations and his lips were chapped to such an extreme that they cracked and bled when he smiled, but everything he had endured to bring him to this point in time had been worth it. The feeling of knowing he had conquered some of the most treacherous terrain on the planet while standing six hundred feet from an untouched biome, where few beyond the most devout and revered of Buddhist monks ever set foot, was almost euphoric. He wanted to breathe it all in and commit how he felt right now to memory, but the excitement was simply too great. He turned to face the others and recognized the same expression of awe and wonder he must have been wearing.

He reached up and straightened a ripped prayer flag that had tangled with one of the ropes that supported the bridge. It was yellow and the words printed on it were faded, but he recognized the wisdom it imparted as that of harmony. He smiled and stepped out onto the wooden bridge. The planks had been laid in a crosshatch pattern: three-foot lengths laid horizontally from one side to the other and two long planks staggered right down the middle. The Yarlung Tsangpo flowed far below, a shade of blue generally reserved for the most placid of tropical seas. It thundered from the sheer cliffs along its banks, down the faces of which vines slithered through a preponderance of bromeliads. The far end of the bridge appeared to terminate against a solid mass of camphorwoods.

The bridge shook beneath him and even the most gentle of breezes made it sway. He used both hands on the rope rails and leaned forward to brace the weight of his pack.

This was positively surreal. He'd explored and excavated some of the oldest and most remote anthropological sites in the world, but even they had been accessible by road or by trail from nearby towns. A part of him had almost built this up to be a mythical place in his mind during the course of nearly the full week it had taken him to get here after his plane landed in India. It was no wonder so many myths about this area had sprung up through the eons. Even as he stepped from the bridge and into the dense thicket, he found it difficult to believe he was actually here, and now that he was, he found the prospect of locating what he was looking for in nearly nineteen thousand square miles of rugged terrain — encompassing everything from sub-tropical jungles to temperate forests to tundra and spanning nearly thirteen thousand vertical feet — more than a little daunting.

Fortunately, Brandt had told him where to start.

He shoved through the branches into an emerald world of blossoming rhododendrons and overbearingly fragrant sandalwood trees. Crimson and olive-backed sunbirds chirped and flitted through the upper canopy with flashes of red and gold. Langurs barked a warning from uphill to his right. A cairn of flat stones marked a sharp bend in the path. The faint smell of incense hovered around it from a carbon-scored natural indentation in the uppermost stone. He had no more than turned his back to it when he heard a clattering sound and an enormous bird reminiscent of a pheasant, with red feathers and white spots, shot past his feet and into the underbrush. He looked back to find Warren picking himself up from the pile of toppled stones.

"Lost my balance," he said.

"That tragopan ran out of the bushes and spooked him so badly he threw himself from the path," Julian said.

"You should have seen the look on his face," Adrianne said. "You'd have thought it was a tiger for as wide as his eyes—"

"All right. You've all had your fun," Warren said.

"We keep moving," Zhang said. "Camp still far and it soon be dark."

He stepped past the others, nodded to Brooks, and assumed the lead without another word. His customary grin was conspicuously absent.

Brooks tried to drink it all in as he walked. Only occasionally did the sun perforate the upper canopy in thin columns of sparkling light. Condensation clung to the tips of the leaves and shivered loose with little more than the air of their passage. It was staggering how day and night — time itself, for that matter — seemed to lose meaning in the eternal twilight beneath a canopy alive with birds and insects. He noticed anomalies in their behavior he couldn't at first define, until he finally realized they had merely yet to learn to fear man and were as curious about him as he was about them. Juvenile langurs with leathery black faces and gray fur that curled like chocolate chips on top of their heads followed them from a distance, swinging from branch to branch at the edges of sight before simply losing interest and fading behind them. A red deer — a species believed to have been extinct for nearly half a century — exploded from the shrubs and bounded past him in a blur.

The others traveled in something of an awed silence behind him, making little more noise than the crunching of detritus, the snapping of twigs, the whistling sounds of branches whipping back into place behind them, and the occasional groan when someone stepped in the omnipresent yak excrement. An aura of reverence surrounded them, an indescribable sensation that made speech nearly impossible. For most of them, anyway.

"I won't have a drop of blood left in me by the time we make camp if these bloody mosquitoes have anything to say about it," Warren said. "So much for being at the top of the food chain."

"There are tigers up here that would undoubtedly dispute your assertion," Brooks said.

"Assuming the mosquitoes haven't hunted them to extinction." He swore and fanned at the whining cloud around his head. "Even if you're right, surely they've learned to keep their distance from humans."

Zhang chuckled and shouldered through a wall of branches that had overgrown the trail. Despite his outward attempts to hide it, something was making him nervous. His head was on a swivel and his right hand continually sought a better grip on the wooden handle of his old ice ax. Brooks found himself increasing his pace to keep up with their guide. He had to remind himself that westerners were prohibited from entering Motuo and that coming upon a group of Tibetan monks bore dramatically different consequences than encountering a patrol of Chinese soldiers. Especially for Zhang.

The columns of light faded from gold to gray. Mist crept silently through the treetops. Brooks tracked its slow descent and for the first time noticed the complete and utter lack of birdsong. In conjunction with Zhang's behavior, that realization caused the hackles to rise on the back of his neck.

He stopped and listened for the grunting of monkeys or the whistling of ground birds, for the sounds of animals moving unseen through the wilderness, but heard only the ruckus of his companions. He held up a hand to halt their advance.

How long had it been since he last heard the *che-chewee* of the sunbirds or the almost metallic screech of the parakeets or the chirping of the wagtails?

"What's wrong?" Adrianne asked.

Brooks shushed her and closed his eyes.

The sound of the river had faded to a distant rumble. He didn't know how far they had traveled, only that darkness was falling on a steady drizzle that made a faint pattering noise far overhead. He'd been so focused on thoughts of what lay ahead and on the mystery and beauty of this isolated world that he hadn't noticed the birdsong wane or the curious monkeys that followed them fade into the trees. He might have been completely unfamiliar with Motuo, but he knew enough about nature to understand that sudden silence meant one thing.

There was a predator in the forest.

He turned to find Zhang frozen ahead of him on the path, at the edge of sight, nearly swallowed by the forest. So still Brooks couldn't even tell he was breathing.

Brooks walked toward him. Even the crackling of the dead leaves underfoot was too loud in his ears.

Clattering in the branches above as the first ambitious raindrops preceded the storm.

"Jordan," Warren whispered from behind him.

Brooks shot him a look that could have stopped a charging bull. When he turned back, Zhang was gone and only the gently shivering branches marked his passage. They had nearly stilled when Brooks ducked through.

A tug on his arm and he dropped to a crouch. Zhang closed a hand over his mouth to prevent him from speaking and pointed into a small, dark clearing ahead.

A biological smell wafted into his face. Warm and metallic. Meat on the verge of spoiling.

A clump of fur was tangled around the end of a branch, from the leaves of which a dark fluid swelled and dripped with the viscosity of syrup. And beyond it, Brooks saw the source of both the smell and all of the blood.

And for the first time, realized just how isolated from the rest of the world they truly were.

PART III

SHAMBHALA

11

Yarlung Tsangpo River Basin
Motuo County
Tibet Autonomous Region
People's Republic of China
October 15ᵗʰ

Two Days Ago

Years ago, as a graduate student at the University of Chicago, Brooks participated in a dig in the South African province of Limpopo, during which they exhumed the maxillae and lower orbital framework of the skull of *Australopithecus robustus*. The excitement of being party to such a tremendous discovery had been almost euphoric. He and the other grad students had pounded *unqombothi* — a South African beer made from a slurry of maize and sorghum malt — into the wee hours of the morning, reveling in the kind of success few ever experienced in the field, let alone as twenty-three year-olds who hadn't done anything to earn the right. He'd stumbled away from the ring of tents around the fire to relieve himself and remembered hearing a crinkling sound from a stand of sickle bushes maybe twenty feet away, past where a trio of wildebeests had bedded down in the tall grasses.

Were it not for the noise, he never would have seen their horns rising from the wavering field or the reflection of the firelight from their eyes. More crinkling sounds and they'd turned to face the shrubs.

He'd zipped up and rejoined the revelry without sparing the encounter a second thought, until the next morning when he crawled out of his tent, slipped through the same bushes to the same spot to relieve himself again, and found the remains of what was once a wildebeest strewn everywhere. The carcass looked like it had been attacked by an entire pride of lions. There was fur and blood everywhere. Gnawed bones and appendages scattered through the high weeds. He'd looked up to find a pack of jackals staring back at him with the early morning sun reflecting from the blood covering their snouts and bared teeth and vultures hopping through the grass with their wings spread and their heads lowered.

That had been nothing compared to what he saw in the clearing before him now.

At a guess, he was looking at the remains of three Tibetan red deer like the one that had blown past him maybe a mile and a half back, but it was impossible to tell for sure. There were brick-red swatches of fur everywhere, tattered pelts with greasy yellow adipose layers. Violently broken and disarticulated bones. Dismembered carcasses on the matted grass, swarming with flies. The flowers and weeds were trampled and covered in black spatters where the blood had yet to fully dry.

Brooks had never seen anything like it. It was one thing to come upon what was left of a lone deer that a predator stalked and overcame, but this was another thing entirely. Deer were fast animals, especially these Tibetan morphs, which had to be able to bound over great distances and often even greater heights. Whatever had come upon them had caught them completely unaware and overwhelmed them before they could react. Their bodies were no more than a single stride from the impressions in the grass that were only now beginning to spring back into place.

He pushed through the trees and stepped out into the clearing. Both hands came away smeared with blood. He looked back to see the leaves of the trees spattered with crimson droplets.

Zhang grabbed his arm with a ferocious grip that bit into his biceps.

Brooks looked down at the hand, and then pointedly at Zhang, who released it and whispered something in Sichuanese under his breath. Brooks's

Chinese was limited to the Mandarin he'd picked up from his colleagues during a three-month dig in the Liaoning Province, but the two dialects were similar enough that he was certain Zhang had said something about a forest ghost.

He watched the trees for the slightest hint of movement. Between the roiling clouds of flies and mosquitoes and the way the leaves twitched with the rainfall dripping from the upper canopy, everything seemed to be alive. Tigers were intelligent animals that knew well enough to make themselves scarce when they caught the scent of man. Most of them, anyway. There were areas on the southern slope of the Himalayas where the occasional Bengal tiger developed a taste for human flesh, but he felt confident that if this was the work of a tiger, its appetite was surely already sated, and it would be unlikely to attack him, especially in the company of four others. Bears, on the other hand, where unpredictable, especially in an area like this where they rarely encountered human beings. This slaughter, however, didn't look like the work of a bear. And he didn't know enough about dholes to have any idea what to expect as far as the wild canines were concerned. Still, the dead silence of the forest meant that whatever was responsible was still somewhere nearby, and Zhang's reaction, superstitious though it seemed, made him uneasy.

He recalled the plaster mask Brandt had shown him and shivered.

"We'd better keep moving," Warren said from behind him. "We need to pitch camp before dark and I think we're all in agreement that the farther we get from this area the better."

"It won't matter if this is the work of a tiger," Julian said. "If it decides to hunt us, it will stalk us for weeks — or longer — if that's what it takes."

"This from our resident tiger expert," Adrianne said.

"Tell me I'm the only one who bothered to do his research before hopping on a plane and traveling halfway around the world to sneak into one of the most isolated regions on the entire freaking planet."

"Natural predators are the least of our worries," Warren said. "Our greater concern would be encountering either Tibetan or Chinese patrols. We'd have a hard time explaining our presence in a restricted area like this. Besides, I brought along — shall we say — a little protection."

He pulled open the left side of his khaki cargo vest to reveal a hunting knife with a thermoplastic handle and six-inch blade in a leather shoulder sheath and gave Julian a practiced wink.

"What are you, Crocodile Dundee?" Adrianne said.

Brooks sighed and wondered not only if Warren had any experience with the enormous knife, but how he had managed to get it through customs. He imagined the four-day trek back to Pai carrying Warren after he inadvertently disemboweled himself. It wasn't nearly as amusing as he would have thought.

"You think a buck knife is going to stop a tiger?" Julian said. "The Thak man-eater killed four people before they finally tracked her down. You know what they found? She'd already been shot twice. And that was in the Eastern Kumoan Division of India, maybe fifty miles from here."

"This is no mere buck knife," Warren said. "With a mere flick of the wrist, I can embed this three inches into the trunk of a tree."

"Trees aren't the most elusive of targets. You think you could hit a jungle cat running low to the ground at thirty-five miles an hour when it bursts from the brush fifteen feet away?"

"A flash of the blade and a chilling battle cry ought to dissuade it from attacking."

"If by battle cry you mean screaming like a little girl," Adrianne said.

Brooks sighed and turned around. The arguing was getting on his nerves. They'd been constantly going back and forth about something patently ridiculous since Lage. It was one thing for Adrianne and Julian, who — for all intents and purposes — were still kids, but Warren never failed to rise to the bait when by all rights he should have been above doing so.

"You think a five hundred pound tiger's greatest natural enemy is loud noises? We're talking about India, where there are ten people per square foot and another five standing on their shoulders. There's never a moment of silence."

"Now you're just being silly."

"All I'm saying is there are more than enough examples of man-eating tigers to warrant taking extra precautions. The Champawat Tiger killed more than four hundred people in Nepal and northern India. The man-eaters of Chowgarh and Bhimashankar each killed more than fifty."

"There's obviously an ample supply of prey species in this area to sustain them," Adrianne said.

"The same could be said of the Sunderbans, where villagers are considered part of the tiger's food web and their relationship has evolved into a supplementary model."

"We're wasting time," Brooks said. "And even if we are dealing with a tiger that's somehow overcome it's trepidation around man and developed a taste for human flesh, I figure the last thing we want to do is hang around in a clearing full of freshly-killed prey for any length of time."

Julian nodded reluctantly, but waited for Adrianne before heading into the mouth of the path on the opposite side of the clearing. Warren watched their packs disappear into the brush before following. Brooks waited until they were gone before taking one last look at the carcasses of the deer.

The claw marks of the predator were easy enough to discern. The dentition of the bites, however, was substantially harder to envision. There were no clear ridges, and the meat appeared to have been torn from the bones, suggesting whatever killed them hadn't sat down with its meal and worked it over like lions would have. These animals had been quickly attacked and overwhelmed and eaten in a manner that could only be described as violent.

He raised his stare to the forest once more, but, despite the distinct sensation of being watched, saw nothing.

Like he himself had said, they were wasting time, and they were going to have a hard enough time pitching their tents in the darkness. Besides, they were going to need as much rest as they could get. They had a big day ahead of them tomorrow.

"Zhang," he called.

The Sichuanese trail boss turned to face him from where he still stood near the point where they'd initially entered the clearing. He extricated the clump of long white fur he'd been examining from the branch of a tree and tucked it into his pack.

Brooks was reminded of the white fur that framed the face of a tiger and hung from its belly.

Zhang slung his pack over his shoulders once more and walked past Brooks toward where the trees still shook from Warren's passage.

"We need go far as we can before make camp," he said.

Brooks again felt the weight of eyes upon him and realized what an excellent suggestion that was.

12

Eighteen Months Ago

"Can anyone tell me what causes evolution?" Brooks asked.

He scanned the faces of the small group of graduate students trailing him through the west wing of the Brandt Institute. They made him feel older with each passing year. Or maybe it was just the disconnect between his generation and the next. He was barely over thirty and could still turn heads at the gym, but his dark hair wasn't quite as thick as it once was and the lines around his eyes were more defined. Character, they called it. More likely too much time spent out in the sun on some remote dig or other. At least he still had the deep blue eyes. They compensated for the rest of the flaws in an overall comfortable package.

These kids, though, with their tattoos all over their arms and up their necks were a different breed, although one he found more than a little intriguing, especially when it came to the way they used their quasi-individuality to identify themselves as part of a tribe, but then dyed their hair or added piercings to distinguish themselves from it. Not that they were really kids. They were all in their twenties and the very brightest in their respective graduating classes.

All of them knew the answer to his question, but feared the consequences of answering in inexact terminology. The JBIEA only had two internships available for the twelve hopeful candidates for whom this would be the crown jewel of their educational careers. They were all exceptionally qualified and would undoubtedly each do a magnificent job. Brooks was looking for the intangibles, though. The ability to think outside of the box and view the world in a unique way that could one day lead to revolutionary breakthroughs in the field of anthropology. He didn't have a checklist and he couldn't even clearly define the criteria in his own mind. All he knew was he'd recognize what he was looking for when he saw it.

"Environmental pressure," one spoke up. He wore a suit so expensive there was no way he actually owned it.

"Climactic change," a girl who'd been doing her best to flaunt her ample bosom said.

"Predation," said a skinny kid who hardly looked old enough to drive.

"Entropy," said a short girl with a pink stripe in her blond hair. She'd been trailing the group while her competition jockeyed for position at his heels.

Brooks raised an eyebrow.

"Qualify."

"The world is in a constant state of change. No two seasons are alike, let alone years. As such, species must remain in a constant state of adaptation to combat it. It's that constancy of variability that triggers mutations of a completely random — and yet statistically predictable — nature, most of which are so subtle their genetic expression goes unnoticed. The minority are dramatic, and, more often than not, turn out to be disadvantageous. The few that prove advantageous are integrated into the gene pool by selective reproduction."

"Are those evolutionary changes rapid or do they take a great deal of time?"

"Both."

"Give me examples."

"An example of a rapid change would be the peppered moth, which evolved a black-and white-marbled pattern on their wings to camouflage themselves with the indigenous lichens on the trees. During the Industrial Revolution, pollutants killed the lichens and darkened the trees with soot, which made the lighter-colored moths increasingly visible to predators that hunted them to the verge of extinction, while those with the melanistic mutation thrived when they otherwise would have been the first eaten. Thus, the population as a whole shifted to the darker coloration in a matter of generations."

"Very good. And how about slow?"

"Pick any species and you'll be able to trace its lineage through the eons. *Homo sapiens*, for example, branched from the same evolutionary tree as primates and great apes. All three of these branches diverged from a common ancestor seven million years ago."

"What proof can you offer to support this hypothesis?"

"Besides common knowledge and every textbook printed after 1960?" suit-and-tie said. "Except in the South."

The others chuckled.

Brooks smiled at the joke, but he was curious to hear pink hair's justification.

"Structurally, commonalities can be found between nearly all bones in modern-day species and in fossils. Physiologically, we share nearly ninety-nine percent of our DNA across the board, which can be corroborated through the samples obtained from our shared lineage."

"And how do we know which genes we share and for which proteins they're coded?"

"Genomic mapping."

"And how is that genetic material passed from one generation to the next?"

"Through the germ line DNA. Sperm and egg."

"So if the same genes are being passed down from one generation to the next, what impetus is required to trigger evolutionary change?"

"Mutation of the DNA itself."

"It's believed that spontaneous mutation of DNA accounts for only three-tenths of a percent of the difference between humans and our closest living relative, the bonobo, which shares 98.7 percent of our DNA. What constitutes the remainder?"

"Junk."

"And what is junk?"

"Proteins coded into our DNA for which there's no established function or direct intraspecies correlation."

"Good. And how do those proteins get into our DNA?"

"They're encoded there by the RNA, which transcribes them directly into the mitochondrial DNA."

"And where does that anomalous RNA come from?"

"Transcription?"

"True, but from what source?"

She opened her mouth, but closed it when nothing came out. The sea of faces went blank, as he expected.

"What if I told you the majority was encoded from primitive retroviruses and 'fossilized' in our DNA?"

Whispers of disbelief rippled through the group.

Brooks smirked. He lived for this moment.

"A full eight percent of our genome is composed of 'junk' segments that can be directly matched to historic retroviruses, which evolve both within and alongside their host populations. Once they integrate themselves into a species, they become what we call endogenous retroviruses, or ERVs, which are then passed along to our offspring in their DNA. Now, these retroviruses have more than fifty thousand possible points of insertion, which means that the same sequence of DNA found at the same site in different species means it's more than coincidence, right? The odds against it are astronomical. So to find the same sequence in all three branches of our evolutionary tree means that all three received that same segment of DNA from a common ancestor.

"For as many identical segments as we find, there are even more than don't match. A classic example is *Papovaviridae*, which can be used to trace migration patterns within the human species. Its various genotypes diverged at the same time as our primitive tribes, essentially creating geographically distinct subspecies. There are even much more recent retroviral segments you'll find in Europeans, but not Americans, and Africans, but not African-Americans. It is by this means that we continue to evolve as a species as a whole and — more importantly — as geographically-distinct subspecies."

"So you're saying viruses are primarily responsible for our evolution," suit-and-tie said.

"I'm saying viruses are one large component."

"What doesn't kill us makes us stronger," pink streak said.

"Is that not exactly what Darwin proposed? Think about it this way. The timeframe from initial retroviral infection to the first replication inside a cell can be measured in days, not generations. There is no faster way to alter the genome of an individual and no more certain way to pass it on to the next generation. The vast majority of mutations are recessive, and might not even appear in subsequent generations for centuries. If ever. Now, consider that a French paleovirologist was able to revive a virus that had been dead for hundreds of thousands of years. The Phoenix Virus, as he called it, easily inserted itself into a sample of human cells and began replicating its RNA. That's the crucial point you need to understand: A virus acts upon one cell and spreads like wildfire to others, rapidly altering the entire individual — including his germ line — from the inside out, with the sole intention of creating an environment conducive to its own breeding efforts, altering the host's entire genetic code in the process. And so, as Darwin said, what doesn't kill us makes us stronger, but in a way unique to the resulting proteins produced by the replication and translation of the viral DNA inside the human body."

"And it's the expression of those discrete proteins in the gene line that establishes the foundation for any given population model, while simultaneously contributing to its inherent volatility." She smiled. "Thus . . . entropy."

Brooks offered a half-smile of approval.

"What's your name, Ms. . . . ?"

"Grayson. Adrianne Grayson."

Brooks nodded and returned his attention to the task at hand, namely the tour of the facility. There was still much to see before the individual interviews commenced.

"Now over here—"

His words faltered when he turned and looked up the grand staircase to the second level. Johann Brandt himself stood on the landing, leaning heavily on his cane, his head cocked in a curious manner like a bird. He stared at Brooks as though weighing a decision of great importance, then shook his head as though to clear his thoughts. His eyes sparkled and his expression transformed into one of amusement. He gestured for Brooks to proceed with a roll of his right hand.

"Ladies and gentlemen, revolutionary anthropologist and founder of this institute, Dr. Johann Brandt."

Brandt swelled with the attention and waved away their applause.

"All right," Brooks said. "Now over here you'll see the different hominin skulls. Can anyone tell me which one belonged to the most evolutionary advantageous based solely on the shape of the cranial vault?"

He glanced back to see Brandt still staring at him with an expression he could no longer interpret. The old anthropologist winked at him and headed toward his office with the hollow tapping sound of his cane echoing down the hallway.

13

Yarlung Tsangpo River Basin
Motuo County
Tibet Autonomous Region
People's Republic of China
October 15th

Two Days Ago

The view from the campsite was breathtaking. The rainfall had waned to a gentle patter, which caused the lake far below to glimmer in the dying aura of the setting sun. It felt good to be out of the confines of the jungle and even better to be free of the horrible cold of the higher elevations. The gentle breeze blowing through the valley dispelled the mist and felt positively divine. Goosebumps rose from Brooks's skin underneath his damp clothing. The frogs and insects and birds of night croaked and whined and chirped from their mossy enclaves beneath the shrubs and from high in the treetops. Raptors rode the thermals below the cliff top on which he sat, reveling in the sensation of knowing that tomorrow would bring him one step closer to realizing his dreams.

He looked uphill toward the ridgeline far above their camp, where an evergreen-crowned precipice stood apart from the daunting white peaks he could only occasionally see through the clouds. He had insisted that Brandt describe exactly how to get to their destination, which he thought would prove all but impossible to find in this secluded valley. But Brandt's description had been perfect. Brooks could nearly see the spot that haunted his every waking thought since Brandt first described it: the sheer face of perilously smooth limestone hidden from nearly every vantage point by overhanging vegetation. One thousand vertical feet of rock virtually inaccessible from every approach and to all but the most ambitious climbers.

A crackling sound off to his left and he nearly came out of his skin. He whirled to see a red panda trundle out of the brush. It appeared every bit as surprised to see him and scampered quickly back into the shadows.

Brooks shook his head. Something about the nature of the slaughter of the deer in that clearing still made him uneasy. Not necessarily the savageness of the attack, per se, but something he couldn't quite define. Carnage like that was part of the natural order of things. He saw it in some capacity everywhere he traveled, from the Amazon to the Nile and everywhere in between. Those who've never left society behind wouldn't be able to understand. The first time he witnessed it, back in Limpopo, had been almost overwhelming. The mere thought that the wildebeests had been torn apart scant feet from where he'd been standing, and no more than fifty from where he'd been unconscious behind a single layer of fabric, had really done a number on his head. The reality that the lioness could have been crouching in the tall grasses, sneaking silently up on the wildebeests as he fumbled with his zipper, had taken years to get past. Worse still was the knowledge that he hadn't heard a sound as the animals had been torn apart. And then there had been the hyenas and the vultures the following morning, vying for the scraps.

That was it. That was what plagued him. It was the complete lack of scavengers. There hadn't been so much as a single carrion bird.

For the life of him, though, he couldn't fathom what that might mean. A disease maybe? Surely it couldn't have been solely the proximity of the tiger that held them all at bay.

And if it was a tiger that had somehow developed a predilection for human flesh, then was it out there at this very moment, watching them from the cover of the shrubs like the lions had all those years ago?

He shivered at the thought and climbed to his feet.

The Himalayas encircling him finally swallowed the setting sun. It was astounding how a place like this could form deep in one of the most daunting mountain ranges on the planet and exist to this day in such isolation. It was no wonder the Tibetans considered it the most holy of places and why it was revered by Buddhists everywhere as the "hidden lotus."

A crashing sound from the bushes behind him and the wash of a flashlight spread around his feet.

"There you are," Adrianne said. "We were starting to wonder what happened to you."

"Just enjoying the view."

She walked past him and stared upon the valley as the mist crept down from the mountaintops to cloak the lake. It looked almost ethereal in the moonlight.

"How long do you think someplace like this will last before mankind ruins it?" she asked.

Brooks stepped up to the ledge beside her. The wings of bats whistled past, just overhead.

"Nature perseveres. One way or another. The mudslides wash away the roads and the avalanches seal off the passes. If there's one thing I've learned through the course of my work, it's that nature never fails to rise to a challenge. It either outright wins or finds a way to adapt."

"And that's where we come in."

"Millions of years too late."

Adrianne laughed.

"Better late than never, I guess." She turned to face him. "Now. Seriously. You really should get back before Dr. Murray and Julian polish off dinner."

"If it's more of that root soup, then they're welcome to my share. I don't know if it didn't agree with me or if it was actively trying to kill me."

He followed her through the maze of beeches, sandalwoods, and laurels toward the flickering light of the fire, which made the trees cast strange shadows that danced through the underbrush. It was remarkable just how much the patterns of light passing through the branches looked like the stripes of a tiger.

"Can I ask you something, Dr. Brooks?"

"For the thousandth time, while we're in the field you can call me Jordan."

"All right, Jordan. I'll ask you straight up." She stopped and turned to face him. "What aren't you telling us?"

"What do you mean?"

"Pretty much exactly that. Here we are, halfway around the world in the land that time forgot and we're not taking in the sights, you know? We're making a beeline for something and I, for one, would like to know what."

"What makes you think there's anything I'm not telling you?"

"For starters, Dr. Murray was last in the field when Bush was in office, and we all know he's the kind of guy who wouldn't risk getting his L.L. Bean's dirty if it weren't guaranteed to get his face in front of a camera. Then there's Julian, whose research focus is so far removed from the rest of ours that I can only assume he's been brought along because of that specialty specifically. Assuming, of course, that his old man isn't funding the entire expedition. And our guide? I don't know if you've noticed, but he has knives strapped to every appendage and a military-issue Type 54 semiautomatic under his parka. Trust me. I know. I'm an Army brat. I've lived on just about every base around the globe with a father and two brothers. The only thing they loved more than talking about shooting stuff was actually shooting stuff."

"You seem to have this whole thing figured out. What about you then? Why do you think you're here?"

"Because I'm brilliant." She flashed a smile and winked. "And because you expect to need my expertise. More precisely, my knowledge of population models in the wake of evolutionary divergence and speciation. You don't haphazardly throw together such a potentially prestigious and expensive expedition in so little time without knowing exactly who you want and why you want them before you even set out. So I ask you again, what aren't you telling us?"

"All will be revealed tomorrow." He tried to step past her on the narrow game trail, but she moved to block him. He ended up face to face with her, so close he felt her breath on his chin when she looked up at him and stared right into his eyes. "I promise. Tomorrow. And don't worry. It'll be more than worth the wait."

Brooks squeezed her shoulder and eased past her. She smelled of jasmine and lotus blossoms and sweat. The lines between professor and student often blurred in the field, but the last thing he wanted right now was a distraction, no matter how enticing. Not with history awaiting him.

When he didn't immediately hear her following, he knew what was coming and kept walking so she had to speak to his back, denying her the ability to read his expression.

"You have a mercenary guide leading four evolutionary anthropologists with very narrow fields of focus directly to something you already know you'll find. Your expertise is the influence of viruses on physical evolution, while mine is the subsequent prediction of how that population fits into its ecosystem and the dynamics of either its ultimate proliferation or extinction. But my specialty, like yours, is in vector-borne evolutionary impetus, which brings us to the necessity to bring along someone who — regardless of his outward idiocy — is a genius when it comes to understanding the physiological effects of plants on the human body. Throw in someone as camera-friendly as Dr. Murray and you have all the makings of a highly-publicized discovery that will not only change the field, but make a whole lot of corporate interests a butt-load of money in the process."

Brooks smiled to himself. She'd hit the nail on the head, but the truth was even more extraordinary than she imagined. Instead of giving her the credit she deserved, though, he decided to have a little fun at her expense.

"That's a fantastic theory. Assuming you're right, what do you expect to find?"

She hesitated before speaking.

"I'm not entirely sure."

"Then I guess you'll just have to wait and see." He nearly chuckled out loud. She was going to be up all night agonizing over what they would find. "Sleep well."

He stepped from the forest into the glow of the fire. The clearing appeared to have been designed specifically as a campsite. The upper canopy overhung the circle of bare earth to spare the tents from the brunt of whatever rain might come and left just enough space between the branches for the smoke from the fire to rise unobstructed into the sky. He sat on a stone by the fire and waved away the flies hovering over the plate of food they'd saved for him.

The light inside Warren's tent threw his shadow against the fabric as he rolled out his sleeping bag. Julian was already way ahead of him. He leaned against the broad trunk of an oak tree with his eyes closed and a contented smile on his face. Only Zhang appeared restless. He sat on a fallen log to Brooks's right with a pensive expression on his face as he studied something he held up to the firelight between his fingers. Brooks recognized it as the clump of white fur Zhang had untangled from the branch near where the deer had been killed. Or at least he initially thought so. It almost looked like he'd unraveled it and stretched it out to make it longer than he would have expected, even from the belly fur of a tiger. In fact, it was thinner, more like hair than fur.

Zhang caught him looking and held it closer to the fire. It smoldered and shriveled upward toward his fingers. He rubbed them together and dropped the remains into the flames.

He rose and struck off into the darkness without saying a word, leaving Brooks alone by the fire with the smell of burnt hair.

14

Excerpt from the journal of
Hermann G. Wolff

Courtesy of Johann Brandt, Private Collection
Chicago, Illinois
(Translated from original handwritten German text)

January 1939

We spent three days wandering aimlessly — *in my estimation, anyway — during which time we did not encounter another living soul. While König grew increasingly distant, Brandt's frustration built to an almost maddening crescendo. He was accustomed to being able to take his measurements of villagers even while waiting out storms and the customary diplomatic snags. The only evidence of human intrusion were the sporadic cairns and chortens, which supposedly spoke some secret Buddhist tongue in which none of us was versed. Most had been reclaimed by the vegetation centuries ago, but a few demonstrated more recent carbon scoring from the burning of incense, which fueled Brandt's frantic search for where those respon-sible might have gone.*

König vanished into the brush before any of us rose for the day, leaving us to wonder if today would be the day he didn't return. Despite his arrival every night with wild game upon which to feast, he continued to look more and more gaunt. He said little, contrary to his nature, and appeared to be in the process of consumption by some malady or other. Its evidence was in his eyes, which never quite seemed to focus upon you when he spoke, but rather upon some point in the distance that only he could see. While I had not known him as long as some of the others, I knew him well enough to recognize that whatever it was that called him to the hunt every day was something he viewed as his personal mission in life to collect. We all recognized the air of obsession about him, and something more perhaps, something which, were we dealing with anyone else, we might have called fear.

That left Eberhardt, Metzger, and me to essentially plot our course without the direction of our leader or our anthropologist. Metzger proved exceptional at harvesting the pelts of the animals König left for us to tend to as though we were his man-servants, not his colleagues. He was also quite adept at tanning the hides and curing the meat. The benefits of a Bavarian upbringing, he claimed. And Eberhardt turned out to have a nose for exploration, as well. It was his instincts that led us to search the higher ground, rather than merely content ourselves with the relative comforts of the lowlands, where we enjoyed both the occasional spot of sunlight and the tea leaves and fresh berries it produced.

Of course, we also had our own jobs to do. Despite the loss of the vast majority of his supplies, Eberhardt created maps of stunning quality and detail on whatever paper he could scrounge — including hard-bargained pages from this very journal — for later transposition onto more fitting media. He fashioned a drawing compass from the whittled bones of waterfowl and constructed a magnetic compass from the needle in our surgical kit and the treasured lodestone he found beneath the Himalayan ice. He also became increasingly fascinated with the Buddhist relics we encountered and would often waste precious hours meticulously drawing them, while we all knew that this was a subject of considerable contention between our generous benefactors in the Ahnenerbe and the Christian beliefs of our Führer, who outwardly condemned the worship of such false prophets while not-so-secretly borrowing from their symbology. It was one such drawing that sent König into a fit of rage when he saw it. He held it to the fire and waved it in front of Eberhardt as it burned, claiming the SS did not fund this expedition to commemorate the blasphemous idolatry of these godforsaken heathens. According to König, ours was a simple task: Find evidence of our Aryan ancestry, catalogue every minute detail about the location, and return to the Fatherland with incontestable proof. Eberhardt had suggested the task would be much easier to complete if König were to actually help us on occasion, rather than vanishing into the forest before each new dawn, to which König merely smiled and said that was exactly what he was doing.

It was at that point we first began to question his sanity.

We did not see König for two days after that. Not until we discovered the cliffs.

Brandt, on the other hand, abandoned his one-man search for the mysterious race he was certain was somewhere out here, waiting to be found, in an effort to help expedite our progress. He assisted Eberhardt with his drawings and noted the differences between the various chortens we had failed to appreciate, like the petal designs and seven steps of the Heaped Lotus Stupa, which commemorated the birth of the Buddha, and the octagonal steps of the Stupa of Reconciliation. His anthropological insights allowed us to paint a picture by which to better understand the sanctity of this valley and its importance to the surrounding peoples.

Metzger's mood darkened seemingly by the hour as his magnetic readings, which at first had been wildly encouraging, became inconsistent and arbitrary. The composition of the rocks and soil varied from one kilometer to the next, despite the constancy of Eberhardt's primitive directional compass. He speculated the equipment had been damaged by the careless Sherpas, but had been unable to diagnose the problems, let alone fix them. In the end, his only option had been to precisely record the readings and hope time and perspective would allow him to understand them. The rest of us were outwardly supportive, but knew exactly how failures of such magnitude were perceived and plotted to distance ourselves from him upon our return, even though privately we knew there was no better geologist in all of Germany.

I collected samples of the flora, both pressed and dried, in hopes of publishing a collection to coincide with the release of the film of our explorations, tentatively titled Erstaunen [Astonishing] Tibet. *Unfortunately, the lack of anything truly amazing would probably necessitate a change to something along the lines of*

Langweilig [Boring] Tibet, *for all of the lackluster footage I had obtained. At least up until we found the remains of the shapi.*

Not coincidentally, that's also where we caught up with König.

We came upon him standing in the middle of a clearing at the base of a sheer limestone cliff perhaps three hundred meters tall, his rifle pointed into the forest opposite us. Brandt hailed him and nearly received a bullet for his courtesy. I will never forget König's wide eyes staring down the sightline of his Browning as he took aim at us, nor the sweat beading his brow or the way the barrel trembled in the grasp of our master hunter. He gasped for air when he finally pulled the stock from his shoulder, as though he had been holding his breath for a great length of time. When he turned away from us, we looked to one another in confusion before comprehension dawned.

Arches of blood climbed the stone wall at such an angle as to suggest violent force. Nearly that of a bullet passing through a deer at close range, I speculated, and yet we had heard no shot. Considering we nearly always heard the sound of König's rifle fire, which echoed through the deep valley in such a way as to make the origin of the sound impossible to divine, the fact that we hadn't heard anything, coupled with the freshness of the blood, proved the animal had been dispatched by other means. And Lord only knew what those means might have been, judging by the condition of the shapi's remains. The once mythical goat-antelope had been rendered as though by a ferocious beast twice its size, perhaps even several of them. Its long fur was tangled in the azaleas and lotus flowers, its customary golden locks discolored by blood, which, Metzger noted, miraculously dripped from the leaves of a birch tree high above it. Its carcass was hollowed and bare, its bony framework devoid of musculature in the least aesthetically pleasing way possible. Only its blunted head and snout remained remotely intact, despite its broken horns.

We had all read the fantastic accounts of the Champawat Tiger killed by the British hunter Jim Corbett thirty years ago, not far from where we entered Tibet, in fact. The monster had killed more than four hundred men from Nepal to East India before it was eventually tracked using the trail of blood left by the young villager it had carried off to devour. It was said to have entered villages in broad daylight, roared to cause panic, and then plucked off its victims one by one in the ensuing chaos. We had even heard tell of a tiger leaping onto the back of an elephant and carrying off its mahout as we were leaving Gangtok.

I am certain we all believed ourselves invulnerable to a large extent, or at least that such things only happened to the primitive villagers of this godless land. It wasn't until that moment when we realized that such beasts undoubtedly knew no distinction between heathen and Christian meat. I saw the truth etched upon König's face as he knelt and studied something on the ground, as I had witnessed him doing with the odd footprint I filmed on the way into the valley. He traced it with his bare fingers, then turned and looked straight up the rock cliff. He stood, cocked his head, and then pointed at a ledge perhaps ten meters above our heads.

It took him a good fifteen minutes to reach it, by which time the smell of the carcass had drawn nearly every fly in the Old World and things I had no desire to confront skulked and scurried through the underbrush. König crouched upon the narrow ledge with vultures wheeling overhead and nodded to himself as if in confirmation of an inner suspicion we believed to mean the beast had waited up there for the shapi to graze within range before pouncing. It was impossible to interpret König's body language when he vanished inside of himself as he did then, possessed as he was by the primal hunter within him.

He looked to either side as though gauging how best to descend before cautiously turning, bracing himself against the escarpment, and peering upward. He stayed in that position for the longest time before once more turning to face us so quickly he nearly fell from his perch. There was no mistaking the excitement on his face. It wasn't until I was standing nearly directly beneath him and staring past him, hundreds of meters up the face of the cliff, that I saw what he had discovered and felt the same surge of exhilaration.

15

Yarlung Tsangpo River Basin
Motuo County
Tibet Autonomous Region
People's Republic of China
October 16th

Yesterday

"Y ou sure you're up for this, prof?" Julian asked.

Brooks stared straight up at the sheer limestone face and had to focus all of his energy on mustering his resolve. The cliff was much steeper than he'd envisioned and their route up it significantly less obvious. Had Brandt's directions not been so accurate and had he not seen the proof that the old man had been here, he would have found it hard to believe that anyone from the König Expedition would have not only seen what could only be viewed from this one vantage point, but would have had the courage to go up there after it. He adjusted his climbing harness over his thighs and groin and nodded his readiness to Julian.

"All right, Jordan." Adrianne repositioned the digital video camera mounted to his helmet so its line of sight was as close to Brooks's point of view

as possible. "You'll have to factor in displacement of roughly two inches laterally, but, all in all, I think this is going to work perfectly."

"And you're certain we can strip his audio from the footage?" Warren said.

"This is the twenty-first century, Dr. Murray. Anything the microphone
picks up is recorded on a separate track, so you don't have to worry about
anything he says ruining your voiceover. Unless the camera incurs significant
physical damage while it's recording, anyway."

"Like from a fall?"

"Ooh," Julian said. "If you do fall, will you try to make a sound like this?"
He made a long, high-pitched whistling noise that culminated in a splat.
Brooks had watched enough Roadrunner cartoons as a kid to recognize the
sound effect.

"Funny." He looked up at their destination, a thousand feet up, and tried
to rationalize the distance, but failed to equate it to anything that lent a less
intimidating perspective. That was a hell of a long way to climb and an eter-
nity to fall. And worse, there would be times when his life would literally be in
the hands of a grad student whose sole reason for being was to find new ways
to get high. "Let's get on with it."

"We'll be able to see everything you see on this monitor over here." Adrianne gestured to the hard shell case where the small viewscreen showed an
image of itself. "And we'll be able to hear everything you say, but you won't be
able to hear us."

"If we see something on the monitor you might have missed, we'll flash up
to you with this mirror." Warren tilted what looked like a pocket compact
until the light hit Brooks in the face and he had to shield his eyes. "That'll be
your cue. Verbally acknowledge you've seen our signal and we'll be able to
communicate with yes or no answers. Flash for yes; nothing for no.
Understand?"

"He's got it already," Julian said. "That mountain's not going to climb
itself."

He wore fluorescent orange climbing shoes with blinding yellow laces and
black rubber soles and a pair of gray climbing shorts with a fully integrated
harness system already built in. The legs in between were uncomfortably hairy,
at least for the rest of them, and covered with scabs he couldn't resist picking
at. His shirt was one of those skintight, moisture-wicking spandex numbers
with built-in padding on his elbows and over his shoulders where the straps of

a backpack would ride. The graphic on his chest was of five fictional stages of evolution from a monkey to stooped men of varying degree to an erect man and finally to a man climbing a rock wall. He caught Brooks looking and beamed.

"I can hook you up with one just like it when we get back home, prof."

"Don't tease me, Julian." Brooks tugged on his harness and the attached rope. Checked and double-checked his supply of quickdraws, hexes, and spring-loaded cams. Ensured the ice axes on either hip were secure. Looked up at the cliff and watched the vines hanging from the precipice above their destination whip sideways on a gust of wind he couldn't even feel from the forest floor. "I'm going to hold you to it."

Julian smiled and nodded as though Brooks had passed some crucial test in his mind. He opened the pouch hanging from his waist, dumped chalk into his palms, and produced a cloud of blue when he clapped them together. Warren coughed and Adrianne waved it away. Brooks turned to find Zhang crouching several feet away, extricating one of the hundreds of jagged fragments of petrified wood from where they'd worked their way into the earth. He fingered it as he looked up to the very top of the cliff. He felt the weight of Brooks's gaze and hurriedly stood. The expression on his face was one Brooks couldn't read.

"Let's do this thing," Julian said. He rolled his head on his shoulders, stretched his arms, cracked his knuckles, and scurried up the talus slope at the base of the mountain.

"Are you going to tell us what's up there now?" Adrianne asked.

"You've come this far already, what's a few more minutes?"

He winked at her and bounded up the slickrock after Julian. While he'd never be accused of being a great climber, Brooks could hold his own in a pinch. It was one of those skills he'd taken upon himself to learn as an undergrad after declaring his major and being exposed to the overwhelming field of competition for the few highly coveted positions. He'd needed to do anything and everything he could to distinguish himself from the countless others like himself, some of whom were undoubtedly smarter, wealthier, or willing to use their physical endowments to secure the rare spots on the more prestigious digs. A willingness to work for free and receive no credit when the findings were published was no longer enough. He'd learned rock climbing from a seventh-year senior who viewed it as a religion; skydiving and BASE jumping from a former Ranger who lost a leg in Desert Storm; and enough of about a dozen different languages from the generous proprietors of local restaurants to stumble through casual conversations, and, most importantly, fake his way through an interview.

He felt his climbing skills returning, but not nearly at the pace he would have liked. Too many years as an administrator had softened him, dulled his instincts. Or perhaps he was simply too excited by the knowledge that what he had traveled all this way to find was nearly within his reach. His stomach tingled like a teenager on a first date and his pulse throbbed in his temples. He was grateful for the gloves because he could feel the dampness on his palms beneath them. Thanks to what he fully intended to bring back down with him, he would find the world into which he descended afterward one on the brink of monumental change.

Julian scaled the limestone like a gecko, with even more grace and confidence than he exhibited on the ground. He unconsciously hummed the theme song from *Spider-Man* over and over. While amusing at first, it quickly lost its charm and Brooks began to wonder if sinking his ice ax into Julian's calf might not be the most effective means of silencing him. Or at least the most satisfying, anyway.

The others fell farther and farther below as they ascended. His legs started to tremble and his muscles burned, but he savored the sensations. There was simply something about being so close to realizing his life's goal and simultaneously one misstep from a gruesome end that made him feel alive in a way he hadn't in a long time.

Julian paused on the larger ledges and shelves to take in the view of the mist-blanketed valley while Brooks caught up. He hammered anchors so quickly it was as though he'd been doing it all his life. He gripped crimps with just his fingertips and scurried upward to lunge for edges, all the while fixing the rope for Brooks, who struggled by comparison. They reached a point where the wind grew stronger with every vertical foot while the handholds diminished in size from buckets to crimps, and finally to finger cracks that Brooks barely had the strength to hold, let alone use to pull himself upward. For every foot they climbed, they moved half a dozen laterally, seeking anything resembling purchase.

Brooks was suddenly all too aware of his exposure and just how reliant he was becoming on the anchors seated by a grad student who was probably last fully sober a decade ago. If then. The others were mere dots far below, craning to see them.

Julian shouted something, but the wind swept his words away.

Brooks braced himself and looked up. Julian had crawled into a hollow carved into the cliff and held out his arm. Above him, the ledge loomed like a wave preparing to crash down on them both. Vegetation flowed over it and swayed on the wind. Branches and leaves and vines. Contorted trunks grew straight from crevices in the rock, their leaves sparse and withered. He could no longer see the valley through the vegetative screen, only the ground directly below them.

Another few feet and he clasped Julian's wrist, shoved with his quivering legs, and crawled into the tiny manmade cave.

It was roughly eight feet long and three feet high and still bore the chisel marks where what had once been a mere oblong impression in the limestone created by the receding seas billions of years ago had been reshaped for the purposes of ancestors so ancient their precise reasons for doing so were lost to the annals of time. Although how they had accomplished this amazing feat defied explanation. This was where the source of the broken and nearly petrified wood half-buried below them had once resided.

Brooks removed his flashlight from his belt and shined it at the back wall. It was slanted and tapered to a crevice that reached deeper into the rock. Petroglyphs had been etched into the rock so long ago they were now indecipherable impressions. He leaned back out over the nothingness and twisted his torso in order to see upward, where a dozen more holes just like this one were concealed from the outside world by the natural screen of plant life, only they appeared to be barricaded by large rectangular blocks of wood.

They were much more than that, though. They were entire lengths of alpine oak trunks planed smooth on the outside and hollowed on the inside to accommodate the contents sealed beneath the fitted lids. And inside of them was what had changed Brandt's life all those years ago and what had brought Brooks halfway around the globe.

They were coffins. Right where Brandt had said they would be. And inside of each was the key to unlocking the mysteries of evolution.

He drew his legs up beneath him, braced his feet, and reached for a ledge he could use to pull himself up to the next hollow, maybe four feet up and another five to his right. His strength and energy revitalized by the prospect of looking inside with his own eyes, he scaled the distance with ease.

The coffins were part of a mysterious burial practice that flourished nearly a thousand years ago in the ages between the dawn of the Song Dynasty in 960 C.E. and the sunset of the Ming Dynasty in 1644. Although credited to an ethnic Chinese minority known as the Bo, this strange burial rite, known collectively as hanging graves, appeared not only throughout the mountains of China, but in the Philippines and Indonesia, as well. The Bo primarily utilized a method of balancing the coffins on wooden posts staked directly into the rock, while these hollows more closely resembled the practices of the Igorot of Sagada and the Torajans of Tana Toraja. Like the valley itself, they were an inexplicable anomaly. Some believed the revered were buried as high as possible to bring them closer to the heavens, while pragmatists theorized it was simply to prevent looting, and all of the various and bizarre shades of speculation in between, from cannibalism to necromancy to vampirism. These, Brooks believed, had been hidden up here for all of these centuries in the hopes that they would never be found, deep inside the most remote and isolated place on the planet.

Brooks squeezed his upper body into the gap beside the head of the coffin and braced his feet on the edge. Julian did the same thing at the other end and looked at him expectantly.

"Are you guys ready down there?" Brooks asked.

After a moment, he caught a flash of light from a thousand feet below.

He smiled at Julian.

"How about you? Ready to change the world as we know it?"

If he replied, Brooks didn't hear it over the scraping sound of the lid as he shoved it deeper into the cave. The echo of the sound made it louder still. A haze of dust billowed out of the coffin and swirled in the beam of his flashlight as he shined it onto his destiny.

"Sweet Jesus," Julian said. "What the hell happened to him?"

Brooks stared down at the desiccated face and realized that the camera wasn't recording his triumph in all its glory, but rather something else entirely.

This wasn't what he'd expected to find.

Not even close.

PART IV

DESECRATION

16

Yarlung Tsangpo River Basin
Motuo County
Tibet Autonomous Region
People's Republic of China
October 16th

Yesterday

The face of the dead man looked nothing at all like the plaster cast. In fact, there was nothing extraordinary about him, outside of the brutal manner of his death, anyway. And the smell. Dear Lord. Brooks had never encountered anything so vile. It was all he could do to close his eyes and concentrate on his breathing to keep from expunging the contents of his stomach. He was accustomed to examining remains, although not nearly this fresh. The decedent hadn't been dead for a decade, let alone millennia.

He opened his eyes and focused on taking a clinical approach. His subject was male and appeared to be in his mid to late thirties. The bone structure of his face was decidedly Caucasian. Maybe six feet in height. Weight indeterminate. His eyes were sunken, his hair and beard as dry as straw. His teeth were bared, the front two on top broken. His right zygomatic arch and temporal bone were fractured, as though from a direct blow with a heavy object. The overlying skin had receded from the bony framework. His wool sweater was torn and crisp with black blood, his ribs exposed underneath. His hands were folded over his deflated abdomen, the fingers skeletal and articulated. The denim of his pants was brittle with the dried fluids of decomposition, which had congealed at the bottom of the hand-carved casket amid a scattering of insect carcasses. His hiking boots formed a triangle where his toes touched.

"He's wearing Levi's and Wolverine boots," Julian said.

Brooks could only look at him blankly, unable to find any words. He returned his attention to the body and fingered the shredded wool. The tears were parallel and inflicted at an angle from the left shoulder, across the chest, and to the upper right abdomen. The skin underneath had decomposed, leaving no indication of the resultant superficial trauma. The anterior ribs to the left of the sternum were deeply scored and thick with congealed dissolution.

"The wounds on his chest were deep and would have caused significant loss of blood," Brooks said. "Those on his legs appear relatively superficial, although based on the quantity of blood retained by the denim, I believe they would have required emergent medical attention."

He caught a flash of the mirror from the corner of his eye. Whoever controlled it was going crazy trying to get his attention.

"What about his head?" Julian asked.

"The blow would have been fatal. The impact shattered his cheekbone, the lateral rim of his orbit, and depressed his temple to such an extent that the injury to the brain would undoubtedly have caused severe hemorrhaging."

"What the hell happened to him?"

Brooks shook his head and looked out over the nothingness. They were thousands of miles away from home and hundreds from the nearest cell tower. Whoever entombed this body had fully expected it never to be found. He craned his neck and looked upward at all of the other coffins hidden in the mountainside, suddenly uncertain of what they would find inside.

He'd seen the proof that Brandt's expedition had been here in the form of the wooden shrapnel on the ground where the coffin had fallen, as he described, but not what Brandt had told him he would find inside. Was it possible this coffin had served as an ordinary burial? If so, how had a

Caucasian man of obvious western origin ended up entombed a thousand feet above the ground in one of the most remote regions on the planet?

"Help me check his pockets," Brooks said.

"I'm not touching him. You do it."

Brooks forced his fingers into each of the front pockets in turn. One produced a Swiss Army knife, the other a golden Sacagawea dollar. He set both down on the ledge and gripped the body by the sweater in one hand and the jeans in the other.

"What are you doing?" Julian asked.

"I'm rolling him over so you can check his back pockets."

The corpse peeled from the bottom with a crackling sound. Brooks was surprised by how light it was. The bones with which he usually worked were fossilized to some degree and as hard as rock. These were probably so brittle they would shatter if he even looked at them too hard.

"Ohh. This is bad. This is really bad."

"Just stick your fingers in there."

"When has anything good ever come from that statement?"

Julian swept his fingers through one pocket, then the other, breaking apart the waxy adipocere. He jerked them back empty and wiped them frantically on his shirt.

"What were you hoping to find?"

"An ID of some kind."

"Who gets buried with his passport? I can't think of one good reason why we don't just close the lid and head back down with the others."

"How about this? This man was literally ripped apart and whoever interred him went to about the greatest lengths possible to hide his body. The way I see it, that's the best possible reason to figure out what in the name of God is going on here."

"You think the Chinese could have done this?"

"Does he look like he was attacked by a military patrol?"

Julian looked away.

Brooks thought back to his initial reaction to the old man's treasured cast. Why hadn't Brandt come back here during the last seventy years? Why hadn't he claimed the discovery as his own? And he thought about how he'd contemplated whether or not Brandt has sent any others like himself as he looked down at a man who couldn't have been dead for more than eight years, judging by the date on the coin.

"Help me close this thing up," Brooks said.

"Now we're on the same wavelength, Dr. Brooks."

They seated the wooden slab back in place and Julian unspooled the rope below them.

"Wrong direction," Brooks said.

"What do you mean?"

"We need to see what's in the rest of them."

"You're out of your mind."

"Maybe," Brooks said, and maneuvered himself so he could reach up over the top of the cave. He didn't wait for Julian this time. He climbed upward on finger- and toeholds that barely qualified as such. All the while, his thoughts raced at the potential implications. The problem was that none of them made a bit of sense.

He hauled himself over the ledge on trembling arms and shoved off the lid before he even got both knees under him. Again, what he found defied explanation. The dead man wore camouflaged fatigues and was every bit as badly mangled as the first. The insignia on the patch on his right sleeve identified him as an enlisted infantryman of the Chinese People's Liberation Army. His wide, flat cheekbones and blunt nasal protuberance were undeniably Asian. Whatever skin he once possessed had dissolved into the sludge on the bottom, where insect carcasses were entombed as though in amber.

"Dr. Brooks," Julian said when he caught up, but Brooks didn't stick around to hear what the grad student had to say.

He climbed upward, hand over hand, his mind driving his shaking body higher. His grip slipped as he pulled himself up onto the next ledge and for a moment he hung by a single hand over a horrible death.

His heart jackhammered and his shoulders ached as he crawled up into the hollow, well aware of his lack of caution and the consequences he'd narrowly averted. His professional curiosity had simply gotten the better of him. He struggled to shove the lid off of the wooden coffin. He fell to his haunches and rested his elbows on the lip. He experienced a sensation of vertigo as he stared down at the remains.

Another male of Caucasian descent. This one couldn't have been out of his twenties. His body was significantly older than the previous two and his journey to decomposition was essentially complete. Only his bones remained, and they had taken on a manila cast. The man's sweater was a sickly shade of gray and deteriorated to woolen swatches. His pants were baggy and tucked into ankle-high hobnail boots, the soles of which appeared uniformly rusted. There were no brand names on anything and Brooks hadn't seen anyone use what looked like an ACE bandage to seal his pants to his boots outside of black and white photographs.

"Are you out of your freaking mind?" Julian clambered over the edge and shoved him farther away from the edge. "You see this?" He tugged on the rope that bound them together. "If you'd fallen, you would have taken me with you."

Brooks looked into Julian's wild eyes.

"You're right. I got carried away."

"Damn straight you did."

"It won't happen again."

"You'd better believe it won't. Down there you're in charge. But up here? Up here you'll do exactly what I say or so help me I'll . . . "

The screaming wind swept away his words.

Brooks crawled back to the coffin. He'd seen something metallic near the bottom right before Julian tackled him. It took him a moment to find it again, in the crust near the dead man's thigh, where the disarticulated phalanges of his fingers and the carpals of his wrist were jumbled near the fractured end of his radius.

He reached in and extricated a ring from the dried sludge. It came a away with a single phalanx that fell out while he examined it.

It was silver and covered with the foul-smelling adipocere. He scraped at the surface with his thumbnail and revealed a triangular design with a backward N inside of it, beside which was a skull and crossbones.

"Dr. Brooks," Julian said.

Brooks continued scraping, exposing a hexagonal design, then a circle inside of which were what looked like a lightning bolt and an arrow. No, it was more than that. It was a Gibor rune and a Bind rune. All of the designs were runes. The hexagon was the Hagal rune and the backward N was the Sig rune. He'd seen them all before. And the skull . . .

"Dr. Brooks, you really need to see this."

There was no doubt about it. It was a *Totenkopfring*. The *SS-Ehrenring* bestowed upon members of Heinrich Himmler's *Shutzstaffel*, one that couldn't have been issued before the late 1930s and one no one on the planet would have been caught dead wearing after 1945.

"Son of a bitch," Brooks said. "What else didn't he tell me?"

"Dr. Brooks!"

He closed the ring in his fist and turned to find Julian lying on his belly at the back of the hollow, ducking underneath the lid Brooks had cast aside, which now leaned against the tapered rock wall.

"What is it, Julian?"

The grad student pushed the lid aside and gestured at the bare stone with an enormous grin on his face.

"What?"

"You have to come closer."

Brooks tucked the ring in his pocket and crawled away from the edge, toward the deep shadows. He had to lower his head and shoulders. He was nearly right beside Julian when a shape resolved from the shadows, down near where the ceiling met the floor.

"Well, what do you know."

Brooks flipped on the light mounted to the opposite side of his helmet from the camera and shined it into the hole, illuminating a dark passage leading deeper into the mountain.

17

Johann Brandt Institute for Evolutionary Anthropology
Chicago, Illinois
October 7ᵗʰ

Ten Days Ago

"Tell me about that initial expedition," Brooks said.

"That was *so* long ago, my boy. Where do I start?"

"How about at the beginning?"

Brandt wheeled out from behind his desk and positioned himself in front of the window, his back to Brooks. Even in his diminished form, he struck a powerful silhouette against the gray skyline.

"There is never just one beginning to any story. You of all people should understand that. Any point in history is a random convergence of timelines that intersect for but the briefest of moments and from which an unlimited number of futures emanate like the rays of the sun. Why don't you ask me what you *really* want to know?"

Brooks thought about the plaster cast as it turned on its stand inside the climate-controlled case. He'd scrutinized every inch of it for the inconsistency that would prove it was a fake. There was just the right amount of asymmetry to the facial features and imperfections obviously caused by the application of the plaster. If it was a hoax, everything about it was perfect.

Brandt turned and looked at him with his fingers tented underneath his chin, his eyes alight with a youthful fire that seemed sorely out of place in his withering frame.

"Is it real?"

"Of course it's real. Why else would I take you down there in the first place? I know how all of the rest of what you saw makes me look. I would have gladly taken the secrets of that room with me to the grave. But that's not the question, or if it is, maybe you aren't the man I thought you were."

Brooks again thought of the plaster face. He'd committed every detail to memory. He recalled the wide, flared nostrils and the eyes that had been memorialized in such a way that he couldn't tell if they were open or closed.

"Was it alive when you cast it?"

"Good heavens, no! Why don't you take a moment to formulate your thoughts."

"I didn't come here to verbally spar with you. I'm in the process of putting together an expedition, which is easier said than done considering I'm not allowed to show any of them what I've seen. What I need to know, more than anything else, is if it's real. And I need a straight answer."

"You've evaluated it for yourself; what is your assessment?"

"If it's a fake, then it's the most elaborate one I've ever seen."

"Instead of approaching this with the intention of disproving its authenticity, why not approach it from a purely scientific perspective? Treat it as you would any discovery in the field and go from there."

"It's just so fantastic."

"Imagine how the man who first exhumed the skull of *Tyrannosaurus rex* must have felt. Did he spend all of his time trying to prove it was fake or did he rush out and tell the world?"

"That's what bothers me most about this whole thing. Why didn't you share your discovery with the entire world?"

"I already told you."

"Try telling me again."

"The answer is simple, my boy. The time simply wasn't right."

"When has any discovery of this magnitude ever been suppressed because of the timing?"

"You'd be amazed the truths the world is unprepared to accept. You can't just shine a light in people's eyes and expect them to accept that until that moment they've been blind. Imagine the religious implications."

"This isn't the Middle Ages. People are able to reason for themselves."

"Not at the cost of their faith." Brandt's smile and tone of voice were patronizing, as though Brooks were a child. "Think about the timing of my initial expedition. We were dispatched by the Ahnenerbe to trace our Aryan roots. Back then, it wasn't the joke that it is now. People actually believed in the existence of a mythical race of Atlanteans and the nobility of the bloodline we, as Germans, inherited from them. Not just the masses, but educated men and women who believed with all of their hearts because they were desperate to believe in something, anything other than the demoralizing realities of our daily existence."

Brandt again turned his chair so he could look down upon the hedge maze. He continued in a faraway voice.

"Ours was suddenly an impoverished country, fractured and dismantled by forces that didn't just defeat us in the first *Weltkrieg*, they ground us beneath their heels like insects and demanded crippling reparations designed to make it so we could never reunite as a Germanic people, let alone rise from our ashes. You understand the power of belief, the feeling of being a part of something greater than yourself. It's a euphoric feeling, one that galvanizes communities. Entire nations for that matter. We all needed to believe in something, no matter how fantastic, as you said. Even Himmler, arguably the second most powerful man in Germany, believed with such fervor that he was certain that not only would we find the proof of our superior lineage high in the Himalayas, we would return with it and show our oppressors once and for all through whose lineage the blood of kings flowed."

"That doesn't answer my question."

"Imagine what would have happened if we returned from the mystical land of Tibet instead with proof that everyone was wrong, that their beliefs were misguided and not only were they not superior, they were inherently *inferior*. It would have been a crushing blow that derailed more than the war efforts. Our country was drunk with power and high on nationalism. God help me, I was, too. Our economy was stronger than it had ever been. It was like one big party we thought would never end. And those of us who'd seen in the flesh what you saw downstairs...we elected not to crash that party."

"What about the others from your expedition? Surely at least one of them would have wanted to take credit for the discovery."

"I was the only one who returned to Germany after we left Tibet. We had something of a falling out, I suppose you might say. And the prospect of returning to a country at war wasn't necessarily appealing to all, especially while we still had *carte blanche* to pursue our individual research. So I guess you could say that I was the one who ultimately made the decision, and there was a juncture when I probably should have shared our discovery with the Ahnenerbe, but what do you think Himmler would have done with that knowledge? He would have twisted it to fit his narrative, making lie of scientific truth. Worse, he would have used it as a rallying cry to send more of our youth to be slaughtered on the front lines."

"What about anytime during the intervening seventy years?"

"What can I say? I am a vain and selfish man. I've lived my entire life knowing the answer to a riddle few believe we will ever solve. Do you have any idea how powerful that can make a man feel?"

"So why share this now? Better yet, why share it with me?"

"That's the real question, isn't it?" Brandt sighed and turned away from the window, beyond which a flock of starlings settled onto the hedge maze. "I am a man both out of time and out of synch with it. I no longer understand the world around me and, truth be told, would really rather not. There is no longer a sense of scientific wonder and enlightenment, but rather one of entitlement. The quest for answers has mutated into the determination to force the will of man onto everything in his dominion. If anyone else saw the plaster cast and recognized the implications, we would lay bare one of the last natural mysteries in the world and in our race to understand it would throw caution to the wind and experiment with forces man was never meant to command."

"You mean we'd attempt to clone it."

"You asked me why I chose you. In answer, allow me to pose a question of my own." He wheeled back behind his desk and stared Brooks directly in the eyes for so long he became uncomfortable. "What is the significance of viruses of the *Popovaviridae* family?"

"*Popovaviridae* is an archaic term for a family of viruses known to cause neoplasms. It's since been divided into two distinct families: *Polyomaviridae* and *Papillomaviridae*. As far as its significance to human genetics, one specific polyomavirus — the JC Virus — can be used to trace historical human migration patterns."

"How so?"

The corner of Brandt's mouth curled upward in an expression Brooks interpreted as one of amusement. They both knew Brooks could answer the question. The director was leading him toward an epiphany of some kind, but Brook was tired of speaking in code. If Brandt had something to say, he wished he'd just come out and say it.

"There are fourteen discrete subtypes of the virus, each corresponding to a specific geographic location, without more than transient overlap. Roughly three-quarters of the global population is infected with subtle variations upon what we consider to be the base genotype of the virus, variations we speculate were caused by mutations within the indigenous populations during the generations following the initial infection at a common site of origin, thus allowing us to trace the history of human expansion using the commonalities of their viral-coded DNA."

"And how does that theory relate to population models?"

"That's not my area of expertise."

"Take a crack at it anyway. Just for fun."

"Polyomaviruses are DNA based, unlike retroviruses, which utilize RNA to directly incorporate their genetic code into ours. As such, they require a much more complex process of transcription in order to insert their genetic code into the host cell's DNA. They're rather unique in the sense that their genome possesses both early and late genetic expression. Initial infection can cause immediate oncogenesis in immune-compromised individuals, or the infection can remain latent for many years before stimulating tumor growth. Once transcribed, the virus' DNA is incorporated into our somatic cells, but not our germ line. Thus, as an exogenous infection, it continues to mutate within each host and through subsequent generations the farther one gets from its geographical site of origin. In a sense, you could say that its continued evolution as a subspecies not only mirrors, but corresponds with our own. As our gene pools become increasingly isolated around the world, our genomes continue to diverge considerably from one another, positing the debate for subspecies classification of the extant lineage of *Homo sapiens*."

"Evolutionarily speaking, what else will you find if you go back far enough historically, to the point of common genomic expression?"

Brooks could sense where he was going with this line of thought.

"Related viruses of the same genus, species with similar physical and genetic makeup. Species like the Chimpanzee Polyomavirus and Simian Virus 40. Similar viruses that infect the cells of lower order primates in a nearly identical manner, all of which cause neoplastic growth in parallel evolutionary lines and become increasingly complex as the host and virus coevolve."

And then it hit him where Brandt was leading him. He imagined the plaster cast and the microscopic imperfections in its surface.

"You were able to extract DNA."

"If only that were the case. I'm afraid that a lifetime ago we never dreamed such things would ever be possible. And believe me, I've tried every available means of gathering viable samples from that plaster, but what little trace we could find was degraded to such an extent that it was beyond worthless."

"So you want me because you believe I'll be able to sample its DNA in the field and be able to recognize the viral patterns in the junk DNA that separates it from us and identify the causative viral infection?"

"If such a correlation exists. Or perhaps we'll just find a random mutation of the proteins with no attributable cause. And if we do find a recognizable viral chain of proteins in its DNA, I have no doubt that you are the one man on the planet qualified to not only decipher its code, but isolate the virus itself."

"You want me to find the virus?"

"For every virus there is a vector of transmission. If you can isolate the virus, I have complete confidence that you will be able to find the vector."

"And what if I can't? It's one thing sampling your traditional array of vectors like mosquitoes and mites, but in a case like the JC Virus, they suspect the mode of transmission is something as benign as contaminated water. For all we know, the source could be an environmental reservoir in soil with a specific pH or on any random species of plant."

"I'm sure I can find someone on staff qualified to evaluate such contingencies."

"And you have to consider the possibility that even if such a virus exists, it could be long dead by now. The vast majority of our endogenous viral proteins were coded by species that have been extinct for millennia."

"Perhaps that's the case. If so, you'll have invested nothing more than your time, and you'll still return with the kind of discovery that will blow the doors off the establishment. Metaphorically speaking, of course."

Brooks sighed and looked out the window. The sun peeked through the clouds, if only for a moment. The first snowflakes tapped against the glass before swirling off into oblivion. He stared into Brandt's eyes and carefully formulated his thoughts.

"What I don't get is what you intend to do with the virus. Let's say we get lucky and we find the remains you left behind seventy years ago. And luckier still, we're able to isolate its DNA, run a real-time PCR screening in the field, and isolate the vector . . . what do you expect me to do, collect it?"

"Exactly."

"To what end? So we can be exposed to it and infect ourselves? So we can isolate the genes responsible for the physical expression and create more beings like it? Man was never meant to play God, and that's exactly what you're proposing we do."

Brandt beamed.

"That's why I chose you, Jordan. You have the knowledge base to understand how it works and the ethical foundation to know where to draw the line between morality and divinity."

He leaned forward and took Brooks by the hand. The old man's fingers felt like they were composed of bones as hollow as those of a bird. He smelled vaguely of ammonia.

"I'm not going to be around forever, but I fully intend for this institution to be. This isn't about playing God. This is about accomplishing what each of us set out to accomplish. This is about knowledge and understanding. This is about answering the most fundamental question in the field of anthropology. This is about learning, specifically, what causes a species to evolve and by which mechanism it does so."

"That knowledge could destroy the world in the wrong hands."

"Which is why I believe if anyone is qualified to safeguard that information, it is you, my boy."

18

Yesterday

Inside the mountain was a karst formation reminiscent of the cave where they'd found the Buddhist grotto. Speleothems dripped from the walls like wax and the stalactites at the edge of sight high above had to be at least as tall as Brooks was. The wall through which he and Julian had crawled was honeycombed with small openings, some natural, others either carved through the flowstone or widened from existing fissures. He could only draw the conclusion that whoever interred the bodies had excavated the tombs from the inside and helped place the coffins from the top of the cliff using a series of ropes. The mystery of how the coffins were "hung" solved, he moved on to the more pressing question of why. Every bit as important was figuring out who had done so. If there were an indigenous tribe that didn't take kindly to intrusion in such a sacred place, were their lives even now in danger?

He thought of the condition of the remains. The wounds hadn't been inflicted by men. The victims looked like they'd been attacked by a tiger or similar large animal with ferocious claws, although Brooks could think of few other native species that qualified. Again, he reflected on the plaster cast and possibilities he was unprepared to consider. He realized he was going to have to tell the others about it and deal with the fallout, but he would have to do so carefully. He was going to need their help if he had any hope of finding out what was going on here.

"Look up there." Brooks pointed to where his light shined on the wall opposite the tombs. "That's how they get down here."

A series of ladders led from one steppe to another, clear up into the darkness beyond his light's reach. They were old and made from wood lashed together by faded leather and spotted with near-petrified bat guano.

Brooks tested the first with his weight, then tentatively climbed up to the first ledge, which was maybe three feet deep and artificially leveled. A golden urn filled with white sand and sticks of incense rested beneath a recess in the cavern wall, where a metallic prayer wheel imprinted with hundreds of tiny incantations and prayers was mounted. It squeaked when Brooks spun it, the sound echoing through the chamber. He turned to face the opposite wall.

"I hope you guys are getting this."

He turned his head slowly and deliberately, allowing the camera to sweep across at least fifty openings, even more than he would have guessed from the ground. If there were a body entombed inside each of them, it would take days to examine them on the off chance that one held a body like Brandt had cast. Maybe the German expedition had simply gotten lucky with the first coffin. Then again, as he'd seen with the corpse that undoubtedly belonged to one of the men traveling with Brandt, there were definitely details the old man had neglected to share with him.

Another ladder led from the first ledge to the second, maybe twenty feet from the ground. There was another prayer wheel covered with Tibetan characters and the faint residual scent of sandalwood. It was the same with the third level. On the fourth, they found themselves even with the highest excavations opposite them and nearly to the stalactites they had seen from the ground. Above them, the cavern roof narrowed to a fissure above the fifth ledge, from which an even longer ladder led upward into utter darkness. The gentle movement of air caressed his face as he looked up.

"I thought you wanted to examine more of the coffins?" Julian's voice echoed from the cavern below them.

"We'll get through them faster if we have help."

Brooks ascended to the final ledge, then climbed upward into a narrow chimney barely wide enough to accommodate his shoulders. There were actually several ladders tied together, maybe twenty feet tall.

He found the entryway sealed when he reached the top and traced his fingertips along the underside of a heavy stone. It felt like the same yellow granite as the outer cliff wall. He placed his palms against it and pressed upward. The stone didn't even budge.

He braced his feet on the rung, leaned his back against the side of the chute, and pushed, harder this time.

The stone rose just far enough to admit a sliver of light. There was no way they would be able to lift it up, even if he and Julian somehow managed to both squeeze into the top of the fissure and push together.

He gathered his strength to try again, only this time, instead of attempting to raise it, he did his best to slide it. He was rewarded with a scraping sound and a pinprick of light. Each exertion produced the grinding sound of stone rubbing against stone and even more light. Pebbles rained down on him. As soon as he'd slid it far enough, he reached though the orifice and pulled himself out onto a slope positively covered with lotus flowers. To one side was the edge of the cliff and the source of the vines that cascaded over the edge, to the other a birch- and pine-crowned peak against the backdrop of the Himalayas.

He trudged through the lotuses and stood at the precipice, trying to figure out the easiest route for the others to take to climb up here. To his right, the dense forest clung to the sheer slope by the force of will alone. To his left, he detected what could have been a trail running through the sandalwood and durian trees. Or at least an impression in the canopy that he hoped corresponded with a trail near their trunks.

"Check it out," Julian said. He crouched beside a plant with large leaves like an elephant's ears and tall stalks covered with scarlet blossoms. "*Persicaria affinis*. Himalayan fleece flower. It's almost unheard of to find one at such a low altitude. Can you believe the roots of this one plant can he ingested to cure the stomach flu or ground into a salve with more potent healing properties than Neosporin?"

"It looks like rhubarb."

"That's the beauty of it. All of these natural cures . . . just sitting there, waiting to be found. It's like a treasure hunt trying to figure out which species are responsible for treating which ailments. I'm convinced that the cures to every disease are out there somewhere, hiding in plain sight. Can you imagine what it must have been like to be the first to discover its miraculous healing properties?"

Brooks looked at Julian in a new light. That was exactly why he did what he did.

"That must have been a pretty amazing feeling."

They found the trail hidden in the jungle. Infrequent use had allowed the shrubs to close over the path, nearly sealing it in sections and rerouting them into the underbrush. They couldn't see a thing through the trees. Brooks figured as long as they followed the topography and continued to work their way downward, they'd eventually reach the valley floor, where the others waited and watched the feed from the helmet-mounted camera.

Julian interpreted Brooks's tacit approval as an invitation to point out every even remotely interesting species of plant. While he did his best to tune out the running narrative, Brooks had to admit the grad student had an almost encyclopedic knowledge base when it came to the identification and medicinal uses of plants and weeds that all looked alike to him.

"And that one there's *Urtica dioica*. The stinging nettle. Its leaves and stems are covered with tiny hairs called trichomes, which act like the stingers of so many wasps. All it takes is the slightest contact, and next thing you know — *boom* — you're being injected with histamine, acetylcholine, and formic acid. But if you dry out those same leaves, grind them to powder, and apply them directly to an open wound, they'll help stanch the flow of blood and stimulate clotting. Imagine the medical applications. I'm talking about paramedics and military field medics. Think about how many lives could be saved with something as simple — and cheap — as a vial of powder you can just sprinkle on a laceration when there's no time for sutures."

He extracted a plastic baggie from his pocket, inverted it, and collected the entire plant, roots and all, without being stung.

"Oh. And there's a cluster of Alpine bistort. *Polygonum viviparum*. You can eat its roots raw — although I recommend roasting them with some of these pink bulblets for a nuttier flavor — or boil them to make a bitter tea.

They produce a potent anti-inflammatory response every bit as effective as ibuprofen. Maybe even more so, especially when it comes to the treatment of chronic inflammatory conditions like arthritis."

Julian crouched in front of the plant and brushed aside leaves reminiscent of a dandelion's and what looked like cattails composed of pink flowers to reveal the moldering detritus from which it grew.

"Nature provides everything you need to survive in any given environment," Julian said. "You just have to know where to look for it." He turned and grinned at Brooks. "Speaking of which, check this out. Pretty freaking amazing, right?"

Brooks stared blankly at the ground for a long moment. He didn't see anything out of the ordinary. When he looked up at Julian, the younger man was smiling patiently at him as though he were the student.

"Do you see these brownish projections that almost look like little sprouts?" He pinched one and plucked it from the ground. Rather than roots, its bottom half was composed of a yellowish worm. "What you see here is actually two distinct species. *Hepialus humuli* — the ghost moth — spends the majority of the larval stage of its life cycle underground, feeding on the roots of plants like this bistort, where it inadvertently comes into contact with a fungus known as *Ophiocordyceps sinensis*. It either ingests a spore or inhales the mycelium, which allows the fungus to colonize the caterpillar's body and turn it into one big reproductive vessel. This little sprout is actually the fruiting body of the fungus. Essentially one really ugly mushroom."

"Tell me you're not supposed to eat it."

"People in Tibet and China have been eating them for their anti-aging and aphrodisiac effects for thousands of years. Only recently have we discovered that they increase the production of ATP in the body, dramatically improving stamina and physical endurance, and their cancer fighting properties are off the charts."

He popped it in his mouth and started crunching it between his teeth.

Brooks had to look away. He resumed walking and pretended the crackling sounds coming from behind him were Julian's boots on the trail.

Brooks was starting to wonder if the path were actually leading them in an entirely different direction than he'd thought when he heard a crashing sound from downhill and saw a silhouette pass through the branches of a tree. Then another. And another still. His mind automatically recalled the plaster mask in

Brandt's basement and his heart nearly stopped. He flinched when Warren burst through the foliage, his eyes wide with panic.

"Couldn't you see me flashing the mirror?"

Brooks remembered the frantic flashing from below as he examined the first body.

"Yeah, but we were hundreds of feet up and we weren't about to turn around—"

"The man in the coffin," Warren interrupted, and doubled over to catch his breath.

Adrianne emerged from the trees, followed by Zhang, whose right hand was tucked under his jacket, near where he kept his hidden weapon.

"I recognized him," Warren said. "I know who the dead man in the coffin is."

19

Excerpt from the journal of
Hermann G. Wolff

Courtesy of Johann Brandt, Private Collection
Chicago, Illinois
(Translated from original handwritten German text)

January 1939

I t took the majority of the day for König to scale the face of the cliff. Our
ears rang with the hammering of anchors while we moved the shapi's
carcass to a location far enough downwind that we were no longer pestered
by the smell or the flies. The rain had only just begun to fall when König
whooped in triumph and crawled out of sight into one of the hollows nearly invisible from every angle. By then we were sitting under an umbrella of tree
branches, resting impatiently. Metzger smoked a cigarette while I filmed Brandt
and Eberhardt tossing bits of dried meat to a once-mythical red panda.

I rushed out into the open, the rain drumming on my pith helmet, and tried to shield the lens of the camera as I raised it toward where I had last seen König. He shouted something I could not understand and dropped what looked like a bomb from the hollow. I barely had time to duck out of the way, and even then I was struck across the back by wooden shrapnel with such force that I feared I'd been impaled.

The others lifted me from the mud — as my hands were preoccupied with protecting the camera — and together we approached the mess of broken wood, amid puddles dimpled by the rain. We all stared at the body that had formerly been contained inside of it for several minutes without saying a word. We had recognized that the hollows served as primitive tombs, but we had all expected the remains to belong to monks, or maybe revered regents or government ministers. Even Brandt was surprised by the body upon which we dumbly stared as König rappelled down the cliff.

I hesitate to describe the condition of the remains in the kind of meticulous detail Brandt reserves for his anatomical surveys and sketches. Suffice it to say, the body was in the advanced stages of rot and recognizable as little more than a skeleton with a brittle layer of skin and an almost comical moustache somehow still curled by wax. It was the uniform that confounded us most, though. Not that we didn't recognize it, mind you. Its mere presence in such a place was an inexplicable juxtaposition. The man was of undeniable Anglo-Saxon descent and his uniform clearly identified him as British. The flash on his sun helmet marked him as an officer of the British Indian Army, the kind who populate our history books.

König believed the man was party to the Younghusband Expedition of 1903, which he claims was in actuality an invasion by the British that culminated in the Massacre of Chumik Shenko, where more than six hundred Tibetans were slaughtered. Brandt argued that he was surely mistaken, for why would an enemy officer be interred in such a reverential manner when the crimes of his countrymen were so reprehensible? It was a question for which we could posit no answer. The only facts to which we were privy merely served to add to our confusion. After all, not only was it impossible to refute his affiliation, it was readily apparent that his suffering had been tremendous. Although none of us gave voice to our fears, there was no denying he had been attacked with a savagery one could only ascribe to a man-eating tiger.

Despite my initial reservations, I filmed the remains, careful not to dwell on any one detail for too long, while the others argued about what to do with them.

In the end, a decision was reached to leave the body at the foot of a nearby chorten for the monks we assumed were responsible for the incense we kept seeing. Surely they were better equipped to deal with the spiritual and physical demands of the dead man than we were.

The sky opened then and released a deluge of almost biblical proportions. Were it not for our strict adherence to the tenets of our Christianity, we would have left the body for the animals, if they would even still have it, but despite our surroundings, we were not savages. We rolled the remains in a tarpaulin and sheltered them from the elements as best we could. By the time we were finished, a star-less night had descended. Despite being soaked to the bone, both Brandt and König were eager to return to the tombs in hopes of examining the contents of the other coffins. For them, this was a mystery of the highest order and one, I'm convinced, they would have risked life and limb to solve were it not for the fact that we were several kilometers from our camp and continued exposure to the elements risked the onset of fevers we would be unable to break given our primitive surroundings.

I believe we might have argued all night beneath an enclave of ficus trees, with the attenuated rain pattering the forest floor around us, had König not abruptly stiffened and silenced us. I will always remember the expression on his face when he looked past me and into the vast expanse of dark jungle at my back. His eyes grew wide and reflected an emotion I had never seen there before and one I am certain felt entirely foreign to a man who until that moment had never truly experienced fear. And that unspoken admission frightened me more than anything ever had in my life.

We stood in silence, listening to the dysrhythmic patter of the rain and the thunder grumbling through the valley for several interminable minutes, during which time we scrutinized the darkness for any sign of movement and listened for a recurrence of whatever sound had so unsettled our ordinarily unflappable expeditionist. After a time, he spoke in a whisper, although his eyes never once ceased roving the forest. There was a cave nearby, one he had discovered earlier in the day prior to encountering the carcass of the shapi. We could bed down for the night and dry ourselves by a fire, if we could manage to gather enough dry wood. The way he gripped his rifle made me wonder if he were truly concerned with our physical well-being or if we were being drawn into the hunt.

I was reminded of a story he told us prior to our arrival in Gangtok about his father, the famous huntsman. The elder König had been on safari in North

Rhodesia when he heard tell of a man-eating lion responsible for dragging villagers from their homes and missionaries from their tents. König's father hired a cadre of locals, who flocked to him when they heard how much he had offered for brave men willing to guide him into the heart of the lion's range so he could end its bloody rampage. He selected only the largest and the strongest among them, those who cared more for the promise of financial gain than for their own lives.

They traveled on foot in the most haphazard manner possible, their lack of caution and fearlessness drawing attention to them wherever they went. They hung fresh kills from the trees surrounding their campsite at night and invited death into their midst. It went on like this for weeks, until the men grew cocky in their invincibility and began to doubt the very existence of the man-eater. Not Walther König, though. Unbeknownst to his men, König spent his nights with his rifle in the trees overlooking their tents, waiting for the beast to show itself. The night it finally did, Walther watched it creep into the tents and listened to the screams of his men as it slaughtered them. The following morning, he followed the trail of carnage to the den of the lion, where he killed it while it slept.

König had then laughed himself nearly to tears when he said his father had only carried a fraction of the amount he had offered the men who led him into the hunting grounds and had never expected to pay so much as a single pfennig. The men had been convinced to serve as bait by the promise of money. As we walked through the silent forest behind König and his rifle, I could not help but wonder if he were using us in much the same way.

There was no doubt he suspected something was out there, but he uttered no words of warning. In fact, quite the opposite. Whenever he met my stare, he attempted a smile that I could tell was for my benefit alone.

The cave was smaller than I'd envisioned, but it was dry inside and situated beneath a rocky crag that sheltered our fire, which, thanks to the damp wood, produced more smoke than flame. The warmth was a godsend, though, if the moving shadows it cast were not. And finding storage space for our supplies out of the elements was an additional blessing, especially for Brandt, who obsessed about his plaster powder and the prospect of it getting wet and hardening. He claimed it was more valuable than gold and irreplaceable, and despite its weight carried it personally with his most prized possessions. I felt the same way about my reels, and yet I somehow managed not to burden the others with my incessant whining.

As I sit here now, chronicling the events of the day so as to refresh my memory when it comes time to edit these cans of film into a single coherent feature, I feel increasingly anxious. The air is electric with a sensation I cannot quite describe in my mind, let alone in words. There is no birdsong, no chirruping of insects or frogs. Only the violent sounds of the storm lashing the canopy and the raindrops assailing the shrubbery and puddles. Metzger and Eberhardt breathe softly as they sleep, while Brandt studies his anatomical drawings by the wan light, occasionally grunting to himself as though reaching some internal conclusion that launches a riffling search through the preceding pages. All the while König remains vigilant. He sits at the farthest reaches of the fire's warmth, on top of a stone formation nearly as tall as he, his knees drawn to his chest. His rifle rests in his lap as his eyes dissect the shadows, moving from left to right and back again, occasionally darting toward the origin of a sound nearly indistinguishable from the storm.

I draw no comfort from his protection, only a growing sense of unease, for I fear whatever demons plague him are contagious. I find myself dwelling upon the footprint we discovered prior to crossing the bridge into Motuo, the obsessive nature of our resident zoologist's secretive daily forays into the unknown territory, and the horrific wounds inflicted upon the British soldier. Perhaps it is merely König's paranoia that is catching, for even as I write this, I am certain I hear the subtle noises of some unseen predator moving through the jungle and feel the weight of its eyes upon me.

Whatever creature stalks us is becoming increasingly brazen and, I fear, will soon reveal itself to us in a flurry of teeth and claws.

20

Yarlung Tsangpo River Basin
Motuo County
Tibet Autonomous Region
People's Republic of China
October 16ᵗʰ

Yesterday

"His name is — *was* — Kaspar Andreessen," Warren said, pointing at the small video monitor. He'd located the point on the digital recording where Brooks had isolated the man's face and chest, captured the frame, and enhanced it to the best of the equipment's limited capability. They all stood in a half-circle around it, staring in silence at the corpse of a man whose death had surely been as terrifying as it had been painful. "I met him at the Max Plank Institute in Leipzig back in 2002. Or maybe it was 2003. It doesn't matter. He was chair of the research group on Great Ape Evolutionary Ecology and Conservation. I interviewed him for the Discovery Channel about the impact of toxic chemicals on the environment and the alarming rise in oncogenesis among native ape populations following the death of Snowflake, the albino gorilla, from skin cancer."

Adrianne asked the question they were all thinking.

"So how did he get here?"

"He was German?" Brooks said.

"If I remember correctly, he was actually Swedish. Or maybe Dutch."

"He had a Sacagawea dollar in his pocket. That's not the kind of coin you can pick up — let alone spend — just anywhere. He had to have been in America prior to coming here."

"A lot of people carry talismans," Adrianne said. "Maybe it was his lucky coin."

"It certainly doesn't look like it was very lucky from where I'm standing," Julian said.

"Even if he was dispatched from America," Warren said, "there's no telling where he was or if there's any connection to how he ended up here."

"Do you know if he was ever on staff at the Brandt Institute?"

"How should I know?"

"You've been affiliated with the institution for the longest."

"And you're the bloody director. If anyone should know, it's you. And don't you think Johann would have told you if he commissioned another expedition before ours?"

Brooks didn't reply. He was starting to think Brandt had only told him what he wanted to hear. And the truth was he probably should have known if Andreessen had ties to the institute, but, with the exception of files related to current staff and interns, all personnel files were stored off-site. Most weren't even computerized yet. When Brooks was promoted to director, he inherited a daunting organizational system defined by its disorganization. His only choice had been to blame it on his predecessors, wipe the slate clean, and implement his own system. When it came to matters prior to the start of his administration, he wouldn't even know where to begin.

"You said he specialized in great apes, right?" Adrianne said. "There definitely aren't any of those around here. The last known great ape in Tibet was *Gigantopithecus blacki*, and it's been extinct for three hundred thousand years. I did my master's thesis on radical environmental changes and their effects on both migration and extinction. *Gigantopithecus* is a classic example of extinction as a consequence of a species' failure to adapt. When a climactic event killed off the bamboo forests, it was unable to convert to a frugivorous diet."

"Technically, *Gigantopithecus* has been reclassified so that it falls into the subfamily *Ponginae*," Warren said. "It's more closely related to orangutans than gorillas."

"Regardless, there wouldn't be any professional reason for him to be here, would there?"

Brooks looked at the dead man, and for the briefest of moments saw his own face. *Gigantopithecus* had initially been classified as a hominin, more closely related to primitive man than his simian forebears. Based on the size of its molars, experts believe it stood somewhere between six and nine feet tall and moved bipedally, although that conclusion was largely speculative considering no pelvic or lower extremity bones had ever been found.

Again, he recalled the plaster cast and realized just how easy it would have been to use it to manipulate a primatologist.

"I thought that *Giganto*-whatever was just a myth," Julian said.

"You're thinking of the yeti," Warren said with a sigh.

"Yeti no myth," Zhang said. They were the first words he'd spoken since Brooks returned. "I know people who see it."

"I'm sure," Warren said.

"They say they see it attack animals. Even kill yak and mule and drag them off."

"We need to focus on what we're supposed to do with this knowledge," Brooks said. "This man's been dead for a long time. I find it hard to believe no one would come looking for him when he didn't return."

"Maybe they did and just couldn't find him," Adrianne said. "I mean, what are the odds that anyone would find those tombs all the way up there unless they knew exactly what they were looking for."

Brooks felt the weight of her stare upon him and shifted uneasily. He had to tell them everything, especially now that he had reason to question all Brandt had told him.

"You're assuming anyone knew he was here in the first place," Julian said. "For all we know, whoever sent him made him sign a non-disclosure agreement like we did. I guess when you think about it like that, who all even knows that *we're* here?"

"What about the others?" Adrianne said. "How in the world did a Nazi end up here?"

"I find the nature of their wounds more disconcerting," Warren said. "Is it possible the victims were buried in such a manner to protect the identity of the animal that killed them? To hide the evidence?"

"I can see it," Adrianne said. "If anyone found out, this place would be crawling with people trying to either capture or kill it, and we've all seen how little the natives like outsiders."

"You're missing the point," Julian said. "We're talking about different people killed in the exact same manner over the span of three-quarters of a century. How many animals live that long? I'm not the expert on population dynamics, but surely that means whatever it is has been breeding and if it's managed to stay hidden for so many years, then what are the odds that it's still out there right now? Remember what I told you about the tigers in the Sunderbans? People are just another type of meat on the freaking menu. Who's to say we aren't dealing with the same thing here?"

"Then why weren't they eaten?" Brooks said. They all stood in silence. That was the question, wasn't it? The only predator in the natural world that killed without consuming its prey was man, and it was obvious the victims had been killed by something entirely unrelated to human beings. "We need to examine the other bodies."

"I'm not going anywhere until you tell us what's really going on," Adrianne said. "And this time none of that 'you'll find out soon enough' crap. We walked straight through the middle of the jungle to the foot of a cliff filled with tombs we would never have seen if we didn't already know they were there. They're the reason we traveled halfway around the world. The bodies inside the coffins. And yet you seem as surprised as the rest of us about what's inside. So I ask you again, what aren't you telling us?"

The others stared at him expectantly.

"You're right. I knew the coffins were here. I was given detailed directions and knew what I would find inside of them. Only I wasn't prepared to find human remains."

"What else would you expect to find in a coffin?" Warren asked.

"An unclassified hominin," Adrianne said. "He expected to find intact remains preserved by some primitive burial rite. That's why we have an evolutionary anthropologist, an expert on population models, a botanist who can climb like a monkey, and a glory hound who'd do anything to get his face on TV. No offense, Dr. Murray."

"None taken."

"So how did you know, Jordan? How did you know this place would be here?"

"Brandt told me."

"How did Brandt know?"

"He was the one who found it."

"So if such a discovery really exists, then why didn't he take credit for it himself?"

"It's a long story."

"I don't know about you, but I don't have anywhere else to be."

"This would have been so much easier if I'd been able to show you."

"Show us what?" Warren asked.

"Trust me, I didn't believe him at first either. Even after seeing it with my own eyes." He paused and furrowed his brow. "Wait a minute."

He looked around until he found his backpack buried under all of the others and set about extricating it. The first raindrops pattered the ground and slapped the leaves in the upper reaches.

Zhang tilted his face to the sky and shielded his eyes from raindrops that fell like marbles.

"Big storm coming."

And just like that, the sky opened and they were seemingly immersed in water.

Brooks helped the others frantically pack the sensitive electronic equipment into padded, hard-shell cases and load them into their packs. They were all drenched by the time they shrugged them on and made a break for the cover of the trees. The rain seemed to pour unabated through the canopy, making it difficult to see. Even the largest of trees provided little shelter from the storm, forcing them to continue on their current course toward where they occasionally glimpsed sheer granite cliffs rising above the foliage. The ground grew steeper and channels of water raced past them, eroding through the slick mud.

"Over there!" Julian shouted.

Brooks looked up just long enough to see the grad student pointing through the dense forest toward a towering escarpment, then hurriedly looked back down to keep the rain out of his eyes.

They ran for everything they were worth and ducked under the shelter of an outcropping from which the rain poured like a waterfall.

"Where the hell did that come from?" Julian gasped. He stripped off his shirt and wrung it out. His skin prickled with goosebumps and he wrapped his arms around his chest to stifle a shiver.

"I tell you big storm come," Zhang said with a shrug.

"A little more than a second's warning would have been nice."

Brooks took off his own shirt and draped it over a boulder. He was just about to peel off his pants when he looked up to find the others staring at him expectantly.

"Fine. Let me change out of these wet clothes and I'll tell you everything I know. Better yet, I'll show you."

He grabbed his backpack and ducked behind a stone formation that must have fallen from the cliff eons ago and toppled backward into the recess. There was what appeared to be the mouth of a cave set into the wall behind it, one completely hidden from the forest by the massive rock. He took off his backpack and carried it into the darkness. Water dripped from somewhere ahead of him with a metronomic *plip . . . plip . . .* and he smelled a combination of mildew and something that reminded him of the time his basement flooded.

He changed into a dry pair of boxers and pants that had been spared the rain by the waterproof fabric and silently thanked the heavens for the small favor. He wrung the water from his others and was just about to head back out when he caught something from the corner of his eye. A reflection from metal, possibly. Maybe just quartz embedded in the granite wall.

He removed his mini LED Maglite from his backpack and shined it toward the rear of the cave. The flashlight fell from his hand and clattered to the ground. The beam highlighted the rocks to his left, barely illuminating the deeper reaches.

Brooks stared at the scene before him in the dim light for several moments before he finally found his voice.

"Hey." He cleared his throat and tried again. "Hey!"

"What is it?" Warren asked.

"You guys need to see this."

PART V

CONDEMNED

21

Yarlung Tsangpo River Basin
Motuo County
Tibet Autonomous Region
People's Republic of China
October 16th

Yesterday

Brooks retrieved his flashlight and shined it deeper into the cave once more. He heard the clamor of footsteps on the stone behind him.

"What is—?" Adrianne started, but silenced herself with a sharp intake of breath. "What in the name of God happened in here?"

"Is that all blood?" Julian asked.

Brooks advanced cautiously. The cave widened to either side of the narrow stone corridor that served as an entryway, making it hard to determine how large it truly was and impossible to see anything hiding directly beside the outlet. He swept the beam slowly from one side to the other, the column of light shrinking against the earthen wall and the old tarp draped over the objects stacked against it. He made a conscious effort not to focus on what had obviously been stored in here for an incredibly long time. At least not yet. Not until he made sure that nothing else was in there with them.

He thought of his ice axes inside his backpack, the serrated picks folded down and useless to him now. They were the only items in his possession that even remotely resembled weapons. If he were walking into a tiger's den as he suspected, then he had no conceivable means of defending himself. He knew he should turn around and get the hell out of there. His curiosity had always been his Achilles' heel, though, and right now it was beyond piqued.

He stopped near the end of the tunnel and listened.

"What do you—?"

Brooks shushed Warren and concentrated on hearing any sound that might betray the presence of something lurking just outside of his range of sight. The whisper of soft breathing, the wet, slathering noises of a predator licking blood from its fur, anything at all other than the *plip . . . plip . . .* of the rain slowly working its way through the fissures in the mountain, the faint buzzing of insects, and the nervous shuffling from behind him that made it increasingly difficult to hear the subtle sounds that could prove to be the difference between life and death.

There was blood everywhere, but it wasn't fresh. The cave didn't smell like an abattoir, nor did the spatters on the walls shimmer in the light. They had dried and begun to flake away in spots, lending the appearance of brick-red lichen.

He glanced back to see Adrianne's pale face right behind him. Julian and Warren shadowed her, as though in an attempt to keep as many bodies between them and whatever might be in the cave. Zhang was silhouetted in the mouth of the cave. He made no effort to enter, which, considering he not only had a weapon, but the training to use it, undoubtedly spoke volumes about their situation.

Brooks returned his attention to the cave ahead of him. He swallowed hard and willed his hands to stop shaking. He took a deep breath, blew it out slowly, then quickly stepped out into the open.

He swung the light to his left.

No movement.

To his right.

Nothing.

He expelled such a forceful sigh of relief that he could almost feel the adrenaline fleeing his system and took in his surroundings. Another step forward and something crunched beneath his feet. The occasional fly passed through his beam, casting a magnified shadow. He stood in a cavern roughly twenty feet wide, ten feet deep, and vaguely ovular in shape. The uneven ceiling was maybe eight feet high and bristled with stalactites that formed columns to either side at the periphery of his light's reach. The tips of the stalactites nearest him were at eye-level. Several had arches of blood that had dribbled into drops that clung to the tips, unable to succumb to gravity before they congealed. The walls were positively covered with the kind of high-velocity spatters that resulted from violence of significant force and brutality. They climbed the ancient burlap tarp, where the blood beaded in the sheer amount of dust. The upper half had fallen down to reveal an old leather locker, the copper corners and latch thick with greenish rust.

Brooks took another step forward and felt as much as heard something snap underfoot. He shined his beam at the ground and recoiled. There were bones everywhere. Broken pieces of them, anyway. Most were old and yellowed and largely unidentifiable chunks of calcium. Others, however, were fresher, the articular ends of the long bones knotted with tendons and carti-lage. They were broken and gnawed where whatever consumed them had attempted to gain access to the marrow. And hardened into the thin layer of congealed blood were long white hairs that reminded him of the ones Zhang had burnt over the campfire, the fur he thought must have come from the belly of a tiger. He was about to say as much when he shined his light farther to the left and highlighted a swatch of orange and black fur and the source of the buzzing sound.

"Christ!" Brooks stumbled in reverse and nearly tripped over an intact portion of a deer's ribcage. His pulse thudded in his ears. He had to force himself to breathe. "That scared the bejesus out of me."

"I told you there were tigers here," Julian said.

"'Were' being the operative word." Warren turned on his own flashlight and added his beam to Brooks's. "This one hasn't been among the living in quite some time."

Its remaining fur was coarse and attached to straps of greasy, desiccated skin scattered around the largely intact framework. The fur on its face was brown with dried blood, the softer tissue of its eyes and nose long since consumed. Flies crawled in and out of the holes where they'd been. It wore orange and white booties on its otherwise skeletal appendages. It rested in a significant pool of dried blood, but there was no sign of the viscera that had spilled out in it.

"Whatever scavenged it did a first-rate job," Julian said. "They didn't leave a single bite of meat behind."

"This doesn't look like the work of scavengers." Brooks thought about the remains of the wildebeest in Limpopo after the vultures and hyenas were finished. "It's too neat. Too thorough. I think whatever killed it did so inside of this cave and proceeded to eat right here."

"That would explain the blood all over everything," Adrianne said.

"It could have been shot by a poacher and somehow managed to drag itself back here to its den to die," Warren said.

"No . . . it was definitely killed here." Brooks shined his light on the exposed bones of the tiger's neck, from which the fur curled forward as though in an attempt to unmask the animal. "The vertebrae are visibly misaligned. And there are fracture lines right there and . . . there. Whatever killed it broke its neck and then consumed it."

"Those injuries could have been inflicted postmortem," Adrianne said.

"Look at the way the second vertebra is retrolisthesed in relation to the first and how the zygoapophyseal joints are out of alignment in the oblique plane. The fractures of the spinous processes all but confirm it. The tiger's head was wrenched backward, then its neck was twisted sharply to the side."

"What kind of animal is strong enough to attack and overcome a full-grown tiger?" Adrianne asked.

Brooks looked back at her in the darkness, but said nothing.

"You guys will never believe this," Warren said.

Brooks turned to find Warren standing on his toes so he could see into the trunk that had formerly been covered by the tarp. He lost his balance and inadvertently pulled it down from its perch. He danced out of the way before it could land on his feet. It burst open on the ground and scattered its contents amid the bones.

Both men swept their lights across artifacts that couldn't have seen the light of day in decades. There were heaps of moth-eaten clothes and leather boots with rusted buckles. Brooks nudged them aside with his foot and exposed a bent aluminum scale ruler, a collection of miniature trowels and brushes, rusted pliers, a stone pick, and cardboard squares warped by the damp. He picked one up and held it under the flashlight. Most of the ink had faded, but he could still see the outlines of eyes of various shapes, sizes, and colors. These were the primitive tools of an early anthropologist.

"Whoa," Julian said. "Would you look at this?"

He held a piece of plaster to his face, then turned it around so they could see the details on the inside. There was the ridge of a brow, the half-sphere of a closed eye, a cheekbone, and the upper conch of an ear.

"Is that what I think it is?" Adriane snatched it out of his hands and ran her fingertips along the smooth inside, tracing the contours of the face. "It's an actual plaster cast of a human face. Do you have any idea how rare this is?"

"Or how about this?" Warren held up a metal contraption made of three rulers and several long calipers attached to what looked like a dome that could be screwed down onto a man's head. "Did you ever think you'd get to see a real craniometer? A part of me almost didn't believe they were real. I mean, just look at it. Who in his right mind is going to let someone clamp this thing down on his head?" He turned it over and over in his hands then scraped at the rust with his thumbnail. "Cranium size as the measure of intelligence . . . it's astonishing how far we've come in such a short . . ."

His words trailed off and his brow furrowed. He chipped even harder at the rust.

"JGB," he said. "It's engraved right here." He looked Brooks dead in the eyes. "Johann Gerhardt Brandt. This is his trunk, isn't it?"

There was nothing Brooks could say.

"You know who the biggest proponents of using anthropometric tools like these was? The Germans. And these devices were all antiquated by the 1950s. Are you telling me that Brandt was a—"

"Nazi," Julian finished for him.

He held up a pitted pith helmet. The tan fabric had turned brown with water and blackened with mold, but the twin insignia on the sides were unmistakable. Four slanted rectangles in an almost checkerboard-like pattern forming twin lightning bolts. Or, more accurately, the stylized Sig runes of the Schutzstaffel, the paramilitary arm of Hitler's regime.

"I think it's high time you told us what we've all gotten ourselves into here, Jordan," Warren said.

Brooks nodded and carried his backpack out of the cave. He set it down at the base of the large boulder and removed a piece of paper from one of the inner pockets. It was folded and creased and crackled when he opened it.

Behind him, the rain continued to pour unimpeded from the ledge with a thunderous roar. Zhang stared through the curtain of water with his semiautomatic pistol drawn, all pretense of civility abandoned. He made no indication that he'd heard them. He just watched the outside world as though he could see something that none of the rest of them could.

Brooks sighed and offered the computer printout to Adrianne, who snatched it from his hand. She glanced at it, then right back up at him, her eyes wide.

"This wasn't how I planned for you to learn about this. I thought you'd be able to see it for yourselves. It wasn't my intention to mislead you."

Adrianne looked back down, brought the paper close to her face, then drew it farther away.

"This can't be real."

"I've examined it myself. I have no doubt about its authenticity whatsoever."

Warren grabbed the printout from Adrianne and studied the picture Brooks had printed weeks ago, one at which he'd spent countless hours staring while plotting the expedition. Julian leaned over Warren's shoulder to better see.

When Warren looked up at Brooks, there was no animosity in his eyes, no hint of the anger that had been there just seconds before. In its place was a crooked smirk.

"Well," he said. "This changes everything, doesn't it?"

22

Johann Brandt Institute for Evolutionary Anthropology
Chicago, Illinois
October 10th

Seven Days Ago

Brooks stood under the banks of halogen lights, watching the mask turn in its protective case. Less than twelve hours from now, he and his team would board a 28-hour international flight bound for Kathmandu, where they would catch a series of buses across Nepal and Sikkim to the southern border of Tibet. From there, he had no idea what to expect. Brandt had told him every detail he could remember about the original Ahnenerbe-sponsored expedition, from how they had been initially stonewalled by the British in Gangtok and forced to travel days out of their way to cross the Tibetan border from Bhutan to how they followed the Yarlung Tsangpo through perilous valleys and over ice-capped mountains, all the while trailing unwieldy trains of Sherpas and overburdened mules.

But this was a different world now.

Seventy years ago, Tibet had been a mystery to the Western world, a primitive land steeped in mysticism and superstition ruled by an almost mythological hierarchy of silk-clad regents and ministers beholden to the spiritual rule of the Dalai Lama from his majestic hilltop shrine, the Potala Palace. It was a country under constant siege by the Chinese forces of the ruthless Chiang Kaishek and the deceptive advances of the colonial British, whose dreams of creating an entire world under the imperial rule of a small gray island in the Atlantic would soon be shattered by the sound of the skies over London filling with the roar of the Luftwaffe and the screams of the bombs.

Back then there were few cars and even fewer paved roads. Bandits roamed the hills while merchants traveled the Ancient Tea Horse Road with hundreds of pounds of tea on their backs and a steady stream of monks made pilgrimages on dirt roads upon which they prostrated themselves in the mud and snow. It was an age of innocence, or perhaps merely naiveté, that was never destined to last, no matter how fervently the citizenry believed or how hard they prayed.

Now it was a pseudo-autonomous Chinese territory unable to secure even third world status for its lack of sovereignty. While neighboring Bhutan's economy boomed and American business interests blossomed in India, Tibet clung to a bygone age of spiritual enlightenment in which monks bound by tradition found themselves blinking under a steady barrage of flashes from cell phone cameras and wrenched into a world where tourists flocked to marvel at the beauty of their country, while turning a blind eye to their suffering.

Brooks wished he could have been a member of that earlier expedition, when the globe had been riddled with blank sections just waiting to be explored by daring men and women willing to risk their lives in the name of knowledge. Nearly every nook and cranny were now mapped by satellites, from the highest peaks to the deepest oceanic trenches. There were few uncharted regions and even fewer mysteries left to be solved, one of which continued to turn as the case rose from the pedestal, no longer separating him from the mask, which a part of him had almost expected to vanish like smoke.

Brandt pressed another button on the console and the rotation ceased. The blank eyes stared up at Brooks from another place and time. He glanced at Brandt, who smiled and gave him permission with a nod.

Brooks reached toward the mask and stopped inches short. He rubbed his gloved fingers together. He could feel the sweat beneath his sterile gloves, the oils from this skin that would start an unstoppable process of deterioration were they to come into contact with the miraculous specimen. He turned his head and blew out a long breath, then carefully lifted the mask from the stainless steel mount that had been machined to fit its every contour.

"Have a seat, my boy," Brandt said. "The way your hands are shaking I fear I might have a heart attack."

His voice was full of playfulness and mirth. He knew what it was like to hold such an amazing piece of work in his hands. Surely it was how Moses must have felt when he first hefted the stone tablets carved by the hand of God. It was like peering through the keyhole of a door beyond which lay the secrets of the universe.

"It was even more impressive in the flesh." Brandt winked. "Too bad we weren't able to get out of Tibet with any footage. Can you imagine the kind of stir that would have caused?"

Brandt chuckled and started to cough. He doubled over and gasped into the oxygen mask in an effort to catch his breath. It almost seemed as though his condition had deteriorated significantly in the last week alone. For not the first time, Brooks wondered if the old man would still be alive when they returned from Tibet.

"To think that this was once a living, breathing creature is almost beyond comprehension," Brooks said. "It's magnificent."

Brooks sat down at a stainless steel table, which appeared to have been recently sterilized. The mask weighed next to nothing in his hands and felt as delicate as an eggshell. It was a uniform gray in color and so detailed that it was unnerving not to be able to feel the weight of the skull underneath.

Some anthropomorphic masks had been molded with all the care of a manikin's head and painted with gaudy colors outside the normal palette of human coloration, while others, like this one, had been created with the utmost care and precision. The fact that they were originally cast in the field was staggering. The sheer level of artisanship made their best modern digital models look like a child's sketchbook by comparison. Despite the controversial nature of the science and the inhumane methods by which they were known to work, what the Nazis had done for the field of anthropology was nothing short of revolutionary. If only they'd elected to follow the path to enlightenment rather than succumbing to the purest distillation of evil mankind has ever known and perpetrating the kind of atrocities beyond even the capacity of a god of fire and brimstone to forgive.

There was another stainless steel manikin's head on the table, this one displaying features presumably generic enough to allow for any of the masks in the room to be placed upon it for closer evaluation. The thought of Brandt down here running his fingertips over the faces of men and women who'd been subsequently gassed and incinerated made him shiver, even as he seated his mask on the holder and prepared to do the same thing to an unknown hominin that couldn't have been dead for very long at the time of casting. To think that such an amazing specimen had survived into the twentieth century. Was it the last of its kind or were there more like it out there, hiding in the few remaining refuges man had yet to exploit? Or was it something different, an aberration or mutation of an existing bloodline isolated by time and geography? The possibilities were seemingly infinite. If only Brandt had been able to take a sample of its genetic material . . .

Brooks worked from the outside in, tracing the uneven edges. They'd been left ragged, not filed down and smoothed into ovular shapes like most of the other masks, lending it an additional air of legitimacy, as though someone had just curled their fingers underneath it and lifted it from the face of the creature. Its hairline was low on it forehead and formed a widow's peak barely above the ridge of its brow. It similarly grew inward along the lines of the cheekbones, nearly to the nose, framing the eyes in a manner reminiscent of a gorilla. The hairs on its head and face formed individual impressions in the plaster so detailed it almost looked like he could comb them. They were much longer than those of a great ape, more like a cross between a human and an orangutan, which was why he'd initially suspected that it might be an extant species of *Gigantopithecus*, but the remaining features were far too humanlike for there to be any doubt as to its lineage.

Its brow was sloped and formed a distinct ridge. Extrapolating the curves over the top of the frontal bone and around the temporal bones to the sides produced what he imaged to be a cranial vault similar to his own in both shape and size. The eyes could have come from any human being, although based on their dimensions, appeared to fall somewhere between Caucasian and Asian, as did the almost aquiline nose and the fleshy nostrils.

The lower half of the face, however, more closely resembled that of a gorilla. The jaws were prominent and bulged outward nearly to the tip of the nose. It was the only part of the skeletal architecture that wasn't distinctly human, as though its face had been molded while biting down on an enormous slice of orange, peel and all. The lips were nearly hidden beneath a heavy mustache; its beard covered the entirety of its cheeks and chin all the way down to the bottom of the mold.

Brooks traced the lips with his index finger, willing them to part, or to at least betray a hint of the size and shape of the teeth inside. He understood now exactly what Brandt had meant when he drew the parallels between the evolution of man and his teeth. If he were to wager a guess, he would have said the teeth hidden behind the lips were a carnivorous progression, although to what end he could only speculate. Assuming this evolutionary leap was triggered by environmental pressures, he had to wonder why a creature with the potential for higher thought would need to develop something that closer aligned it with predatory species than civilized man.

He closed his eyes and tried to picture it. The head was roughly ten inches tall. The average human was approximately seven and a half heads tall, making this individual six-foot-three if traditional human proportions were applied. Shorter and heavier with the proportions of a gorilla and significantly taller if judged by orangutan standards. Without any other dimensions to help define it, there was no way of knowing for sure and Brandt seemed curiously unwilling to commit to any details beyond those physically provided by the mask.

Brooks imagined a hominin more closely resembling a man standing knee-deep in Himalayan snow, the howling wind whipping his long hair back from his face while the snow lashed his features.

If all myths were rooted in fact, then was it possible this was the legendary yeti of Nepalese and Tibetan lore? Was the abominable snowman in fact more than a mere anthropoid ape and instead an actual evolutionary branch of the tree of mankind?

After all, if a species like *Homo floresiensis*, a hobbit-like race of miniature humans, could survive on an Indonesian island until so recently, was it so hard to believe that another branch could have arisen in one of the most remote and geographically isolated regions on the planet?

23

Yesterday

Brooks explained everything while they catalogued the remaining trunks from the German expedition. They were reluctant to let him off the hook for his deception, but they conceded the fact that they likely wouldn't have signed on had he broached the idea without offering the kind of proof he himself had required from Brandt. Nor did they believe they would have done anything differently if they were in his shoes. The discovery was simply too fantastic to apply the normal rules of logic and convention.

They asked the same questions that Brooks had: Why didn't Brandt allow all of them to inspect the mask in person? Why hadn't he claimed the credit for his discovery and why had he waited so long to send another expedition? Or had he? Warren was certain the man in the coffin was Dr. Andreessen from the Max Planck Institute. Surely finding the prominent primatologist's remains in a burial where Brooks had expected to find an unclassified hominin couldn't be coincidental. And if that were the case, then surely he hadn't traveled all this way alone. Where was the rest of his party? And were Brooks and his team even now in danger of meeting whatever fate befell them?

Fortunately for Brooks, they didn't believe he'd been deliberately trying to mislead them, only to reserve an unbelievable truth until they were in a position to be able to judge for themselves. The problem was that it was readily apparent to all that Brandt had either manipulated or outright lied to him. Little had been as Brandt had described, more than could be attributed to the fading memories of an old man. After all, he'd been able to provide perfect directions to a specific point halfway around the world in the middle of a foreign land where he'd only been once, and a lifetime ago at that. He'd been right about the broken coffin, the fragments of which had been right where he said they'd be. Was it so hard to believe he should have been able to recall commissioning another expedition prior to theirs or something as potentially traumatic as leaving one of his German colleagues behind with the supplies they must have fought tooth and nail to haul over the Himalayas?

Like Brooks had held back information with the intention of leading his team to a revelation of the highest magnitude, was it possible Brandt was doing the exact same thing to him? And if so, what were they ultimately going to find in this valley, miles away from the nearest human settlement?

If the abandoned trunks held any clues, they were unable to recognize them. There was enough ragged and tattered clothing to serve as kindling for a fire, beside which they warmed themselves and dried their drenched outerwear while they examined some of the objects they'd carried out of the cave with them.

They'd found hand-drawn maps on paper so brittle it nearly disintegrated in their hands, a needle-compass and a lodestone, and drafting tools that appeared to be crafted from the hollow bones of some species of fowl in one trunk. Another held ammunition for a rifle they couldn't find and individual animals that had been gutted and wrapped in burlap. They were nearly mummified and reminded Brooks of the earliest exhibits he had seen as a child; there was nothing remotely lifelike about the birds and small mammals shriveled inside that case. Another still contained an assortment of rocks and minerals and dented collection trays filled with pressed vegetation, some of which was already preserved in what felt like wax. There were small containers covered with dust and filled with crisp insects that would undoubtedly break apart with even a gentle shake. Other crates held various tools of more mundane use, from hammers and ice axes to rotted fruit leather and jerky. They even found a tin of Atikah brand cigarettes that appeared well preserved, if so stale they were like wooden dowels. But it was in the bottom trunks in the pile, the heaviest of them all, that they made the most interesting discovery.

They were filled with photographic equipment, from box-style still-life cameras to archaic reel-to-reel motion picture cameras. There were dipping trays and handling tongs and bottles of developer chemicals that had eaten through their containers and fused the bottoms of the trunks to the stone floor. There had to be easily fifty rolls of undeveloped film and stacks of negatives that had fused together over time. The few developed pictures were stuck together in a folder. The final case had been packed with circular cans of exposed 8mm film, more than two hundred hours' worth of footage at a guess.

Brooks carefully peeled apart the pictures. Some of the emulsification came away on the backs of the other photos, leaving behind gaps in the pictures, while the others held up lengths of film in front of the fire. There were five men in the pictures, none of whom Brooks immediately recognized. Men in khaki shirts and socks without elastic that bunched around their ankles in what looked like the wharves of Calcutta; mugging for the camera from where they sat on crates of equipment; wearing wool hats with ice in their beards; outside a tent on the windswept Tibetan plateau; candid shots by themselves and in formal attire with foreign dignitaries ensconced in silk.

After the first pass, Brooks turned them over and read the captions someone had written in delicate cursive. The words had largely faded, but he could tell by those that remained intact that they were German. Brooks had learned enough about the language to identify names, places, and dates and the more frequently used words. He recognized Brandt's name immediately; the others he had only heard in passing, if at all. He knew Augustus König had led the expedition, but he was unfamiliar with the roles handled by Kurt Eberhardt, Otto Metzger, and Hermann Wolff.

He flipped over the picture of the men seated on the crates. He recognized the word "*warten,*" which meant "to wait," and presumably the "gtok" was the last for letters of Gangtok, which made sense considering what Brandt had told him. There were five names below the caption, from left to right, although when he flipped it back over, the one face he could scarcely believe belonged to the old man he had known for the past decade didn't correspond to his name. They must have been written in an order known only to their author.

He continued to flip through them until he found the individual pictures. The first was of a bearded man with a pipe in his mouth and a rifle against his shoulder. He crouched over a red panda, holding its head up so the camera could better photograph it. This was undoubtedly their adventurer and zoologist Augustus König; however, the caption beneath him identified him only as "*Unsere Furchtlosen Anführer.*" *Our something leader.* Fearless, probably.

The only picture of Brandt showed him staring across a field of snow with ice in his beard and his frosted breath blowing back over his shoulder, lost in thought. He squinted as though in need of his trademark glasses he either hadn't brought or had yet to be prescribed. The words on the back were illegible.

Another was of a man with startlingly light eyes and a birthmark on his temple. He wore a huge grin and had his arm around the shoulders of a native, who looked more than a little uncomfortable. There were only a few legible words, none of which Brooks recognized: *Arzt, einen Weg*, and *Einheim Isch-* something.

The next featured a man wearing the pointed silk hat of a regent and a goofy expression on his face. The caption read simply "*Der Narr.*"

The final photograph was of the fifth man and showed him slurping a black noodle from a bowl of soup, his eyes alight with mischief. His skinny face was leathered from the elements and he looked several years older than the others. Brooks read the words on the back: "*Blutegel Suppe.*" Brooks knew *blut* was blood and *suppe* was self-explanatory. He looked again at the black noodle and the comical expression on the man's face.

"Leech soup," he said out loud.

Adrianne leaned over his shoulder.

"That's disgusting. I've seen enough leeches to last me a dozen lifetimes."

"All either of these films show is the view from the window of a train," Julian said, tossing the cans into the stack at his feet.

"You're lucky," Warren said. "I have an hour of a man trying to get a mule out of some mud and another of wild asses swatting flies with their tails."

"They obviously filmed everything they saw with the intention of editing it down later," Adrianne said.

"What did you get?" Julian asked.

"A pervy film of a couple of natives bathing in a lake. A cold lake by the looks of it."

"Give it here!" Julian grabbed it from her and stretched it out. "What the hell? They're dudes!"

"I never said they weren't."

Brooks laughed for what felt like the first time in forever.

"You're still not off the hook, Jordan." Adrianne shouldered him to the side and he nearly toppled from the rock they shared as a seat. "You still have a lot of making up to do."

He glanced over to find her blushing. She peeked at him from the corner of her eye and his heart rate accelerated. He was about to ask what she had in mind when Warren leapt to his feet.

"I think this is what we're looking for."

He crouched by the fire between Brooks and Adrianne and stretched the film in front of the fire so they could see.

Brooks leaned closer and saw dozens of tiny 8 mm images of what he at first mistook for an ordinary rock. It took him a moment to realize that he was looking at the same cliff he and Julian had just climbed. The image was hazy, as though it were either foggy or raining. Nothing happened for frames on end until a torpedo-shaped projectile materialized and grew increasingly larger as it streaked toward the camera.

The perspective veered wildly until the camera focused on the muddy ground. The picture drew out of focus for a moment, then zoomed in on the ground as the cameraman followed a trail of wooden pieces to where a shadowed body lay folded in the mud.

"This is it," Brooks said. "This is what Dr. Brandt told me . . . "

His words died as the camera focused on the body. It wasn't at all what he expected. The man was Caucasian and wore a military uniform of some kind. His face looked nothing like the mask.

"This . . . this can't be right."

"I think we've been sent on a wild goose chase," Warren said.

"Keep going. There has to be something more."

"I watched it to the end before I said anything, Jordan. Trust me. There's nothing else there."

"I'm telling you there has to be."

Brooks grabbed the reel and brought the film nearly to the tip of his nose. There was no doubt that not only was the man Caucasian, he'd been dead for quite some time, judging by his level of decomposition.

He unraveled the film onto the ground without the slightest concern for its preservation. Nothing made sense. Brandt had described this exact scene to him in painstaking detail, only the body had belonged to something completely different. If Brandt had lied about this, then what else had he lied about? Where had the cast of the hominin face come from?

The last of the film unspooled onto the ground and he stared at the final series of images. The man who could be seen in the background rappelling down the cliff approached the body until he could only be seen from the waist down. The camera caught a reflection from something in his hand. No...something on his hand.

Brooks dropped the film and flipped through the photographs until he found the picture of the bearded man with the pipe and the rifle. He looked at the man's right hand, which he used to hold up the head of the dead panda for the camera. Right beneath its furry jaw was a silver ring engraved with a skull and crossbones.

24

Excerpt from the journal of
Hermann G. Wolff

Courtesy of Johann Brandt, Private Collection
Chicago, Illinois
(Translated from original handwritten German text)

February 1939

Metzger is missing.
 I have no idea how long he has been gone or in which direction he went, or even if he left under his own power. Thus far our best efforts to locate him have proved ineffective and we have yet to find any sign of his passage. As the shadows now lengthen, we must consider the possibility that night will fall on Metzger alone in the wilds, and if my suspicions about the nature of his vanishing prove correct, I fear we must begin making our own preparations if we are to avoid sharing whatever cruel fate has befallen him.

I've spent every moment since discovering him missing scouring my memories for some clue I might have missed, some warning we should have heeded. Surely there is some precaution we should take ourselves before the sun sets and we are again at the mercy of the creatures that stalk this strange land.

I awakened before dawn on the floor of the cave, my knees drawn to my chest beneath my parka. Brandt had fallen asleep sitting against the cave wall, his notebook open on his lap. Eberhardt was still cocooned inside his sleeping bag. I assumed Metzger and König had already risen as I did not see their sleeping bags, but I could smell neither wood smoke nor the aroma of anything cooking. It was not until I walked outside the cave to find down feathers and tattered fabric scattered across the ground that I realized something was wrong.

The rain continued to fall, turning footprints into puddles of ill-defined shape, some of which were reddened by what I could only conclude was blood.

I saw no trace of König either, although his disappearances were not uncommon. Wherever he went, he had taken his rifle with him. I recalled my earlier thought that König was using us to bait whatever hunted us and roused Brandt and Eberhardt, who initially dismissed my concerns. Until they saw the down and the blood diluting into the rainwater.

Even then, neither was willing to subscribe to the notion that Metzger had been dragged from the cave, sleeping bag and all, and set upon by some animal while König watched. If anything, they said, the blood must have belonged to whatever foolish creature dared wander within our master hunter's range. Surely his shot had wounded the beast and sent it crashing off into the forest to die. Metzger had probably helped him track it and even now they were dressing its carcass. I reminded them that none of us had awakened to the sound of gunfire, but that detail seemed of no consequence to them. Brandt had his mind set on further examining the unusual burials, while Eberhardt had already catalogued two unknown species of rhubarb and was intent upon naming everything he found after himself, as if the world were simply clamoring for a bitter-tasting Rheum eberhardtii *or a potentially malarial* Anopheles kurtii.

They humored me in the end and together we struck off into the wilderness, following the tracks we were able to identify as König's once we were out of the brunt of the rain. He left clear impressions where he crouched or knelt behind the various clumps of trees and shrubs he used as cover. From the same vantage points, I was able to determine he was observing a path that ran parallel to our wending course. I left the others to König's path, while I traveled the one he had been watching.

The tracks I found there were faint, barely appreciable indentations smoothed away by the weight of something heavy being dragged behind whatever left them. For meters at a time I found them obstructed by detritus or washed away by the elements.

The others called for our missing colleagues, their voices echoing from the valley walls, while I grew ever more convinced that the last thing we wanted was to draw attention to ourselves. König might have ignored our shouts, but I have no doubt Metzger would have hailed us were he able.

We lost both trails on an incline where the runoff had carved an impromptu gully into the hillside, uprooting trees and snarling them into a tangled mass where the water fell into a waiting tributary of the Yarlung Tsang-po [sic]. We traversed its abrupt banks uphill in search of a narrowing we could cross and instead encountered mud so slick it might as well have been ice. Fortunately, we also found König, standing high atop a rocky crag, shielding his eyes from the heavy rain as he stared down upon the vast, unmoving forest.

He didn't seem to hear our calls, nor did he acknowledge us until we were nearly upon him, and then only with a flinch. When he faced us, I could see it in his eyes. He had seen something, the kind of sight that could no more be repressed than it could be un-seen. His entire body was smeared with mud, from the top of his head to his once-polished boots. The rain had eroded stripes through the coating on his face. He appeared not to see us at first, and when recognition finally dawned, his initial expression was quickly replaced by a disarming smile. I had seen it, though. Even in that fleeting moment, I had seen not the face of the hunter, but that of the prey.

The others denied they had seen anything amiss. Even König's theory that Metzger had risen early to take his magnetic readings in hopes of rationalizing the unusual discrepancies made a certain amount of sense. The way he said it sounded rehearsed to my ear, though, as if he had been practicing just how he would present it to the rest of us. There was no proof to give lie to his words; however, I am near-certain I saw a patch of dried blood in the conch of his ear, where neither the mud nor the rain had been able to reach it. By the time I convinced Brandt to look, it was gone.

I have no doubt that König knows more about Metzger's disappearance than he claims. There is a sense of resignation in the way he searches, unlike Eberhardt and Brandt, who shout Otto's name loud enough to startle the birds from their roosts and the wild hogs from the brush, as though he realizes that no matter how long or hard we search, we will not find him. God help me, I am beginning to believe that will be the case.

I try not to think about the fact that if I was right and something had taken him from the cave in his sleeping bag, it had stood less than a meter from where I slept, blissfully oblivious. Had it stared down upon my slumbering form before ultimately deciding that Metzger would make a better meal? Had it savored the smell of us all in its nostrils before selecting its intended victim? Was it even now watching us from the shadows of the forest, its stripes a perfect match for the saplings growing in the wan light that perforated the canopy?

I recall the footprints I first saw upon exiting the cave and how they melted in the rain as I watched. I could not distinguish König's tracks from those of the Other, not by size or by gait. And that is what most troubles me. Should not the prints of a tiger be plainly distinct from those of a man? Should not their prints be grouped together in some fashion? Surely such a large cat's stride could not be as evenly spaced as König's. I have no doubt that not all of the tracks belong to our fearless leader. I do, however, believe that whatever else was out there had walked on two feet like a man. Or at least that is what the evidence suggests.

I am unprepared to share that conclusion with the others. Not yet, anyway. Eberhardt is only now coming to grips with the fact that his friend might not return before sunset and Brandt is otherwise preoccupied, although with what is anyone's guess. His face is flush and beaded with perspiration despite the cool breeze and I do not think I have seen him eat anything all day.

It is König who worries me most, though. After spending the majority of the afternoon searching on his own, he returned with a sack full of macaques and weasels, which he meticulously skinned by the fire. He speared one of the monkeys on a spit and turned it over the flames. The pelts he tanned from the branches of the trees; the remaining carcasses he placed in a sack, although I saw him add no salt or preservatives. It was only by chance that I stumbled upon one of the weasels, bloody and stinking, staked to the ground on a post with a tin can tied to its ankle. I found another not far away, hidden among the bushes. I have not seen him set traps like these before. They are the kind meant to attract predators, although not to entice them into our midst as they had been the night before. Just close enough that König would hear the tinkle of a can rattling against a wooden post.

There is something he is not telling us, something that does not make sense to me, no matter how hard I try. I cannot fathom how he let the Other get past him last night, or if indeed that was the case. It would have had to walk within mere meters of him, a range at which he could not have missed if he tried.

There will be no rest for me this night, not if I intend to learn König's secret.

25

Yarlung Tsangpo River Basin
Motuo County
Tibet Autonomous Region
People's Republic of China
October 16th

Yesterday

B rooks was exhausted, but he knew he wouldn't be able to fall asleep, no matter how hard he tried. There were simply times when he couldn't shut off his brain, and this was undoubtedly one of them. A part of him knew they would be better served regrouping and returning to Motuo when they were better prepared. It was obvious Brandt had lied to him about everything from start to finish, but for the life of him, he couldn't figure out why or what Brandt had to gain by doing so. And that problem would only be compounded upon their return. Even if they confronted him and demanded the truth, they wouldn't be able to trust his answer. If they wanted to know what was going on, then they were going to have to find out for themselves, and Brooks could think of no better place to start than the coffins.

Someone had gone to great lengths to hide the bodies and Brandt had done the same thing to ensure they were found. The question now wasn't so much why, but what secrets did they contain and how were they supposed to unlock them.

While Brooks questioned Brandt's integrity, there was no denying the man's brilliance. This team hadn't been assembled by accident. Brandt had known exactly who he wanted and why he wanted them, and had made sure they were contracted. It would only be by utilizing their individual specialties that they would uncover the answers, and Brooks was more than ready to begin with his own.

They had only brought what they could carry on the trip. They had none of the standard lighting arrays by which to work, only their flashlights and a single 15-watt solar-powered portable work light that wasn't going to last much longer without a recharge. Brooks and Adrianne had to frequently rearrange their lights as there was so little space to work in the recess and their bodies constantly blocked the lights and cast shadows onto their subject.

A cold wind rose from the east and howled across the opening.

Adrianne helped Brooks catalogue their findings while preparing the primer-mediated standard *Taq* DNA polymerase solution they needed for PCR evaluation, the results of which would then be compared against the control samples. If there was anything even remotely out of the ordinary in the genetic assays of the dead men, they would be able to detect it.

Brooks stared down at the broken body of Augustus König. This man had spent months traversing the unexplored Tibetan wilds with Brandt, leading his team on an adventure of historical proportions. What happened to him? How did Brandt survive to continue the work that brought him international acclaim, while this man now resided in an anonymous grave where likely no one would have ever found him were it not for Brandt, who in seventy-some years never mentioned the fate of his colleague or any of the details about what happened here. He had simply returned to Germany, where he was posted at Dachau and pursued his anthropological agenda on subjects of a much different nature. Had he gone to Dachau to disappear or was it an opportunity he couldn't pass up?

Brooks could only imagine that once someone participated in the perpetration of that kind of evil, it left an indelible mark on his soul that no amount of contrition could erase. Some had undoubtedly even embraced it. Perhaps Brandt's status in the field and his accomplishments had blinded Brooks to the true nature of a man willing to do absolutely anything for the sake of knowledge. Worse still, Brooks feared they were more alike than he was willing to admit.

"Are you ready to do this?" Adrianne asked.

Brooks nodded and passed her the sample of bone he had collected from König's humerus. She expertly added it to the solution and used a micropipette to transfer it into several different receiving containers, then loaded them into a miniature centrifuge, which would spin them down and help the polymerase break apart the strands of DNA. The fragments would then be loaded into the PCR system, where a chain reaction of replication would occur.

She'd already prepared the samples they had taken from the long bone in Andreessen's arm while he was hacking into König's for comparison.

While the battery-powered centrifuge hummed, Brooks pondered what was capable of killing these men in such a manner and over such a significant length of time. No larger order of mammal had a lifespan exceeding a century, nor was there a predator capable of passing along to its offspring a predilection for slaughtering its prey without consuming it. There were too many contradictions in the nature of the beast, too many traits conflicting with the natural order. And why, if its existence was the sole reason Brandt had dispatched the expedition, had he sent two evolutionary anthropologists with such narrow specialties involving viruses?

Pebbles rained past the opening and Warren cursed from above them. He and Julian were performing a cursory examination of the other remains, cataloguing the approximate age, race, nationality, stage of decomposition, and anything else they could think of in hopes of finding at least a superficial relationship between the bodies, one they could further exploit by comparing the genomes. There was something here; they just weren't able to see it yet.

"Which templates do you want me to load?"

"Genomic, viral, and plasmid."

Adrianne placed the control samples into the slots in the Palm PCR instrument with the samples from Andreessen and König and closed the lid.

"What do you expect to find?" she asked.

"I really don't know."

"Surely you have a theory."

"I believe we were sent here to find a virus, but I have no clue whatsoever how that relates to Brandt's mask."

"Don't you think that if a virus were responsible for its evolution we'd need the original subject in order to isolate the virus fossilized in its DNA and not just a random assortment of bodies we just happened to find entombed up here?"

"That's the thing. I don't think we just *happened* to find them. Brandt knew what we'd find in these tombs when he sent us. We saw the evidence of that on the film. Wherever he found the body he cast, it wasn't here and he knew it. He wanted us to find these bodies specifically."

"If he already knew what we were going to find, why send us in the first place?"

"That's the real question, isn't it?"

She removed the samples from the Palm PCR, placed them in a holder, and used a micropipette to transfer them, one by one and drop by drop, into a single row of wells in the portable gel electrophoresis machine. She closed the lid and turned on the battery pack, which sent a current through the agar. The negative electrical charge caused the DNA of the samples and the controls to separate by size and travel through the gelatinous medium.

"That doesn't change the fact that something's out there. We all saw what it did to those deer and the tiger in the cave. Not to mention what it did to these guys. So I have to ask what we're all thinking . . . is it possible the creature Dr. Brandt used to create the mask is still alive?"

Brooks didn't know how to answer her question. It was one he had so far refrained from analyzing too closely himself. The idea itself was positively fantastic, and yet what little evidence they had pointed to that conclusion. And if that were the case, then were they in serious danger of meeting with the same fate as these men? Wouldn't the safest thing be to leave Motuo while they still could?

Logically, he knew he was jumping at shadows. Other people frequented this area. They'd seen ample evidence of that in the form of the incense and the offerings in the grotto. Surely if they could travel safely through here, then Brooks and his team could, too. The flaw with that logic was the proof to the contrary in the open coffin right in front of him.

Adrianne lifted the small sheet of gel from the machine and placed it on top of the lid. She turned on a handheld black light and Brooks killed the other lights. The sheet of gel glowed faintly purple, while several rows of horizontal lines fluoresced bright pink. Each of those lines corresponded with a discrete segment of DNA. The largest segments remained near the top of the lanes, while the smaller segments were propelled by the negative charge away from the wells and toward the positive anode.

Dozens of parallel pink lines appeared in the lanes beneath the human control template in the first lane and the samples taken from Andreessen and König beside it. The fourth lane featured a viral template, beneath which there was only a fraction of the number of DNA segments, nearly all of them so small they ended up closer to the bottom of the agar. The fifth, an undigested plasmid containing a polyoma virus-like protein, or VLP, produced a mere three bands, the heaviest of which corresponded directly to the DNA of the virus itself.

By comparing all five side-by-side, they would be able to see which segments of DNA matched in the same way a child's DNA was compared against a potential father's. Theoretically, Brooks was looking for the segments that varied from the human control sample, matched both Andreessen and König, and whether or not they correlated with any of the viral bands. He was looking for evidence of the presence of an unknown virus somehow incorporated into their very genetic codes.

The physical comparison of the lines was painstaking and tedious. All of the larger segments matched the human template, as expected, with the exception of a single band with an approximate length of 2.5 kilobase pairs, which was more than large enough to produce the physical expression of the mutation, especially if you consider it takes only three base pairs to determine eye color.

He glanced at the body and saw no overt manifestations of any anomalies, but mutations could come in any form and didn't necessarily involve an external component. For all he knew, the men could have developed tumors that rotted away during the process of decomposition.

The smaller bands were much harder to correlate, largely because most of them were fainter and packed much more closely together. Again, there was only one of the many lines where the samples of the two victims matched a viral segment not found on the standard human template. Not coincidentally, they also fell nearly in line with the polyomavirus plasmid. The difference between them couldn't have been more than fifty base pairs. While that was essentially an insignificant alteration when compared to the three billion base pairs in the human genome, it represented an enormous mutation in a viral organism comprised of a mere five thousand.

The bodies had been exposed to a mutated version of the polyomavirus all humans possessed to a varying degree, only this one contained one percent more DNA, which was responsible for the alteration of 2,500 base pairs in the two dead men, a mutation that had obviously been triggered by the exact same virus at a common site of infection. It had replicated itself into their genetic codes and spread like wildfire clear up until the moment of their deaths.

Their DNA — the fundamental building blocks of their very existence — had been changing and Lord only knows how a mutation of such magnitude might have physically expressed itself given enough time to do so.

Brooks looked up at Adrianne and saw the same comprehension dawn in her eyes.

Considering humans shared 99.9% of their DNA, that meant individuals differed by a mere three million base pairs. A variation of 2,500 base pairs was not only statistically significant, it produced a genetic variation of 0.08% from the common human genome, the same genetic difference between modern *Homo sapiens sapiens* and its closest extinct ancestor, *Homo neanderthalensis*.

"Do you know what this means?" Adrianne asked, her voice quivering with excitement.

Brooks stared at the decomposed face of the dead man, a face that looked deceptively similar to his own.

"It means these men are of a completely different species."

PART VI

Tooth and Nail

26

Yarlung Tsangpo River Basin
Motuo County
Tibet Autonomous Region
People's Republic of China
October 17ᵗʰ

Today

The rain started to fall once more. What started as a sprinkle they heard spatter on the face of the cliff when the wind gusted quickly turned into a tempestuous deluge that flung the overhanging vegetation against the mouth of the hollow and pelted them with raindrops. Brooks and Adrianne hurriedly gathered their equipment and bundled it back into their packs before the water could ruin it. They scurried back through the tunnel and into the cavern, where the wind blowing through the honeycombed stone sounded like a hundred different voices chanting without pausing for breath.

Brooks caught movement from the corner of his eye and looked up at the first ledge, where Zhang stood in the flickering glow of a handful of candles melted nearly to nubs on random outcroppings on the wall. A great gust howled through the mountain and extinguished them. He'd seen their trail boss's face in that brief moment and recognized the expression on his face.

Fear.

The expression was as universal as it was unmistakable.

Brooks set down his backpack and rummaged in the darkness until he found his flashlight and clicked it on. When he shined it up toward the ledge where Zhang had been, it illuminated nothing more than a faint haze of swirling smoke from the candles. He raised his light and opened his mouth to call for Zhang, but was cut off by a shout from behind and above him.

He whirled and saw the weak glow emanating from inside one of the passages near the top brighten steadily until Julian's face peeked out.

"There you are." His eyes were wide with excitement. "You won't believe this. No, wait. I can't describe it. You have to see it."

He ducked back into the hole, then appeared once more.

"You guys coming or what?"

A single ladder connected each level to the next. The ledges outside the rows of holes were maybe three feet wide, at the most, just wide enough to walk precariously from one hole to the next and to accommodate another ladder. With his Maglite shining sideways from the pocket of his jacket, he could barely see the rungs well enough to grab them. He ascended three different ledges, each roughly ten feet above the other. By the time he neared the fourth, he was glad he couldn't see the bottom below him in the darkness. A single misstep or broken rung and he could easily break both legs. Or worse.

The light intensified above him before Julian once again thrust his head from the hole directly above the top of the ladder. The ledge here was much narrower. Long sections had broken off, leaving no means of entering the crypts to the right, at least not from the inside.

"What's taking you so long?" He looked down and saw Brooks mere feet below him. "I could have built an elevator in the time it's taken you to get here."

"We're not all part monkey like you, Julian."

"If you really believe that, prof, you might want to think about changing professions."

He grinned and vanished back into the tunnel.

Brooks smiled as he climbed up to the thin ledge, braced himself, and grabbed for the lip of the orifice. Despite his frequent bouts with idiocy, he was starting to genuinely like Julian. There was something simultaneously endearing and maddening about him that reminded Brooks that the grad student was far brighter than he wanted people to think he was. There was an inherent advantage in being routinely underestimated.

And then there were times when Brooks wondered if he wasn't way off base with that assessment and metaphorically ascribing human traits to a pet rock.

"We can't get through if you don't move," Brooks said, his face so close to Julian's that he appeared to have a single eye.

"Oh, yeah." Julian shook his head as though to rattle his brain back into place. "Right. You got it, prof."

He wriggled backward and into the recess while Brooks slithered forward. The ground was damp from the rain blowing into the cave. Once he cleared the egress, he turned around and went back in, face-first. Adrianne was just peering over the edge from the inside, looking for the best place to get a grip to pull herself up. Since she was shorter than the rest of them, she couldn't quite find purchase without transferring her weight out over the abyss.

Brooks extended his hand and she gratefully took it, their eyes meeting in the faint light. Brooks felt a tingle in the pit of his stomach as he pulled her into the tunnel. As with Julian, their faces were only inches apart. He felt the warmth of her breath on his lips and the line he'd drawn momentarily grew blurry.

She smiled as though she could read his mind and said, "I'm getting wet."

Brooks stared at her without the slightest idea how to respond.

"The rain," she said. Her hand made a soft splashing sound when she patted the ground in front of his face. "It's getting my clothes wet."

Brooks's cheeks flushed with heat.

She winked playfully and tapped the tip of his nose with her wet finger.

He smiled and wiped it on his shoulder, then scooted backward into the recess, where Warren and Julian had squeezed as far as they could to either side to make room for them. They both looked curiously at Brooks when he sat up.

"What?" he asked.

Warren rolled his eyes theatrically and shined his light into the coffin. There was barely room for all four of them in the tiny recess. As it was, they were forced to crouch on the lid of the coffin, which wobbled and made cracking sounds under their combined weight. The back of Brooks's head grazed the low stone roof as he leaned over the body. He caught one whiff of the smell, covered his nose with his hand, and started breathing through his mouth.

The remains were skeletal, the bones dark brown from absorbing the fluids of decomposition, which adhered to the bottom of the coffin in a thick black crust. The tatters of a robe partially covered its ribcage and pelvis, the straps of fabric black and crisp. The broad cheekbones, U-shaped jaw, and low, slanted frontal bone were definitively male. The circular orbital openings, rounded ridge and prominent nasal spine, and slight mandibular protrusion suggested he was of Asian descent. There were obvious fractures of his left humerus, anterior third through eighth ribs, and ilium. His joints demonstrated average wear and just the faintest hint of inflammatory remodeling, meaning he was probably somewhere in his mid to late thirties. He wore a mala necklace with plain brown beads and a single discolored tassel.

"He was a monk," Adrianne said.

"That's what I thought at first." Warren shined his beam onto a tangle of desiccated dark hair maybe four inches long under the skull. "Until I saw all of that hair. Have you ever seen a monk who didn't shave his head?"

"Hair and nails continue to grow after death."

Warren smirked and abruptly turned his face away from the wind, which screamed through the vines and pelted them with rain. When it waned, he shined his light at the man's skeletal hand.

"That much though?"

Resting near the disarticulated fingers were long, thick nails. They were yellowish-brown, deeply ridged, and tapered to ragged points.

Brooks leaned in and picked one up. He recoiled from the stench and the repulsive sensation of the rain-dampened grunge on his fingertips. He turned the nail over and over, then aligned it with the nail on his index finger. The condition resembled *onychogryposis*, or "ram's-horn nail," which caused the nail to grow hard and thick and made it nearly impossible to cut, but it lacked the telltale curvature of its namesake. It looked more like the claw of an old world primate like a baboon, a more aggressive species known to prey upon other small mammals, like the chimpanzee from the hominin tree.

He passed it to Adrianne and shielded his eyes from another assault of raindrops. A grumble of thunder rolled down from the high country like an avalanche. Beneath it he heard what sounded like a shrill cry that blended into the screaming wind.

"And now for the *pièce de résistance*," Warren said. He leaned over the side of the coffin and shined his light underneath the mandible and onto the roof of the dead monk's mouth. At first Brooks didn't see what had his colleague so excited, so he leaned nearly all the way down, until his ear nearly touched the corpse's chest. There was no mistaking it from that angle. He should have noticed right away that the teeth projected slightly too far forward for a man of Asian origin. From the inside he could see that the tiniest bits of the roots were exposed, and between those prongs, which served to plug the teeth into the sockets, were calcifications that almost resembled bone, although human beings had no ancillary bones in their alveolar sockets.

The truth hit him with another gust of freezing rain.

He glanced at Warren, who offered his smuggest smile and held up one of his ice axes.

"Do you know how hard it was waiting for you guys?" Julian said.

"Would you care to do the honors, Jordan?" Warren said.

Brooks's hand felt weightless when he accepted the ice ax. He stared at the extended pick for several seconds while he set aside his reservations. An anthropologist was tasked with the preservation of his discoveries in the field. What he now contemplated was a violation of his core beliefs, but his curiosity was simply too great. He *had* to know if his speculations were correct. If so, what he was about to do would change the world forever.

He aligned the pick with the left maxillary bone, beside the nose and below the rim of the orbit, raised it several inches, and struck the brittle bone with a loud *crack*. The pick made a small hole, from which the bone splintered away like cracks in an eggshell. He inserted the tip through the hole again and pried the broken fragments outward until he'd exposed the entirety of the maxillary sinus.

Warren leaned closer and shined his light into the roughly trapezoidal space, which had once helped filter the air and equalize pressure changes inside the skull. Now sharp protrusions of bone jutted upward from the floor of the sinus.

"They're teeth," Julian said.

Brooks could only stare at them, his pulse thrumming in his ears.

The bases of the teeth were barely visible and the roots were still in the early stages of development. The bulk of the tooth was deep inside the bone, pressing down on the monk's permanent teeth from above, just as they had once forced out the baby teeth.

Brooks had never seen anything like it in his entire life. He had discovered remains from time to time that CT scans revealed had additional teeth trapped above the permanent teeth, but this appeared to be nearly a full set, minus the central and lateral incisors. Everything from the canines to the molars. He was witnessing spontaneous odontogenesis, the formation of teeth where no teeth should exist.

In normal children, the permanent teeth started to develop sometime between three months and two and a half years of age. They began as microscopic germ cells derived from the ectoderm of the first branchial arch and the ectomesenchyme of the neural crest, although the mechanism by which those germ cells were first stimulated to grow remained a mystery. Like any seed, the germ grew roots and an external projection, in this case composed of both inner and outer layers of enamel and *odontoblasts*, which formed the dentin. And thus, what started as a random aggregation of cells transformed into a highly specialized structure by means of a biological impetus beyond the limited understanding of science.

The virus had activated whatever mechanism caused these germ cells to grow and proliferate.

Brooks reached into the sinus in the monk's face and pinched the roots of the tooth closest to the nose, presumably the canine, and gently applied upward traction. It didn't budge. A little wiggle and more pressure produced a cracking sound. It came right out after that.

He held it up for all to see. Warren shined his light on it. It was maybe an inch and a half long with the roots, making it somewhere between a quarter- and a half-inch longer than the incisors. It reminded Brooks of the canines of a chimpanzee, only with more exaggerated inward curvature.

"How the hell did he grow that?" Julian asked.

Brooks pressed the tip of the tooth against the pad of his thumb and winced at how sharp it was.

He recalled his conversation with Brandt regarding the coevolution of hominins and their teeth and how each iteration of man served to bring humanity closer to the top of the food chain, closer to becoming the perfect predator.

"We have to check the others," Brooks said.

In his mind he saw the plaster mask and experienced the revelation toward which Brandt had been guiding him from the very beginning. The species they were here to find wasn't a historical offshoot of the human line, but an extant species only now beginning to evolve. Truly the next step in their own evolution. And if these physical mutations were the connection between all of the victims entombed here where someone hoped they would never be found, then Brandt had known König was infected by the virus and had potentially sent Andreessen to his death with full knowledge of what the primatologist would be exposed to.

Just as he had dispatched Brooks's team.

He imagined the picture of Brandt with a smile on his face at Dachau and realized just how completely he'd fooled them all.

27

Johann Brandt Institute for Evolutionary Anthropology
Chicago, Illinois
October 9ᵗʰ

Eight Days Ago

"I trust you've reviewed your itinerary and found all of the arrangements satisfactory," Brandt said.

"Everything appears to be in order." Brooks leaned back in his chair and ran his fingers through his hair. They'd been discussing every detail of the expedition in Brandt's office for nearly four hours and his head was positively spinning from trying to keep track of them all. He could hardly keep them straight in his own mind, let alone well enough to present them to his team. "There's really only one variable that concerns me."

"Which one is that?"

"The guide you hired to get us from Gangtok to Motuo. What do you know about him?"

"He comes highly recommended by an old friend of mine, a man who doesn't take such matters lightly. I trust his word implicitly."

"Surely you can appreciate my position, though. We'll be four Americans traveling in China without having filed formal travel plans with the consulate. You know the Chinese can spin anything to their advantage. We could wind up being treated like an invading army and find ourselves in the middle of a political maelstrom."

"I've been assured your guide can get you safely through Sikkim and into Tibet without causing an international incident," Brandt said with a smirk.

"You mock me, but it won't be your ass on the line if anything goes wrong. We'll be in the middle of nowhere and hundreds of miles from anything resembling help. Not to mention the fact that — thanks to the non-disclosure clause in our contracts — no one other than you will even know we're there."

"Your guide has performed his services admirably for my colleague, who has utilized him on numerous occasions to safely move liberated antiquities into India."

"Your friend's a smuggler?"

"Dear heavens, no." Brandt chuckled. "He's the director of the Modern Tibetan Studies program at Columbia."

"So where did he find this . . . what's his name, Zhang?"

"From what I understand, Mr. Zhang comes from a long line of merchants who've traveled these routes since the days of the Han Dynasty."

"Has he made the trek to Motuo before?"

"I've been assured he can get you there."

"That doesn't answer my question."

"I worry less about your ability to navigate the trail through the Himalayas than I do you meeting with unsavory elements along the way. After all, were it not for our fearless leader and master hunter, we undoubtedly would have fallen prey to bandits on more than one occasion."

"So Zhang's some sort of mercenary?"

"You make it sound so sordid. He served in the PLA long enough to learn how to circumvent their patrols and how to handle a weapon. It's not as though you'll be able to get any of your own through customs. You'd be amazed how many permits needed to be filled out to get your ice axes through."

"They're called 'ice tools' now."

"Perhaps that explains the sheer volume of paperwork."

"What kind of trouble do you expect us to get into?"

"None you can't handle, if I've made the proper arrangements."

Brooks sighed. Talking to Brandt was a maddening experience. No matter how he phrased his questions, he could never get a straight answer. So much of what the old man told him he had to accept on faith. At least, if nothing else, he trusted Brandt, and if Brandt trusted his friend's recommendation of Zhang, then that was going to have to be good enough. Whatever the guide's qualifications, at least he knew Zhang wouldn't abandon them in the middle of the Himalayas, at least not with the bulk of his fee being paid upon their safe return to Gangtok.

"What about the other members of the expedition?" Brooks asked. "I've been poring over their resumes and I have to admit I'm a little surprised by their selection, even considering how quickly we had to throw this together."

"Do go on."

"Let's start with Adrianne Grayson. While I can see where her specialty could be beneficial, her contribution could be made entirely upon our return. You don't have to be physically in the environment to predict the population dynamics of an extinct organism."

"Who says the organism is extinct?" Brandt said, and raised his eyebrow.

"You said the subject wasn't alive when you cast it."

"Relax, my boy. You mustn't take everything so seriously if you intend to live as long as I have." He smiled indulgently. "Ms. Grayson is highly skilled in the lab and has experience working with the portable PCR, which, if I understand correctly, has a pretty steep learning curve, especially for someone, shall we say . . . set in his ways?"

"I worry about the safety of an attractive female in the field."

"Attractive, you say?"

"You know what I mean."

"It says here that Ms. Grayson was raised in a military family. I find it hard to believe she could be entirely without the ability to protect herself. Besides, should you be so fortunate as to discover the theorized virus responsible for the mutations, would you not be best served to have one among you capable of establishing a formal range and pattern of population distribution? I can't see you having much success randomly collecting environmental samples and testing them for the virus. If there's a locus of exposure, you and I both know it won't be easy to find. And believe me, you could stay there for the rest of your life and still not see the entirety of Motuo."

"What about Julian Armstead? Outside of his climbing ability, I really see no benefit to his inclusion."

"Answer me this, my boy . . . how much food can you carry?"

"I don't know. Why?"

"How about while also shouldering a pack full of heavy scientific equipment? You'll be traveling light, with only what you can carry on your person. On my expedition, we led a train of more than thirty mules, and even then we were burdened by our own clothing and personal supplies. You'd be surprised how heavy even an empty pack can be when hauling it over the highest mountain range in the world. You're going to need someone capable of distinguishing the edible plants from the poisonous ones, and, from what I understand, Mr. Armstead is something of a savant when it comes to the identification of different species of flora. And remember, not all viruses are transmitted by higher order life forms. You're familiar, of course, with the transmission of the pepper mild mottle virus directly to human beings without an insect intermediary? Or perhaps the *Bunyaviridae* family of hemorrhagic viruses or the *Rhabdoviridae* family of pathogens, which can infect both plants and animals?"

"Not to mention his father's business standing and money."

"The institute is keeping a close eye on the boy because of his potential, not his father's. His proposed pharmacopeia of ancient holistic treatments could revolutionize the field of modern medicine and break the stranglehold the pharmaceutical corporations have on the entire system. And you never know . . . he could be the one who discovers the secrets of the fountain of youth. You'd better believe I'll be the first in line if he does."

Brandt laughed, but the humor didn't reach his eyes. This was a man accustomed to staring his mortality in the eye and for whom every day was a withdrawal from an ever-diminishing supply of tomorrows.

"And Dr. Murray?"

"You mean why did I choose someone with so little actual field experience?"

"The thought did cross my mind."

"What Warren lacks in experience he makes up for in knowledge. There is no one on this planet more thoroughly versed in the evolutionary minutiae of the human race. Did you see his interview last year in the documentary about the discovery of that hominin skull in the Republic of Georgia?"

"Bits and pieces."

"I thought his theory regarding consolidation of ancestral lines was remarkable. Rather than viewing each new discovery as a species in a state of completion, he proposed that each be considered a species in transition, a snapshot of a single moment in evolutionary time, if you will, thus minimizing the number of distinct branches on the hominin tree. If you consider the differences between *Homo habilis* and other contemporaries like *Homo erectus* could simply be the variations among individuals of a single, evolving line, then suddenly the entire field narrows to the study of evolving structures and features, not necessarily the leaps from one incarnation to the next."

"If I remember correctly, he compared his theory to the evolution of the automobile."

"Sometimes the simplest answer can be the right one."

"So he's my complement. I find the source of the mutation in the DNA, he identifies the corresponding traits, and from there we work backwards to isolate the genes responsible for each."

"Precisely."

"And it has nothing to do with Dr. Murray's relationship with the media and his ability to get the institute under the international spotlight?"

"I never said I completely lacked vanity, my boy. Can you think of any better sendoff for an old man than to see his life's dream realized in front of the entire world?"

"I think we're glossing over one very crucial fact."

"And what, pray tell, is that?"

"The body you found. Assuming it's even still where you say—"

"It is."

"—you left it, then it's experienced a lifetime's worth of decomposition. There'll be nothing left of it but bones by now."

"Exactly. And you can take samples of its DNA from its long bones, like any other skeletal remains."

"A lot can happen in seventy years. Floods, tornados, earthquakes. Any number of natural disasters could have destroyed the remains. That's not even factoring in the human component. We're talking about a country that's basically been at war with the Chinese since its inception. And — no offense, Dr. Brandt — you have to allow some margin of error—"

"For the fading memories of an old man?"

"I can't even remember what I wore yesterday, let alone which classes I took in high school or what my favorite cereal was in second grade."

"Tell me, Jordan. If you saw what I did — in the flesh — would you be able to forget a single detail, no matter how much time passed? Could you go a single day without thinking about it in every spare moment?"

There was nothing Brooks could say.

"I didn't think so. Now, if you wouldn't mind, this senile old man would like to finish going through the final preparations for an expedition he's funding entirely by himself—"

"I would have gone back for it," Brooks said. "You're right. I can't imagine a day would come when I forgot a single detail, but I would have gone back for it. Maybe not right away. I can't speak for what I would have done in your shoes at the time, but once the war was over and the Nazis were all gone, I would have gone back for it."

"We are two different men, you and I, from two different ages and schools of thought. Mine was a generation that earned its knowledge, while yours inherited it. For you, evolution was a demonstrable fact from the moment you opened your first biology book. For us, it was a miraculous theory beyond our wildest imaginations and one we laid bare the globe in an effort to prove. We never dreamed it would be accepted as scientific fact, especially in educated circles."

"What about the others?"

"What others?"

"The men from your expedition. Surely you didn't all feel the same way about keeping your discovery a secret. Any one of them could have gone back for the remains in the last seventy years. For all we know, the corpse is in some government warehouse with the Ark of the Covenant."

"I assure you, none of them went back."

"How can you be so sure?"

"Trust me, my boy, there's no way on this earth that any of them went back there."

"Not even to curry favor with the Nazis? Surely a discovery of that magnitude would have been worth its weight in gold to Himmler."

"None of them would have done that."

"And yet you plied your trade in a concentration camp."

"How easy it must be to judge when you have the benefit of history on your side."

"What happened to the others?"

"I don't know. Not for sure. We parted ways with König in Sikkim. Last I knew, he was intent on continuing his explorations into Mongolia, where the Communist Russians were busy slaughtering everything that moved, but I don't even know if he made it that far. A part of me fears his allegiance to the SS drew him back to the Fatherland and into the war. If that was the case, I have no doubt he went down firing.

"Eberhardt and Metzger were academics. They undoubtedly walked right back into their teaching posts upon their return. You have to understand that their specialties were in the natural sciences and not what, at the time, was considered largely theoretical. Their lives were rooted in the concrete world of the easily quantifiable. Things they could touch, taste, smell, feel. Anything that didn't fit neatly in their organized little worlds upset the balance and had no place in their lives."

"You never spoke to them after you left Motuo?"

"Perhaps as an American you have no frame of reference as to what it is like living in a country besieged by air raids and ground troops, day and night. Or even trying to find your way home from another continent when every man you passed would gladly kill you if he knew your nationality. We split up in Calcutta so as not to draw attention to ourselves. Even passing through the Suez Canal was a considerable risk with the war raging in Egypt. Four Germans would have been seen as a threat, while a single road-weary academic would seem harmless enough."

"And what about the photographer?"

"Hermann Wolff was more than a mere photographer. He was a cinematographer whose work was every bit as inspired as my own. I have no doubt he went on to much acclaim, although I never saw any of his films. The Ministry of Public Enlightenment and Propaganda undoubtedly appropriated his skills and likely got him killed in the process."

"What about the footage he filmed in Motuo? Surely he captured images of the remains."

"Of course he did, but we made a pact that none of us would bring to light the true nature of our discovery, no matter the consequences. And do you know how five men are able to keep a secret?"

"To paraphrase Ben Franklin . . . if four of them are dead?"

Brandt smiled sadly.

"It only works if they trust each other, my boy, which is exactly what I'm asking you to do. Trust me when I say that everything is going to work out exactly as planned."

28

Yesterday

Brooks scurried out of the tunnel, swung over the ledge, and scampered down the ladder so quickly he nearly toppled the whole works. He hit the next ladder and the next, aware only peripherally of the others descending more cautiously above him. His mind was racing and he seemed incapable of catching a single thought. All he knew was that he needed to see the other bodies, knowing full well what he would find, but praying he was wrong.

He threw himself into the passage leading to the recess where Augustus König was entombed and slid across the wet stone. The moment he cleared the opening he was on his hands and knees, the wind and the rain assaulting him with such force he could barely keep his eyes open. He shoved off the lid and shined his light at the face of the man Brandt had claimed must have been killed in the war, when he never even left Motuo.

König's teeth appeared normal from the front. Brooks nearly had to crawl into the coffin to manipulate the light in such a way as to see inside König's mouth. Still, the teeth appeared well seated in their sockets. He gripped one and pulled it toward him until it broke with a snap. If there was another tooth forcing its way through the bone, he couldn't see it.

Scuffling sounds behind him.

Julian crawled from the tunnel as Brooks snapped open the pick of Warren's ice ax again and swung it toward König's face. The tip tore through the desiccated skin and shattered the maxillary bone. The light shook in his hand when he shined it into the sinus, revealing tiny chips of bone, but no roots protruding from below. He swung again and struck the maxillary ridges between the teeth and the sinus. Wedged the tip into the fractured bone and pried off the cortex until he exposed a section of the spongy inner trabeculum. And the teardrop-shaped teeth only now beginning to form.

Brooks dropped the ice ax and collapsed to his haunches.

Everything Brandt had told him was a lie. König had not only never left the valley, he'd been exposed to a mutagenic virus and beaten to death before any of the genes outwardly manifested. What about the others from Brandt's party? Were they entombed here, too? Were they similarly infected? How had Brandt left here unscathed? And what did he hope to accomplish by sending Brooks and his team now?

The answer was painfully simple and probably the only grain of truth in Brandt's story. He wanted them to isolate the virus and bring it back with them.

Brooks shivered and turned to face the others.

"We should go."

"What do you mean?" Adrianne asked. "Think about the implications of everything we've seen. This is the Garden of Eden for an entirely new species."

"No," Warren said. "This is the point of divergence, and for any given species there are numerous such points, most of them false starts. Not every evolutionary step is beneficial to the species. If this one were, this mountain wouldn't be filled with their corpses, but rather with ours."

"Save it for the cameras, Dr. Murray."

"You think I'm being melodramatic? Ask yourself this: If the people entombed here were about to take the next great evolutionary leap, then who in the name of God beat them to death? It defies the established principles of natural selection."

"It's never that simple and you know it. If it were, the oceans would be filled with nothing but an ever-evolving lineage of progressively larger sharks. Every organism has to serve a specific function and have an established niche in its ecosystem."

"You're making my point. Man has no established role in his ecosystem; he bends it to his will and colonizes it like a virus."

"Which is exactly what I'm saying. Any environment is a living, breathing entity distinct from every other. Think of it as an infinitely more complex human being. What happens in the human body when it's attacked by a virus?"

"The immune system creates antibodies to combat it."

"Exactly, which is precisely what the environment does. The environment was not ready for this particular incarnation of the human virus and neutralized it as a threat to the delicate balance of the ecosystem. That's Population Dynamics 101."

"Biology always trumps the environment. Every organism either succumbs to external pressures and dies or adapts and thrives. That's Evolution 101. Nature always finds a way to persevere. The oceans *were* once filled with predators of increasing size until the competition for resources became too fierce and the requisite dieback occurred. Only those species most adept at hunting the limited prey species survived. And mankind is no different. His progression from hunter-gatherer has accelerated at an astronomical rate toward the rabid consumption of all his natural resources and the ultimate destruction of his environment."

"Guys," Julian said.

"Which is why, based on your own logic, the inevitable dieback has to occur. Like you said, nature perseveres, but in its own best interests, not in those of any particular species. The ecosystem must always remain in a state of balance. Any major shift would prove catastrophic."

"True," Brooks said, "but are we talking about the dieback of a species only beginning to evolve or one that's spread like a virus and forced the environment to develop antibodies."

"Guys!" Julian said.

All eyes turned toward him. He had his ear cocked to the outside world and his eyes closed.

"Did you hear that?"

"Hear what?" Brooks asked.

"It sounded like gunfire."

"That's just the thunder," Warren said.

"I'm not an idiot. I can tell the difference between thunder and gunshots."

"From your days on the mean streets, Mr. Trust fund?"

"Blow it out your ass, Dr. Murray."

"Where's Zhang?" Adrianne asked.

"I saw him heading topside a while back," Brooks said.

"I don't like this," Warren said. "We shouldn't be here. Can't you feel it? Something's not right."

"You mean other than your theories?" Adrianne said.

"If I'm right, we're all in serious danger."

"And if you're wrong, we'd be running away from the greatest discovery of the twenty-first century. Try to think about this rationally."

"I *am* thinking about this rationally."

"You're Christopher Columbus turning back at the edge of the map. What if he'd decided not to sail just a little bit farther?"

"Would you guys quiet down so I can hear," Julian said.

Brooks listened, but heard nothing over the howling wind and the sheeting rain. Adrianne's argument was compelling, but his gut told him Warren was right. He could feel it, too. The air was electric with potential. But if they left now, it didn't necessarily mean they would never return.

He wondered if Brandt believed the same thing when he left their leader behind, whatever the circumstances surrounding his decision.

"You guys are arguing theory when the only real question we need to ask is who killed and interred these people and are they still out there?" Brooks said. "And until we learn that answer, I'm with Warren. We should leave now and return when we're better prepared. I'm not going to be responsible for risking your lives."

"Something's wrong," Julian said. "I'm telling you. I heard shooting and now . . . nothing."

"We're not accomplishing anything sitting here. We need to get moving."

Brooks crawled back toward the tunnel and had just ducked his head inside when Adrianne spoke.

"There's something important we need to consider." He knew what she was going to say because he'd been thinking it, too. "What if we've already been exposed to the virus?"

Brooks continued crawling. There was no answer to her question that didn't potentially end in an unmarked burial in this very cliff.

When he reached the bottom of the ladder he discreetly felt his gums. There was nothing out of the ordinary. No palpable anomalies or localized points of tenderness. In fact, other than the progressive symptoms of exhaustion, he felt perfectly fine.

He crossed the narrow cavern and ascended from one ledge to the next. The others remained close behind him, barely allowing one to reach the top before mounting the ladder below them.

Brooks thought about the grotto while he climbed, about the teeth in the Buddha's hand. They weren't a mix of human and animal like he'd first thought. He knew exactly where they'd come from now. He just wasn't entirely certain of the implications. The people who traveled through here had left offerings of absurd amounts. Did they know what lay ahead of them in this valley? And if so, how long had they known? Some of the fabrics draped over the walls looked like they were hundreds of years old, nearly as old as the burials themselves. Were those the people who were responsible for hiding the remains? Were they also the ones who killed them? How far were they willing to go to make sure the secrets of this place never reached the outside world?

He hit the top ledge and climbed upward through the narrow chute. The rock that concealed the opening had been left off, allowing the rain to fall through unimpeded and the walls to run with slick mud. Traction on the wooden rungs grew increasingly worse as he neared the surface. It didn't help that the entire works shook with the others coming up behind him. He had to shield his eyes against the deluge when he finally poked his head out.

Runoff channeled through the lotus flowers, making the ground so slippery he could barely brace his elbows to haul himself out. He stood on the exposed precipice, the wind snapping his drenched clothes, and shouted for their guide.

The storm swallowed his words.

He was about to try again when lightning flared and something caught his eye. A reflection. On the ground, in the bushes to his right.

He leaned over and scrutinized it as he walked toward where he'd seen the reflected lightning. He brushed aside the leaves of the fleece flower Julian had identified earlier and saw what had caught his eye. He pinched it between his fingers and held it up so he could better see it.

"It's a Tokarev cartridge," Adrianne said. "You can tell by the steel casing and the distinct bottleneck shape. Not to mention the fact that it's significantly smaller than the nine-millimeter rounds used by nearly all other modern semiautomatic weapons. The kind you would use in a Chinese-issue Type 54 semiautomatic pistol." She shrugged. "Trust me. I know these things."

Brooks sniffed the open end and smelled the sulfurous residue of gunpowder. He passed it to Adrianne, who confirmed his suspicions with a nod.

"I knew I heard gunfire," Julian said. "How come no one ever believes—?"

"Shh!"

Adrianne silenced him and sifted through the lotus flowers until she found another casing, and another still. She faced the tree line at the top of the hill and turned slowly from one side to the other before returning to a spot where a dense thicket of birch trees was almost indistinguishable from the darkness, were it not for the way its leaves shimmered like the scales of a trout.

"He stood here and fired toward those trees."

She trudged uphill through the flowers, her arms out to her sides for balance on the slick slope. About halfway to the thicket, she crouched and collected three more steel casings, these ones more closely arranged.

Brooks caught up with her and walked at her side as they neared the trees. The rain had beaten a carpet of leaves from the canopy, concealing whatever tracks the water hadn't washed away. He wanted to shout for Zhang, but something prevented him from doing so. Maybe it was how the shadows near the ground appeared almost sentient, as though lying in wait for them. Or perhaps it was the fact that Adrianne, who mere minutes ago had refused to walk away from their findings, pulled up short and stopped altogether.

He glanced back at her and saw it in her face. She felt it, too. And if there was one thing Brooks knew, it was that no species evolved without developing a highly sophisticated set of survival instincts. Right now, his were screaming for him not to take another step.

"Do you think he abandoned us?" Warren asked in a voice barely audible over the rain.

Brooks shook his head. That's not at all what he thought. True, there was no way of knowing if Zhang was shooting as he advanced up the mountain or as he fell back toward the valley, but that didn't change the fact that Zhang had been firing toward the thicket, where he surely must have seen something more menacing than the shadows.

Brooks took a step closer and shined his light into the trees. The branches bounced up and down and swayed violently from one side to the other. The bushes surrounding their trunks positively shook.

He eased closer and closer until he was mere feet away and his light cast wildly shifting shadows into the depths of the thicket. He braced a leafy branch on his left forearm and ducked out of the worst of the storm. The trees attenuated the brunt of the wind and rain. A mat of moldering leaves covered the ground. Several steps ahead was another steel casing, this one all by itself.

He knelt and shined his light across the detritus. Zhang's footprints were distinguishable by the faint impressions and the way the leaves around the outside edges stood slightly upward in the mud.

Brooks stood once more and shined his beam ahead of him. The trees grew so closely together that he couldn't even see the shadows behind them. Zhang wouldn't have had a clear shot at much of anything more than a few feet away, if then. So what had he been shooting at?

And then it hit him.

Brooks slowly raised his light up into the canopy overhead. A branch as thick as his arm ran nearly directly above him, its papery bark torn where claws had bitten into the pulp. Fresh sap glistened in his beam near what looked like the point of impact from a bullet. The trunk was riddled with punctures and scratches from which amber oozed toward a deep crimson spatter. The rainwater had eroded clear white lines through it on its way toward the ground, where a semiautomatic pistol was partially buried beneath the mud and leaves.

29

Excerpt from the journal of
Hermann G. Wolff

Courtesy of Johann Brandt, Private Collection
Chicago, Illinois
(Translated from original handwritten German text)

February 1939

T he others slept restlessly. Eberhardt remained vigilant until his exhaustion became too great and claimed him in the mouth of the cave, where he awaited his friend's return. He had faith that since Metzger had been raised in the Bavarian Alps he had at least learned rudimentary survival skills. He said we should not prematurely concern ourselves, although the expression on his face even as he spoke the words suggested they rang hollow in his own ears.

Brandt was febrile, his skin beaded with sweat. The aspirin diminished his fever, but never entirely eased it, and he was burning through our limited supply at an alarming rate. I fear it will be gone by the time the rest of us need it, should his malady be catching.

My curiosity got the better of me while I was forced to wait out the sunset and the gloaming. As he was in no position to deny my request, I seized the opportunity to page through his notebooks. I read them with abject fascination as I covertly watched König, who again perched on his rock, surveying the night without appearing to so much as breathe.

I find Brandt's work revelatory. Never have I imagined the complexities of the anatomical arts. His theories regarding the relationship between the size of the cranium and intelligence strikes me as brilliant in its simplicity. Not to mention the categorical differences between races. There is nary a blue-eyed Tibetan among the hundreds he has studied, nor does a single man among them have blond hair. He has even gathered detailed statistics regarding how nearly every aspect of their anatomy differs from our own. The width of their noses and cheekbones, the proportional lengths of their appendages, the size and shape of their teeth, even the way they walk differs greatly from those of us of decidedly Nordic descent.

While his science is largely observational — and thus, arguably, not a science at all — I can see exactly which conclusions he intends to draw. The differences between races are much more significant than mere skin color alone. A case can and rightly should be made for separate sub-species classification, for his subjects are as alike one another as they are unlike us. If this can be proven — and I suspect it will take more detailed anatomic investigation than can be accomplished with mere calipers and eye charts — then can not a case be made that we have indeed evolved from disparate lineages? Can the same theory be applied to other races beside the Tibetans? Will it hold up to scrutiny when applied to Africans and Orientals? Or even Arabs and Jews? Are we not a single species of man, but rather many species of unrelated ancestry isolated by nature and geography, like so many dogs? And if this is indeed true, then is it possible that Himmler is in fact right and we are truly the descendants of a superior race?

My mind reels with the possibilities. Mere days ago I laughed at the notion of finding proof of the existence of an Aryan race. And now . . . I am no longer convinced of anything beyond my lack of knowledge. I feel like a newborn opening his eyes to see the world around him for the first time. I am simultaneously terrified and exhilarated. Why could I not have learned such things while I was still at university?

I replaced the notebooks in Brandt's trunk and pretended to sleep. There was even a time when I might have dozed, and yet upon opening my eyes found König only then descending from his perch as silently as a shadow. I knew he would not be able to see me beyond the dying embers of the fire and watched him gather several boxes of ammunition, rub dirt into the skin of his face and hands, and dart off into the trees with his rifle. I wasted no more time on false pretense. Had I not moved as quickly as I did, he would have been lost to me.

The night was cold; however, no rain fell, nor did the wind blow. To my own ears I made the ruckus of a yak thrashing through the forest and surprisingly did not give myself away. Neither did I prove especially adept at tracking our master hunter in the dark, though. He made no sound, at least none that I could hear, and left barely the occasional track to point me in the right direction.

The first of his traps I encountered stood untouched. The monkey staked to it had drawn an audience of flies, but little else beyond the smell of rot. I wondered at König's use of bait, for was not the definition of a predator its instinct to hunt? Would a beast as noble and ferocious as a tiger be so easily fooled?

It was these thoughts upon which I dwelled when I heard the clanking of a tin can from the distance. It was a sound that reminded me of my utter lack of a long-range weapon of any kind. My knife would serve me well in close quarters, but nowhere near well enough to slow the beating of my heart or the trembling of my hands.

I found the next stake on the ground near the severed twine and the can to which it had been tied. The animal's carcass was nowhere to be seen. Only the flies remained, drifting through the clearing with no clear scent to follow. The tracks were more distinct here, if no more defined. I could at least tell they did not belong to König, for they more closely resembled the print I had filmed earlier and that I believed our fearless leader had been tracking for several days prior to that. It struck me that perhaps it was not we who were the hunters, but rather those being hunted.

I heard another sharp clang and the snap of a stick. I moved more cautiously this time, remaining close to the trunks of the trees to hide my silhouette and scampering from one to the next to minimize my exposure. I was nearly upon the source of the sound when a hand closed over my mouth and I was dragged unceremoniously into the underbrush.

A voice whispered into my ear to hold still and remain silent. König's eyes were wild and stood apart from his face when he released me and crawled past where I lay to better view his trap. I heard the softest of crunching sounds, like those made by a man walking across kindling. As I focused on them, however, the sounds resolved and I heard them for what they truly were. They were the sounds of an animal chewing, of bones breaking between powerful jaws.

I risked a peek over the top of the bushes and König shot me a glance of warning.

The chewing abruptly ceased and I heard a sound that will haunt me until my dying days, assuming my days are not already numbered. It was a long, deep inhalation as whatever was out there tested the air for our scents. It was not a sniff, as one would expect from an animal, but an inhalation of the type one could only ascribe to a human being.

In the silence that followed, I did not move so much as a single muscle, for I knew the slightest noise would betray me. I held my breath until it grew stale in my chest, my ribs ached, and I started to swoon. I could barely see König as he seated his rifle against his shoulder and sighted the clearing through his scope. I do not know what he saw, only that what he did caused him to turn to me and utter a single word.

Run.

Which is exactly what I did. I sprinted blindly through the forest without any regard for direction, my arms in front of my face to shield them from the branches that cut my skin and sought to blind me. I listened for the sounds of pursuit behind me, but could hear nothing over the ruckus of my own creation. I could not even tell if König was at my heels. For all I knew, he had used me once more as bait to draw out our attacker and I had proved an eager accomplice. And still I could not bring myself to turn around. For all my misgivings, I had seen the expression of genuine mortification on his face, an expression I once believed to be outside of his range of emotion.

I ran until I was on the verge of collapse, my exertions burning in my chest. Every thicket was identical to the last and I could no more tell where I was than see where I was going. In retrospect, I should have used the position of the moon to guide me or, failing at that, utilized my other senses. I should have heard the monotonous buzz of the flies or smelled the carnage that had summoned them. Maybe then I would not have run headlong into that clearing and seen the condition of the remains.

Where the moonlight touched the ground the vegetation was black with blood. The bones were heaped in no discernible formation, as though merely cast aside. I could at first not identify which species of animal they had once assembled and might never have had I not seen the shape of the skull and what little the animals had left of Metzger's face.

I made no conscious decision to stop, and yet I found myself staring down at what had only a day prior been a man with whom I had shared every moment of the last four months. The buzzing stillness was unmarred by so much as the wind rustling through the trees.

It was at that precise moment that I reached the decision to leave this godforsaken land. It was not so much the death of a colleague — for such things are not unknown on expeditions like ours — as much as the manner of his death. This was not the work of animals, at least not any I have ever encountered. Even the feared tiger, for all its ferocity, was incapable of such utter destruction. Metzger had been rent limb from limb in a fashion that defied the natural order and expressed an inherent brutality beyond the capacity of mere animals, which would not have left so much meat for the scavengers.

Despite absorbing these details in a matter of heartbeats, the scene is still fresh in my mind, as though in some way a part of me is still standing there, regardless of how many days and kilometers have passed in the interim. If I survive to return to the Fatherland, I swear I will take the secrets of this vile land with me to the grave, for if what I have seen is indeed our Master Race, then I have no doubt we are all damned.

30

Yarlung Tsangpo River Basin
Motuo County
Tibet Autonomous Region
People's Republic of China
October 16th

Yesterday

"If he's still alive, he'll know where to find us," Brooks said.

"And if he's not?" Warren said.

"We can't just leave him," Adrianne said. "What if he's hurt and needs our help?"

"You were there. We didn't see a single footprint leading away from there in any direction."

"We barely searched for half an hour."

"Which was more than long enough to learn we weren't going to find anything, no matter how long we looked."

They emerged from the winding path through the forest and struck off across the wet plain. The cliff was barely visible to the right through the driving rain. They'd left nearly all of their equipment in the tombs, but at this point it didn't matter. They could come back for it. Right now, the only thing that mattered was getting as far away from this place as possible.

"Besides," Warren said, "how can we be sure he didn't stage that whole scene so he could abandon us?"

"Because he doesn't get the remaining three-quarters of his fee until we arrive safely back in Gangtok," Brooks said.

"Even what he's made so far is surely a small fortune for people up here. Maybe the Chinese are paying him even more to turn us in. Lord only knows what would happen if they leaked word they caught four Americans in a restricted area. Our own embassy wouldn't even acknowledge us."

"He wouldn't have left his pistol," Adrianne said. "You can tell how much he loves it by how well maintained it is."

She'd commandeered the weapon and cleaned off the mud to reveal the Chinese factory markings and the distinctive star of the PLA engraved in the grip. She'd expertly ejected the empty eight-round magazine and jacked the breech to show them the solitary bullet left in the chamber. If any of them objected to her taking charge of the pistol, no one said a word. Brooks had experience with firearms in general, but none with handguns of the semiautomatic variety, although firing a single shot wouldn't require an extensive amount of training.

The earth was slick with mud, the bushes and flowers beaten to the ground. The path that had been so evident earlier in the day was now invisible. Brooks trusted his sense of direction and prayed it held true. They needed to take the fastest and most direct route back to their camp if they intended to distance themselves from whatever took Zhang. The last thing they could afford was to be outflanked and cut off from their supplies. They had no chance of surviving the frigid Himalayas dressed as they were now.

The logical part of him insisted they were overreacting. So far all they had seen was a smear of blood where Zhang's trail ended and the remains of the deer and the tiger. There was more to it than that, though. He recalled the white fur Zhang had collected and how it had more closely resembled hair, how it had smelled when he incinerated it over the flames. More importantly, he remembered the expression on the trail boss' face when he did so. He'd known that something was wrong in this valley, but he'd said nothing. Was it because of the money he'd been promised or some other reason only he would ever know?

And then there were the mutated bodies in the coffins. The sharp teeth forcing their way down through the trabeculum and the claw-like nails that had fallen from the decomposed fingers.

Brooks could sort through it all later. His only objective now was to get them all clear to safety. Later they could share a laugh at how easily they'd been frightened off, but Brooks's gut was telling him they'd never get the chance if they stayed here a moment longer than they absolutely had to.

The familiar mountain reared up over the treetops ahead, its entire face running with water. The clearing in front of it had become a lake. Its surface popped with raindrops and a small stream had formed where there had been only a shallow depression before.

They sloshed through the shin-deep water toward the cave. The roar of the runoff splashing into the standing water made it impossible to hear anything else.

Brooks ducked his head and shielded his flashlight when he passed through the waterfall.

Their backpacks were in the mouth of the cave where they'd left them, although they were much wetter than he'd anticipated. He hoped the water-resistant fabric kept the clothes inside at least somewhat dry.

He grabbed Adrianne's pack and handed it to her, then tossed Warren's to him. They were remarkably light without the cases of scientific gear they were leaving behind. He was reminded of something Brandt had said: *You'd be surprised how heavy even an empty pack can be when hauling it over the highest mountain range in the world.* He should have recognized it then. It wasn't hyperbole; the only reason to carry an empty pack was if you were wearing everything that had been inside it and you'd left everything else behind.

Julian shrugged on his pack and looked at Brooks with the face of a child. His hair hung over his eyes and his beard was stringy with water. In that moment, he looked positively terrified.

"Are you all right?" Brooks asked.

Julian nodded, but couldn't maintain eye contact with him. He looked more than just scared. He looked sick.

Brooks reached out and laid his palm against the grad student's forehead.

"You're burning up."

"We don't have time for this," Warren said. "If we keep moving, we ought to be able to make the bridge by early afternoon."

Brooks had no idea what time it was. With as dark as the storm clouds made the sky, the sun could have risen hours ago for all he knew.

"What about Zhang's supplies?" Adrianne asked.

"Just take the whole pack and we'll divvy them up along the way."

"We leave them," Brooks said. "If he's still alive, he'll come looking for them and see that we've gone. He'll know where to find us."

"He's dead and you all know it!"

"What if it were you, Warren? Would you want us to leave you with absolutely no means of survival?"

"Of course, I would."

"You're full of crap, Dr. Murray," Adrianne said.

"What use would they be to me if I were dead?"

"I think maybe he's right," Julian said. "I've been climbing all my life and on every continent. One of the few benefits of having a trust fund instead of a father. And what I've seen is that no matter where you go, the birds don't just stop chirping because of a little rain. This place is too quiet. Tell me you haven't noticed the same thing. The only time the woods in Sonora weren't near deafening with squawking was when there was a cougar on the prowl. And then not even the coyotes dared to make a sound."

No one spoke, for even now they could hear nothing over the rumble of the water falling mere feet away.

"Regardless," Brooks finally said, "we leave his supplies. Even if he doesn't return to claim them, they'll only slow us down."

He didn't bother looking at Warren. This wasn't a democracy. This was survival.

"I'll go out first. You wait here until I signal you that everything's clear, then you come out fast and stay together. Got it?"

He shouldered his pack, drew a deep breath, and slowly eased just far enough through the waterfall that he could see the muddy clearing. He could barely keep his eyes open with the water spattering from his head and shoulders. There was nothing in the flooded field or the muddy flats leading up to the tree line.

His feet sank into the soft mud under the standing water as he stepped out from the waterfall and into the open. He shielded his eyes from the rain and turned in a full circle, watching for anything resembling movement, before focusing once again on the forest ahead, where deep shadows formed under the canopy.

He reached back through the waterfall and gestured for the others to follow him. He'd barely begun to slog through the mire when he heard a loud splash behind him and whirled in time to catch Adrianne's hand before she fell into the water. He pulled her toward him as Julian jumped through the waterfall and nearly bowled both of them over.

Warren's silhouette appeared on the other side through the curtain of water. He stood mere feet away, his shape distorted by the flowing water, then retreated and merged into the darkness.

"Hurry up!" Brooks said.

"He's probably rummaging through Zhang's pack," Adrianne said.

"Damn it, Warren!"

There was movement on the other side, at the very edge of sight and low to the ground.

"What the hell?" Julian said. "The water suddenly got warm."

Brooks looked down at the murky water around Julian's legs. Tendrils of a darker fluid spread out from where the water splashed down into the lake. He shined his light into the water and watched the thicker fluid diffuse around their ankles before being whisked away by the current.

"Go," Brooks whispered. "Now!"

He looked back up at the thin layer of flowing water that separated him from the cave, this time certain he could see frenetic movement near the mouth of the cave. How could anything have gotten past them while they were standing right there? Unless . . .

"It was already in there!" Brooks shouted into Adrianne's face. He jerked on her arm and sprinted in the opposite direction, water churning up in front of his knees.

Behind him, he heard a roaring sound he was certain originated from something other than the runoff thundering down the face of the cliff.

PART VII

DELUGE

31

Yarlung Tsangpo River Basin
Motuo County
Tibet Autonomous Region
People's Republic of China
October 17th

Today

West.

All Brooks could think was that they needed to go west.

Somewhere ahead of them was their initial campsite and the path that would lead them through the forest and to the bridge over the Yarlung Tsangpo River. From there, the real trek began.

If they made it that far.

Crashing in the underbrush behind them. Or maybe uphill. The acoustics made it impossible to divine their location. Not that it mattered from which direction death came. His lungs burned and his legs ached and he felt as though he were dragging Adrianne behind him. He knew full well that when she went down, she was taking him with her. And through it all the sounds of their pursuit grew ever closer. It was only a matter of time before the gap closed completely.

The ruckus of snapping branches melded with the rumble of water tearing down the hillside. He could no longer hear the sounds of their hunters and, worse, realized they were being chased toward a natural barrier they might not be able to cross. Even slowing down to try could prove their undoing.

He couldn't help but think about how Warren had been overcome before he could even cry out in alarm and slain without making a sound. It could have been any one of them. If whatever killed Warren was the same thing that got Zhang, then how had it managed to beat them back to the cave, unless it had known exactly where to go and had been on its way before they even followed the spent casings into the forest? That implied a level of intelligence Brooks refused to consider, for to even acknowledge the potential was to admit that there was no hope of them leaving Motuo alive.

A tree stripped of leaves cartwheeled ahead of them through the forest. A great wave of brown water rose up in the distance and a chunk of the trail simply vanished. The shrubs growing from it toppled into the runoff.

He glanced uphill. Floodwaters thundered down from the high country, eroding the gully before his very eyes. Debris tumbled end over end with such speed that trees were pummeled and broken in half with resounding cracking sounds and showers of splinters.

They weren't going to make it.

He looked back. Past Adrianne and Julian, whose fatigue showed on their faces, and toward the forest behind them. A dark shape eclipsed the path and bounded up into the trees uphill, maybe thirty feet back and heading for a crest of rock that rose above the point where the path intersected the impromptu river. He caught even more movement through the trees downhill as he turned back.

"How well can you swim?" he shouted.

"What?" Adrianne said.

"How well can you swim?"

"You're out of your mind!"

"If you have a better idea, now's the time!"

"We'll drown!" Julian yelled.

"All we have to do is survive the runoff."

"That's all?"

"The river will be running high and fast when we reach it. Keep your legs in front of you and brace for impact!"

"The debris is moving at thirty miles an hour. Any of those trunks would hit us like a truck!"

"Then don't get hit!"

Brooks peeked uphill to his right in time to see a silhouette dart behind the rock formation that channeled the water down through the uprooted forest.

Stumps with serpentine roots bounded down the hillside, thrown before the rapids. Entire shrubs caught on trunks that could only stand against the assault for so much longer.

To his left, the violent water flowed down the eroding gully toward a stone precipice from which it fired out over the distant treetops below. Another silhouette flashed from behind the trunk of one fig tree and vanished behind another.

The roar was deafening. The water was running so high and fast it would sweep them under and propel them a quarter mile downhill before they were able to catch their first breath while plummeting down into the mist.

It was at least a dozen feet wide, far wider than any of them could jump. A broken trunk screamed past, crashed downstream, and flipped out over the valley below. The sound of its impact, when it finally came, was like a head-on collision.

This was suicide.

Movement to his left. A white blur streaking through the forest, ascending the slope as it went. He caught a glimpse of long fur as it drew parallel with them.

To his right, a hunched silhouette rose from the top of the rocks, crouched as though about to pounce.

They were out of options. If they so much as slowed in an attempt to turn around, their pursuit would close from either side. Whatever they were, their movements were coordinated. It was a pack-hunting mentality reserved almost exclusively for higher order predators. One of them must have gone after Zhang, while the other lay in wait for them in the cave. As though they had done that very thing before.

Ten feet and closing fast.

A section of the path crumbled into the water before his very eyes.

"It's right behind me!" Julian shouted.

Brooks couldn't bring himself to look back. His heart raced and his eyes tried to keep up with the debris speeding past.

Five feet.

He looked uphill and prayed not to be impaled by a tree trunk.

Two feet.

A dark shape leapt from the top of the cliff in his peripheral vision as he focused on the stream.

The ground gave way under his left foot before he could launch himself away from the bank. He saw brown water churning with vegetation and then he was immersed.

His mouth filled with water even as he tried to close it. The shock of the sudden cold paralyzed him. Adrianne's hand wrenched from his grasp. He struck the ground and his head filled with sparks. His feet flipped up over his head. Something grabbed his side. Tore through his shirt, the skin beneath. It was gone by the time he grabbed for it. He opened his eyes and saw only darkness. Something struck his shoulder. His back. He could no longer tell which way was up. His lungs rejected the fluid he'd inhaled, forcing him to open his mouth to cough.

He inhaled the slightest amount of air with the water. For the most fleeting of moments he saw treetops and storm clouds. And then he was weightless.

Falling.

He saw the waiting river from which boulders stood like massive breakers, surrounded by the broken remains of shattered trunks boiling in the flume. Then the mist, and a body plummeting through it. Arms and legs limp.

He struck the river with such force that he was certain he'd hit one of the boulders. The air, what little there was, exploded from his chest. He couldn't even draw a mouthful of the vile water. The current dragged him under and bounced him along the bottom, repeatedly smacking his head against all manner of rocks and debris.

In desperation he reached for what he thought was the surface and drove his hand down into the ground. His vision darkened as the pressure in his chest increased exponentially. When the seal broke, he was going to inhale his death.

He flipped over and felt his heels strike the bottom. Used the momentary traction to propel himself upward toward water that grew incrementally brighter as he reached through tangles of roots and branches.

He breached the surface with a gasp and a wave slammed right down on his face. He grabbed for anything he could reach and found himself once more submerged when the shrub he attempted to climb rolled over. Again, he fought to the surface and caught just enough air to survive the impact with a boulder, which sent him careening off to the side. He felt his eyes roll upward and realized in a moment of sheer panic that if he went under again he wouldn't be coming back up.

His right hand caught a snarl of branches. Before he could pull, his arm was nearly yanked from the socket. He faced upstream, the water battering his face, but he was no longer at its mercy. The branches bowed over the rocky bank. The trunk to which they were attached split right down the center with a loud snap.

He grabbed on with his left hand and pulled himself toward the shore, all the while watching the trunk come apart and the roots rise from the crumbling ground.

The moment his torso was out of the water, he gasped for air and ended up vomiting the horrible water onto the mud. He curled his fingers into the soft earth and dragged himself all the way out, where he lay on his side, staring through the overgrowth of shrubs into the dense forest.

He remembered the others with a start and struggled to his hands and knees.

The river raced past at a staggering speed, dragging with it whole trees and debris moving so fast he couldn't identify it. He managed to get his feet under him and grabbed his side. His own warmth sluiced through his fingers and down his ribs.

Nothing looked familiar and yet everything looked exactly the same. Several streams cascaded down the escarpment across the river from him, although none of them was nearly as large as the one that had carried him here, which could easily be miles away by now. As were whatever he had seen moving through the trees, those white blurs, but they wouldn't remain that way for long.

A flash of blue from ahead of him.

Adrianne's backpack.

He sprinted headlong through the bushes lining the bank, barely keeping his eyes open as the branches slashed at his face. He burst from the trees and nearly leapt right back into the river. The bank had collapsed and in its stead was a collection of branches and trunks where the river bent. He leapt for the sturdiest looking section and grabbed for Adrianne's backpack as it rushed past. His right hand caught a strap and he pulled for everything he was worth. His legs fell through the dam, but he maintained his leverage and dragged her up beside him.

Her face was pale, her eyelids and lips blue. Her head lolled forward and water dribbled from her mouth.

"No, no, no."

He pulled her toward the bank and started giving compressions. Her body bucked with his exertions, but didn't respond. More and more water gushed from her mouth.

Shouting.

He looked up to see Julian on the other side, maybe a hundred feet upstream, staggering through the underbrush.

Again with the compressions, hard and fast. He felt her sternum sink deeply into her breast, forcing spurts of water from her mouth. His fingers were too cold to feel for a pulse, even if he could afford to spare them.

She retched and gagged. Turned her head and vomited all over him.

He pulled her to him and smeared her wet hair from her face. Kissed her forehead over and over.

She curled her fingers into the shirt on his back and started to cry.

32

Johann Brandt Institute for Evolutionary Anthropology
Chicago, Illinois
October 8ᵗʰ

Nine Days Ago

"You can ask me anything you want, but I can only tell you what I remember," Brandt said. "And even then I often wonder how much is actual memory and how much is the product of an overactive imagination. Maybe the two aren't mutually exclusive. When you're young, you're convinced you will recall every event with complete clarity, only to find that it isn't so much the database that corrodes as it is the hardware you use to retrieve it becoming increasingly antiquated. In my case, I often feel as though my memories are indexed in a card catalogue sorted by a blind librarian."

Brooks strolled down the main aisle, for the first time truly seeing the pictures on the walls and the faces of the men and woman for whom death had come shortly thereafter and served as the low-water mark in the history of a species that had only begun to fathom the depths of its capacity for evil. Until now, whether consciously or not, he had chosen not to look at them, as though to acknowledge them in his own mind would taint the majesty of the central display, but to look away from the suffering was every bit as monstrous as the initial infliction of cruelty. These were people whose lives had been inexorably altered and whose lips, if they could move, would tell tales too horrible to hear. And yet they were a part of the journey he prepared to take, and from their ashes a field of study to which he'd devoted much of his life had risen.

There were few actual photographs from those early years, unlike the preponderance from the latter half of the century, when cameras became affordable enough that everyone could own one and the development of negatives became an automated industry, stripping the artistry from the craft. Those early pictures, though, they weren't haphazardly snapped with the mindset of deleting those that didn't make the cut; they were composed, still-lifes captured by an artist on a photographic tapestry. Brooks almost felt as though he could see into the subjects themselves, rather than merely observing them from afar.

He stood before a picture of five men in suits and ties and leaned across the glass display case filled with masks cast from faces of obvious Tibetan or Nepalese origin to better see it. The men posed in a line beside a very formal British officer wearing a helmet with a cock's comb crest and several shorter dignitaries in silk robes and strange hats that reminded him of an ostrich's rump.

"That was our second night in Gangtok, if memory serves, and our first formal meeting with the political officer from the British Mission and the local regent. Thapa was his name, although I recall none of the names of those in his entourage."

Brooks didn't immediately recognize Brandt, who seemed to have not grown into himself yet. He stood off to the side as though called into the picture as an afterthought. Not like the others, who did their very best to look more important than the dignitaries receiving them. He'd come to recognize König by his rugged features and physique and Eberhardt by his scarecrow-frame. Metzger was shorter and stockier and his eyebrows were so thick and dark they drew the eye away from his bulbous nose. Wolff had eyes so blue they appeared almost white, a birthmark near his hairline, and a cocky air about him, as though he kept a secret to which none of the others were privy. Brooks chalked it up to the arrogance of an artist who fancied himself to be on a different level than his peers, in much the same way an academic could often appear arrogant when surrounded by company he considered inferior.

"We thought all we would have to do is smile and hand out gifts and we would be on the road to Lhasa in no time. To think there was a time when the British held the keys to all kingdoms. It's a wonder we aren't still there trying to hack through their myriad layers of bureaucracy. I suppose the end of the empire was one of the few redeeming outcomes of the war."

The picture beside it featured the same men in their uniforms with hobnail boots and bouffant trousers, as though they were about to goosestep right down the dirt road crowded with much shorter peasants. Brandt grinned around the pipe clenched between his teeth. Beside him, the others posed in ways meant to appear very serious; however, the overall impression was one of boys attempting to put on airs before the picture was taken. Eberhardt and Metzger stood close, as they always did, while König appeared both with the group and apart from it, a faraway look in his eyes. Wolff stood tall and proud, his chin held high.

Brooks was about to move on to the next picture when something caught his eye. He scoured the photograph until he saw what had drawn his attention. A piece of metal poked from the breast pocket of Wolff's jacket, its head shaped like a T-square with pincers. They were calipers, the kind early anthropologists used. Why the expedition's photographer had them was a matter of speculation, though.

The next picture was of the five men on the windswept Tibetan plateau in heavy winter garb. Behind them, strings of prayer flags flew from a cairn of rocks stacked so tall it was a miracle they didn't fall. König wore a game bag from which the feathered tails of birds protruded. His rifle was the only clean thing about him. Eberhardt wore a fur-rimmed hat pulled so low over his forehead that only his nose and chin were visible. Metzger was hunched against the frigid breeze, one eye closed. Brandt wore a wool hat with an enormous pack on his back from which three bound poles projected. Wolff towered over him, against his chest a large brown sack that sagged over his arms like grain or cement powder.

Those were the only pictures commemorating the König Expedition into Tibet. The remainder of the photographs featured Brandt, no longer accompanied by men accustomed to laughter and adventure. They were either uniformed men subordinate to him or emaciated prisoners being subjected to the tools of his trade.

Brooks had always known that this part of the story would have to be addressed. Brandt had marched off into the Himalayas as a wide-eyed scientist and returned a man obsessed, one who devoted himself not only to the Nazi party, but to its beliefs. The expression on his face was more than that of a man taking advantage of the times to further his research as he claimed, it was the expression of a true convert. It was his eyes that gave him away. Whatever Brandt said in an attempt to diminish his role in the atrocities or to justify his actions as the inescapable realities of a country held captive by the prejudices of its chancellor, his eyes gave lie to his words. The more Brooks thought about them, the more he firmly believed that whatever happened to Brandt's party in Tibet, he'd returned a changed man driven by forces outside of his understanding or control.

Brooks forced himself to look at the gaunt faces of people who'd been wrenched from their lives, treated like cattle, abused as slaves, and then subjected to horrors beyond his imagination when he spoke.

"How anyone can deny the Holocaust happened with proof like this is beyond me."

"It's not so much about denial as repression. In the aftermath of the war, mine became a country ashamed of itself, not for its actions, but for the actions it allowed to be taken in its name."

"How were you not arrested and tried?"

"Be careful reading history backwards, my boy. In retrospect, mine were crimes of opportunity. At the time, they were not crimes at all. Would you prosecute the scientists who inject mice with carcinogens or kill rabbits with cosmetics?"

"It's not the same thing."

"Oh, but it is. In the proper context."

"There is no context capable of justifying mass murder."

"Like I said, I've taken full responsibility for the decisions I made at the time, even knowing I was taking advantage of a bad situation."

Brooks stared at the photographs of a much younger Brandt. His bearing was erect and his chin held high in such a way that he appeared to be looking down his nose at those around him, almost like Wolff had in the previous pictures. His cap sat high and proud on his head. No matter how Brooks looked at them, he couldn't see Brandt as a victim.

"Why did you do it?"

Brooks couldn't bring himself to look at Brandt, who rolled down the aisle behind him. The electric hum of the chair abruptly ceased and the room became preternaturally quiet, save for the buzz of the overhead lights.

Brandt said nothing for the longest time, while Brooks stared at the photograph of a much younger version of the man outside of a building into which railroad tracks converged from seemingly every direction at once.

"The world was a different place back then. The political climate—"

"Enough!" Brooks shouted, his voice echoing through the sublevel.

He turned to Brandt in the ensuing silence and stared at the diminished man, curled in upon himself in his wheelchair, the aura of death hanging over him.

"Stop trying to tell me what you think I want to hear. Tell me the truth, no matter how ugly it is. There's something I'm missing. Something I need to understand. What happened on your expedition that caused you to return home to do . . . " — he made a sweeping gesture toward the faces of the starving Jews — " . . . this? You're asking me to lead an expedition into the very same place and for every answer you give me, I'm faced with a dozen more questions. There are too many inconsistencies in your story. Too many holes I can't seem to fill."

"What would you like to hear? That I became so focused on my research that I didn't care about anything or anyone else?"

"That's a start."

"Or how I was dispatched on an expedition to find ancestors that sounded like they were ripped from a fairy tale, and not a very good one at that? I found the whole notion of the Aryan race patently ridiculous. How anyone could speak of it aloud with a straight face was beyond me. We were looking for the mythical survivors of a fictional land in order to prove we were superior to the rest of the world, all of whom looked exactly like us. We might as well have been hunting leprechauns for all we expected to find. We climbed into those mountains already trying to figure out how we would break the truth to Herr Himmler that his *master race* didn't exist in such a way that didn't get us all expelled from the party. Or worse. But do you know what happened next?

The last thing any of us expected. We found exactly what we were looking for."

Brandt looked past him toward the end of the room. Brooks followed his stare to the case containing the rotating mask.

"I entered Tibet a skeptic and returned a believer. And until you've experienced it for yourself, you have no idea the power of belief. It's strong enough to override any compunctions. There is no greater ally to have on your side, no more formidable weapon. Maybe I didn't fully subscribe to the Nazi propaganda. I'd be surprised if anyone did. I was raised to question everything and only believe what I could see with my own eyes. And I had seen the master race. I had seen not our mythical roots, but our very real future. I knew not how such mutations worked, for genetics was a field in its infancy. I knew heredity and that any aberration was a product of its breeding, so I set about learning everything I could about our species and its potential. I did things I will take with me to my grave and for which I know I will eventually be brought into account, and all because I believed as fervently then as I believe now. Humanity stands at an evolutionary crossroads. With the knowledge we've accumulated over the last seventy years and the technology at our disposal, we are finally in a position to take control of the destiny of our very species."

"Maybe there are some things we were never meant to control."

"You're saying you wouldn't open Pandora's box?"

Brooks stared at the face slowly turning in its Plexiglas housing and wondered what price he placed on his own soul.

33

Yarlung Tsangpo River Basin
Motuo County
Tibet Autonomous Region
People's Republic of China
October 17th

Today

Brooks could only guess as to where they were and the river had risen so high that whatever game trails might once have existed on its banks were now several feet underwater. Picking their way through the shrubs and overgrowth was a maddening proposition, especially knowing there was only one way into and out of this valley and surely whatever stalked them knew as much, too. To make matters worse, right now they were heading in the wrong direction.

Julian was still on the other side. Swimming across the river wasn't a realistic option any more than walking back into the teeth of their pursuit was. Their only choice was to continue deeper into the valley and hope to find a place narrow enough to either ford or toss a line across. If Julian could get them his rope, they could pull him through the water and to the opposite shore.

The rain still fell, although nowhere near as hard. They were spared the majority of it beneath the canopy; however, the sound of even the diminished downpour on the leaves made it impossible to hear anything approaching. The humidity wouldn't allow their clothes to dry, either. It was reasonably warm and yet their teeth chattered and the fine hairs on their bodies stood on end. They were going to be in serious trouble when the sun went down if the rain didn't cease. They couldn't afford to change into dry clothes only to get them wet, too. They were damned one way or the other and their only hope for survival lay in getting out of this infernal valley and across the highest mountain range on the face of the earth.

Brooks tried not to think about what happened to Warren. It seemed positively unreal. One moment they were arguing over what to do with Zhang's supplies and the next his blood was diffusing into the water around them. And whatever killed him had stood mere feet away on the other side of the waterfall, close enough that he could have reached through and touched it. He remembered how human-like its silhouette had been with a shiver.

Adrianne clung to his hand as though for dear life. He found the physical contact reassuring and drew strength from the gesture as they scoured the flooded forest for anything resembling a stricture narrow enough to cross.

Julian had an even harder time on the far side, where the sheer escarpment often bordered the river, forcing him to climb its slick surface, where venomous snakes had sought refuge from the rising water. And all the while they could feel that something else was still out there, its presence betrayed by the silence of birdsong and the absence of game.

Brooks battled through a thicket of durian and lychee trees and turned to see Julian across the river, gesturing toward something ahead of him. Another dozen feet and he saw why the grad student was so excited. Several tree trunks had piled up at a bend in the river, narrowing it by a third. The rushing water thumped against them with enough force to fill the air with a dense mist of spume, nearly concealing the rock formation against which the trunks were pinned. It was by far the best option they'd seen in the entire time they'd been walking and likely the best they would encounter, especially with the knowledge that time was now working against them. The clouds in the eastern sky were already beginning to darken, while to the west they were imbued with the faintest hint of red from the setting sun.

Brooks sloshed onto the floodplain, wading as deep as he dared without sacrificing the leverage provided by the trees still firmly rooted in the ground. Across from him, Julian was little more than a silhouette through the rain and mist as he eased along a collection of boulders that appeared to have once formed a great outcropping from the top of the cliff and onto the slick logs, his rope wound in his hand. He made it a single step away from the rocks before a stump rose from the depths and slammed into the trunks.

"Throw us the rope!" Adrianne called.

If Julian replied, they couldn't hear him over the roaring river. He held out his arms, bent his knees, and inched away from the bank. The trunks rolled and sank beneath his weight as he advanced. He reached a point where he had no choice but to carefully lower himself to his hands and knees, and even then barely managed to keep himself above water. He paused and looked up at them, his eyes wide, his lips a grim line. He was maybe ten feet from the far side and rapidly running out of room to crawl. Smaller trunks slowly twisted out of the logjam in front of him and drifted away on the current, accelerating as they sank.

"Try throwing the rope!" Brooks shouted.

Julian nodded, raised the bundle from the water, and braced himself as well as he could. In one jerky motion, he hurled the rope, which unspooled in the air as it arced out over the water. It splashed into the river well shy of where Brooks clung to the branch of a durian, reaching for it.

Julian reeled it in and tried again. The rope flew farther, but still fell a good five feet short. Brooks might have been able to catch it if he dove. With as quickly as the water swept it away, if he missed he would be at its mercy. Even if he managed to grab it, there was no guarantee he wouldn't just end up pulling Julian in with him.

A cluster of trees shook across the river, near where the largest boulder leaned against the sheer cliff.

Julian bellowed with the exertion of a third try, which didn't even make it as far as his previous effort and cost him his balance. His entire left side dipped underwater and he clung to the log through sheer force of will. A section of the dam broke away and he scurried backward as fast as he could. He was nearly to the boulders when he was finally able to stand again.

"I have an idea!" he shouted.

He slid off his backpack, rummaged around inside until he found his ice tool, and shouldered it once more. He snapped the pick into place and stared at it for a long moment before looking up at them through the spume.

"I'm only going to get one shot at this! If I miss . . . " His words were swallowed by the raging river.

"What?" Adrianne yelled.

"If I miss, you guys are going to have to go on without me!"

Brooks watched Julian tie the end of his rope to the handle of the small pickax and recognized what he was doing. If his throw fell short like the previous ones, the pick could snag some debris rushing through the water or sink to the bottom and embed itself in the rocks, likely costing Julian his rope and his best means of scaling the cliff again.

"We'll find another place to cross!" Brooks shouted. "It's not worth the risk!"

Julian glanced back over his shoulder toward where the trees met with the fallen boulders. When he looked back, it was with determination on his face. He tied the free end of the rope to his climbing belt.

"I don't have a choice!"

His shoulders rose as he took a deep breath. He flexed his legs and tested his balance.

"Jesus," Brooks said. "He's going to run for it."

Adrianne looked at Brooks, then back at Julian. They both knew what he intended to do. Whether his ax cleared the river or not, he was going in and it was up to them to get him back out.

"Wait!" she shouted, but it was too late.

He took off at a sprint, his right arm reaching back with the ice tool, preparing to hurl it as far as he could.

The tool weighed roughly two pounds, twice the weight of a football and nowhere near as aerodynamically designed. Brooks figured he could make the throw himself, but didn't know if he was confident enough to stake his life on it, especially with the additional six to eight pounds of rope attached to it. The river was maybe thirty-five feet wide and Julian was going to have to throw it at least twenty-five with the rope creating all sorts of downward drag. And while Brooks had no qualms about diving for the rope, the last thing he wanted to do was try to catch the ax. It was designed to pass through several inches of ice hardened by the arctic winds. Lord only knew what it would do to him.

Julian cried out as he ran toward the end of the logs and launched the ice tool high into the air.

Brooks watched it arch out over the river, the rope unraveling behind it. The tool flipped end over end until the rope weighed it down. The pick streaked straight toward the flooded area to his left.

It was going to make it.

The ground over there was submerged and didn't appear nearly as stable. Most of the trees had been carried off, leaving pits of mud above which swirling eddies formed. The pick would undoubtedly stick, but how long would it be able to remain in place when the river pulled Julian's weight against it.

Brooks pushed off from the tree and splashed toward where it would land. His feet sank into the mud past his ankles and the deceptive current tugged at his legs with greater force than he anticipated. He'd barely taken two strides when the rope tightened and jerked the ax in reverse.

He looked toward the opposite side of the river as Adrianne screamed behind him.

Julian left his feet and flew backward into the spume, his arms and legs extended out in front of him like the appendages of a doll. He hit a boulder and tumbled over the side, vanishing into the impenetrable shadows in the crevices between the rock and the cliff.

The ice tool struck the river with a splash before Brooks could even think about diving for it. The rope slithered across the surface and streaked straight down toward the bottom, drawing taut as it stretched back over the rocks. It went suddenly slack and vanished into the water.

"Julian!" Brooks shouted. He strode toward the river and sank to his knees in the mud. The current battered him and he had to drive his hand into the ground to keep from being carried away. When he looked up again, an arc of blood spattered the escarpment and a dark shape moved quickly through the mist.

He flipped over and saw the fear in Adrianne's eyes.

"Run!" he shouted.

Brooks pushed himself up from the mud and barreled blindly into the forest after her.

34

Excerpt from the journal of
Hermann G. Wolff

Courtesy of Johann Brandt, Private Collection
Chicago, Illinois
(Translated from original handwritten German text)

February 1939

A better man than I would have gone back for the others. I have come to terms with my cowardice, and yet I fear I might never learn the fates of my colleagues Johann Brandt and Kurt Eberhardt. I will never forget the war cry of our Master Hunter, who managed to hold the beasts at bay until the sun had risen into the sky. Nor will I forget his sacrifice, for were it not for his bravery and unparalleled skill with a rifle, I likely never would have escaped the accursed valley with my life, such that it is. I can only imagine my father's shame. He is a man who returned from the Great War against his will, kicking and screaming for another go at the forces of King George. Only his scorn *and public disgrace await me in the Fatherland, where there will be questions for which even my best answers are insufficient.*

So I squat on the trail in the home of a Luoba [sic] *farmer, who allows me to stay in his barn in exchange for my labor in the cassava fields, while I patiently wait for my colleagues to emerge from the valley. It has been three weeks now. Three infernal weeks of eating rice with tapioca and bolting the doors at night against a threat the old man calls Yeh-Teh* [sic]*, which can be heard clawing at the wooden doors and walls, even over the braying of the mules kind enough to share their stables with me.*

I know in my heart that my friends are all dead, but I still pray they found their way safely from the clutches of Motuo and through the mountains to the south into Bootan [sic]*. Only monks frequent the trail, herding hairy yaks with the devil's horns, their red robes sweet with the smell of incense. They pass me in the fields without a glance, as though I do not exist in their eyes. It is a feeling with which I am intimately acquainted, for unlike König and Brandt, who have an aura of greatness about them, I am but the simple son of a soldier whose only potential claim to glory now sits inside trunks in the back of a cave, the cans rusting and the film beginning to disintegrate.*

I might as well not return at all without the film our benefactor commissioned and the rest of my team, from whom such amazing discoveries had been expected. My welcome would undoubtedly consist of prompt dismissal from the ranks of the SS and reassignment to the lowliest position available in the Ministry of Propaganda, assuming I escaped service as cannon fodder for the Soviet Russians. I have a mind to stay here with the mules until I have worn out my welcome and the bitter winter claims me. Let them find my frozen corpse a thousand years from now and wonder which manner of primitive life form I was to have passed from this world sitting still enough to freeze to ice.

Had König survived, he would have returned to a parade in his honor and his own personal ladder through the ranks of the Ahnenerbe. Eberhardt and Metzger could have staked their claim to any university position they fancied. After reading a mere fraction of his research, I have no doubt Brandt would have been able to write his own ticket to whatever hallowed halls of academia awaited such men of vision. Even had I my films, my reward would have been relegation to a darkroom where countless hours of splicing and editing awaited me and where thousands of hours of uneventful footage could be cobbled into a single unremarkable travelogue featuring five mildly enter-

taining men, the most uninteresting of whom left the others behind to save his own skin.

I recall our time on the ship bound for Ceylon and the dreams of grandeur we shared, while strange foreign lands passed over the rails. Five boys with the mysteries of the world waiting to be laid bare before them. I remember the wine and the laughter we could no longer suppress at the comedic notion of finding some primitive Eden filled with perfect physical specimens of Nordic heritage, whose ancestry we claimed despite our complete lack of physical resemblance.

Metzger had been engaged to marry the daughter of a farmer, whose lands would have one day made him wealthy. Eberhardt's family owned a percentage of an Austrian salt mine and König's father had left him the keys to the kingdom. Only Brandt — who was orphaned as a boy — and I had come from nothing, while only I would return to it, and with even less than I had initially set out. If only I could return the wealthy son of a heroic adventurer or a brilliant anthropologist whose observations would provide a rallying cry for our entire nation. Then it would not matter if I returned empty-handed or alone, for having nothing was vastly different than being nothing. Had I the slightest ambition I would have filmed our final hours in Motuo or collected König's rifle or salvaged the work of the other three. Then I would have at least had something of value beyond this pathetic notebook filled with this often-incoherent drivel.

We have failed in our mission. More to the point, I have failed in mine. At least the others have an excuse. What is mine? I ran because König told me to and I never once looked back? The sound of his murder so traumatized me that I waited a dozen kilometers away until I finally gave up and abandoned my colleagues without even bothering to learn their fates? That I had potentially left them in dire straits, to die at the hands of something I never once saw, not even when all I had to do was press my eye to the gap between slats in the door while I was safely bolted behind it? Something that might very well have been exactly what we had been dispatched to find? Oh, yes, I am sure the Reichsführer-SS and I would share a haughty laugh as I regaled him with those tales.

I find myself wondering if a death by freezing in these horrible mountains or in a British cell in Sikkim or by ostracization in the Fatherland could be any worse than the one offered in the valley below, which on a clear day appears as a benign green smudge through the notch between snowcapped peaks. Was not a swift death preferable to a protracted one? Would an admitted coward not seek out the more swift and merciful end?

There is a certain logic to the course of action I now ponder. The last place the eagle would look for the fish is on dry land. The wolf would never expect to find the rabbit in its own den. Perhaps there is still the possibility of reward greater than that offered by a quick death. If I could collect my cans of films, the notes and research of the others, and the trophies of our expeditionist, then I would not be returning empty-handed, but rather with the fruits of all of our labors. I would be the sole heir to the rewards each entitled us. Failing at that, I would at least be spared an agonizing death in the cold or from the shame of a coward's homecoming.

Perhaps I should invest further thought into this notion, for at this moment I have nothing but time. These monks who come and go with impunity . . . surely there is something I can learn from them, whatever tool allows them to survive where we, as a group, failed. And what better distraction than a man in a bright red robe when attempting to sneak through the land of the bull?

I will seize the next opportunity to follow from afar.

Maybe the heavens will smile upon me just this once.

35

Yarlung Tsangpo River Basin
Motuo County
Tibet Autonomous Region
People's Republic of China
October 17th

Today

A crashing sound ahead of him and Adrianne went down hard. She finally allowed the terror to catch up with her and started to cry. Her back shuddered as she buried her face in her hands and kicked at the detritus.

Brooks collapsed to the ground beside her, exhausted. He'd burned through every ounce of energy long ago and was running on adrenaline fumes that weren't going to last much longer.

"We need to keep moving."

He took her by the arm and attempted to help guide her to her feet. She rose only as far as her hands and knees.

"Did you see his face?" she whispered.

Brooks looked away. The expression of horror on Julian's face was the last thing he wanted to think about now.

"Come on. We can't afford to stay still for very long."

"It doesn't matter. They'll find us soon enough. We're dealing with an apex predator. Its instinct isn't to colonize or spread its seed. Its dynamics are very simple. It hunts and it feeds. That's all. We represent competition for resources, and that's one thing it can't allow."

"We're also easy prey."

"I don't necessarily think that's the case. Remember the tiger in the cave? It was killed, but its remains weren't consumed, they were scavenged. And think about the men entombed in the cliff. They were all brutally beaten to death, but not so much as a bite had been taken from any of them. They'd been killed and left to rot, then someone collected them and interred them where they weren't likely to be found. If you were to encounter our civilization for the first time, it would appear exactly the same."

"But we're dealing with animals, and animals kill will with the sole intention of consuming their prey."

"You know as well as I do that we aren't dealing with animals."

Brooks said nothing. He had been fighting that admission with everything he had. To accept that they were dealing with a species evolved from a higher order mammal like *Homo sapiens* was to concede every slim advantage they held, if only in his mind. The most effective predators were those that killed without thought or conscience. Sharks were the perfect example of nature's most effective hunters. They were always in motion and attacked anything that moved. They never overpopulated their own ecosystems. They savaged their prey without mercy or pity. The prospect of dealing with a hominin version capable of higher thought was the most frightening idea Brooks had ever considered.

Adrianne struggled to her feet and turned in a circle. The dark forest closed around them like a fist, making it impossible to see more than a dozen feet in any direction.

"Where are we?" she finally asked.

"I'd guess roughly three miles south of the point where we pitched camp. If I'm right, then the bridge that will take us out of here is about six or seven miles . . . that way."

He pointed toward what he estimated to be northwest.

"We're already on the other side of the river. We should just keep heading south and take our chances in Nepal or Burma."

"It's one thing crossing the Himalayas on an established route. Attempting a blind crossing is another thing entirely. Mt. Everest is nearly thirty thousand feet and lies directly between us and Nepal. We couldn't make that climb on our best day, let alone the way either of us feels right now."

"I'm fine." She turned away, but he'd already seen the sweat pouring from her hairline and the flush of her cheeks. There was no hiding her ragged breathing or the way she unconsciously massaged her temples. "What about heading due east until the river doubles back into India?"

"Think about the canyons we had to navigate to get here. If there was another way around, don't you think someone would have found it by now? There's a reason the Chinese haven't been able to build a road through here, even with the modern equipment at their disposal."

"Stop shooting down every suggestion I make!"

"I'm just being realistic."

"You're being an asshole!"

Brooks took her by the hand, but she jerked it away. Her skin was startlingly warm.

"I want to get out of here just as badly as you do. Believe me. We can't afford to make a mistake, though. Whatever's out there not only knows where we are, but where we need to go. And every second we waste arguing costs us what little lead we have."

"So what do you propose then?"

"They know we have to head for the bridge and they'll expect us to come from this side of the river. They won't expect us to double back."

"There's no way we'll be able to cross the river again, let alone climb up the cliffs lining it."

"And yet that's exactly what we're going to do."

This time when he took her hand, she didn't resist. He guided her through the forest, toward the mountains to the east, the white slopes of which rose into the storm clouds through the canopy. All of the mountains encircling them looked the same; it would be exceedingly easy to get turned around and head off in the wrong direction. If countless generations of Sherpas and Lhobas and any number of smaller tribes hadn't found an alternate egress through the Himalayas, then what were their chances? They would freeze to death in the treacherous valleys, where no one would even know to look for them.

It suddenly struck Brooks just how unlikely it was that any of them would be missed.

Their guide was a paid mercenary who smuggled Lord only knew what across some of the most dangerous borders on the planet. Warren was single and often repulsively arrogant. Julian was estranged from his family and fearless to the point of recklessness when it came to climbing. Adrianne was a driven grad student whose work was her life. Brooks's only real attachment was to an institute whose founder was the only man alive who knew where they were. And Brandt had already demonstrated his powers of deception and manipulation.

How many teams had he sent into these very hills to be slaughtered by a species only he had somehow survived? And more importantly, why had he sent them here *now*?

What did he have to gain from their deaths? Brooks couldn't fathom a single thing. The real question was what did he have to gain if they managed to accomplish their objective and return with the viral DNA they'd been sent to acquire? It wasn't about obtaining the proof he could hold up for the world to see; the plaster cast could have easily been used to that effect, if not as conclusively. There had to be something more to it, some motivation that Brooks was missing. And therein, he feared, lay the key to their survival.

The mountains rose even higher above them as they ran. The mist receded toward the peaks as the sun ascended somewhere above the clouds. Every time they burst from the cover of the trees and into a clearing, he expected death to be waiting for them, and every time he was surprised to find only another dense thicket waiting for them. The river grew louder to their left as it slowly worked its way southeast. Between the ruckus of their passage and the thunder of the Yarlung Tsangpo echoing from the cliffs it had spent eons eroding, they wouldn't have been able to hear anything crashing toward them through the underbrush, let alone stealthily stalking them, until it was too late.

They'd never made it this far east. Beyond the sheer cliffs and the icy mountains, which served as an impasse and had thwarted every invading horde and army, lay the People's Republic of China. Were the river navigable, it would eventually take them south into India and the slums of Calcutta on the Bay of Bengal. This far to the north, though, it was a wild, white-capped beast filled with uncategorizable rapids and waterfalls that had defied commerce for millennia. Even if they had a vessel, it would be smashed to bits — and them right along with it — before they were even out of Motuo.

The ground grew steeper and the deciduous trees gave way to bushy pines, which thinned enough to reveal a series of towering yellow granite escarpments from the crevices of which the gnarled trunks of dead trees protruded. Carrion birds wheeled overhead in the drizzle, their black forms intermittently vanishing into the clouds and reappearing again. The river advanced ever closer. The occasional *thoom* marked the descent of a tree from the runoff on the opposite side.

The forest abruptly gave way to the granite cliffs that served as the barrier to the Himalayas to the east. To either side of the river were now sheer faces of granite that had to be at least a hundred feet tall and served to channel the water between them into rapids and troughs that collided with such force that the air was opaque with spume. Anyone unfortunate enough to be swept into the gorge would find himself beaten and broken against the rocks and drowned even before he could be gored by the wooden projectiles fired downstream by the current.

Brooks had other ideas, though.

He looked up at the cliffs. They were the orange of rust and riddled with fissures and cracks. Granite was a climber's best friend: it had a high friction coefficient and naturally formed step-like ledges. Without Julian to spot him, he was going to need all the help he could get.

"You're not really contemplating what I think you are," Adrianne said.

"Better here where they're just wet than up there where they're covered in ice."

"If we fall—"

"I've heard drowning's one of the more peaceful ways to go."

"That's not funny."

"It wasn't meant to be."

Brooks shed his backpack, snapped on his climbing belt, and attached his ice axes to the bungee cords affixed to either hip. He pointed through the sparkling mist toward a vague shadow maybe thirty feet from the top.

"When I get up there, I'm going to toss a rope down. I want you to put on the harness in my backpack and tie the rope to it. Then run it through this clip and tie it like . . . this. Do you understand?"

"I've got it."

"Tie it wrong and you *will* fall." He mounted the rock wall and looked back at her. "And if you see anything, take the shot and climb like hell."

The granite was slick, but not as slick as he'd feared. The narrow ledges offered solid traction and coincided with the various sedimentary layers, almost like an irregular ladder with inch-thick rungs spaced six feet apart. As he climbed sideways out over the river, he became increasingly conscious of the consequences of a single misstep. The roar of the river was so powerful that even the rock trembled. Occasional flumes grabbed at his feet and slapped the rock around him. The boughs of a fig tree swatted his legs and nearly pried him from the wall. He leapt for the next ledge up and pulled himself higher, out of the reach of the debris. Already his arms and legs trembled with the exertion as a consequence of the prior day's arduous climb and the lack of sleep.

For every foot he ascended, he took three sideways, picking his way along the narrow edges in search of crimps of diminishing size and frequency. He could barely see Adrianne through the mist and even then tried not to look back too often for fear he might throw off his balance. His fingertips bled freely, forcing him to pay close attention to where he placed his toes so as not to slip in his own blood. The rock became dryer as he climbed, until he was above the spume and nearing the cave he had barely been able to see from below. Whether it was large enough to comfortably accommodate both of them he couldn't tell, but at least it would serve as a resting point and give him the leverage he needed to belay Adrianne up. The longer she remained out in the open, the better their chances of having their ruse prematurely discovered.

He skirted a vulture's nest built into a dead tree growing from a crevice and noted the sheer amount of bones among the feathers. He recognized the skeletal remains of rodents and smaller birds, and even the distinct carpals and phalanges from a human hand. The owner of the nest was probably one of those that had been circling overhead and now perched in the branches of the dead pines lording over the top of the cliff, their exposed roots projecting out over the nothingness. They flapped and jostled for position, craning their bowed necks in an effort to better see him directly beneath them.

By the time he reached the mouth of the cave, the pain in his hands had become unbearable. His shoulders and calves felt like hooks had been looped into the muscles and twisted to the point of snapping. Tears ran from the corners of his eyes. He gave everything he had left to haul himself up and over the ledge and into the cool darkness. He barely had the strength left to draw his legs inside.

Brooks moaned in relief. He lay there on the cold stone only long enough to catch his breath and pushed himself up to all fours with trembling arms. He started to turn around and stopped abruptly.

The smell.

There was something in there with him. Something with which he was intimately familiar. Something that by all rights shouldn't have been here in the humid darkness.

He unclipped his flashlight and shined it deeper into the darkness.

"Jesus," he whispered.

The light fell from his hand and clattered to the stone.

PART VIII

THE HUNT

36

Yarlung Tsangpo River Basin
Motuo County
Tibet Autonomous Region
People's Republic of China
October 17ᵗʰ

Today

Brooks had been on digs all over the world and while they all differed in terms of composition of the soil and the relative age of the subjects, the remains all had a similar smell. It was one he considered almost archival, an ancient scent as unique to the human species as it was distinct from all other animals. It was the ultimate fulfillment of an individual's biological destiny, when everything susceptible to rot had decomposed to nothing and even the dissolution had dried and wasted away, leaving only the porous bones to absorb the various aromas of their surroundings, in much the same way tea leaves absorb the flavors of their unique environments.

He knew there were bones in the darkness before he even saw them, and yet he was still unprepared for the condition of the remains. He'd seen everything from warriors fallen in battle and left to sink into the fields to the most revered, ensconced in silk and soaked with scented oils, inside their gilded tombs. He'd unearthed those wrapped in fetal position and interred in funereal bundles and those who'd starved to death and simply fallen apart. Even the remains of human ancestors so ancient all they left behind were partial skulls that had become more rock than bone. None of them had displayed this level of violence, though.

These bones were heaped in a pile in no apparent order or design, as though they'd merely been cast aside after outliving their usefulness, the primitive midden heap of a predatory species. All of the long bones were scored by teeth marks and snapped in half to scrape out the marrow. Even the irregular bones of the hands and feet were disarticulated and gnawed. Only the skulls appeared marginally preserved, but they were riddled with fracture lines and missing everything from teeth to entire jaws, their cranial vaults broken open and pried apart to access the brains in the most expeditious manner possible.

No anthropologist could work in this field for very long without encountering the earmarks of cannibalism. The ends of bones smoothed by the contours of the pot in which they'd been boiled, the denaturation of the bony matrices by flames, the telltale scoring of the sharp instruments used to carve off slabs of muscle. After all, morality was a more recent evolutionary adaptation within a species that collectively no longer feared its next meal might never come.

These were different, though. There was no indication that any attempt had been made to cook them. They looked like they'd been savaged by wild animals, but rather than scattered and left to work their way into the ground, they'd been gathered and entombed where only the vultures would ever find them.

It was impossible to tell how many individuals had been crammed back into that recess, only that they were all of varying age. Without the ability to carbon date them, he could only estimate that they were anywhere from several hundred to several thousand years old. Some of them near the back were maybe even older than that.

Brooks picked up his light and shined it onto the surrounding walls. They were covered with petroglyphs of men and animals, of hunting parties and fallen warriors, and creatures that walked on two legs, but looked nothing like the other men. They were represented as hairy, like the yaks with their unmistakable horns. There was even primitive writing reminiscent of ornate Tibetan script, with its swooping curves and accent marks, if poorly chiseled by an unsteady hand.

He backed away and tried not to think about the implications of what he'd found. As an evolutionary anthropologist, he could spend months in this one cave alone, sifting through the remains and cataloguing every minute imperfection and injury, poring over the petroglyphs and determining their place in the chronology of human evolutionary development and charting the course of divergence, but now was not the time. Adrianne was still down there and a species he now feared was capable of higher thought and written communication would only be fooled for so long.

He quickly hammered several anchors into the ground and attached a belay device with carabiners to each. He fed the ropes through each in turn and tethered them to his harness. A few solid tugs confirmed it was properly seated. He gathered the remaining length of rope, leaned out over the river, and saw Adrianne already creeping out over the river. From this height, it looked like it might swallow her whole. She was barely moving and appeared to be on the verge of slipping with every jerky movement she made. The plan had been for her to wait for him on level ground. The only reason she would have taken her life into her own hands by venturing out onto the cliff was—

He glanced toward where he had left her and saw only their backpacks through the spume. They'd been opened and the contents spilled out onto the bank, as though in an effort to make it appear as if they'd washed up onto dry ground at the point where the river wound into the canyon, which could only mean one thing.

Their pursuit was closing in on them and she'd made a desperate play to buy them more time.

When he looked back down, his eyes met hers through the mist and he saw the sheer terror on her face. She clung to the tiny ledge for dear life and there was no way she would be able to do so for much longer.

"Hold on," he said, and dropped the rope.

It uncoiled as it fell and snapped like a whip maybe six feet to her left. It swayed on the breeze, just out of reach. He watched her grab for it, terrified to extend her arm to its full length.

He swung the rope from his end in the hopes that he could get it close enough. Even if he did, though, it would take two hands to tie the knot he'd shown her and she wouldn't be able to do so without letting go.

The rope bounced off her palm and seemed to momentarily dislodge her from the wall. She scrabbled for purchase and pressed herself flat against the granite. The rope slapped her shoulder and she reached for it too late.

He glanced again toward the bank of the river and saw motion through the mist. The branches of the trees shook as something moved through the forest.

"Come on, Adrianne," he said, and swung the rope once more.

It hit her shoulder again, only this time she grabbed it before it rebounded out of reach. She fed it through her harness, wrapped it around several times, then fed it back through to form the kind of knot used to tie a sinker to a fishing line. It wasn't ideal, but it was going to have to work. She wound the rope around her forearm several times and gripped it as tightly as she could.

She looked to her right, then quickly back up at him with tears in her eyes. He read her intention on her face and threw himself backward into the cave as she let go of the ledge. He caught a glimpse of her grabbing the rope with both hands as she fell toward the waiting river. He barely had time to brace his feet against the stone to either side of the opening before the rope drew taut and yanked him forward. He cried out with the strain of straightening his legs and reeling the rope through the carabiners, which served as a system of pulleys to distribute her weight.

The rope swung from side to side over the ledge while the stone worked at it like a dull saw blade. It was rated for five falls, but there was no way it could have been tested under these conditions.

He gave it everything he had, pulling hand over fist until it felt as though his biceps would tear and his elbows would snap, and still he belayed her higher until finally her right arm appeared over the ledge. He dove for her, grabbed her by the back of her jacket, and dragged her inside.

Several silhouettes materialized from the mist.

He threw himself deeper into the cave, hauling her up on top of him. He pursed his lips to shush her and felt her mouth against his. She kissed him long and hard, her tears falling onto his cheeks. He kissed her back and drew her to him in a desperate embrace that only those who've narrowly survived a brush with death could understand. The pistol tucked underneath her waistband pressed against his abdomen, but he wasn't about to complain. When she finally withdrew, she remained right above him, her breath warm on his lips.

She closed her eyes and turned her right ear toward the outside world. Brooks listened, but couldn't hear anything over the thunder of the river.

"Did they see you?" he whispered.

She shook her head. "I'm not sure. I . . . I don't think so."

"We can't stay here."

"There's nowhere to go from here."

She started to cry again. This time he kissed her, only softer, a gesture from which he hoped she drew reassurance. She broke away more quickly this time and leaned her forehead against his. Her skin was startlingly hot.

"It's about time," she whispered, and looked up for the first time. "Amazing."

"Thank you," he said with a smirk.

"Not you — although that wasn't half bad — I mean . . . that."

He rolled out from beneath her and followed her eyes to the pile of bones, barely illuminated by the glow of the flashlight he'd dropped on the ground. From this vantage point, he saw something even more amazing than the accumulation of remains.

He crawled forward and right up onto the bones, then looked up at the roof of the cave.

"Well, what do you know?" he said.

A great roar echoed from the canyon, only this time he was certain it wasn't the river. He was again reminded of Limpopo, only this time it wasn't the remains of the wildebeests he recalled, but rather the sounds of the lions that had killed them.

37

Yarlung Tsangpo River Basin
Motuo County
Tibet Autonomous Region
People's Republic of China
October 17th

Today

There was a chute above the pile of bones, a narrow crevice leading upward into the darkness. Brooks understood now why the bones had been broken to such an astounding degree. They'd been thrown down the hole from somewhere high above them. And if they could get down here, then surely he and Adrianne could get up there.

He shined his flashlight up into the shadows, but the beam diffused before reaching the top. The chute itself was obviously the product of erosion and not the work of man. The walls were smooth and appeared to offer nothing resembling hand or foot holds, or even the tiniest finger cracks.

"I can't see anything down there," Adrianne said. She lay flat on her stomach against the side of the cave's mouth, just far enough out into the open to see the ground where their supplies were still scattered around their backpacks.

Not being able to see them was worse. He and Adrienne didn't know where they were or in which direction they'd gone. They could be heading upriver toward the lone bridge exiting Motuo or circling around to descend upon them through whatever warren of tunnels and caves connected them to the unknown above. Whatever the case, they were already on borrowed time.

He scooted the bones out of the way and carefully stood up. His shoulders barely fit into the chimney and it was all he could do to manipulate his arms so that he could raise the light over his head. At the farthest reaches, he saw the hint of stone and the faintest silhouette of what might have been a ledge. He ducked back down and found his face inches from Adrianne's.

"We're going to have to climb for it. Once I get to the top, I'll lower the rope—"

"We don't have that kind of time and you know it."

Her left forearm was circled with bruises and there were even sections where the rope had bitten through the fabric and into her flesh. She'd torn the ripped sleeves and fashioned the straps into bandages that were already wet with blood.

"The offer stands."

He stood up once more and clamped the mini Maglite between his teeth. He pressed his back against one side, his forearms against the other, and inched upward until he could get his knees into the chute. The pressure on his shoulders was phenomenal, as was this pain in his elbows and knees, which he pushed into the bare rock with every ounce of strength he possessed. His body shook with muscular contractions. He wasn't going to be able to maintain this level of exertion for very long.

He focused on the movement of one appendage at a time. One arm, one leg. Another arm, another leg. He couldn't lean his head far enough back to gauge his progress above him and resisted the urge to look down. Not that he would have been able to see much of anything with Adrianne's body blocking out the light. She grunted and groaned at first, then started to whimper with every movement. For as difficult as it was for him, her shorter limbs made it exponentially harder, especially considering her injured arm. He had to admire her courage and determination, but he knew they would only take her so far. With each passing second, her body grew weaker and it was only a matter of time before it gave out completely. If it did so too soon, she would plummet straight down the chute and likely shatter both ankles, leaving him to carry her across the Himalayas on his back.

The thought stimulated a surge of adrenaline and Brooks moved faster. Forearm, knee. Forearm, knee. He felt the back of his jacket rip and the spinous processes of his vertebrae scrape against the rock. He had to bite his lip to keep from crying out with every vertical inch he gained.

If his body gave out first, they would both fall down onto the jagged bones. His weight crashing down on top of her from this height would undoubtedly break her neck. The image grew even more real as the pain in his shoulders caused him to bite through his lip and fill his mouth with blood. He was nearly resigned to that fate when his right forearm rounded over the ledge and he was able to raise his elbow onto level ground. His entire body shook when he pulled himself up into a cavern with a ceiling so low he could barely crawl out on all fours.

He turned around and reached for Adrianne, who clasped his wrist with the last of her strength. Her palm was slick with blood. Were it not for his grasp on her wrist, she would have fallen. As it was, he barely lifted her high enough to wrap his other arm around her torso and awkwardly drag her up beside him.

She gingerly plucked the flashlight from between his teeth and shined it into the waiting darkness. The light lent little more than the impression of space. As she crawled toward the larger cavern, leaving smears of blood on ground already thick with it, the ceiling rose and they were eventually able to stand on legs that hardly seemed able.

The floor was carpeted with a layer of blood that had long ago dried and curled up like the silt in an evaporated lakebed. It turned to powder underfoot as they advanced. Whatever lived in here must have just shoved the bloody remains across the floor and down into the chute to dispose of them. And whatever had done so was likely the source of the long white hairs all over the ground amid the desiccated reeds and vegetation. It reminded Brooks of a bird's nest, or perhaps more like the warren of a mammal, although one that hadn't been used in quite some time. It smelled of age and fecal dust, with the faint scent of ammonia. He recognized it as the smell of a tomb even before Adrianne shined the light onto the bodies arranged supine on the ground, side-by-side, their arms crossed over their sunken chests. The silk robes that had once covered their bodies had rotted to black tatters and now revealed more than they concealed.

Here was the species Brandt had cast, although these individuals had been dead for a long, long time.

Their skin had pulled tightly to their bones and become the texture of leather. Their lips were drawn back from bared teeth reminiscent of those of a chimpanzee, only sharper. Their foreheads were more steeply sloped, but the remainder of their facial architecture was surprisingly human. Their hair grew to widow's peaks just above the bridges of their noses and followed the contours their cheekbones beneath their eyes. Their beards were wiry and long and more closely resembled the hair on their heads than the whiskers of an ordinary man. Even their necks, shoulders, and the remainder of the skin showing through the silk was covered with a layer of white hair every bit as thick, lending them the overall appearance of albino orangutans crossed with human beings.

Adrianne knelt beside the nearest one and reached tentatively toward its face. She stopped, steadied her nerves, and brushed its cheek with the backs of her fingers. Her long nails combed through its beard. She looked up at Brooks with tears in her eyes. There were simply no words for the emotions they both felt. It was like awakening inside of a dream rather than from one. This was the moment they'd spent their entire lives working toward, all the while content in the knowledge that it would never arrive.

"Is this what Dr. Brandt cast?" she finally asked.

"No," Brooks whispered. "All of these are too gaunt. The face he cast was much more . . . alive."

"That was seventy years ago."

"And these have all been dead for at least twice that long. Probably longer."

"So this is just a tomb."

"That's my guess. Only more like a crypt. I would wager this is some sort of familial unit or clan and generations of them were all laid to rest together."

"You think they're capable of breeding?"

Brooks could only shake his head. He hadn't considered that the mutations, if that was indeed the source of the physical changes, could be passed through the germ line in addition to manifesting from viral insertion into the DNA. That was a terrifying line of thought, for if these creatures could breed and found a way to cross the barrier of the Himalayas, then humanity's days at the top of the food chain were numbered.

Adrianne raised the light to the walls. Hundreds of tiny nooks had been carved into the stone and filled with trinkets, all of them concealed under a layer of dust. The majority were *Śartra*, Buddhist relics of all shapes and sizes. There were bowls filled with pearls and beads, items of jewelry, miniature statues of the Buddha in various poses, and every type of stupa. What little space remained was etched with the same stylized script as they had seen in the room below. The grave goods in this one cavern alone had to be worth several million dollars.

The notion that religious relics like these were in some way important to these dead creatures was beyond comprehension. Perhaps like the modern remains hidden in the cliffs, someone else had entombed them here and left the *Śartra* as an offering of sorts. Or maybe these . . . things had collected the artifacts like birds gather foil and string for their nests. The idea that these creatures were capable of comprehending religious dogma on any level implied more than mere intelligence; it implied the kind of imaginative thinking and reasoning that would make them more terrifying than any predator the world had ever seen.

Adrianne turned in a circle until the light settled upon twin columns of empty recesses, staggered to form a primitive staircase, like those prominent in the ruins of the Pueblo II Era tribes of the American Southwest. She shined it upward and illuminated another fissure, this one even narrower than the last, but fortunately the toe-trail continued upward into the darkness.

Brooks stepped in front of her before she could mount the ladder. He was the better climber and could use the rope to belay her up once more if she reached her physical limits. Besides, he had the ice axes, which were probably the best weapons they had in such close quarters. And he had a feeling that before the day was through, he was going to have to use them.

He climbed as fast as he dared. Adrianne had affixed the flashlight under the right sleeve of her jacket so that it shined upward. He passed several slender fissures to either side, but their ultimate goal was to climb out of the darkness, not find themselves further lost in it. The smell that wafted from each was the same as the one from below. Perhaps this series of caverns had once served as a home to these creatures; now it was one enormous tomb that didn't smell as if it had been disturbed in many years. The extant species obviously dwelled somewhere else.

The tunnel terminated abruptly at the top. Like the other burials, this one had been sealed from the outside by a large stone.

Brooks braced himself and shoved against it.

The rock didn't budge.

He pushed again.

And again and again.

There was no give at all. He thought about how long the bodies had been down there and how much dust had accumulated on the artifacts. It was a distinct possibility that this boulder hadn't been moved in decades.

Panic set in.

He bucked his shoulders against the stone and shoved with his legs until the pressure broke one of the footholds and he started to fall.

38

Yarlung Tsangpo River Basin
Motuo County
Tibet Autonomous Region
People's Republic of China
October 17th

Today

Brooks caught himself on the next handhold and immediately looked down at Adrianne. Her hair and shoulders were covered with rocky debris, but at least the broken rock hadn't knocked her off the wall. He took a deep breath and forced himself to approach this rationally.

The blasted boulder was either extraordinarily heavy or wedged in there tightly. He used the pick of his ice ax to scrape around the edges. Gravel and dirt rained down on Adrianne below him before clattering to the ground seconds later. As he chiseled, more and more light shined down onto him and muddy water dribbled through the seams. He reholstered his pick, braced himself again, and pushed upward with all his might. The stone made a cracking sound, then abruptly slid away from the earth that had held it so tight. Gray light and rain flooded the darkness. He saw the branches of pines overhead as he continued to shove the rock out of the way. When the gap was large enough to accommodate his shoulders, he pulled himself out on shaking arms and crawled onto a mat of flattened grasses and dead needles.

A gust of wind howled past him, assaulting him with raindrops and tossing the branches of the trees before once more resuming the steady drizzle. His heart thudded in his ears as he quickly surveyed his surroundings. They were on the top of the cliff and exposed to the elements from which they'd largely been shielded in the canyon below. Maybe twenty feet to the west was the edge of the cliff and a surprised group of vultures. Some took to flight from the dead trees, while others huffed and hopped away into the underbrush. The forest limited his view in every direction, save for the high, mist-shrouded peaks that towered over the upper canopy, which bowed to the will of the wind. If there was anything else out here, he couldn't see it.

"Come on," he said, and reached down to help Adrianne out of the hole.

She collapsed onto the ground and struggled to rise to her feet. He took her by the hand and pulled her toward the forest to the north, keeping the river within sight to his left. They still needed to cross it if they were to have any hope of reaching the bridge.

"We're looking at two distinct population models." Adrianne spoke just loudly enough that he could hear her over the river. "The one entombed down there appears to be a terminal branch, one steeped in an entirely different culture and dynamic. How old would you say the bodies were?"

"The most recent couldn't have been interred much less than a century ago."

"Like maybe seventy or eighty years?"

Brooks saw where she was going with that line of thought.

"You think we're dealing with a population evolved from the first wave of Europeans to explore this region?"

"The timing would be right. It would also coincide with the bodies in the coffins and fit with a marked and dramatic shift in population models, living arrangements, and funereal practices."

"You're suggesting a Caucasian lineage usurped the habitat from one arisen from native Tibetans?"

"Does that not fit with the entire colonial mindset of the early twentieth century?"

Brooks shouldered aside pine branches and birch saplings, keeping one eye on the cliff to his left, the other on the thick forest. With as loud as the river was, they wouldn't hear anything approaching until it was too late. They needed to find a place to cross the gorge — and soon — or there was no way they'd be able to reach the bridge before nightfall.

"That would at least explain the artifacts entombed with the bodies, but it still doesn't tell us what we need to know about the extant population."

"Of course it does. Think about it. We're dealing with a more loosely bound clan potentially evolved from soldiers from the British Indian Army and the Nazis. When you factor that into the equation, it gives their instincts and actions a measure of predictability."

"You're assuming their human instincts somehow translate to their mutated state."

"Instincts are ingrained in your hindbrain. They're the result of millions of years of evolution, of ancestors surviving any number of threats and environmental factors. Even if the cerebrum is destroyed, the body retains the knowledge of how to keep itself alive in much the same way birds inherently know to fly south for the winter. It's not a conscious decision, but rather one that's been passed down through successive generations, which, if they learned one thing, it's how to survive."

Brooks parted a stand of saplings and stopped dead in his tracks. The thicket ahead of him looked like a tornado had torn through it. The tall pines were uprooted and smashed and snarled into a mess of broken and tangled wood where the floodwaters had washed down from the high country, bringing with them enormous boulders from the granite escarpment to the east. It wasn't the devastation ahead of him that had caught his attention, though.

He glanced back at Adrianne, then headed for the cliff. The water had hit the trees with the force of a runaway train, throwing fifty- to eighty-foot-tall pines ahead of it as though they were mere blades of grass. Several had been swept over the edge and now rested across the chasm, tangled with shrubbery and vegetation.

They couldn't have asked for better luck.

Adrianne's hand tightened on his when she realized what he intended to do.

The Yunnan pine was a transitional species that filled the elevation gap between the smaller and broader chir pines and the sturdier Himalayan pines. It grew much taller than either of its cousins and had much longer needles. Unfortunately, it also had a much thinner trunk.

Brooks cautiously approached the precipice on the slick rocks and mud. He released Adrianne's hand for balance and gingerly placed his right foot on the trunk, near where its severed roots projected upward, taller even than he was. The wood was waterlogged and gave slightly under his weight.

His heartbeat thumped in his temples.

Several trees had fallen on top of one another, their lower branches tangled and stripped to the bare wood. The upper reaches were a seemingly impenetrable bushy snarl of needles that completely hid the tapering trunks underneath them and the opposite edge beyond. Through the gaps between the trunks he could barely see the brown water rushing past through the mist and spume.

He took hold of one of the roots and eased both feet up onto the trunk. Even at its widest point, it couldn't have been more than eighteen inches in diameter. The thought of balancing along its tapering length caused his hands to shake.

"We can find another place to cross," Adrianne said. "Surely there's—"

"There's no time. We can do this. We'll just go across one at a time so it can handle our weight. I'll go first. I can belay you across if it falls."

"But what if it falls while you're on it?"

He opened his mouth to say something reassuring, but the words never came out. He caught motion from the corner of his eye and whirled uphill toward the forest. A clump of branches maybe thirty feet from the ground swayed harder than the rest of those around it. He watched for several seconds before returning his attention to Adrianne.

"We're out of time."

Brooks stepped away from the roots and out over the nothingness. The deceptive wind battered him from his left. He thrust out both arms for balance, slowly lowered himself to his hands and knees, and crawled toward the opposite edge. Below him, the river roared and debris raced past like cars on a freeway. He forced himself to look up and concentrate on the far side. The tree bowed beneath his weight, subtly at first, but visibly as he neared the middle and started picking his way around the branches, transferring his weight from one trunk to the next and back again. Another few feet and he would crawl into the dense canopy, where the going would be slow and dangerous, and worse, he wouldn't be able to see much of anything through the heavily-needled boughs. He looked back over his shoulder in time to see Adrianne step up onto the trunk. He was about to shout for her to get back down when he saw the expression on her face. Behind her, the pine trees shook as though blown by a tempest, raining needles and pinecones onto the ground. Shadows launched from one tree to the next as the crashing sounds reached his ears even over the river.

"Run!" he shouted, and crawled back toward her as fast as he could.

Adrianne pushed off from the roots and managed several long strides before her right foot glanced from the bark and vanished out of sight. She slammed down onto the trunk with a resounding *crack*.

The tree shuddered and noticeably dropped beneath him. He dove for her as she toppled to the side and grabbed her hand.

Behind her, branches exploded from the trees and white blurs streaked toward the ground from the upper reaches.

"Come on!" he shouted, and pulled her up onto the log behind him.

He stood and hopped from one trunk to the next as he worked his way into the smothering foliage. He released Adrianne's hand and prayed she stayed on his heels. They were barely halfway across when the trunks shuddered and started to shake.

They weren't going to make it.

Brooks grabbed the branches and used them to propel himself forward. He lunged from one trunk to another, conscious of certain death rushing past beneath him and the narrowing of the trunks even as the branches grew closer together. The tree bounced underneath him and clumps of bark broke off where the wet wood splintered and cracked beneath their weight.

A roar behind him and a loud snapping sound.

One of the narrower trees to his right wrenched away from the others and plummeted into the mist.

He could see the forest on the opposite side through the branches and realized that it didn't matter if they reached them. Their pursuit would overtake them long before they reached the cover of the forest, if they even made it across the makeshift bridge, which bucked underneath him, making it nearly impossible to know where it would be when he stepped down. He tried not to think about how many of them must have been behind him to cause the trunks to shake so violently.

The moment he saw solid ground he drew his ice ax. Two more strides and he could make the jump. He lowered his shoulder against the branches, came down on his right foot, and lunged with his left. The instant it landed on a section of trunk narrower than it, he dove for the rock ledge. He landed hard on his shoulder and popped right back up, ax in hand.

He swung it at the largest tree even as Adrianne struggled toward him, her eyes wide, a scream he couldn't hear on her lips.

White blurs streaked through the branches, barely ten feet behind her.

He swung the ax again and again. Wood chips and bark flew. A crack formed and widened, then collapsed in upon itself with a sharp *thack*.

The tree dropped suddenly.

He looked up to see Adrianne leaping toward him with her arms extended. The trunk fell away from her feet. The branches grabbed for her legs.

Brooks caught her hand and threw himself backward, pulling her along with him. She landed squarely on his chest, knocking the wind out of him. He rolled out from beneath her and crawled toward the ledge, his vision throbbing, his body convulsing in a desperate attempt to refill his lungs.

White bodies became entangled in the branches of the falling pine as it dropped out of sight, while others still advanced along the lone remaining tree.

He collapsed to the ground and rolled onto his side. Drew the ax and swung it for the tree, but there was no force behind the blow.

Adrianne leapt over him and sat on the ground, braced her feet against the trunk, and screamed as she pushed. The tree slid a good foot along the ledge. She scooted closer and tried again.

Brooks saw white hair clearly now as arms shoved branches out of the way for bodies moving low to the trunk, humanoid feet gripping almost like hands.

Adrianne shoved again with her legs and the trunk slid. The uppermost branches bent and the treetop dropped over the edge.

Brooks saw a flash of terror in a pair of blue eyes through the needles, and then they were gone. The tree canted downward and dove into the river with a splash of water that passed through the mist.

His breath returned with a high-pitched wheeze and he crawled over to where Adrianne stared down at the river. Far across on the other side, a silhouette stood apart from the forest, its long fur blowing on the wind like flames. It raised its face to the sky and drew several deep inhalations. Its head snapped back down and it turned in their general direction. Again it rose to its full height and sniffed. It abruptly dropped to a crouch and bared its teeth at them. And then it was gone, leaving only a trail of shaking branches in its wake.

39

Excerpt from the journal of
Hermann G. Wolff

Courtesy of Johann Brandt, Private Collection
Chicago, Illinois
(Translated from original handwritten German text)

March 1939

O n the twenty-fourth day I followed them. Three monks arrived with
the dawn. Two led oxen by the reins while the third carried what I at
first believed to be a lantern from a distance. As they neared I saw
the smoke issuing from the openings in the golden housing and smelled the
distinct aroma of sandalwood. The monk swung it gently from side to side like a
priest with his thurible.

I waited at the top of the cliff beside the path, hidden behind the same rhododendron for the third straight day since concocting my suicidal plan. I watched
them chain the first yak to the cairn at the edge of the farmer's land. My gracious

host — a man I knew by the name of Wang-chuck [sic] *— remained inside his home behind the battened shutters until they were gone before he finally came out to inspect the offering. He fed it fresh vegetables of a quality better than he reserved for his own table and served it fresh water from the stream. He was still singing its blessings when I passed him on his knees and followed the scent of sandalwood into the forest.*

They moved at a slow, steady pace thanks to the yak, which allowed me to sneak from behind one tree to the next at a comfortable speed that minimized my exposure. The grunting of the beast allowed me to keep track of them even when they were outside of my range of sight.

Only a fool would not recognize what they intended to do with the yaks. I had already listened to several being slaughtered from where I awakened to their screams in the relative safety of the barn. They were sacrifices to the creatures, flesh and blood in exchange for their safe passage. After all, could not even the mighty lion be tamed in such a manner?

There were several times when I feared they sensed my presence. I hid as best I could and waited with baited breath until they contented themselves once more that they were alone and again resumed their trek, all the while burning that infernal incense, which after a time came to blend with the smell of the forest itself.

I do not remember how long we walked, only that by the time we reached the bridge where what seemed a lifetime ago I filmed König examining the footprint of the monster that killed him, it felt like days had passed. The mere act of returning to that awful place caused me such anxiety that my heart pounded and my legs trembled. My mouth became so dry that no amount of fluid would slake my thirst. My head hurt and my palms sweat and I worried my breathing would give me away.

Never had I imagined I possessed the kind of courage I required to cross that bridge, while every fiber of my being resisted with such vehemence that I was in tears before I set foot on the weathered planks.

Every tree, it seemed, was alive with movement and beneath the sound of the river was the roar of something else. I knew this was not the case, for if death came for me, I knew I would not see it coming. I lacked the skills of a hunter, at least when it came to animals of a lower order. I was able to track the monks without much difficulty and followed them for the better part of the day, until the sun was beginning its descent and lengthening the shadows. They were halfway across the clearing by the time I reached the end of the path, and still oblivious to my presence. I could tell where they were going by the course they plotted through the tall grasses. As I expected, they intended to chain the beast to the chorten where we had left the remains of the man from the broken coffin. Once they did, I had every cause to believe they would expedite their departure before the feeding commenced, which meant I had precious little time to enact my plan.

I knew this part of the valley better than any other and made my way to the cave where we had left all of our supplies. They remained precisely as we had left them, only then was not the time to gather those for which I had come. This trip was to collect one solitary item I found in its own case with the rest of König's belongings. With it in my possession, I followed the path around the circumference of the field until I heard the lowing of the yak, at which point I slowed my progress and approached the monks with an element of stealth.

By the time they heard me coming, I was already in their midst with the Erfurt Luger our master hunter inherited from his father in my fist. My plan had been to disrobe them, relieve them of the incense-burning censer, and disguise myself as one of them long enough to gather everything of importance and facilitate my departure. As they were holy men, I expected immediate compliance with my demands, not the chaos that ensued.

Everything happened so fast that even now I am uncertain of the sequence of events or how they came to pass. I know only that one of the monks made a move to disarm me of the pistol and another was shot in the ensuing fracas. The first monk disengaged when his brother fell and before I realized what I intended to do, I had shot him in the back, leaving me alone in the clearing with the last monk, who turned and ran before I got a look at his face.

I called after him that I meant him no harm and that events had simply spiraled out of my control. Even if he heard me, I am certain the sight of his brothers on the ground and me wearing their blood spoke louder.

It was only when he disappeared into the jungle that I realized the monastery from which he hailed was somewhere along the path I would need to travel to pass through the Himalayas. If he were allowed to reach it, his entire order would be waiting to intercept me on my return to the Fatherland.

He put up a furious chase, but in the end his red robe betrayed him through the trees and I shot him from thirty meters. When I finally reached the point where he had fallen, all that was left of him was a pattern of blood on the ground. I did not have the time to further track him, not with the rate at which the sun was sinking toward the mountains. I was confident, however, that with as badly as he was wounded, he would not be able to outpace me indefinitely.

I returned to the clearing where the dead men lay on the ground before the yak, stripped out of my clothes, and left them with the dead monks, one of whose robes fit me well enough. I was surprised the beasts had not yet been summoned by the smell of the carnage. It was only then that I understood what König had recognized from the start: These creatures preferred to hunt under the cover of darkness or in the deep shadows of the darkest sections of the forest.

I remember gauging the distance from the sun to the peaks before running back to the cave. There were so many things I wanted to take, and yet only so much I could carry. A single trunk filled with film canisters and samples of the flora was my physical limit, at least across a distance of any length, which meant I would be forced to leave behind the crates of specimens König collected and entire trunks overflowing with the research of our scientists. I did not comprehend their work well enough to quickly sort out the most important pieces, either. If I returned with only a fraction of my own work, none of which detailed the Aryan race we had been sent here to find or corroborated my fantastic stories of the hairy beasts that killed the rest of my team, I would undoubtedly incur the wrath of Herr Himmler. I was running out of time and there was no way I could salvage this plan without carrying well more than I could move, even with the aid of a mule.

It was from this thought that inspiration struck.

I realized I had something better than a mule, something that would allow me to carry everything I needed.

I conservatively estimated the sun to be three hours from setting, which meant I was already running behind schedule. I was going to need every minute of that three hours and even then I would be reliant upon a significant amount of luck.

The yak was still in one piece when I arrived and came with me willingly enough once I unchained him, although at a maddeningly slow pace. By the time we returned to the cave, I was on the verge of panic. The animal grazed while I burdened it with everything of importance: a case of König's rarest pelts; Metzger's magnetic readings and gemstones; Eberhardt's maps and sketchbooks; a case of what I hoped were my best films; and Brandt's prized trunk with his cherished journals and irreplaceable supplies. I tied it all down as I had seen the

Sherpas do so many times and swung the censer in front of me as I drove the yak toward the setting sun, which I watched darken from gold to orange, and orange to red through the canopy above me, all the while knowing I would never reach the bridge in time.

The shadows grew bolder and from their depths I heard the crackle of movement, sounds that became less subtle with each passing minute until they were all I could hear. The branches visibly shook and I recognized that I had run out of time.

The sun was still a blood-red stain on the mountaintops when the yak brayed and dug in its heels. It was only then that I deciphered the sounds of footsteps from the ruckus, footsteps that blossomed into riotous crashing as the forest came to life. The animal shrieked. I heard the sudden rush of blood spattering the forest floor, then the heavy slop of viscera following suit.

I turned to see it collapse to its knees, then topple to its side. The rope snapped and spilled its cargo into the bushes.

And then all was quiet, save for the rumble of the river.

Warm blood crept over the tops of my sandals and onto my bare feet. I held the censer in front of me like a shield, the smoke drifting from the vessel into tentacles that searched the night air for the creatures I could not see, and yet knew were somewhere nearby.

I stood perfectly still as one by one they emerged from the shadows of the forest, man-apes that approached their meal with caution before attacking it with a savagery the likes of which I'd never seen before.

I watched them in abject horror, flaying the animal with their claws and thrusting their teeth into its flesh. I was certain when they were done with it, they would turn their hunger upon me, but I didn't dare move. I was paralyzed by fear to such an extent that I lost control over my own body. I could not run, even if I tried.

And then they looked up at me from their meal, their hairy faces and beards clotted with blood, and I realized just how horrible of a mistake I had made.

40

Yarlung Tsangpo River Basin
Motuo County
Tibet Autonomous Region
People's Republic of China
October 17th

Today

Brooks and Adrianne ran to the northwest. If they could survive the swollen river, then so could whatever those things had been.

Brooks thought of the way he'd seen those muddy feet gripping the thin trunks and realized just how easy it would be for them to climb back up the cliffs. They needed to put as much distance between themselves and the river as they could, and they needed to maintain an element of unpredictability. The creature he had seen on the other side had taken off to the west. At the rate it was moving, it would easily beat them to the bridge.

They burst from a thicket of larches and sprinted across a meadow spotted with locus flowers and puddles dappled with rain. The rugged foothills rose ahead of them, maybe a mile through the dense forest of sandalwoods and lychees. Somewhere up there was the escarpment with the hanging graves. If they could just find it, he would be able to pinpoint their location well enough that they could work down through the hills and approach the bridge from the north along the rocky bank where the cover was thicker. And even then there were no guarantees, but unspoken between them was the understanding that if they couldn't cross the bridge, then they'd rather go out with their lungs filled with water than in the same manner as Julian and Warren.

Adrianne's hand slipped from his and she collapsed onto her chest.

Brooks turned around, took her by the hand again, and helped her up to her knees. There was blood on her lips and chin and her eyes didn't quite focus on his.

He pulled his sleeve over his hand and used it to wipe away the blood.

"Are you all right?"

"Just tired."

She offered him a weak smile and he saw the blood on her teeth and along her gums. He tried not to let the surprise show on his face.

"I can't possibly look that bad," she said.

He placed his palm on her forehead and looked directly into her eyes. Her skin was waxy and she was burning up.

"How long have you known?" he asked.

She shrugged.

"It's coming on faster now. I can feel it. The pain in my mouth is getting worse by the minute."

"We need to get you to a hospital."

She rested her palm against his cheek. He felt her long nails against his ear.

"I was so desperate to impress you when we first met. Do you remember that day?"

"Don't talk like that."

"At first I wanted you to see how brilliant I was, how perfect I was for the institute. I wanted you to need me. And then . . . and then I just wanted you."

"I'll carry you out of here myself if I have to."

"The problem is we've been looking at this species all wrong. The Lotka-Volterra equation doesn't apply because we're not dealing with the traditional predator-prey relationship. We're looking at them from our perspective, not theirs. What we're dealing with is a complex dynamic more closely resembling that of a host-parasite relationship, which is governed by the Nicholson-Bailey model. The parasite — or virus in this case — searched for and chooses its hosts at random, but only those that are genetically susceptible to it become infected, which is why the model is inherently unstable. It's that instability that allows for coevolution in the first place. We need to stop thinking about them as a discrete species and start thinking of them as human beings. We have to ask ourselves what we would do if we were them."

"We would leave here."

"So why haven't they? All of these years and they're still here."

Brooks thought of the house with the shutters and doors that looked like they'd been attacked by animals.

"I think they do leave."

"So why do they come back? Why do they stay here?"

Brooks had no answer.

He pulled her to her feet and plucked a lotus flower. Its petals cradled a small amount of rainwater. He offered it to Adrianne, who thanked him with a nod and swished the water around in her mouth before swallowing it. She licked her teeth and smiled again. The blood was gone, but her gums were red and swollen.

He had ibuprofen in his pack, but there was no way they could go back for it now. Maybe they could sneak into the cave where Warren died and raid his supplies. They needed to find a way to lower her fever and reduce the inflammation . . .

He furrowed his brow and turned in a circle. It took a moment, but he eventually saw what he was looking for. He guided her toward a cluster of plants, one of which had a stalk covered with tiny pink bulbs and leaves reminiscent of those of a dandelion. He gripped it near the base and pulled it out of the ground.

"Thank you, Julian," he said, brushing the dirt from the roots and handing it to Adrianne. "Alpine bistort. Eating the roots produces an anti-inflammatory response every bit as potent as ibuprofen."

She stared down at it for several seconds before bringing it first to her nose, then to her lips. Her eyes met his when she took the first bite. She winced and took another. Then another still.

He took her hand and pulled her again toward the northwest and the waiting cliffs.

Something she'd said continued to bother him as they entered the forest. If these creatures — these new men — retained even a small amount of their humanity, they would want to go home. It was the most powerful instinct and one common to every species. They would have been terrified by the physical transformation and crippled by the pain. In their position, his lone thought would be of crossing the Himalayas by any means and finding his way back home. The only way he would have stayed here in this horrible place was if he no longer knew where home was. And the only way that could happen while he maintained even the smallest semblance of cognitive function was if he no longer remembered where home was.

Suddenly, everything became clear.

"Profound retrograde amnesia," he said.

"What?"

She was panting and out of breath. He slowed and looped her arm over his shoulders so he could ease her burden.

"It's a condition generally attributed to severe head trauma; however, there've been a ton of documented cases caused by viral sources like encephalitis and even herpes simplex, the common cold sore. They not only cause memory impairment, but extreme agitation and dramatic changes in personality."

"The virus attacks the central nervous system."

"Specifically the thalamus and the hippocampal formations of the temporal lobes in the brain."

"Meaning it affects the cerebrum while leaving the brainstem intact. But they still have some residual language comprehension, so Broca's area and the frontal lobe must not be affected to the same degree. They're capable of emotion and complex problem solving without the restraints of conscience. They're running on instinct and emotion, and that's the surest recipe for violence and aggression."

"That violence is generally indiscriminate, though. These things attacked as a pack. Their movements were coordinated. That's more suggestive of, at worst, localized brain damage. And if you think about infections like encephalitis and herpes, it's the acute swelling of the brain itself that poses the greatest threat. It's possible the chronic inflammatory nature of this viral infection is responsible for increased and sustained pressure on the lateral parts of the brain, if not for shunting blood flow entirely to the areas in question."

"So if we can effectively combat the swelling—"

"We can theoretically prevent the localized brain damage."

"But for how long?"

Brooks knew the answer to her question was of significant personal consequence, but without any pharmaceutical-grade anti-inflammatories, they were
counting on finding a large quantity of roots that might not even work. The
prospect was depressing, and yet he couldn't allow her to give up hope.

"As long as it takes."

He squeezed her hand and guided her through a maze of longan and
durian trees, which opened onto a clearing that afforded him a better view of
their surroundings. The river was a clearly delineated line through the treetops
of the valley below them and to the south. The hills grew steeper and more
heavily forested to the west, forming a transition zone of sorts between the
river and the mountains. The main path ran somewhere through there,
although from here he couldn't quite tell where. The trees to the northwest
blocked his view of the plateau where they had camped and the broad meadow
at the base of the cliff honeycombed with tombs. Maybe another half-mile to
the north and then back to the west and they could approach the escarpment
from the forest above it, instead of walking out into the open field.

It seemed like a logical course of action, but to get there they would have
to pick their way through the woods where Zhang had been taken.

The drizzle waned and the humidity skyrocketed. The clouds thinned
enough that he could see the sun already sinking toward the rugged western
horizon. No matter how hard he wished, he couldn't slow its descent. They
needed to cross that bridge while they could still see well enough to do so.
They wouldn't be able to survive another night in this awful place, nor would
they be able to indefinitely stall the progression of the virus.

They walked in a silence marred only by the crunching of their footsteps
on the wet detritus. Already Adrianne's hand was starting to feel warmer.
They had to find more of the bistort root. Brooks tried to remember anything
else Julian had showed him that could prove helpful. He wished he'd been
paying closer attention.

The dull headache that had been with him most of the day had blossomed
into a throbbing migraine. He'd always been prone to headaches when he
didn't get enough sleep, though, and he couldn't remember the last time he
had anything even remotely resembling a decent night's rest. Maybe Pai
Village, which had been what, five days ago? That was too long for anyone to
go without allowing his body to recuperate. It was no wonder every muscle

and joint in his body ached. And with the way the storms came and went, bringing with them warring pressure fronts, it would be abnormal if his sinuses didn't hurt. There was no point in analyzing every little ache and pain, even if he did have the subtle metallic taste of blood in his mouth.

He spat on the ground and was relieved to see little more than the faintest pink hue.

The hills sloped sharply away from them to the west, forcing them to climb higher if they intended to follow the topography and utilize the diminishing cover. Massive rock formations reared up from the trees, which grew sparser as they walked. They had a much better view of the valley below them, where they could now clearly see the grasslands and the sheer cliffs that enclosed them, among them the one housing the cave where Warren had been killed. The waterfall no longer flowed and the pond had shrunk to a quarter of its former size, leaving behind a ring of muddy weeds and debris. While he still couldn't see the escarpment where they'd left their equipment inside the tombs, he had a good enough feel for where they were to find his way there.

Maybe he hadn't fully formulated a plan for what they would do once they reached it, but at least he knew where they could find more bistort when they . . .

In his mind he saw Julian, kneeling in front of the pink-flowered plant. Something about the image set off alarm bells and derailed his line of thought, yet, for the life of him, he couldn't figure out why. He remembered the grad student sifting through the dead leaves and weeds around its roots, then looking up at him with a huge grin on his face.

Nature provides everything you need to survive in any given environment. You just have to know where to look for it.

Brooks nearly had it when Adrianne gasped and tugged on his hand.

He stopped and followed her line of sight to the northwest, toward where he could now see the crest of the hill on top of the escarpment where he had first climbed out of the tombs.

"You still have that gun?" he asked.

"There's only one bullet."

"If we have to use it, we're dead already."

He struck off through the trees as quietly as possible toward where two wooden caskets now rested beside the hole in the earth.

PART IX

Speciation

41

Today

They approached the ledge from the east. Cautiously. Quietly. The scent of sandalwood wafted from the orifice, but they could neither see nor hear anything transpiring below. Brooks raised his ax as he neared the coffins. They were the same as all of the others: hand-carved from a single trunk. Coils of rope were heaped on the ground beside them, presumably the means by which they would be lowered over the ledge, through the vegetative screen, and into the tombs.

Adrianne covered him with the pistol, although they'd agreed that she would only fire as a last resort. They needed to hold on to that lone bullet for as long as they could.

There were partial footprints in the mud with smooth, rounded edges. They could have been left by any kind of shoe or sandal. The flattened weeds and bare granite gave no indication of how the caskets had come to be here or who had brought them. Only the incense suggested that anyone was still here.

Brooks watched the mouth of the chute as he quietly slid back the lid of the nearest coffin. He glanced down and then quickly at Adrianne, who surveyed the tree line uphill along the barrel of the gun before joining him. He held up a hand to stop her, but she brushed it aside and stared down at the remains.

Warren wasn't immediately recognizable. The left side of his face was crushed and the right was a mask of blood. His skin was pale and waxy and bloated with absorbed water. Flies crawled all over him, as though oblivious to the intrusion on their meal. His arms had been crossed almost peacefully over his chest. His clothes were still wet and muddy and his gut distended with the gasses of early decomposition. It was hard to believe that mere hours ago this had been the same living, breathing entity with whom they had spent every moment of the last week. And now he was dead.

Brooks felt a surge of anger and helplessness.

He closed the lid with tears in his eyes and opened the other coffin.

Zhang had fared no better. His jaw was broken and jutted to the side, where his cheek had been torn back to his ear. The ends of broken ribs protruded from the front of his sweater, which was black with blood. His arms were similarly crossed over his chest, although the left had been placed over the right to hide the stubs where two of his fingers appeared to have been bitten off. His abdomen—

Brooks turned away. He could think of no worse way to die. Whoever gathered his remains had at least managed to stuff most of him back inside.

A clattering sound from the hole.

Adrianne silently closed the lid while Brooks walked toward the hole. He wanted nothing more than to drive the pick straight through the skull of whoever was down there. Two men lay dead in the coffins that would be used to hide their remains where they would theoretically never be found. And whoever was down there was responsible for keeping the secrets of this horrible place.

The clattering grew louder.

Brooks waved Adrianne back. She ducked behind Zhang's coffin and peered around the side. He crouched between the hole and the edge of the cliff. If he was right and the sounds were the result of someone ascending the ladder, then whoever it was would have his back to him when he climbed out.

He adjusted his sweaty grip on the handle of the ice ax. Tensed the muscles in his legs in anticipation of lunging.

The crown of a bald head appeared, followed by a slender neck, and shoulders draped with the sashes of a red robe.

Brooks sprung and wrapped his left arm around the man's neck. He jerked him backward and partially out of the hole, and pressed the tip of the pick against his throat, right under the curve of his jaw.

The man made a gagging sound and grabbed Brooks's left arm.

"How many more of you are there?" Brooks whispered.

The man didn't respond.

Brooks pressed harder on the pick and felt the warmth of blood trickle onto his arm. He asked again, but still the man said nothing, so he forced the tip even deeper, caught the edge of the man's jaw, and used it to turn his face.

The man made more gagging sounds, but didn't say a word. The skin on his head and neck were nearly black with *sak yant* tattoos, the kind tapped into the skin using a sharpened bamboo stick. He recognized the *Ongk Phra*, or Buddha's Body, meant to provide insight and guidance; the *Sii Yord*, or Four Spires, designed for protection; the *Ha Thaew*, or Five Rows, which promised good luck; the *Paed Tidt*, or Eight Points, which granted protection in the eight directions of the universe; and the *Yord Mongkut*, or Spired Crown, which promised good fortune in combat. Read together, they told the tale of a long-suffering monk whose battles with both the inner and the outer worlds were equally real. They also spoke of a man whose spiritual beliefs were of greater consequence than any amount of pain he could experience in the flesh.

"How many others are down there?" Brooks whispered directly into the monk's ear.

When no answer came, he wrenched the man all the way out of the hole, pinned him on his back, and pressed his forearm against the man's throat with all of his weight. The man's pale skin immediately started to redden, highlighting the perfectly symmetrical *Suea*, the twin tiger tattoos facing each other from opposite sides of his face. Their tails framed his eyes like question marks and their serpentine bodies curled around his nose. His lips fit perfectly between their ferocious jaws and slashing claws. It was a tattoo meant to demonstrate power and authority, but it wasn't nearly as striking as the blue of his eyes or the birthmark on his right temple. The same blue eyes and birthmark he recognized from the pictures of Brandt's expedition they had found inside the cave.

Brooks could only stare at the face hidden beneath the tigers. The monk had shaved his head so recently that not even the stubble showed. His skin was taut and leathered by the sun. There were crow's feet beside his eyes, but few other wrinkles or signs of aging. Even his eyes themselves held the intangible quality of youth.

He imagined Brandt wasting away in his wheelchair, his flesh clinging to his bones like melting taffy. There was no way this could be the same man from the photographs. Birthmarks themselves were hereditary, but Brooks had never known one to appear in the exact same place in subsequent generations. This man couldn't have been more than fifty-some years old, if that. He barely looked older than the man in the old black and white pictures.

"Jesus," Adrianne whispered from behind him.

Brooks looked back to see her pointing the pistol over his shoulder and at the monk's face. She wore the same expression of surprise he must have been wearing.

He stared again at the man. His robe marked him as a monk of the Mahayana or Tibetan tradition, who wore red as a symbol of their compassion and kindness toward all other beings. Even with the tattoos altering his face, he would have sworn this was the same man.

Brooks knew enough German to bumble his way through simple conversations. He pointed at the hole and looked the monk right in the eyes when he spoke.

"*Wieviel?*"

The man's face showed a flash of recognition, but he said nothing. Brooks raised the ax into striking position. A droplet of blood fell from the tip of the pick, landed on one of the tigers, and dribbled into the well of his ear.

The monk's eyes widened and he held up three fingers.

"*Drei?*" Brooks said.

He felt the monk try to nod against his forearm and lessened the pressure just enough for him to accomplish the gesture. Brooks's head was spinning. Here was a man who was physically identical to a scientist that never returned from an expedition nearly three-quarters of a century ago and who spoke the same language, and yet this man appeared barely older than he was and nowhere near as frail as Brandt.

"Ask him if he was part of the König Expedition," Adrianne said.

The monk glanced at her from the corner of his eye.

"You understand what she said, don't you?"

The man looked back at Brooks, but communicated nothing with his eyes.

"He recognized the name," Adrianne said.

"We found König's body in the tombs," Brooks said, and pointed down into the hole beside them.

The monk couldn't hide the comprehension in his eyes.

Brooks struggled to recall anything and everything he had learned in German, rudimentary though his knowledge was.

"*Was ist ... deine ... Name?*"

The man's brow wrinkled and he looked almost confused.

Brooks removed his arm from the monk's neck, but kept the ax raised in striking position. The monk rubbed his throat and the blood slowly drained from his face.

"*Mein Name ist Jordan.*"

The man tapped his lips and made a gesture like sound coming out. He opened his mouth and Brooks saw the nub where his tongue had been cut out.

"You have no tongue ... *no Zunge?*"

The man nodded cautiously.

"So you can't speak ... *nicht sprechen?*"

Again, the monk nodded and held up his hands. He glanced at the ax, then at Brooks, and then back at the ax.

Brooks lowered the ax without breaking eye contact.

"*Was ist deine Name?*"

The man looked at him without blinking.

Brooks had recognized both Brandt and König in the pictures, but he couldn't be certain about the others, especially considering the names had been written out of order.

"Eberhardt?" he said.

The man shook his head. There was an element of sadness in his eyes.

"Metzger?"

Again, he shook his head.

"Wolff?"

Another shake.

"Well, it can't be König or Brandt."

The monk nodded. A wistful smile formed on his lips.

A clattering sound arose from the hole.

Brooks realized they'd been too loud, but he couldn't give up. Not yet. Not while they were so close to finally getting some answers.

"König?"

Adrianne aimed the gun at the hole as a face appeared. It bore the same *Suea* tattoo.

"It can't be Brandt."

The man glanced at the other tattooed monk and held up a hand. The second man stopped where he was, but never took his eyes off Adrianne's gun.

More clattering sounds from below them as feet struck the rungs of the ladders.

"You're not Brandt," Brooks said. "I know Johann Brandt. You aren't his son and you certainly aren't him. You look nothing like him."

"I don't like this," Adrianne said. "He's stalling."

She was right and Brooks knew it. The monk was lying to them in hopes of buying time, but for what?

"Down the hole," Brooks said. *"Zu gehen . . . unter."*

He grabbed the monk by the sash and pushed him toward the earthen orifice. The second monk scrambled down and out of the way. The man who was trying to mislead them into thinking his name was Brandt extended his arms and caught the lip before he fell. Brooks shoved him in the midsection with his foot and the man dropped out of sight.

"Don't let them out of there," Brooks said.

Adrianne stepped forward and aimed the gun down into the darkness while Brooks lunged for the boulder. He shoved it over the hole, grabbed Adrianne's hand, and dragged her toward the trail.

42

Today

The threat of being shot would only buy them so much time, and the boulder even less. They needed to be as far away as possible when the monks made their way out. Tibetan monks weren't known for their pacifism and they outnumbered Brooks and Adrianne two-to-one. Brooks didn't know how they fit into the puzzle that was Motuo, but the way Brooks saw it, the fact that they were responsible for hiding the bodies of the victims made them complicit in the killings.

He couldn't understand what the monk had to gain by lying to them about his identity, which made him question everything the man had attempted to communicate to them, yet there was no denying his staggering resemblance to the man in the old photographs. And how did they manage to travel through this hunting ground without being attacked by the predators?

They slowed only long enough to grab the bistort Julian had initially shown him. Brooks pried it out by the roots and was already starting to run again when he remembered the grad student sifting through the detritus and what he had said.

What you see here is actually two distinct species. Hepialus humuli — the ghost moth — spends the majority of the larval stage of its life cycle underground, feeding on the roots of plants like this bistort, where it inadvertently comes into contact with a fungus known as Ophiocordyceps sinensis. It either ingests a spore or inhales the mycelium, which allows the fungus to colonize the caterpillar's body and turn it into one big reproductive vessel. This little sprout is actually the fruiting body of the fungus. Essentially one really ugly mushroom.

He stopped abruptly and jerked Adrianne to a halt. He passed her the bistort, grabbed a handful of the loam, and shoved it into his pocket.

People in Tibet and China have been eating them for their anti-aging and aphrodisiac effects for thousands of years. Only recently have we discovered that they increase the production of ATP in the body, dramatically improving stamina and physical endurance, and their cancer fighting properties are off the charts.

That's what his subconscious had been trying to make him remember. What was cancer if not the rapid and uncontrollable division of the body's own cells where they had no business growing? That was precisely what was happening with the mutations already beginning to manifest inside of them. The spontaneous genesis of teeth was no different than the proliferation of a tumor. If they could slow — or even stop — their growth, then they could potentially buy themselves enough time to reach medical attention.

If they managed to survive that long.

Brooks lowered his shoulder and barreled through the branches. Once they reached the end of the trail, they would be forced to break cover and cross the open field. It was their point of greatest exposure. Once they crossed it to the northwest, Brooks was confident they could find the northern bend in the river and work their way back south to the bridge. It was just a matter of getting there.

The monks were surely already out of the chute and knew exactly which direction they had gone. While the path was the obvious choice, it was also the route of least resistance and the fastest passage. They couldn't risk allowing the forest to slow them down any more than they could take the chance of it dictating their course.

Branches slashed his forearms and face. He tasted blood in his mouth and prayed the lacerations on his lips were the source. He burst from the forest before he saw the clearing and sprinted through the knee-high grasses. The sun was closer to the horizon than he'd expected and was already beginning to darken from gold to a brilliant bronze. In mere hours, it would sink behind the mountains and strand them in darkness.

He glanced up and to his right and saw the silhouettes of four men on top of the precipice, their robes flagging on the breeze. None of them moved. They just watched as Brooks and Adrianne dashed across the field.

Brooks fixed his eyes upon the opening of a narrow gully and ran straight for it. When he looked back again, the monks were gone.

The bottom of the gully was filled with standing water and uprooted trees above which a cloud of mosquitoes hummed. The slope was slick with mud and they fell repeatedly, but eventually reached higher ground and the traction provided by the moldering detritus and the pine trees. The mosquitoes swarmed around them, but Brooks no longer had reason to fear them. The way he felt now left no doubt that he'd already been infected. His head throbbed and his mouth hurt, and every muscle in his body felt like it was on fire even as his skin grew colder and prickled with goosebumps.

Looking back, there was only one point in time when they all could have been infected at the same time, and that was when they crossed through the leech zone. At the time he hadn't given the slightest thought to the potential for transmission. In his mind, he equated leeches with the act of sucking blood and didn't consider the fact that after doing so they metabolized the blood and became vectors to pass along the infection. They weren't like bees, which could only sting once. They continued to aggressively feed throughout their lifecycles, passing along whatever blood-borne pathogens resided in their digestive tracts through their anticoagulatory enzymes. He'd been so fixated on traditional vectors like the mosquitoes that eagerly made pincushions out of him that he'd neglected to take the proper precautions against the more uncommon species, especially, in this case, one whose intestines produced endogenous exopeptidases — enzymes that broke down proteins one pair of amino acids at a time, essentially unzipping the DNA of the infection and passing it along in various stages of degradation, making its expression in the host not only variable, but unpredictable. It was like playing craps with each of their individual genomes.

That was why their symptoms had all come on in different ways and at different times. None of them had received the exact same version of the virus that was now replicating itself unchecked inside all of their cells. The intact portion of the virus to which each of them had been exposed could have varied by any amount of an estimated five thousand base pairs, depending upon where the peptidases broke the chain of DNA. Considering it took only three base pairs to express something as dramatic as eye color, the physical expression from one individual to the next could be dramatically different.

Adrianne fell, only this time she made no effort to rise.

Brooks dropped to his knees beside her and rolled her onto her back. The left side of her face was brown with mud and she was barely able to keep her eyes open. He could positively feel the heat radiating from her.

"Not much farther now," he said. "You can make it."

The ghost of a smile formed on her lips.

"Go on without me. I'm just . . . slowing you down."

"No chance of that."

She still clung to the bistort, the roots of which were only half consumed. He brushed off the dirt and held it to her lips, then fished around in his pocket until he found several of the larvae with the fungi growing from them.

"Sorry about this," he said, and slipped them into her mouth when she opened it to take a bite of the roots.

The carcasses made crunching sounds between her teeth, but she didn't protest.

He took her by both hands, pulled her to her feet, and wrapped his arm around her back. She managed half a dozen steps before her legs gave out and she dragged both of them down.

"Come on, Adrianne. You have to help me. You can do this."

He rolled onto his side, draped her arms around his neck, and struggled to all fours with her on his back. He grabbed her around the thighs and bellowed with the exertion of standing. Her grip around his neck was weak, forcing him to lean forward as he walked. The strain was phenomenal. He focused on anything and everything else to distract his mind, but the grim reality of the situation was that unless she regained enough strength to walk on her own, there was no way he was going to be able to get her to safety.

Her grip grew weaker by the minute. Her head fell forward and rested on his shoulder. He could feel her fever, even through his clothing and over his own. She had to be well over 104 and still climbing. It was only a matter of time before brain damage started to occur.

He needed to cool her down and fast.

Brooks staggered on. She seemed to become heavier with each step he took. Balance grew increasingly untenable until he finally toppled forward onto the ground underneath her.

"I need you to help me, Adrianne. I know you can hear me. I can't do this without you."

He tried to stand again, but made it only as far as his knees before collapsing onto his side.

Brooks crawled out from beneath her, stood, and dragged her by her wrists. He alternately glanced back over his shoulder to see where he was going and down at her face. Her eyes were closed, her eyelids dark with the early stages of bruising. Her skin was pale . . . so pale. Her mouth hung open and her head bobbed limply. There was blood on her lips and he couldn't tell if she was breathing. The pulse in her wrists was so weak he could barely feel it.

"Stay with me," he said.

Tears cut wet trails through the dirt on his face. He bared his teeth against the awful strain in his back and shoulders. His breath came in shivering bursts from his nose.

Her wrists slipped from his grasp. He stumbled, caught his heels, and fell hard onto his back. His entire body cried out in pain when he attempted to stand. He had to settle for crawling back to where she lay, her hair tangled with pine needles and clotted with mud. Her eyelids had parted just enough to reveal bloodshot crescents of the sclera.

"Hold on. Do you hear me? Just hold on."

He grabbed a fistful of her jacket and dragged her over the rocky rise. The sound of the distant river taunted him.

They were so close now. Just a little farther . . .

And yet he knew there was no way he could even get her as far as the bridge. As it was, he was so exhausted he feared he wouldn't be able to make the trek on his own.

The thought of dying here was more than he could bear. His survival instincts screamed for him to abandon her, but he couldn't bring himself to do it. At least not yet. Not until . . .

Not until what? Until she died? Or worse . . . until she changed?

There was standing water at the bottom of the steep hill and around the trunks of a thicket of birches. Their leaves were already yellowing from the saturation of their roots. The muddy water had to be significantly cooler than the ambient air, and would only get colder as the sun set. It was their only chance.

He heard Julian's voice in his head.

Nature provides everything you need to survive in any given environment.

Brooks dragged Adrianne down the rugged slope. They slid on gravel and mud alike and tumbled through thorn-bushes that tore their clothes and cut their skin. By the time they reached the bottom, Brooks's palms and knees flowed freely with blood. He removed the pistol from beneath her waistband and inserted it under his own. With the last of his strength, he pulled Adrianne through the muddy weeds and into the water.

The cold provided a physical shock and momentarily cleared the fever-induced fog that clouded his thoughts. Mosquitoes swarmed over the stagnant water, which produced a vile smell reminiscent of hardboiled eggs and flatus. He sank deeper into the mud as he worked his way through the maze of trunks until he reached a point where the water was more than a few inches deep. He turned and cradled Adrianne under her head and upper back and scooted until he found an isolated area from which he could barely see through the trees and even the crimson rays of the setting sun hardly reached them. He lowered the base of her skull into the cold water.

Her eyes snapped open and she stared at his face. Her pupils were uneven and her nostrils were crusted with blood. When she spoke, her teeth shimmered with fresh blood.

"It's too . . . late . . . for me. You must . . . must go . . . "

"Shh. Save your strength. We need to cool you off if we hope to break your fever."

Her lips parted as though she were about to speak, but her eyes closed and she let out a long sigh.

Brooks searched through the mud until he found a large stone and used it to prop her head far enough out of the water. He emptied his pocket of the crisp worms and placed one against her lips, but she made no effort to chew it.

He separated the rest from the detritus, tossed a couple into his mouth, and saved the remainder for Adrianne.

He covered her body with leafy branches and found a dry patch on which to set the gun. He lowered himself into the water beside her. It couldn't have been less than sixty degrees, but it felt like an ice bath. The clarity in his mind faded as the cold worked its way through his entire body.

He managed to drag a branch with muddy leaves out of the muck and cover himself with it before his eyes closed of their own accord. He took Adrianne's hand in his as the world ceased to exist.

43

Yarlung Tsangpo River Basin
Motuo County
Tibet Autonomous Region
People's Republic of China
October 17ᵗʰ

Today

Brooks awakened wracked with violent shivers. His teeth chattered so hard it felt like he'd cracked them. The taste of blood in his mouth was overwhelming. He rolled to his side and dribbled a mouthful into the water.

He spat again and focused on his surroundings. The dead leaves draped over his face made it hard to see. He removed the branch and let it sink into the mire.

To his left, Adrianne's shivering created tiny ripples that reflected the moonlight, which barely provided enough illumination for him to tell that the bruising around her eyes hadn't gone away, but it hadn't gotten worse either. Her irises moved restlessly beneath her lids. He cautiously touched her forehead and found it blessedly cool.

Night had fallen, and with it the darkness he would have done anything to avoid. They were now at a distinct disadvantage. Not only could they hardly see and were totally unfamiliar with this part of the forest, but the lost time had surely allowed their pursuit to close whatever gap they had opened. The predators could be anywhere by now.

And then there were the monks, who passed through the killing grounds with impunity. Brooks wished he knew how they accomplished such a feat. He didn't buy into the notion that the tattoos provided some mystical source of protection any more than he believed the men were spared because of their devoutness. The problem was that he knew absolutely nothing about them. He had no idea where they came from or where they went, to which temple they belonged, or even which sect. All he knew was that wherever they went, the scent of sandalwood followed.

Brooks sat up and listened. He heard the faraway grumble of the Yarlung Tsangpo and the whispering of the wind through the leaves. Regardless of whether or not there was anything else out there, they could only stay here for so much longer. They needed to take advantage of their diminished fevers before they spiked again, and already he could feel the resurgence of the heat and the pain that had been mercifully alleviated by the cold water.

He tucked the pistol down the back of his pants, marked the spot where he left Adrianne, and crawled to the edge of the thicket, where he lay in the mud in the tall grass while he surveyed his surroundings.

Nothing moved.

Jackdaws and warblers shrieked in the distance and he heard the solitary hoot of a rhesus monkey from the other side of the river. The boughs of the trees swayed on a gust of wind, then stilled again. He risked climbing out into the open and stood up to better see.

The river was maybe a quarter mile ahead through the trees. He could just barely make out the rocky precipice, beyond which a mist had settled into the canyon. The bridge had to be roughly a mile to the south, a distance that was simultaneously short and seemingly insurmountable. He listened for a full minute longer before crawling back into the water and quietly moving through the trees.

Again, he thought of the monks and how they secured safe passage.

If they were truly dealing with an evolved version of *Homo sapiens*, a predatory offshoot resulting from speciation, then the best place to start was to catalogue the points of divergence. They had obviously followed the established natural progression when it came to their teeth, and yet the growth of hair over their entire bodies felt like a devolution of sorts, a step backward toward their remote forest ape ancestors. Their musculature was advanced, and yet they'd taken to the trees like primates. They had retained at least some amount of their higher mental faculties, while they appeared to hunt by instinct rather than by intelligence or cunning.

Therein lay the key.

How were they hunting them? Surely in the time he and Adrianne were unconscious in the water their tracks could easily have been discovered and followed, unless that wasn't how they hunted. They'd lain in wait in the dense forest where the runoff had piled debris across the path and after the majority of the creatures fell into the river, the lone remaining individual had taken off in the direction of the bridge, or so Brooks had assumed.

Maybe their vision had become sharper and they hunted from the trees to take advantage of their increased visual acuity. If so, then crashing through the dense canopy was almost counterintuitive. They would effectively be blinded by all of the leaves and branches. Besides, primates had evolved stereoscopic vision in order to escape predation, not so they could prey on other animals from above. And no sensory adaptation came without a price. Like blind men developed better hearing to compensate for their loss of sight, primates purchased superior sight at the expense of . . .

"Their sense of smell," Brooks whispered.

Modern humans had roughly twice as many OR pseudogenes — the genetic basis for the sense of smell — than their closest primate relatives. If this trend continued and this new species not only regained functionality of the genes, but acquired even more, then it was a distinct possibility that their sense of smell could rival that of a bloodhound. Was it possible that the monks used the scent of sandalwood, which flourished all around them, to mask their scent from the predators, and if so, could he and Adrianne do the same?

The mud squelched underneath him and issued a bubble that burst on the surface with the stench of rotten eggs. It was so strong it made his eyes water.

He crawled to Adrianne's side and removed the branches he'd used to hide her.

"Time to move," he whispered.

Her eyelids fluttered and parted just far enough to reveal the hint of her irises.

"I c-can't . . . f-feel . . . my l-legs."

Her teeth chattered when she spoke and her body tightened with muscular contractions beyond her control.

"Just hold on to me and don't let go."

She offered a weak smile and touched the side of his face with a hand that felt like ice. Her eyes opened just far enough that she could see him, but she didn't appear to be able to focus on him.

"It's h-happening so . . . f-fast now . . . I c-can f-feel it . . . everywhere . . . It . . . Oh, God . . . it h-hurts—"

"Save your strength. I'm getting you out of here."

Brooks cradled her against his chest and struggled to stand. Her added weight threw off his balance and he fell sideways into the water. He bit his lip to keep from crying out against the strain and tried to rise again. His legs trembled and every muscle protested, but he managed to find his feet. The mud sucked his feet clear past his ankles. Every step was a seemingly superhuman feat that brought with it the boggy stench of sulfur and rot. He made as little noise as he could as he slogged through the water and still it sounded like a herd of bison fording a stream. He had no choice but to throw caution to the wind and trade stealth for speed.

As it was, he was burning through what little strength he'd regained at a staggering rate and Adrianne barely had enough to wrap one arm around his neck. Her other arm hung against his thigh and swung with every movement, toying with his already tenuous balance.

They crashed through the reeds and onto the mercifully dry ground. The river called to them through the trees ahead. He watched the canopy for any sign of movement. The way the breeze riffled the leaves, he probably wouldn't have been able to recognize it regardless. Even if he were, there was nothing he could do about it. He was in no position to protect himself, let alone both of them. The only option was to head for the bridge as fast as he could and pray for a miracle.

And even if they crossed the Yarlung Tsangpo, they were far from in the clear. It wasn't as though the bridge served as some sort of magical barrier the hunters couldn't cross. For Brooks and his party to have been infected by the leeches, they had to have sucked the blood of this new species prior to sucking theirs, which meant they were more than a full day's travel under ideal conditions from the farthest known extent of the predators' range. And the trail through the Himalayas was still another day's hike from there. That was a full two-days' travel and he'd barely made it a hundred feet with Adrianne's dead weight across his chest and his legs were on the verge of giving out.

The reality of the situation came crashing down on him. It was all he could do not to despair.

He looked at Adrianne's pale face, rocking against his shoulder. The bruising around her eyes appeared to grow worse even as he watched. Her mouth hung open and blood dribbled down her chin. He didn't need to see her teeth to know what was happening inside. And even if they did escape and he got her to a hospital, what then? They weren't dealing with something as relatively innocuous as the common cold virus. This one was already making changes to her very genetic code at an alarming rate. There was no cure waiting or any known way to reverse the extent of the mutations. Their best hope was merely to stall the progression in the same way drugs were used to prevent HIV from turning into full-blown AIDS. And looking at her now, how could she hope to live like this for any length of time. She was in obvious pain and barely able to remain conscious for moments at a time. Were it not for the fact that he didn't know to what extent she'd been exposed to the virus, it would almost be a mercy to spare her the continued suffering. But as the virus degraded inside the leeches, this could be the worst the infection might ever get and her body could potentially adapt. Or she could continue to endure a painful physical transformation that ended with her becoming like the others.

The lips he'd kissed so recently glistened with blood and he felt the heat radiating from her. He saw the way her chest shuddered with each breath and the limpness of her appendages. If he left her — just set her down in the grass and walked away — she would die, but there was still a chance he might live. And yet there was no way he was going to leave her behind. Either they both made it or neither of them did. It was as simple as that.

Brooks kissed her on the forehead and steeled his resolve.

He scoured the forest for any sign of a path that might lead to an option he had yet to consider and watched the mist-shrouded canyon to his right for anything that might serve as an alternate means of crossing the river, as the fallen trees had earlier. He had to stop and lean against a pine tree before his legs gave out. His shoulders were on fire and he was losing feeling in his hands. He took a deep breath and propelled himself forward.

Another hundred feet and his legs crumpled underneath him. He fell to his knees and shouldered a tree to keep from landing on top of Adrianne. He feared if he went all the way down, he wouldn't be able to get back up again. Tears of frustration poured down his cheeks. He groaned as he fought back to his feet and staggered in the direction of the bridge.

He was beginning to feel a sense of inevitability. There was no way they were going to survive. Not at this rate and not with as loudly as they crashed through the branches and with the way the detritus crackled underfoot. It was only a matter of time before every animal in the forest knew they were here.

Brooks abruptly stopped and retraced that line of thought.

The corners of his lips curled upward and for the first time he felt something that might even have been hope.

He pressed on with a renewed sense of determination, the wheels in his mind turning as a plan slowly started to come together. It was a desperate gamble and one fraught with danger, but if it worked . . .

They crested a rise and found themselves on top of a granite formation, at the base of which the weak moonlight reflected from the stagnant floodwaters. The forest grew even denser as it approached the river. Mist moved silently through the upper canopy, obscuring the forest floor and all but the faintest hint of the trail. And downhill to his right he saw flickers of color.

Prayer flags.

He remembered how they'd been strung across the river. Somewhere in the mist beneath them was their only hope.

They'd finally reached the bridge.

44

Excerpt from the journal of
Hermann G. Wolff

*Courtesy of Johann Brandt, Private Collection
Chicago, Illinois
(Translated from original handwritten German text)*

March 1939

The censer fell from my hand and spilled cinders onto the ground, where they smoldered with an ethereal orange glow. The beasts stared at me through the smoke with those hideous eyes. They were human eyes. Of that I had no doubt. Not even then, before I knew for certain. These were the mythical people I had been sent to find, only they were anything but the Aryans we believed them to be. Maybe they had been, once upon a time, but now they were little more than animals. Mindless, soulless creatures that cared for nothing beyond the hunt, beyond the taste of blood in their mouths. I could no more share this discovery with my countrymen than I could anything else that had tran-

spired in this godforsaken land. To allow the world to see the Germanic peoples as savages descended from filthy apes would be to destroy what little self-respect we had built since our catastrophic defeat in the Great War.

Or so I thought at the time. It wasn't until later that I understood the truth, a truth I would share with no man for as long as I lived.

And so I stood there in the swirling smoke of the sandalwood and the damp leaves, waiting for my life to be ended. They watched me for several minutes more before returning their attention to their meal. They ate with abandon, tearing meat from bone and entire appendages from the trunk. They snapped and snarled at each other and fought for scraps. And when the carcass had been rendered bone and gristle, they shoved handfuls of the bloody dirt into their mouths.

I did not see the first of them leave; I only noticed that there were fewer of them. Perhaps there had been as many as a dozen. By the time the majority of the skeleton had been carried away, there were only three left to fight over the remaining bones. One grabbed an armful of disarticulated ribs and scampered into the forest, leaving the last two with little more than a broken skull from which the brains had already been consumed and vertebrae hollowed of the marrow.

One had the tangled white fur of an unkempt Maltese, knotted with briars, mud, and feces. Even when it stood its shoulders remained hunched. It looked up at me from beneath its matted hair and I saw the age in its eyes. It bared its yellow teeth and then snatched the skull from the ground and hobbled into the underbrush.

The lone remaining specimen dropped to all fours and dug in the dirt for any morsel it might have missed. It was thinner by half than the others and its hair was much shorter. The growth was patchy, longer on its head and face, shorter on its arms and flanks. Were it a hound I might have thought it afflicted with mange. And then it looked up at me and snarled and I knew . . . I knew right then and there exactly what it was.

It must have detected the change in my expression or scent — or perhaps it was merely at the mercy of its hunger — for it stood and approached me, slowly at first. It raised its head and sniffed the air, savoring it like the bouquet of a fine wine. When it looked at me again, there was recognition in its eyes and an expression of confusion on its face. Somewhere in the mind of the beast it recognized me as I had recognized it.

In retrospect, I believe there was still a part of my old friend Kurt inside of it, for its muscles tensed and I was certain it would run, but it hung its head and slunk toward me, deliberately and with an air of submission. It sniffed again and again as it neared until its face pressed against first the robe, and then my bare skin. When its face reached mine there were tears in its eyes and I knew what needed to be done.

I drew the Luger from beneath my robe and pressed it against the beast's heart. It closed its eyes and issued a hoarse growl, or what sometimes I find myself recalling as the sound of two words flowing together: kill me.

I know that must be a fiction of my mind's creation to justify what I did next, for if I ever for a second think of the beast whose blood decorated the surrounding trees as my fried Eberhardt, then I am wracked with grief. Instead I have come to terms with the fact that Kurt's soul departed his body when it changed, leaving nothing more than a base predator to inhabit what was left.

Without the yak, I could take no more than I could carry, so I was forced to prioritize as quickly as I could. The beasts might have been sated for the time being, but I had no doubt they would return again and this time no amount of incense or yak meat would save me. In that moment I experienced a measure of clarity I ascribed to the adrenaline flowing through my veins. I had seen with my own eyes what had become of Eberhardt. Something had caused that transformation and deep down I understood that I would spend every waking moment of the rest of my life trying to understand it. To that end, no amount of film or fur would help me, nor would any magnetic readings or maps. What I needed were the observations of a man more brilliant than I, a fellow naturalist of sorts whose journals I believed held the keys to proving the theories of revolutionaries like Charles Darwin. In these journals were the secrets to understanding man and God and the very future of our species, if indeed we were a single species. Perhaps the Aryans were not simply human, but rather something else entirely. Something more. Perhaps divinity was not a state of being, but a state of physicality. If men could grow fur and claws, then who was to say they could not grow the wings of an angel. The implications were staggering. There was no limit to the potential of Brandt's pseudo-science, of all of his observations and drawings. This was the future, the dawn of a new age of knowledge, a renaissance of anatomy and spirituality that would lead us to the hand of our Maker.

Brandt's precious case lay broken and emptied on the ground, his notebooks scattered. As I collected them I saw his bag of plaster and set to work without thinking. I had filmed him doing it enough times that it was second nature to me. I applied the plaster to the beast's face, smearing it from one side to the other in such a way as to follow the contours and make the hair lay as its patterns of growth dictated. I covered its entire face from the crown of its head to its neck and from behind one ear to the other. And when it was nearly dry, I pried it from the creature's face, loaded it into the trunk that had once belonged to Eberhardt himself, where I had already collected Brandt's journals, and set out walking.

I crossed the bridge under the cover of darkness and was nearly upon the house where I had spent the last three weeks when it started to rain. I heard the grunting of the yak to the north and understood why they had chained it where they did. It not only served as an offering to protect the household, but to cover the retreat of the monks should the beasts, for whatever reason, prove insatiable.

I found the monk I had shot at the bend where he'd collapsed in the mud, bleeding from a wound in his leg. Another half-kilometer and he would have reached the farm, where they would have treated his wounds and sent word to his monastery. But fortune was on my side this day and destiny decreed that my quest would continue.

He lay facedown in the mud, his robe drenched, his legs far paler than I would have expected, even taking into account the blood loss. I rolled him over and aimed the pistol at his head.

His face was stark white and covered with mud, but I would have recognized it anywhere, especially when he opened his blue eyes and stared first at the Luger and then into my eyes. I fell to my knees beside him and rejoiced that my friend was still alive, but Johann didn't share my enthusiasm. In fact, he looked at me as though I were the monster. He told me he understood what I intended to do, that he too had recognized the truth of what he'd seen in the valley. He said I cannot return to the Fatherland, that I must not share what I had learned here with anyone in a position of power within the Reich. He said they would misuse such wondrous knowledge for their own ends, that they would twist it and corrupt it into something dark and unholy.

He was right, I knew, and yet I had no intention of spending the rest of my life in this awful place as he suggested. I wanted no part of the monastic life or the teachings of any deity that demanded I give up all of my earthly possessions. I intended to learn everything I could not so I could be beholden to anyone's god, but rather so I could look Him in the eyes as his equal, one who had unveiled all of his mysteries and deciphered all of his riddles.

And when Brandt told me he could not allow me to do so, I showed him that he had no way of stopping me. I pointed the gun into his face and pulled the trigger, but the hammer fell upon an empty chamber. So I hit him with it instead, again and again, until I heard the nervous lowing of the yak and realized I had run out of time.

I could not allow him to talk, though, at least not until I was comfortably back on my way to civilization. And despite all evidence to the contrary, I was not a murderer. The first death was an accident, the second self-defense, and the third an act of mercy.

Brandt's calipers were in the trunk. I used them to pinch his tongue and draw it from his mouth. I rolled him onto his side, braced the pincers against his teeth, and raised my heel.

Seconds later I was on the move again, tracking the blood of my old friend on the path, his cry that preceded unconsciousness reverberating in my ears.

45

Today

I t was just under a quarter-mile away. Maybe a thousand feet. They'd come so far and were now so close . . .

From where he stood, clinging to the cover of the trees on the cliff, he watched the prayer flags alternately appear and disappear into the mist. To get there, they'd have to pick their way down the steep, rocky slope to his right, working their way closer to the river and the pitfall into its depths. From there it was a matter of wending through the dense foliage along the edge of the canyon to the mouth of the bridge. He followed the proposed route with his eyes, tracing the topography and working around the largest trees, the trunks of which he couldn't even see through the lush—

A localized section of the canopy swayed. Maybe a hundred feet from the bridge.

The boughs gently stilled. A heartbeat later, the branches of the adjacent tree bowed dramatically before being overtaken by the fog.

They were down there, lurking near the bridge, just as he'd expected.

He watched the trees for several minutes longer, but only the fog moved through the canopy, obscuring it beneath a creeping white haze. There was no way of telling how many of them were down there. For all he knew, it could only be the one he had seen across the chasm after they crossed the fallen pines. Or the trees could literally be crawling with them. If he and Adrianne could survive the river, then surely they could, too. He had to plan on there being at least four and pray the element of surprise worked in his favor.

And that Adrianne would be able to make it across the bridge without him.

Brooks stepped back and merged with the shadows of the trees and whispered into Adrianne's ear.

"I need you to wake up now."

She stirred and turned her face toward his. Her forehead was hot against his neck, despite how badly she shivered. She struggled to keep her eyes open and focused on him.

He knelt, set her on the ground, and propped her back against the trunk of a tree. Her eyes widened with fear and her lashes welled with tears.

"G-go on," she whispered. "I'll be . . . all right."

Brooks felt his heart break. She thought he was leaving her there and continuing without her.

He tipped up her chin so she couldn't look away.

"You're not getting rid of me that easily."

She tried to smile, but only ended up crying harder and clutching his hand.

He placed the rest of the bistort and the larvae in her palm. She stared down at them for a few seconds, then looked him in the eyes as she shoved them all into her mouth and started to chew.

Brooks leaned across her and pointed in such a way that she could see straight down his arm.

"See those flags? That's the bridge. I estimate the distance to be under a quarter-mile. You'll need to go down those rocks over there and cut through the forest along the edge of the gorge until you reach it. Once you cross, go as far as you can before you have to stop and find someplace to hide."

"I don't think—"

"You can do this, Adrianne. You're the most determined woman I've ever met. I need to you be that person now."

"What about you?"

"Just keep going. I'll catch up with you. And if I don't . . . Remember that old farmhouse with the shutters? The one we passed on the way in? Get there. I have a feeling they'll know what to do."

"Come with me."

"You'd better believe I'll be right behind you, but we won't get very far with them right on our heels."

"You can't be thinking of confronting—"

He kissed her with everything he had, willing his strength into her. And in that moment he made an unspoken promise to her that he fully intended to keep.

"Now listen carefully. This is the most important part. When you reach the bottom of this cliff, you need to cover yourself with mud as quickly as you can. Hurry and get as close as you dare, but don't attempt to cross until you hear my signal. Then get your butt across the river. I don't know how much time I'll be able to give you."

"How will I know the signal?"

He reached behind his back and removed the pistol from beneath his waistband.

"It'll be pretty hard to miss."

"But there's only one—"

"You just get yourself across the bridge. Trust me. I have everything worked out." He hoped his smile conveyed more confidence than he felt. "We need to hurry and make our move while we still can."

He stood and offered his hand.

Her hand shook when she reached for his. Her grip was weak, but to her credit she pulled herself up and stared down into the mist.

"Don't you dare leave me now," she whispered.

"Like I said, it's going to take a lot more than this to get rid of me."

He pulled her to him and kissed her one last time. Without a word, he turned and headed away from the river before he lost his nerve. He didn't look back. He had to trust that she would make it on her own or all of this was for naught.

His pulse thrummed so loudly in his ears it reminded him of the sound of primitive war drums. Each breath came faster until he was on the verge of hyperventilation. If this plan failed or the weapon somehow fired prematurely, he was going to get a really good look at whatever these things were.

He suddenly understood why Brandt — the Brandt from the institute bearing his name — had never come back. If he had seen even half of what Brooks had and escaped with his life, then the prospect of ever returning must have scared the living hell out of him. It was no wonder he opted to send others in his stead, especially knowing how close he must have come to one of them in order to cast its face. As it was, Brooks had seen little more than hairy shapes crashing through the branches and a silhouette from the distance. And despite all of the death and the lies and his growing fear, his professional curiosity had never been more aroused. He wanted to see one of them up close before he left or he'd never be able to forgive himself. It would be his greatest regret and one he'd have to live with for the rest of his life . . . because there was no way he was ever coming back.

There was a reason this secret remained so carefully guarded. With all of the technology at their disposal, geneticists could use the virus like a skeleton key to unlock the Pandora's box that was human evolution. Mankind had already demonstrated its willingness to advance science at all costs, even if it meant wielding it like a sword. People of all races and walks of life would be subjected to experimentation, both willingly and against their wills. Governments would set about creating super soldiers and corporations would use the knowledge to enslave humanity.

Brooks recalled Adrianne's words.

Nature perseveres, but in its own best interests, not in those of any particular species. The ecosystem must always remain in a state of balance. Any major shift would prove catastrophic.

Nature had found a way to contain this mutation inside of one of the most isolated regions on the planet. It was never meant to get out, but rather to serve as a small, but integral piece of the complex puzzle that was Motuo. The evolution of some subset of man as an apex predator released upon an unsuspecting world would be more than catastrophic; it would be an extinction-level event.

No evolutionary anthropologist could view it as anything else.

So why had Brandt sent other expeditions into this horrible place knowing that the secrets could never be made public knowledge, when even he had already shown his commitment to suppressing the discovery? It was a contradiction on so many levels. If anyone from Brooks's team managed to return home, they would undoubtedly be in some stage of infection. For whatever reason, Brandt wanted the virus, but he had no intention of sharing it. So what did he intend to do with it?

Brooks followed a game trail down from the high ground, clinging to the bushes that somehow grew from the steep slope. He skinned his knees and thrust his hands into brambles, but he hardly felt it. The throbbing in his head occupied all of his attention. He could feel the source of the pain in three dimensions, from his temples all the way inside to his corpus callosum and along the length of his optic nerves and into his eyes. The pressure in his sinuses was beyond anything he'd ever experienced.

He isolated the course of the main path — and the route of least resistance to the bridge — from just above the level of the canopy.

The rain started to fall once again as he descended into the camphorwoods and elms. The wind arose with a howl and violently tossed the upper reaches, which clamored with the siege of raindrops. He hadn't anticipated this contingency and its potential impact on his plan, but it was too late to worry about it now. Adrianne had to be nearing the bottom of the cliff by now, if not already smearing mud all over herself.

He found his own reeking pool swarming with mosquitos near the path. He had neither the time nor the patience to apply it. He simply dropped to the ground and rolled around in it until he was so covered he had to claw it out of his eyes and off of his lips. Maybe it was an unnecessary precaution, but he could think of no other reason the predators hadn't already found them.

He flung the excess mud from his hands. With as badly as he smelled, he'd want to stay as far away as possible, too.

The path was less than fifty feet away. He approached it with as much caution as he could afford. Even if Adrianne was still holding her own, whatever reserves she'd tapped wouldn't be bottomless.

Brooks stopped within clear sight of the trail. The way the trees shook, he couldn't tell if it was caused by the wind or something else. At least there was nothing standing on the path directly ahead of him, which was about as much as he could have hoped for.

He stepped out onto the trail and looked quickly one way, then the other.

Both directions led into deep darkness and overhanging trees. This section looked somewhat familiar, but not familiar enough to pinpoint his location. Maybe just under a third of a mile to his right was the bridge, now so far away he couldn't hear the river. Of course, with as hard as it was raining now, he probably wouldn't have been able to hear it anyway. At least it helped conceal the less than surreptitious sounds of his movements.

There was standing water on the path and he could feel the rain that penetrated the canopy washing the mud from his hair and down his neck. He couldn't risk staying out in the open for very long.

He drew the pistol from the back of his pants, made sure the safety was on, and then ducked into the bushes on the opposite side of the path. He found a camphorwood tree around which dozens of saplings shot up toward the gap in the canopy. The one he wanted was roughly three feet tall and grew directly beneath a sturdy horizontal branch of the larger tree. He stripped the leaves from the sapling and tore off all of the side branches until it was nothing but a long green stick rooted in the ground. The overhanging branch was roughly the width of his finger and bent easily with the application of pressure. He stripped it, too, and fed it straight through the trigger guard until the Type 54 hung from the branch above the naked sapling. He pushed down on the larger branch and threaded the tip of the sapling through the trigger guard as well, then pulled it back down upon itself. It bent like a stiff cord and pulled the gun downward with it, forcing the upper branch to bow and placing enough pressure on the trigger to fire the gun if the safety were disengaged. He tied the sapling back to itself as tightly as he could and held it in place while he inspected his work.

It wasn't prefect by any means, but it just might work.

He carefully released the sapling and watched the knot draw even tighter. It wouldn't hold forever, which was was the whole point.

He searched the ground around his feet and found a damp twig the width of a paintbrush. He broke off a piece about an inch in length and wedged it inside the trigger guard, only this time in the slim gap behind the trigger itself. It was barely wide enough to stay in place and would undoubtedly either fall out if jostled hard enough by the recoiling branch or snap in half under the steady application of sustained pressure.

Brooks stepped back and did his best to steady his hands. There was only one thing left to do.

He turned to the west and prepared to run for his life is this didn't work like he'd drawn it up in his head.

A deep breath in.

His heart hammered so hard and fast it was all he could hear.

Blew it out slowly.

He reached for the side of the pistol, right above the trigger . . .

And flipped off the safety catch.

PART X

YEH-TEH

46

Today

T he trigger bit down on the tiny stick, which bent against the pressure and made a distinct cracking sound, but didn't break.

It wouldn't last long, though.

Brooks glanced at the knot in the sapling. It was already starting to unravel.

His heart leapt into his throat.

It was going to fire too soon.

He dove away from the booby trap and crawled into the bushes. The ruckus of the storm assailing the upper reaches masked the sounds of his passage. He stayed low to the ground and moved as fast as he dared.

Ten feet.

Twenty.

He lowered himself to his belly to decrease his visibility and dragged himself though the mud with his elbows and knees.

Twenty-five feet.

Thirty.

He rolled over onto his back and used his heels alone.

Thirty-five feet.

Forty.

All the while he searched the trees overhead for any sign of the predators lurking in the shadows. The mud served to decrease the noise of his exertions and reduce the friction, making it so he almost glided across the ground.

He risked a faster pace. His heels squelched in the mud and his shoulders shook the branches. Faster still.

He lost track of his distance from the trap, but the farther he was from it when it went off, the better his chances.

Any second now the twig would snap or the knot would release and the gun would fire. When it did, he needed to be prepared for everything within earshot to converge on the sound.

And then he needed to be ready to run.

The boughs passed in the darkness above him. The shadows were alive with expectation. He saw silhouettes where there were none and movement behind the swaying branches and shivering leaves. He had no doubt that at any moment he would look up and see something looking back down at—

A piercing pain on the back of his head. It traveled through his skin and toward his left ear.

Brooks stopped and reached for his scalp. He felt the warmth of blood. The grime from his fingertips burned the laceration. He traced it toward his ear until he found where the thorny branch was still hooked under the skin.

The pain made his eyes water, but he resisted crying out. He pried it out and put pressure on the wound to stanch the bleeding. If he was right about their evolved sense of smell, then there was one scent that would summon them faster than all others, and that was fresh—

A dark shape materialized from the shaking branches overhead. Leaves and twigs fell to the ground all around him.

Brooks held his breath and watched as the silhouette drew contrast from the shadows. A hunched form crouched on a thick bough maybe twenty feet above him, holding on with both hands and feet. Its wet hair hung in ropes beneath it like Spanish moss. Its knees were bent straight up, its thighs pressed against its chest. Above them loomed a head with human contours and dimensions.

It rocked back, thrust its face to the sky, and drew a long inhalation he could hear from all the way down on the forest floor.

When it made no immediate move, Brooks nearly breathed a sigh of relief.

Its head snapped down and its body stiffened.

Even though he couldn't see its eyes, he could feel them scanning the bushes beneath which he hid.

Lightning flickered in the distance, freezing the raindrops in midair. He caught the merest flash of reflection from its eyes. And then they were gone.

Thunder crashed.

There was no longer anything up there.

Brooks slowly released his breath and held perfectly still. Had it not smelled him and moved on? He slowly bent his knees in preparation of pushing off again and—

Movement from the corner of his eye.

He turned to see the branches to his right part, then fall back into place.

His heart pounded so hard he feared it would give him away.

The bushes moved again, closer this time.

It knew he was in there.

He looked lower to the ground and saw the outline of two hairy legs through the leaves. They took a step closer. Paused. Took another still. He saw a foot with the great toe turned inward — a *hallux varus* configuration common in primates — like an opposable thumb on the foot.

A flurry of sniffing.

Brooks held his breath and pressed the back of his head into the mud in hopes of concealing the smell of his blood.

The branches were again ripped aside and he saw the silhouette of shoulders and the side of a face. Its prominent jaw bulged outward as though closing its lips over a slice of orange.

The leaves fell back into place and again he saw the movement of legs. Barely two feet from his right shoulder.

It would see him this time. There was no doubt in his mind. The leaves directly overhead shook as fingers with long, ragged nails reached into the bush and—

Thoom!

The entire shrub shook as the shadow bolted toward the source of the gunshot. Its legs flew past in a blur.

The report rolled through the valley.

Shadows darted through the canopy high above him, moving with such speed he could barely see them, let alone count how many of them tore through the foliage.

Brooks flipped over and propelled himself through the bushes and toward the path. He hit the trail running and prayed he'd given himself a big enough head start.

The branches whipped at him from either side. He threw his arms up in front of his face and tried to navigate the narrow corridor through the forest. The slick ground did its best to rob him of his balance. He was still so far from the river he could barely hear it.

A booming roar from behind him.

They'd discovered his ruse. The hunt was on.

Ahead, the fog descended through the lower canopy and surrounded the trunks, limiting visibility. The Yarlung Tsangpo called to him from a seemingly insurmountable distance.

He was already panting and the muscles in his legs burned. If he fell now, he feared he wouldn't be able to get up again. And even if he did, any time he lost would cost him what little separation he had.

The sound of the river grew louder until it became a physical force against his chest. The ground sloped steeply downward so abruptly that he left his feet and slid through the runoff into a waiting rhododendron, which helped him to struggle to his feet once more.

Crashing from the trees behind him, but he couldn't spare a backward glance. He knew what it meant.

They'd already caught up with him.

He wasn't going to make it.

More crashing sounds and swaying branches uphill to his left.

A flash of lightning froze the world around him. He saw raindrops and leaves and the pile of stones at the bend ahead, where the cairn had once stood.

The trees all around him positively shook.

He was so close . . .

Thunder pealed as he burst from the forest and sprinted toward the bridge. The wind buffeted him and assaulted him with raindrops. The thinning fog rolled past beneath the bridge at the behest of the gale.

Brooks ducked under the vines and tattered prayer flags and ran toward the far side with the drumming of his boots on the decrepit planks, which shuddered beneath his weight.

He prayed Adrianne had already made it across. If she hadn't, then he might as well have killed her himself.

He drew the ice axes from his belt and snapped the picks into place.

Five hundred feet.

The brown water called to him from so far down he could barely see it through the mist.

Four hundred fifty feet.

The wind hammered the bridge and swung it nearly sideways. He grabbed the rope railing. Slipped. Caught himself on his knees. Looked back.

A shadow emerged from the trees concealing the path.

He wasn't going to make it.

He leapt to his feet and ran for everything he was worth.

Four hundred feet.

Three hundred fifty.

He prepared himself to hack at the ropes the moment he reached the far side. The picks were sharp enough to slice through several inches of ice. Surely they could make short work of a pair of ropes that had to be at least a century old and weakened by the elements.

But he needed to have time to pull it off.

He glanced back again.

The shadow stood silhouetted against the trees, its wet hair flagging on the breeze. Another stepped out of the forest behind it. They made no move to follow him out onto the bridge.

Maybe they recognized what he intended to do with the axes and were smart enough to realize they didn't stand a chance against the river from this height.

Three hundred feet.

Halfway.

No, that wasn't it. They were so fast that they could easily overtake him before he reached the far side, let alone hacked through the ropes. So why didn't they?

He remembered the coordinated manner with which they'd hunted him earlier and suddenly understood.

Brooks stopped dead in his tracks and looked up toward the far end in time to see more shadows advance toward the bridge.

It was all over now.

Even if Adrianne had found the strength to cross, she had surely walked right into their trap.

He turned around and watched the predators start across the bridge toward him, then whirled around and saw the others do the same.

He'd never stood a chance.

He leaned over the rope and looked down at the river. If the fall didn't kill him, the tree trunks firing down the current and the boulders hiding beneath the troughs surely would.

The wind faded and the bridge stood still beneath him. He closed his eyes and raised his face to the sky. The enormous raindrops beat down upon his face and shoulders and he experienced a moment of clarity. He knew what he had to do. It was the only thing he could do. The secrets of this valley could never be allowed to get out.

He lowered his face and felt the cold water run down his cheeks. He opened his eyes and stared first at the ice ax in his left hand, then at the one in his right. He raised them up to either side of his head and turned the picks outward.

The lightning reflected from the sharp tips and illuminated the hunters at either end of the bridge.

"What are you waiting for?" he shouted.

The echo of his voice was swallowed by a clap of thunder and the drumroll of running feet striking the bridge from both sides at once.

47

Yarlung Tsangpo River Basin
Motuo County
Tibet Autonomous Region
People's Republic of China
October 17th

Today

Brooks's heart pounded. His hands trembled.

The bridge shook so hard beneath him he could barely maintain his balance.

They raced toward him from the east, grabbing the rope rails for leverage and hurling their lower bodies forward, faster and faster. He peeked over his shoulder. They were coming every bit as quickly from the west.

He adjusted his sweaty grip on the handles of the ice axes.

To the east, two hundred feet and closing. The same to the west.

He swallowed hard. Tried to regulate his breathing.

A hundred fifty feet and closing.

They'd passed the halfway mark. The point of no return.

He squared his shoulders to those barreling toward him from the west.

A hundred feet.

The long hair snapped from their heads like flames. He saw recessed eyes and savage, bared teeth.

Seventy-five feet.

He swung the picks down and struck the ropes.

The entire bridge lurched. He glanced to his right. The pick had cut halfway through the rope. The frayed edges retracted and started to unravel.

He looked back up.

Fifty feet.

Forty.

He took a deep breath in anticipation of submersion and swung the picks again.

The bridge dropped several feet. The ropes split and snapped back to either side. The vertical support ropes that had been attached to it fell straight down. The arched ropes to which the prayer flags had been tied drew tight.

Twenty-five feet.

Brooks fell to his knees. He'd expected the whole bridge to collapse when he cut the ropes. Without any supports underneath, the decrepit bridge should have immediately given way.

Twenty feet.

He watched his death approaching with both terror and awe. Their facial architecture and expressions were undeniably human. As were the musculature of their chests and the taper of their waists. Their legs were proportionate, and yet they moved more like apes, leaping and swinging rather than running. Their arms were long and hairy and he could see the claws on their fanned fingers.

Fifteen feet.

They were truly magnificent in every way.

Ten feet.

Brooks closed his eyes and tucked his chin to his chest. His hands fell limply to his sides, the picks clattering to the—

The ground dropped out from beneath him. He heard a resounding *crack* as if from far away as he fell. He opened his eyes and saw boards separating beneath him against the backdrop of the river.

He looked up as a hairy shape lunged for him. He spun away and its claws bit into the back of his jacket. He swung the ax toward the western half of the bridge. The pick struck between to horizontal planks even as the bridge fell away from him. He swung the other ax and buried it through another board.

The bridge started to go vertical. Brooks pulled himself tightly against it a heartbeat before he was struck from above by a body that shrieked when it bounced from his shoulders and out over the nothingness.

Another blur streaked past to his right. It grabbed for him and he felt claws carve into the meat of his thigh before they disengaged at the side of his knee. It roared as it plummeted into the mist.

The bridge swung toward the granite wall. He watched it race toward him and braced for impact.

Another one cried out when it lost its grip on the planks. It struck his left shoulder and cartwheeled over the river.

Brooks lost his grip on the ax in his left hand when the bridge struck the escarpment.

The wood snapped and he fell. The pick in his right hand caught several feet down.

He grabbed the bungee on his left hip, reeled the ax up to his hand, and swung it at the bridge. It lodged in the wood with a *thuck*.

Weight on his back. Jerking him downward. Thrashing. He felt feet scrabbling against his legs as the beast attempted to gain enough traction to climb him.

A tearing sound and the creature lurched. Claws pierced his back where his coat had been. He felt the sharp tips inside of him, against his ribs near his spine.

Brooks bellowed in pain and looked up at his hands. They slid down to the very bottoms of the rubber grips.

More clawing against the backs of his legs. And then the claws disengaged from his ribs with a snap and the weight was gone.

An all-too-human scream grew farther and farther away until it was silenced by a splash.

Brooks didn't look down. He focused everything he had left on his survival.

Blood poured down his back and saturated the waistband of his pants. His breathing became ragged, gasping, and he felt an acute tightness in his chest.

The top was so far up he could barely see it.

His arms shook as he pulled himself upward. Pried the ax from the wood.

Swung it higher and impaled the wood. He did the same thing with the other ax. Over and over until he gained traction with the toes of his boots and secured the leverage he needed to climb.

Right hand, left hand.

The warmth of blood diffused across the backs of his thighs and rolled down his calves. His head became light and the world started to spin.

Higher.

Right hand, left hand.

The corners of his vision darkened. The wind swung what little remained of the bridge sideways, bouncing him against the granite.

He poured every last ounce of his strength into the climb. Pulled with his arms; pushed with his legs. He tasted blood in his mouth and knew he was almost out of time.

He heard the clatter of boards striking the rock wall below him and then splashing into the river.

The whole thing was coming apart.

Right hand, left hand.

He swung the ax overhand and met with no resistance. His forearm struck the rocky ledge. He braced his elbow on the level ground and pulled himself up with a grunt. His lungs felt like they collapsed in upon themselves and he had to open his mouth against the blood that rose from his chest.

Water flooded down the path. It ran over his arms and splashed him in the face.

He closed his eyes and struggled against the current, vying for purchase as it threatened to sweep him off. One final push with his legs and he crawled over the ledge between the support posts and collapsed onto his side.

Darkness closed around him. He gasped in an effort to inflate his punctured lungs. His body was cold. So cold. He was peripherally aware that he was losing too much blood, but his only conscious thoughts were of Adrianne.

He pushed himself up to all fours and crawled. Blood dribbled from his mouth and pattered the water flowing over his wrists. He'd told her to run as far as she could. If she'd left any prints, the runoff had already erased them.

The coldness spread to his brain and he could feel it shutting down, like someone walking through a house and flipping off the light switches.

The ground leveled off to a muddy plain spotted with rhododendrons and wild grasses. His arms gave out and dropped him face-first into the mud. He propped himself up on his elbows and dragged himself onward. The earth tilted beneath him and his vision blurred. He fell once more. When he raised his head he saw a footprint in the mud beside the impression of his face. The track was smaller than his and had the distinct tread marks of a hiking boot.

He laughed out loud and crawled faster.

She'd made it. Adrianne had crossed the bridge in time. Tears of happiness streamed from his eyes as his vision dimmed.

There was another footprint. And another.

He collapsed to his chest and clawed his way through the mud and weeds, dragging himself by sheer will alone until he saw the shoe that had left the prints lying on the ground behind a rhododendron. Closer he crawled. A wet sock hung from her foot. Her legs were muddy and cold, her skin a shade of pale bordering on translucence.

"No," he whispered. Then louder, "No, no, no!"

He crawled onto her unresponsive body. She lay prone, one arm crumpled beneath her, the other sprawled out to the side. It looked like she'd made a beeline for the tree and simply collapsed upon reaching it.

The rain pattered her back, which showed no indication that she was even trying to breathe. Her head was turned partway to the side. The rain puddled in her ear.

His strength fled him and dropped him onto her. Her cheek against his was cold. He kissed the corner of her mouth.

The muscles in his neck gave out and his forehead struck the ground beside hers. The last thing he saw before the darkness became complete was the puddle of blood that had dripped from her mouth, its surface unperturbed by her breath.

48

Excerpt from the journal of
Hermann G. Wolff

Courtesy of Johann Brandt, Private Collection
Chicago, Illinois
(Translated from original handwritten German text)

November 1956

I emerged from the Tibetan wilds to find a world at war. Everything had changed since last I was in civilization. The reunification of the Germanic peoples was well underway. The Führer had invaded Poland and in response France and Great Britain declared war. The British had sealed off the gateway to Lhasa and would let no one pass, least of all anyone of Germanic descent, which I kept to myself when I joined the flood of Tibetan refugees across the border into India. It took three months to cross the whole wretched country, but I eventually reached the Bay of Bengal.

The whole of Calcutta was abuzz with British Indian Troops preparing for

*the hostilities that would soon be at their doorstep. The German consulates had
all closed under pressure from the host nation and its ambassadors had been
shipped back to the Fatherland. It took seven weeks to work my way back through
the Suez Canal and across the Mediterranean, where I first saw U-boats
performing maneuvers out in the open in preparation for the campaign to come.*

*The pomp and circumstance of the Nazi Party back home had been replaced
by a well-oiled machine geared for fighting the war. No longer were the streets
filled with revelers and the signs of prosperity, but rather rubble and signs
declaring that Jews were no longer welcome. Storefronts had been smashed and
burned without any effort to rebuild them. The outpouring of nationalism had
been channeled into aggressive imperialism. No longer did the cities abound
with hope, but rather the promise of destruction. The world of discovery and
enlightenment I left behind had become one of bloodshed and suffering. Where
once there had been opportunity, there was now the irresistible pull of the call to
arms.*

*My countrymen no longer cared about the superiority of their Aryan roots
and instead seemed hell-bent on proving it by any and all means. I found the
quest upon which I embarked one nobody cared about, if indeed they ever had. It
was just one of many keys the Reich inserted into the backs of the men and boys
they wound up like tin soldiers and loosed upon an unprepared world. The days
of enlightenment had been just another illusion cast by a villainous empire like
any and every other, not one with the best interests of its people at heart, but one
fueled by hatred and motivated by revenge. Our communal vision to prove we
would not be kept down had mutated into a desire to grind our former oppressors
beneath our hobnailed boots.*

*And yet within that dark time of depression and horror, I found opportunity
of a kind I never anticipated.*

*By the time I reached Berlin, the Office of the Ahnenerbe had been dissolved
and incorporated into the General Ranks of the SS. The country needed soldiers
more than it needed men willing to run around the globe on the whim of the
Reichsführer-SS. His pet projects had been relegated to the scrap heap, or so they
said. Filmmakers were no longer sent directly to the Ministry of Propaganda,
but rather to the front lines where it would be their honor to fight and die beside
their fellow Germans. Scientists, however . . . there were special assignments
waiting for men with vision and an unwavering devotion to both their field and
their Führer. Fortunately, that was exactly what I was. Or so I convinced them,*

as anyone capable of giving lie to my claim had left Berlin to heed the call of war long ago. I was an anthropologist by the name of Johann Brandt, an orphan who had risen from the dust to a position of prominence in Himmler's Ahnenerbe, an academic who was issued new identification and credentials after losing his — along with the remainder of his expedition — in Tibet, a scientist who was free to ply his trade without oversight on a population of subjects who had no choice but to let him.

Maybe there was a point when I believed the cost of the knowledge we gained was simply too high, yet every day I went to work with a smile on my face and a song in my heart as I opened books made of flesh and absorbed every last bit of knowledge they contained. And when I feared for the forfeiture of my soul, all I had to do was look at the mask I had cast from the mutated face of my friend Kurt Eberhardt to realize that what I was doing was of monumental importance. So I catalogued every minute physical detail of every race and set about correlating the similarities and differences, and then conducted experiments to see if I could change them.

By the time the tides of war turned, I had amassed the kind of knowledge that made me invaluable. As they say, to the victor belong the spoils. In our case, it was the scientists and their research the Allied forces were desperate to secure. Their hands were clean of the so-called atrocities we committed, so they felt justified in claiming the fruits of our labors as their own. And in exchange for our full cooperation and allegiance, which we all offered willingly, we were pardoned for our complicity in any wrongdoing and granted not only full citizenship in the Land of the Free, but positions from which we could continue our research unmolested, if not unsupervised.

For my part, I was content to blend into the shadows while others of my kind stepped into the limelight by founding NASA and taking high-ranking posts within the Federal Government. Somewhere out there were people who might recognize me for who I truly was or for the imposter I had become, if they hadn't all been killed during the war. So I pursued my calling overseas, as far away from my posting at the University of Chicago — an honor arranged my David Rockefeller himself — as I could get. I followed the lead of scientists like Raymond Dart, Louis Leakey, and Robert Broom and sought to find my place in the field. I traveled the world with my spade and the inexhaustible financial resources of the Rockefeller Foundation. I unearthed the partial skull of Paranthropus robustus *in South Africa and* Paranthropus boisei *in the Great Rift*

Valley and published my first scholarly piece on the accuracy of Charles Darwin's predictions in The Descent of Man, *in which he speculated the earliest humans and their progenitors would ultimately be found on the Dark Continent, as it encompasses the totality of the range of mankind's nearest living relatives, chimpanzees and gorillas.*

Since then, I have funneled all of my energies into proving that the lineage of man has seen many forms and incarnations. If I can prove that Australopithecus africanus *evolved from a primate, then there will be far less resistance to my theory that* Homo sapiens *descended from such primitive life forms. And eventually, when the world accepts my theories as fact, I will put forth the notion that our species is not the finished product of evolution, but rather just another of many stepping stones along the way, for I have seen what is to come and it both excites and mortifies me.*

Yet no matter where my travels took me, Tibet was never far from my mind. The years following the war brought much instability to the region. All foreign relations were essentially severed and the country retreated into itself. With Communism taking root to the east, there was a sense of impending doom. And inevitability. The Kashag had called for help from anyone who would listen during the Sino-Tibetan War decades prior, but no one came to its rescue then, and they certainly were not about to start when Mao Tse-tung rose to power and any form of aid risked pitting the entire Western world against the butcher Stalin and the military might of the Soviet Russians.

It was during this time I commissioned my first expedition into Tibet. I utilized my own finances and made all of the arrangements from afar to avoid attracting the attention of those tasked with my oversight, a job that became increasingly relaxed with each passing day. Despite everything they had given me, there was simply one thing I would not share with them or anyone else.

Unfortunately, my men were turned away at the border. They lacked the creativity of their predecessors and returned with their tails between their legs. The second expedition penetrated Tibet, only to be captured and escorted across the border and to the American Consulate in Sikkim. The third, and final, expedition was launched in 1951, after the Tibetans signed over their sovereignty and the Communist PLA army commenced its formal occupation.

It was my hope that the country would be so overwhelmed with internal matters that it would be paying less attention to its borders and the presence of foreigners. I was proved wrong when first months passed, then years, without word from any of the men. I tried to convince myself they had been caught by the Chinese, but I knew better. They had made it to Motuo, just as I had years ago, and they had met with the same fate as my colleagues. While I escaped due to the serendipitous alignment of fortune and luck, they did not. And so I resolved not to send another expedition into that murderous valley. The hypocrisy of a man who could not bring himself to return sending others to die in his stead was not lost on me. If I were unwilling — nay, too frightened — to go back, then why should I expect anyone else to do so in my name.

And so I put Motuo out of my mind — at least as well as I could — while I threw myself into my work and began laying the groundwork for what I hope will be a global institute devoted to the understanding and advancement of the human species.

Until today.

The date is 11 November 1956, and the man who identified himself only as a representative of American Government — which, this far from home, I interpret to mean Central Intelligence Agency — has just driven away from our dig site near Lake Turkana in Kenya. In his possession were the effects of a man named George Johnson. They'd been confiscated from a Nepalese merchant who attempted to sell them to a member of the Tibetan resistance, who passed them along through some unknown chain of command that ultimately led to the CIA. No one knew what happened to Mr. Johnson or how his property ended up in the hands of this merchant, only that all attempts to return his effects were thwarted by an inability to locate him or his next of kin. The only other identifier was a phone number they were able to trace to the Anthropology Department at the University of Chicago, which ultimately led this "representative" to me. He claimed his interest was solely out of professional curiosity, for in the worn satchel were bones of indeterminate specific origin, decidedly human remains, and a stack of negatives he had taken the liberty of developing.

I explained that the strangely shaped bones likely belonged to a primate, presumably of African origin, while the teeth were an odd assortment of tiger, gorilla, and human. Despite the subtle scrape marks I attributed to teeth, which I assume matched the dentition of the partial jaw from the satchel, I claimed not to see anything extraordinary about the human remains. The representative was most intrigued by the photographs, for in the background of several were locations of what I assume to be strategic military installations of some importance, and about which I truthfully could offer no useful insight. I apologized for being unable to help him, and while I'm certain each of us was able to see through the other's ruse, he was gracious enough to let me keep one photograph he claimed not to care about in the slightest, one featuring a bald monk of Caucasian origin in a red robe against a backdrop of intertwining sandalwood and fig trees. Even without his brilliant blue eyes, I would have recognized the face of Johann Brandt anywhere, only there was something about the photograph . . .

Had the photograph not obviously been recently developed — and in color — I might have believed it to be much older than it was, for Brandt appeared not to have aged a single day since last I saw him nearly seventeen years ago.

As I sit here now, with the photograph by my side, I find myself on the brink of a revelation of the highest order.

Paranthropus and Australopithecus. One developed as a parallel branch that ended in extinction; the other as one in a long line of evolutionary progressions that culminated in the current form of man. They evolved independently of one another and only the passage of time proved which one held the most advantageous adaptations. Is it not possible that whatever impetus caused the changes in Eberhardt could have stimulated mutations of a completely different type in Brandt? After all, he demonstrated the most acute symptoms of the preliminary stages of the infection. Or perhaps transformation is more apt. Is it possible that while Eberhardt became an outwardly superior physical specimen like Australopithecus, Brandt's mutations developed internally, like those of the ill-fated Paranthropus lineage? Could he have developed an immune system somehow resistant to the rigorous conditions of aging in much the same way the initial infection of chickenpox serves as a life-long inoculation against further outbreaks? And if this is truly the case, then what other miraculous feats is his evolved body capable of?

There is only one way to find out for sure, and if it takes the rest of my days, I will uncover the truth, for deep in the black heart of Motuo mankind is evolving into something more . . . something to which I am no longer content to merely bear witness, but rather a process in which I need to be an active participant.

Whatever the cost.

49

Dbang-po Monastery
Himalayan Mountains
Tibet Autonomous Region
People's Republic of China
October 23rd

Six Days Later

B rooks bolted upright with a loud hiss of air. The pain struck him first, like two knives simultaneously thrust into the sides of his chest. He grabbed for the source and found a small tube projecting from either side, near his armpits. They produced a hissing sound that corresponded with each breath. He traced their length and found them sealed with a gauze-like fabric.

He remembered the claws piercing his back and latching onto his ribs. The subsequent pain of his lungs collapsing, gasping to keep them inflated while his pleural cavity filled with blood.

They were chest tubes of a sort, ports through which the excess fluids could be suctioned from his chest.

His eyes made a crackling sound when he opened them, but he closed them right away. The light was too bright to see anything. He shielded his eyes with his hand and tried again.

The sun blazed through a wood-framed window set high into a wall composed of what looked like hand-carved bricks. He raised his other hand to block out the sun and surveyed the room around him.

He was on a wood slab barely wider than his shoulders. An orange- and red-striped blanket covered his legs. There were candles melted to a crate that served as a nightstand. Images of the Buddha had been painted directly onto the walls so long ago the paint had cracked and fallen off in entire sections. A single golden Buddha statue sat in a recess inside the wall to his left, its right hand raised palm out in the *Abhaya mudra*. The swastika on its chest had been painted red to match the silk drapes hanging to either side of it.

He flung off the blanket and realized he was completely naked beneath it. The room was barely the size of a prison cell and there was no sign of his clothes or any of his other possessions.

"Adrianne."

His throat was so dry the word came out as a croak.

He swung his legs over the side and tried to stand. His feet filled with pins and needles and he promptly crumpled to the floor. He could see the outer hallway through the gap underneath the door. There was no lock on the black iron handle.

Brooks pulled the blanket up over his shoulders, wrapped it around him, and held it closed in front of his waist. After several minutes he was able to stand and went to the window in hopes of identifying where he was. At first he saw only sky. He had to stand on his toes to see the rest of the world far below him. The pine trees could have been a hundred feet tall, but they looked like toothpicks from way up here. They covered the rolling hills and bathed the deep ravines in shadow. Snowcapped mountains rose from the horizon and into the clouds. They looked like the Himalayas, although not from any angle he had seen before.

He pushed the window open and recoiled from the cold air. He leaned out and looked to either side. A sheer escarpment to the left. Tibetan granite. Frosted pine trees growing from every ledge. There were buildings to his right. White pagodas with red tile roofs connected by narrow wooden bridges. Beyond them, nothing but sky and steep mountains covered with trees and granite faces hundreds of feet tall.

Yaks grunted and huffed in the distance.

He tightened his grip on the blanket and shuffled toward the door. The mere act of getting out of bed had sapped him of his energy. He felt as though he were made of ice and might shatter if he fell. His joints were stiff and ached, but not nearly as badly as his head. The fever had broken, though, and he no longer had the taste of blood in his mouth.

The door didn't open onto a hallway as he'd expected, but instead a narrow flagstone terrace with thin wooden rails. He followed it in the only direction he could go, toward a passage in the granite. It led to a karst formation far grander than he would have ever guessed. Candles burned on every natural shelf formed by the flowstone. The stalactites cast flickering shadows across the domed roof. The pillars where the stalactites and stalagmites met had been sculpted into tall chortens and hollowed at waist height to house golden prayer wheels. A dozen monks sat on square pillows on the bare ground, hunched over large books with quills moving in their hands.

They didn't appear to notice him as he passed between them, looking down upon their work. He couldn't read the Tibetan characters, but he could certainly decipher the pictures. He recognized Warren and the markings used to show the wounds he had suffered, which brought back the memory of his colleague in the casket with painful clarity. The drawing reminded him of the kind forensic artists produced for murder victims. He saw Zhang, too, only the artist had moved on to detailed drawings of his hands and face. The various lacerations were marked and connected by straight lines to notations he couldn't decipher.

Other monks labored over anatomical sketches of a different kind. He saw a human brain in both coronal and sagittal cross-section, the structures and functions clearly marked. One demonstrated acute cerebral inflammation and the points of contact with the skull where the cerebrospinal fluid, which protected the delicate tissues, had been shunted by the swelling. The resultant necrosis was largely localized, but also radiated inward toward the thalamus and hippocampus.

Another picture showed a brain both similar and completely different. While the shape remained constant, there was a dramatic increase in the size and depth of the convolutions in the gray matter and a wider layer of CSF to buffer the brain from swelling against the confines of the cranium.

When Brooks looked up again, the man he'd seen earlier stood before him, a scar on the side of his neck where Brooks had cut him with the pick.

"Where's Adrianne?" Brooks asked.

The man stared at him with a vacant expression, his blue eyes affectless.

"The girl I was with. *Das Mädchen. Wo ist das Mädchen?*"

The monk turned and started to walk away.

Brooks grabbed him by the shoulder and spun him around.

All of the monks around him jumped to their feet and stood at attention like soldiers.

Brooks didn't care. He pulled the monk closer and growled right into his face, enunciating each word slowly and carefully.

"*Wo. Ist. Das. Mädchen?*"

The monk glanced over Brooks's shoulder at the others, who hesitated for a moment before sitting down once more. He then looked pointedly at Brooks's fists, balled in his robe, then up into his eyes.

"Please," Brooks whispered. "*Bitte.*"

He released the robe and watched as the monk walked away from him. He followed at a distance, knowing with complete certainty that his body wouldn't hold up to any kind of physical confrontation.

The monk lit a lantern from a candle burning on the wall and ducked through another fissure in the mountain. The tubes in Brooks's chest prodded his insides when he stooped and walked in a crouch for a good ten feet before the walls again receded. The passage wound back to his left and opened onto another terrace.

The monk led him through a sparse room with a wooden slab for a bed and a blanket folded neatly on top of it. There were black and white photographs of Tibetan men and women dressed as though from another age. The young man with them was smiling and proud. Brooks recognized him as the man who'd been drawing what he speculated to be an evolved version of the human brain.

The doorway led to another room. It was identically furnished, only the pictures were of a young man and woman. The man wore the uniform and turban of the British Indian Army, the woman a silk dress. The vehicle behind them looked like it had been ripped right out of the twenties.

A wooden bridge spanned a gap between rock ledges. If it broke, he'd easily fall five hundred feet before encountering the top of the pine-covered slope.

They entered another room. Same bed, same blanket. Same black and white photographs, only these featured a man who couldn't have been out of his twenties, posing with a young woman in a skirt and a swastika pin on her blouse. She wore her hair like Brooks's grandmother had. There was the man again, this time mugging with four other boys, all of whom Brooks recognized from the pictures they'd found in the trunks. He looked up at the monk, who smiled sadly and nodded.

Brooks took the frame down from the wall, turned it over, and removed the backing. He slid the picture out and read the names written on the back. He flipped it over and compared them. Again they didn't match what he expected, but at least they were consistent. Augustus König stood to the left with his rifle propped against his shoulder, a broad smile on his face, and a dead shapi at his feet. Kurt Eberhardt knelt over it, pulling its long hair up to his nose like a beard, his eyes alight with mischief. Otto Metzger stood over him with a crooked half-grin and a canteen of water he prepared to pour down the back of his friend's shirt. Beside him was the man standing before Brooks now, a slender man with a pair of calipers protruding from his breast pocket. A man identified as Johann Brandt. And next to him was the man Brooks had known by that name for nearly a decade, a man whose reputation in the field of anthropology was above reproach, a man whose very life was built upon a lie.

A man named Hermann Wolff.

Brandt took the picture from him and stared at it for a long moment before setting it down on his bed. He led Brooks out the door and down a narrow flagstone stairway toward a building larger than all of the others. The gold eaves and finial and the red roof were faded by exposure to the elements. The whitewash was nearly scoured to the bare stone by the abrasive wind.

It towered three stories over them as they approached along a path through a large garden miraculously held in place against the cliff by a retaining wall of stacked granite. Prayer flags snapped overhead from where they'd been strung from the balustrades to various outcroppings on the cliff and the bridge itself. Lotus flowers of every color and hue bloomed to either side of the path. Amid them stood miniature chortens roughly three feet tall and hand-chiseled with the utmost precision, right down to the finest detail. Some were so old they were nearly worn smooth by the abrasive wind, while others were so new the mica in the granite reflected the sun. They weren't as grand as the two-story chortens erected all across Tibet and India to house the ashes of fallen monks, but Brooks still felt as though he were a giant walking through the land of the dead.

And then the truth hit him.

That was exactly what this was. The chortens were urns housing the ashes of the deceased.

This was where Brandt was leading him. He'd demanded to see Adrianne, and now here he was.

He looked all around and saw a chorten that couldn't have seen more than a couple rains. Incense sticks stood from a sand-filled pot and the prayer flags draped over the lotus plants had yet to wither.

Brandt said something to him, but the words eluded him. He walked from the path in a daze and stared down at the newest chorten. The grass was still dimpled from the footsteps of the mourners who'd cast offerings at the foot of the elaborate urn. He fell to his knees and let his head hang. Tears streamed down his cheeks and welled from his chin.

He remembered how cold her cheeks had been, how her chest hadn't risen as he watched, how her breath didn't even ripple the pool of blood under her mouth, and yet still he'd clung to the hope that she might have survived. And now . . .

Brandt's shadow fell upon him and he turned to find the monk staring at him with an expression he couldn't read. He lowered his gaze to the chorten, touched it gently with his fingertips, and traced the Tibetan script he assumed was some sort of prayer.

Brandt's shadow receded.

The heavy wooden door of the building opened behind him with a squeal.

Brooks felt a swell of anger. At the monks for not helping them escape Motuo, for not saving Adrianne as they had him, for interring her in an unmarked chorten half a world away from her home. But mostly he was mad at himself for failing to protect her. She'd trusted him and he'd let her down. He knew he'd spend the rest of his life dealing with the guilt and the dreams of what might have been.

A shadow fell over him again. This time he didn't look back, at least not until he recognized the voice of the woman standing behind him.

"I was beginning to wonder if you were ever going to wake up."

50

Dbang-po Monastery
Himalayan Mountains
Tibet Autonomous Region
People's Republic of China
October 29ᵗʰ

Twelve Days Later

"Y ou're sure you have to go?" Adrianne said.

"I'll be back before you know it."

Brooks wore a collection of clothes the monks had gathered for him and a pair of sandals. In his pack were boots, a coat, and a hat made from the fur of what looked like a species of husky. He wasn't about to complain, though. The river had claimed his backpack and the supplies Adrianne had scattered on the bank in an effort to mislead what the monks called *yeh-teh* — or "bear from the rocky place" in Sherpa — about which he still had much to learn.

He held Adrianne and kissed her softly. He still couldn't touch her without recalling how she'd felt when he thought she was dead and he would never be able to shake the image of the blood pooled beneath her mouth. Her gums were scarred from where the burgeoning teeth had been excised from the cancellous bone, but they became less noticeable with each passing day. The teeth themselves had reminded Brooks of sprouted chia seeds. It was hard to believe such tiny growths were responsible for so much pain and bleeding. His own had been even smaller and now resided at the bottom of a small vase. Their fingernails were still thick and ridged near the edges, but Brandt assured them they would grow out and it would be as though nothing had ever happened. The remainder of the physical changes, while internal where no one would see them, would never go away. At least not for a very long time.

"Promise me you'll be careful."

"You don't have to worry about me. I have Sdom to get me through the Himalayas."

"That's precisely what worries me."

Brooks stared into her eyes and sighed.

"What?" she asked.

"Nothing." He smiled and kissed her again. "Don't change while I'm gone."

"Is that supposed to be funny?"

He opened the door and looked back one last time before stepping out into the sunlight. Brandt — or Tsering as he was now known — and two other monks, Kunchen and Tenzin, stood in the courtyard in their red robes, waiting to see him off. Over the past few days Brooks had gained a tremendous amount of respect for the devotees of the *Zhed Stag* monastery and all of the personal sacrifices they had made. They were the wardens of Motuo, the keepers of the secrets they would ensure never left the valley. Not to mention the fact that they were all brilliant in their own ways.

The *Dzogchen Dgon-pa* — the large central dwelling around which all of the other buildings had been constructed — was a repository of knowledge pertaining to every aspect of human evolution. The research these monks had assembled was nothing short of miraculous. The first time Brooks entered he felt like a Neanderthal being led through Times Square. There were simply things that had previously been beyond his limited ability to comprehend. He couldn't wait to truly delve into the mysteries when he returned.

Brooks stopped several feet from the monks and bowed in deference. They grinned at the clumsy gesture, or perhaps at his absurd outfit.

"Where's Spider?" he asked. "*Chang khang Sdom?*"

Brandt rolled his eyes and Brooks knew.

He looked straight up the sheer face of the escarpment in time to see Sdom come bounding down the granite, bouncing from the rock as he belayed himself on the rope. He unclipped his harness and looked Brooks up and down.

"Not a word, Julian."

"Come on, prof. Cut me some slack. This is too good to pass up."

They had found Julian a full three days after his attack. He'd managed to climb, bleeding and on the verge of death, into a recess high on the cliff, where he treated his own wounds with the stinging nettle and subsisted on the roots he'd collected until he marshaled enough strength to brave the remainder of the climb. The monk named Tenzin had seen him from a distance and lowered a rope to him. They'd called him "spider" ever since and spoke of him in a tone of reverence. It was a unique situation for Julian, and one he did his best to milk for everything it was worth.

"Better get it out of your system now. We have a long journey ahead of us."

Brooks tuned out the flurry of insults about his wardrobe. He was just happy that Julian had survived, even if his arms and legs were now as hairy as those of a tarantula.

Brandt pulled him aside and gave him a searching look.

"You have my word," Brooks said. "We will return."

Brandt gave a solemn nod. It was hard to believe this man who didn't look a day over fifty was nearly twice that old. It was one of the many benefits of the mutation, or, more precisely, one of the byproducts of it. And one Brooks looked forward to studying in greater detail.

"We're burning daylight," Julian said. "The hell if I'm going to spend another night out in the open."

"Promise me you'll take good care of her," Brooks said.

Again, Brandt nodded. Adrianne was more than just his guest; she was his insurance that Brooks and Julian would come back. While the monk and former SS scientist was hesitant to take the risk of letting them return to the outside world with a somewhat functional understanding of the secrets he'd sworn to keep, he not-so-secretly reveled in the thought of twisting the knife in the back of the man who'd usurped his identity and sent countless expeditions to their deaths in his name.

Brooks didn't give the notion of returning to his old life a second thought.

Every second of it had been devoted to discovering the answers that were contained inside of the building in front of him, where chromosomes were mapped right down to the locus level and matched to the physical traits they controlled, where the functions and emotions of the human brain were isolated with pinpoint precision, and where the genomes of man and his many antecessors were plotted side by side with their differing genetic sequences and the corresponding viral sources. And he'd only just scratched the surface of the knowledge they'd accumulated not with the aid of computers and databases, but with the tools unique to them, and them alone, as he was only now beginning to understand.

He couldn't wait to get back to work, but there was something important he had to do first.

Brooks and Julian left the monks behind. They navigated the passages through the mountain and crossed the bridges between buildings until they reached the narrow trail carved into the rock, which led up to the pasture where the yaks grazed. From there the hike would be long and perilous. He hadn't even been at *Zhed Stag* for two weeks and already he was content to stay here and never return to what he'd once thought of as the real world. He now thought of it in the same way as he'd once viewed a colony of ants, busying themselves with the mere act of staying busy, unaware of the world that existed around them.

Or inside of them.

He stopped halfway up the chiseled staircase and looked back down. The monastery was barely visible among the trees growing from the hillside. There was so much he wanted to learn. Lifetimes' worth. Fortunately, he now had all the time in the world to learn it.

EPILOGUE

Northwestern Memorial Hospital
Chicago, Illinois
November 8ᵗʰ

Twenty-two Days Later

T he man beneath the covers was so frail he was nearly invisible beneath them. He looked far worse than when last Brooks saw him. His eyelashes glistened with salve and his lids were thin and purple with ruptured veins. The nasogastric tube through which they fed him was taped to his upper lip so it wouldn't slide out of his nostril. The ventilator tube that snaked down his throat made his chest rise and fall with a monotonous *click . . . whir . . . click . . . whir.*

Brooks sat in the chair beside him, staring at the old man who had nearly sent them all to their deaths. He thought about Warren and how he was now interred in a coffin where no one would ever find him, and about Zhang, whose final moments had been filled with a level of pain to which no man should have to be subjected. And not because this diminished man wanted to understand the truth about the men who evolved into the predatory *yeh-teh* as he had claimed, but rather those who evolved separately from them, those who had discovered the secrets of longevity.

My boy, if there is one thing I understand, it is the nature of mortality. I may not be afflicted with some fatal disease, but I assure you, I am dying. It is simply the fulfillment of my biological destiny, and my time will come sooner than later.

All of this because one old man was afraid of dying. And rightfully so considering how many he had personally sent to premature graves in Dachau and the forests of Motuo.

He had dispatched Brooks and his team into the Tibetan wilds knowing full well they'd contract the virus. In fact, he'd been counting on it. Surely one of them would be infected by the complete version of the virus and not one corrupted by the digestive system of the leeches. He didn't care if they all suffered the violent transformation caused by the incomplete virus or if they were slaughtered by those who already had. Brooks's expedition had been his last-ditch effort to bring back one of them with the right combination of viral proteins, before he succumbed to his own inevitable fate.

Only he hadn't understood the nature of the mutations. They weren't directly responsible for slowing the aging process, but rather for increasing the mental faculties of those who figured out how to do so for themselves. And it was one of many secrets they would one day in the distant future take to their graves with them. Secrets a man named Hermann Wolff had committed countless atrocities in an effort to learn, as the pictures hanging on the walls in his private exhibition hall attested.

"Can you hear me in there?" Brooks asked.

Click . . . whir . . .

The man he'd once known as Johann Brandt made no reply. His irises twitched underneath his eyelids, whether in response to his voice or of their own accord Brooks couldn't be sure.

"I know who you are. Who you *really* are. Not that it matters now."

Click . . . whir . . .

The spherical lumps beneath his eyelids twitched again.

"I met the real Johann Brandt. Nice enough guy. Not much of a talker, though. But I guess you probably already knew that."

Click . . . whir . . .

"No one will ever question your contributions to the field of evolutionary anthropology, only the means by which you amassed your knowledge. And, rest assured, they will find out."

Click . . . whir . . .

Wolff's eyes darted frantically beneath his lids.

"But for all that knowledge, you forgot the most important aspect of evolution . . . the element of unpredictability. Only in retrospect can evolution be viewed as a straight line. Think of all of the branches that ultimately resulted in extinction, despite their physical adaptations. Only man would be so arrogant as to think he could control his own evolution, or worse, believe himself to be the finished product of it. For as little as you regard *Paranthropus* and the supposed devolution of its teeth, it survived for a million years while *Homo sapiens* have only been around half that long."

Click . . . whir . . .

"And despite all of the knowledge you accumulated, you drew the wrong conclusion. The defining characteristic of our evolution isn't our teeth . . . "

Brooks concentrated on projecting the words as the monks had taught him.

It's our minds.

Wolff's eyelids snapped open and he stared at Brooks from the corner of his bloodshot eyes.

Our brains have more than tripled in size since we descended from the trees. It just took a viral key to unlock their potential.

Brooks rose and walked toward the door. He heard the rhythmic *click . . . whir . . .* of the ventilator behind him and looked back into the old man's terrified eyes one last time.

I'll leave you to think about that while you die.

AUTHOR'S NOTE

It's strange to think that a mere 80 years ago the world was still a relatively unexplored place, that vast swatches of land and the animals living on them were a mystery to us. Even stranger is the idea that we knew so little about our own species.

With all of the advances in science and medicine, we take for granted the hard-earned anatomical, anthropological, and sociological knowledge that had to be learned along the way, much of it obtained through means we now find questionable, if not outright abhorrent. It's imperative we understand that our passion for advancement quite often outpaces the development of our morality. We justify this with the belief that the needs of the many outweigh the needs of the few, that it's okay to break a few eggs to make an omelette. I look back in horror at the lengths to which the Ahnenerbe went in their pursuit of knowledge, the countless eggs they broke for what they believed to be the greater good, and wonder how future generations will judge us for the millions of deaths caused by viruses of our own design and the as-of-yet unknown consequences of a campaign of mandatory vaccinations with an experimental drug.

I hope you enjoyed FEARFUL SYMMETRY and take a chance on some of the other books from my catalog, where you'll find more adventure, science, history, and nightmarish creatures.

ACKNOWLEDGMENTS

Special thanks to Paul Goblirsch, Leigh Haig, John Foley, and Kyle Lybeck at Thunderstorm Books; Shelley Milligan (and hubbie); Gene O'Neill; Matt Schwartz; Jeff Strand; Kimberly Yerina; my amazing family; and all of my friends and readers, without whom this book wouldn't exist. The author is indebted to several works that proved instrumental in preserving the historical accuracy of his fictitious quest: *Himmler's Crusade: The Nazi Expedition to Find the Origins of the Aryan Race*, by Christopher Hale (John Wiley & Sons, Inc., 2003), *The Rise of the Fourth Reich: The Secret Societies That Threaten to Take Over America*, by Jim Marrs (William Morrow, 2008); *The Secret King: The Myth and Reality of Nazi Occultism*, by Stephen E. Flowers and Michael Moynihan (Feral House, 2007); and *Geheimnis Tibet*, the documentary of the 1938 Ernst Schäfer expedition into Tibet, which served as the inspiration for this book.

ABOUT THE AUTHOR

MICHAEL McBRIDE was born in Colorado Springs, Colorado to an engineer and a teacher, who kindled his passions for science and history. He studied biology and creative writing at the University of Colorado and holds multiple advanced certifications in medical imaging. Before becoming a full-time author, he worked as an x-ray/CT/MRI technologist and clinical instructor. He lives in suburban Denver with his wife, kids, and a couple of crazy Labrador Retrievers.

Made in the USA
Middletown, DE
27 May 2023